DOWN BY THE RIVER

George's heart, as he pulled to the roadside, struggled like a trapped hare against his ribs. And when he switched out the car lights, Amy began to weep. Then she began the whispering murmur: "He wouldn't! He wouldn't! He—"

George grabbed the girl and shook her till the swift whisper wavered.

They both listened in a kind of skin-prickling dread to the sound of one another's breathing; drawing apart in mutual terror of each other.

"We never saw it," George said softly after a while and felt old wells of courage filling in his soul again. "We went to the pictures tonight. We didn't drive out the river road."

"Yes!" she whispered. "I hear you, George!"

"We didn't see your daddy and those other two men kill that colored boy! We didn't, Amy. Because it never happened! And even if it did—we weren't there to see it! You understand me?"

"Yes," she said numbly. "We weren't there. We never saw it."

SHADOW
OF MY BROTHER

DAVIS GRUBB

ZEBRA BOOKS
KENSINGTON PUBLISHING CORP.

ZEBRA BOOKS

are published by

Kensington Publishing Corp.
475 Park Avenue South
New York, NY 10016

First Zebra Books printing: April, 1992

Printed in the United States of America

ISBN 0-8217-3734-1

LOY

In times long after that night there were those among them who swore that a single bolt of lightning had slashed the cloudless, starlit sky: lighting the faces of the just and the unjust, of sleepers and the watchers of the night, and of the slain and the slayers. George had seen it and would remember to the day of his death. And so had Amy, who had sat clenched and unweeping and livid with horror all that long ride home. Back to Elizabethtown back along that same road down which in the early dusk glow they had come light-hearted and young and lovegay. Back now in careening, furious flight along the river road, filled with dread and grown old and sick from a moment's witnessing. It seemed to George as he pulled to the roadside twenty minutes later that only then did the thunder of that lightning come rumbling belatedly down the low, dark valleys of the night. But it was only his heart, struggling like a trapped hare against his ribs. And when he switched out the car lights, Amy began to weep. For a while George could not bear her beside him; could not reach out to touch her, to draw her against him and still her sobs. He heard them dumbly and helplessly and heard the whir of locusts in the high elms along the black road and stared, unseeing, at the faint lamps of the town up a mile yonder. And then Amy began it: the shrill, whispering murmur, iterating it to the dry rhythm of her breast's breathing: "He wouldn't! He wouldn't! He wouldn't! He wouldn't! He wouldn't! He—"

George returned suddenly from the hushed death of his own dread and grabbed the girl and shook her till her teeth clicked and the swift whisper wavered.

"—wouldn't! He wouldn't! He wouldn't, George! He wouldn't!"

George smacked her flat across the cheek and the whisper stopped. And they were both still a spell; listening in a kind of skin-prickling dread to the sound of one another's breathing, of one another's slowed, doom-deep heartbeats; drawing apart in mutual terror of each other; of what the other's eyes had seen as if somehow they feared the inevitable testimony of one another's tongues, in some dread time to come.

"We never saw it," George said softly after a while and felt old wells of courage filling in his soul again. "Amy, we weren't there. We never saw it."

And the words began to come stronger and surer now as he felt her heart warm to his strength.

"We went to the pictures tonight," George went on. "We didn't drive out the river road."

"Yes! Yes!" she whispered and he could feel her eyes widen bravely as she clutched his big hand in her cold, slender fingers and squeezed till the nails bit.

"We never saw it, Amy," he said, and the more he talked the more he really believed it: that they had not been parked there on the river road, that they had not seen it, that it had never happened at all.

"In fact," he whispered. "In fact, Amy, it never happened at all! Amy, look round at me!"

And he held her cupped face up in his fingers and stared desperately into the pale loving heart-shape of her face as if searching furiously there for the truth of the lie his mouth was making.

"Yes!" she whispered. "I hear you, George!"

"We went to the pictures!" he said again. "And we weren't there at all! And we didn't see your daddy—"

And he cupped his other hand over her rounded mouth before the scream could issue.

"Hush! Hush, Amy! And listen! We didn't see your daddy and those other two men kill that colored boy! We didn't, Amy! Because it never happened! And even if it had—we weren't there to see it!"

He waited a while before he took his hand from her mouth and poised it an inch before her face, feeling her breath cooling the wetness on his palm where her mouth had been, waiting to see if she had gotten hold of herself, before he took his hand away.

"Amy?"

"Yes."

"You understand me?"

"Yes," she said numbly. "We weren't there. We never saw it. Because it never happened. Because he—wouldn't."

And then they were both still again, in that trance-like dread of one another's knowing, listening to the summer sounds of the night and the faraway bang of a backfire down the river road along which they had so lately fled. The crickets seemed to be stitching up the red wound of it; the gentle night winds against their eyes seemed to be healing from them what had been burned there a bare half-hour before. And though George could lose this terrible vision from his mind's sight, he could not close his mind's ears to some dreadful testimony that seemed implicit in the whisper of moving leaves in the high elms above the car, above the very stars themselves: Amy and me parked in my old car in the place where we always go, the place that is better than any place has ever been on earth for me in all my lonely time, and it is dark because the car lights are out and it is night with the air warm and sweet with river-smell and Amy-smell and green-smell and suddenly I see the shine of the lights first in her hair, against my eyes, and I turn my head and she does, too, and we see the headlights of the truck up on the river road where the state-route sign is. Amy holds me close and gasps and I whisper to her to hush and they won't see us and we watch and behind the truck lights there is a dark knot of movement, men struggling with something, and when the boy yells, we see the flashlights stabbing up and down in the paw-paws and the dark knot moves down in the headlights of the truck toward the river shore. And we see the dark knot take shape and meaning in the slashed wedge of headlight glare. Amy's father. And Lowdy Kelts. And Verge Stafford. And the colored boy. And the guns. And because they are all shouting, none of them hears the little scream from Amy and I clap my palm across her mouth before the rest of it comes out and watch, feeling the sickness and the fear and something else darker and more dreadful than either gathering in my belly. And the three men ring round the skinny, furious, frightened Negro in the cheap sports jacket and the boy is screaming something hoarsely at them and the black shapes of all of them throw long, cold shadows in the wedge of light and Amy's daddy and the other two are lifting their guns and striking and shouting and yet louder than their voices threads the shrilling voice of the Negro boy: "Mother lovers! Goddamned mother lovers! Go ahead, mother lovers! I ain't afraid! Go ahead! Go on! Go—" And then I feel Amy's silent scream vibrating against the palm of my quivering hand and my finger tips pressing hard into the sweet softness of her cheek and the big flat chopping sounds begin: like heavy boards striking flat on each other and I see the little red flashes and the Negro boy's face goes scarlet with shiny running ribbons and he is gone down in the knot of the three men, like four dancers in a strange and ancient forest rite. And there isn't any more need for my hand across Amy's mouth. She has gone limp in a faint and still I keep it there, holding her up, while the men drag something soft and broken

down through the pawpaws to the river, and then the stabbing
flashlights weave back up to the truck and with a roar and a
spray of gravel like buckshot into the leaves it is gone and I am
bending out the car window being sick on the running board
and ashamed, ashamed, ashamed and my being ashamed is
deep and dark and not because Amy might see me being sick.
Ashamed, ashamed of something deep and dark that has struck
and thrummed like a drum in my groin; some answer in the
red heart of my belly to the thing I have seen.

"It never happened," he whispered in sudden terror to himself again. "Or—if it did—we never saw it! Right, Amy?"

"Yes!" she said. "Oh, yes!"

And suddenly they were in each other's arms with a hunger
and a fury that neither had ever known before and their teeth
stuck together in that desperate kiss just as the big truck roared
past them toward the lanterns of the town and the promise of
rain swelled in the quickened river wind which pressed gently
now against their striving faces.

The town tocked. Once again livid lightning washed the sky
and every leaf of every tree, and every stone of the courthouse
yonder, and every dry brick of the deserted street before the
parked Chevrolet was bathed and silvered in an instant, evil
splendor. He leaned on the wheel, breathing, sweating, unseeing, listening to Amy's faint hiccupping sobs beside him.
Down the pavement the coiled, gold neon sign above Grandma
Butcher's Place stuttered against the slate-black night. The town
ticked, and held its breath, as if, unknowing, knew—as if already the havoc of outcry ran bawling down its midnight lanes.
He lifted his head from the wheel then and turned his face
toward her in a kind of hypnosis and stared a spell and smiled,
at last, as if there were nothing else to do but smile then, and
thrust down on the door handle and jumped out and went
round to her side and opened the door and stood a spell more,
holding his hand out for her with the odd courtesy of one

already doomed toward one already doomed, and she stepped onto the sidewalk, without looking at him at all, and they began to walk up Cloud Street under the stammering neon scroll toward the Starbright Opera House. Neither spoke; each moving like one dreaming a dream of the other, toward the steady necklace of lights above the steaming popcorn stand.

"Two," he heard himself say.

"George," the girl face in the ticket window said. "The second feature's already started so there's no sense your paying."

"Two."

"What I mean is—go on in. Free, George. You and Amy both."

And without even thanking her, without even seeing her at all, George, keeping a life-grip on Amy's dead-cold fingers, bought popcorn with his free hand and led her into the flickering dream dark of the picture house; stumbling blindly into seats where they could huddle and hold one another and he heard a dry sound above the voices on the screen and knew that the popcorn box had fallen all over their shoes. And they were at the picture show after all. And whatever was happening up in the quivering square of silver screen before them was the real world. And what they had left behind them in the ticking, waiting streets outside: that was the lie. This was the real. It had to be. Because if it were anything else he would be so horribly afraid that Amy would see and be afraid, too. And that must not be. Because he was a man. He was twenty. And so he lived out the sweet lie in the dark with her till the lights went up and he kept her hand still tight in his, now almost bloodless and senseless in that grip, and crunched blindly through the spilled popcorn and out, like dreamers, into the small town night of Cloud Street. Everything was closed now. The lights of the marquee were dulled and Grandma Butcher's Place had gone dark and the whole village seemed deeper within the dark, knowing of its unknown dream. He walked, feeling her beside him, and hearing the truck again stopped for a moment with the brush of an elm bough upon his head, under the shadowed trees, and saw it round Court Street and head out past the courthouse, down Cloud Street, out of town. But he had seen their faces in the instant's illumination of the street lamp: faces flushed and reddened and high-stuck, Amy's daddy and Lowdy Kelts and the other—Verge Stafford—heading out toward the main road, tired and sullen with the night's manly exertions. He decided it was time he got Amy home.

The lights were on. Gladys was still up. But the truck was there, in the space beyond the single lighted window, so he knew that Loy had stumbled into bed and gone to sleep. He stopped the car a hundred feet up the road and kept the motor idling as if waiting for Amy to tell him what to do. There were clouds now, towering above the orchard, and there was reason for the thunder, and the quickened wind that blew from the fruit boughs was sweet with the impending rain.

"I'm afraid," she said. "Afraid to go in."

He sat an instant, hammering the heel of his hand gently on the wheel and staring at the single window where Gladys would be waiting.

"He's gone to bed most likely," she said, in a high, brave voice. "But I'm afraid."

"There's no cause to be," he said. "Because nothing happened. We were at the pictures. Remember."

She sat a spell, staring at the lantern square of curtained window, and then she shivered and sighed.

"Oh, yes," she said. "You're right, George. We were at the pictures. The whole evening long."

And he jumped out and ran round to open the door before she began to cry again.

"I'll take you in, Amy."

And they walked, dreamers still, through the ripe, fruited air below the orchard, toward the calico-curtained yellow of the single waiting window, and the thunder jumped and bumbled obscurely beyond the still ticking night and, listening, George heard a new sound in the darkness. It was a sound and yet not a sound at all: a voice that was tongueless and a singing that was not song. Up in the orchard, lanterns spun small webs of light in the twin windows of the cabins that Loy Wilson provided his Negroes in the harvest time. Perhaps it was a lantern that moaned this sound that was no moan at all but more the very breath and heartbeat of the night itself: the fabric of the dark's own dreadful and unutterable thoughts. Amy's hand began to leap and quiver in his own.

"It was that boy!" she whispered and flung herself against him, hard and breast-flat, her fingers clutching at his shirt. "It was that boy! The one they call Charley! Charley Pancake! George, that's his mother up yonder! George, she knows and she's crying!"

"Hush, Amy!"

He reached up quick and cupped her gently round the nape of the neck, pressing her face hard into his shirt, into the flesh of his breast, smothering her cries with his body.

"Wait, Amy! Wait, darling!"

And then in a kind of little miracle she grew suddenly still in his embrace, waiting as he had told her to, as children wait, and he lifted her face gently in the tinny lampshine from her mother's single, waiting window and stared into her eyes.

"Amy, we've just got to be real brave about this," he said. "It'll all work out, but we've just got to be real brave that's all!"

"All right."

And he led her to the door.

Morning. George woke from a stormy dream of his coming to the town six years before, just after his release from the children's home. When he was awake he glanced furtively round the shabby disorder of the furnished room and thought gratefully that it was his day off from the job at Busbee's Empire Filling Station, the job he had held since his first chance-coming to Elizabethtown. A glance at Hawk's bed. It was unslept in.

Hawk was not there. George bemoaned that: he would have liked Hawk's company after the terrors of that lonely night lately fled. Not that he would have told; he could never tell. For somehow, to his stampeding wits, the notion of telling was the notion of betraying Amy.

George had had Hawk as best friend during his one, dull, uneventful year in the Army. George had never been overseas, but Hawk had been to Vietnam, had seen fighting. Hawk always seemed to keep cool and quiet about things and he was six years older than George. He had been a prize-fighter, even if that part of his life was all washed-up for him. He had told George when they first became friends and were talking about sharing rooming-house expenses that he was married to a Negro girl from Montgomery and that she might come visit him someday if she was able to forget a couple of things that had happened long before Hawk got sent to Vietnam, and Hawk said he thought George ought to know about his feelings in that regard before he decided to room with him. George didn't feel one way or the other. Besides, since the Army, Hawk was just about the only friend George had in the world. Unless you counted Amy. Or maybe Vinnie, Hawk's old fight manager who lived in a hole of a room down the hall from theirs.

George sat a moment longer on the edge of his bed, remembering how he had first met Amy at a rock'n'roll dance hall two years before. His throat grew tight with love for her. Presently he rose and began dressing quickly, with a reproachful glance now and then at his roommate's empty bed. And after a moment in silence, he went down the black well of the staircase and out into the day. And ran till he was on Cloud Street and kept on running till people in front of the Calhoun Hotel turned and roused from morning boredom to stare at him, wondering why a boy would run as if pursued when there was no single living person in all the green, brooding length of the little street behind him. He slowed to a strolling saunter, feeling all their eyes poking and wondering and feeling at the nape of his neck, and then they looked away and went on about their business and he stopped and leaned against a lamp post and mopped away beads of cold sweat from his upper lip. He kept his eyes shut an instant, gathering himself together again, and when he opened them he saw Amy, across the street, in the window of the five-and-ten. She was shaking her head at him wildly and motioning faintly with her hand, but it didn't matter. It didn't matter that she was warning him away, her dark eyes still haggard with panic and her mouth gray and unrouged. He went inside and walked to her.

"Later!" she whispered, furiously. "Meet me later at Candyland! An hour from now!"

"Why? Have they found . . . ?"

"Mother's with me! She knows something's wrong, George! Oh, I went all to pieces after I got in last night."

"Did he know?"

"No."

"He was asleep."

"Yes! Oh, God, George! Please go! I'll meet you at Candyland! Our booth by the fountain!"

But it was too late. Gladys' high heels clicked behind him and he sensed her, smelled her: the aura of choking but ladylike perfume surrounded him.

"Why it's George Purdy! Good morning, George!"

"Morning, ma'am!"

"A fine hour you brought my baby home last night! A fine, respectable hour, I must say!"

"We were at the pictures," he heard his voice say. She held out a bolt of lace for Amy to take but still she did not take her eyes from George's face.

"Here, Amy baby," she said. "I picked out this one for your slip. See what you think, honey. I think it's real pretty."

Amy gave a nervous giggle.

"You better go, George," she said in a high, strained note of laughter. "You know women when they go shopping together! You better go while there's time, George."

"Sure," said Gladys evenly, her eyes on George's rigid face. "George knows. George knows everything about women, don't you, George? George is a pretty grown-up boy for his age, I'll tell the world!"

Amy stood pale as death, swaying imperceptibly in the breathless air of the forenoon, little drops of perspiration standing on her forehead, under the dark tendrils of her hair.

"Try getting my daughter home at a decent hour next time, George," she said, and although the smile was not gone from her full, dark lips there was something of menace in her narrowed eyes; a razored threat beneath her breath, and an angry quickening of the rise and fall of her full breasts beneath her well-tailored jacket.

He said nothing, and Amy gave her little laugh again and clutched the lace, bending and unraveling it, pretending to be thinking only of that.

"It was a late show," she whispered. "It didn't get out till late, Mother! George is not to blame."

"George knows," said Gladys in a voice like the gentle nudge of a pistol muzzle. "He knows what a decent hour is. Don't you, George?"

"Yes," he sighed. "I'm sorry, Mrs. Wilson. I won't keep Amy out so late next time."

"Right, mister!" she chuckled with a full grin that was somehow hideously intimate, and George caught Amy's eyes and held them for a spell; long enough to know that she would meet him within the hour at their first rendezvous: the marbled booth at Candyland, by the root-beer fountain, where in certain golden hours of afternoons they had known together there, sun-motes from the wind-wild sycamore outside the window on Cloud Street made shapes on their table top: shifting, yellow images which they had traced with their fingertips, and had divined there all the splendid promise of good things to be; of the eternities throughout which they should love, worlds without end.

* * *

He sat waiting in the booth, staring at the marble, but it was not the right hour for sun to come, and he clenched his teeth together until his jaw ached and wondered if she would really come at all, if she would really come ever again; thinking with a kind of choking desperation that perhaps something of the two of them had died in the pawpaws that night. Maybe Gladys would shut her away from him forever. Maybe Amy would never be able to face him, knowing what he knew, knowing what they both knew. And suddenly she came through the door, and toward him through the tables, with that proud, hip-swinging walk that always, curiously, hurt his heart. They sat a moment, while she caught her breath, and held each other with frightened eyes, and then her hand stole across the cold stone and wound her fingers with his, squeezing, holding on like the fingers of someone dying.

"George, do you love me!"

"You know that, Amy."

"I mean really love me!" she whispered fiercely. "I mean enough for anything?"

"Yes, Amy."

"Then, George, take me away. Away from him! Away from Mother! Away from here!"

"Amy, we can stick this out!" he mumbled and looked away.

"No," she said. "You know that's not so, George. Maybe *you* can!" she whispered suddenly, fiercely, furiously and threw his fingers away. "But *I* can't. It's *my* father! Remember?"

"Why did he do it, Amy? Why? Why?"

She shuddered and covered her face with her fingers before she began to speak.

"Yesterday morning," she said, talking as if her lips were stiff with frostbite. "He was in town—at the courthouse—with some of his big, important friends. Mother was in the store. The man from the beer distributor's was there. One of the neighbors—

Collie Moon. She was there—buying coffee. This little kid," she went on numbly. "This little colored kid—"

"He was more than a kid!" George said. "He looked to be a teen-ager!"

"God, that's a kid."

She caught her breath and was still an instant, gulping as if she were sick, and then with dry, wild eyes she stared at him and went on whispering. "He came in—to buy candy. He had a dime and a nickel. His mother is one of the Negroes Daddy hired to pick the apple harvest. He had this dime and a nickel and he spent a long time making up his mind about the candy he wanted. Mother told him to hurry up because the beer distributor's man was waiting to get paid and Collie Moon was waiting to get her coffee ground."

"That's all?" whispered George. "My God, Amy, that's all?"

"No! No! Listen to me! Mother told him to hurry and he— he just kind of leaned against the counter by the window and looked at her. Just looked at her for a minute and she said it was just like he was—she said—undressing her with his eyes! She said there was some kind of fresh Northern Negroes that were so used to white women that they just couldn't help looking at *any* white woman that way!"

"And then," she whispered. "Mother says this kid—this Charley Pancake—he made some smart remark."

"What did he say?"

"I don't remember, George. Something—something sexy— something about she was just about the nicest candy in the store. And she came around the corner and—and she smacked him across the mouth. And the beer distributor was there and he heard it all—and he saw it. And so did Collie Moon."

"That's all?"

"It was enough," she said dully. "Oh, George, you know the way Daddy is! You know the way everybody is! The minute Daddy came in for lunch Mother got hysterical and had a fainting seizure and told Daddy the whole story."

"And they killed him for that?"

"Smart nigger," she whispered. "You know how they think. You know how things are."

And suddenly the first sun of the early afternoon stole shy onto the marble table top beside their hands and brief dry gusts of August wind in the high boughs of the sycamore made leaping sun-leaf shapes upon the veined stone.

"Where's he at now?"

"Daddy?" she said. "He left this morning. Before daybreak."

"Where?"

"To the state capitol."

"With them? With the other two?"

"No. No. They're somewhere. They're still here."

"Was he running?"

"George, you know him. He never runs from anything— from anyone. You know the kind of friends he has in the capitol. He's a little man with a big, long shadow, George. That's why— even if they find the boy—"

"They will," he said numbly. "They'll find him at low water maybe. Or down in the dam by Dogtown."

"—even when they do," she gasped. "And even if there was a tag tied round his neck saying, 'Loy Wilson and Lowdy Kelts and Verge Stafford killed me'—it wouldn't matter. They'd have a trial—like a theater show, George—and nothing would happen. It wouldn't matter."

"But no one will ever find out," said George, watching the watery play of sunlight on her fingers. "No one could know. How could anyone ever know, Amy?"

And with a faint pop like the breaking of an egg the empty Coke glass collapsed in his fist, and Amy gave a cry because a trickle of blood went spiraling down his wrist when he held the fingers open in surprise and let the shards of glass fall tinkling to the marble.

"Oh, my darling! You're bleeding! Oh, my love!"

And she leaned forward and seized his hand and tugging

the silk kerchief from around her head, began binding his wound.

"There! Does it hurt?"

"No. Thanks. It's not deep. But I ruined your scarf."

"That doesn't matter!" she cried, and seemed quivering with new strength at having ministered to his hurt.

"George!" she cried suddenly, her eyes flashing. "We don't have to be martyrs about this thing do we?"

"Hell, no, Amy!"

"We don't, George! We've got our own lives all stretched out beautiful and free and fine in front of us, don't we, George?"

"Yes! We do, Amy!"

"And everything is just like it was—before that night—before it happened? Nothing's changed, George?"

He took his eyes away from hers and stared, sullen and still, at the white columns of the public library across the street and wondered if there shouldn't be some kind of book among all those high and eloquent shelves, among the sunlight columned down among the dust motes in the living alleys of human thought; some book with a small, plain, honest answer to her question; to the question that roared round his mind like the tempests of a wrathful God. She reached over and pulled his gaze back to her with cold fingers.

"We could run away," she whispered, but the sunlight was gone from the table now. "Do you love me enough for that, George? To take me away from here?"

"Where?" he breathed, and felt the vast and helpless uselessness of his years. "Where could you go?"

"I wouldn't go anywhere without you," she whispered fiercely. "Nowhere, darling."

"Wait a minute now," he said. "If things get bad. If they should start to move in on me—Amy, there might not be a choice."

"No, George. I won't think of that."

"But you've got to think of it, Amy. If anything should happen to me—don't you see, Amy? If that should happen—one of us has got to be free. To help the other. I mean, if something should happen to me, Amy—if they should grab me—there'd be no one but you left to try to get help."

She was still a moment, biting her lip.

"I know that," she said presently. "I've thought of that, George. But, George. Oh, honey, the thought of leaving you— going off—running away without you—"

"You wouldn't be running away," he said. "You'd be going for help, that's all. Now think. Where? Who?"

"I've thought," she said gravely. "Yes. I've thought of it. George, there's only one place and it's far from here. There's only two people and they're practically strangers—"

"Who, Amy?"

"My grandfather Isaiah and his daughter—my Aunt Nelly. Grandfather Isaiah hasn't spoken to Daddy for heaven knows how long. He detests him. Or at least that's how I've figured it out. Daddy rarely talks about him or Aunt Nelly—either one. Something happened once, I think—a long time ago. Some terrible, awful thing in the family that Daddy won't ever talk about. All I know is that Mama said something once—something nice about Daddy's people and Daddy slapped her face and told her never to mention his father again. He said that his father hated him and he hated his father and they hadn't spoken for I forget how long exactly—thirty or forty years. So—after what's happened—and from the little bit I know about Grandfather and Aunt Nelly—yes, George. They'd take me in. They're the only ones. The only ones on earth. And I think they'd help us both. Because I've got this feeling that they're the only really decent members of my family. Oh, I know that's pretty awful to say— leaving your own mother and father out—but, yes, they're the best of all my family, George. I've guessed as much from things Mama has said against them through the years."

"Such as what?"

"Oh, for example that they were 'nigger lovers.' That mostly. I've heard Daddy say it, too."

"I see. Yes, they sound like they'd help you."

"Oh, George, you don't think anything's going to happen to you, do you?"

"I don't—Amy, I don't know. I—I don't think so but there's always that chance. We've got to think—to plan. Suppose they should pick me up—throw me away somewhere to keep me prisoner so I couldn't tell."

"George, what would you do?"

"It's funny about me, Amy," he said. "I'm no hero. At first I carry on pretty bad when I'm in a jam. But when the showdown really comes—I hold together pretty well. Don't worry about me. That's something you mustn't do. Just help me think— plan. The main thing is where you could go."

"I know darling. I know. There's Grandfather Isaiah and Aunt Nelly. The only ones I could go to. Yes, the only ones on earth who could help. And somehow I know in my heart that they are ones who *would*."

And she smiled at that, wanly, and hunched her shoulders in a little shrug, and hugged his swathed hand to her cheek, rocking it gently to and fro, while fresh tears gleamed in the folded lashes of her eyes.

"Meanwhile, Amy," George said, suddenly reaching over to squeeze her wrist with his good hand, "you better be getting on home. This is all going to take some thinking and scheming out and we don't want your mother getting upset. Go along now."

"All right," she laughed. "Will you be all right?"

"I'll be all right," he said. "Leave things to me. Nine o'clock. Now get along home! I'll see you at nine!"

She rose swiftly and disappeared out the door and ran off under the trees, down the street without once looking back. George sat alone, watching the hands and arms of the waitress who came to clean up the mess of his broken Coke glass.

"Hurt your hand, honey?" said the girl.

"It's all right," he said, smiling. "It's nothing. I hit it against the table and broke the glass. It's nothing. Thanks."

When the girl was gone George sat a spell longer, staring at the freshly wiped top of the marble table. Some new wellspring of courage seemed to surge remotely up inside him. It was nothing he could name or grasp yet, but he knew somehow that he was going to have the strength to do what was needed to be done. He knew that as long as he had Amy nothing could touch either of them. Separately, they were as nothing; together they would do what was right. It was at that moment that he felt the brush of cloth against his elbow and looked up into the face of Gladys Wilson.

"George," she said quietly. "How nice to find you alone. I have a few things that need talking over with you."

He gasped once, blushed, and stood up.

"You won't mind, I hope, if I join you for a little talk, will you, George?" she said in a soft, oily voice that somehow made him feel revulsion.

"Please do sit down, Mrs. Wilson," he said, gathering himself together, still feeling his newfound courage, and looking into her face with curiosity.

"It's about Amy," Gladys said, settling herself across from him and looking hard into his face, though the mouth beneath the eyes were smiling. "And you," she continued. "It's about my little girl's future. I couldn't talk to you about it today in the store—not with Amy there. And so, George I've waited till you were alone."

He said nothing, still looking at her eyes, thinking for one foolish instant that she knew their dark secret, then dismissing that thought as quickly as it had come.

"If it's about Amy, it concerns me," he said quietly.

"Yes," said Gladys softly. "That's what we must see about, mustn't we, George. About you and Amy. You're in love with her, aren't you George?"

"Yes."

"And she, of course," Gladys went on, "feels she's in love with you. My, my, how our children do grow up. Right under our very noses."

He watched her closely now, sensing her danger, hardening himself for whatever might come.

"Children," Gladys went on, glancing up briefly at the waitress by her side. "Yes, please. I'll have a claret phosphate. Separate checks, please."

She fixed her gaze with almost sensuous savagery on her wedding ring and turned it absently back and forth on her finger.

"Children," she went on. "Particularly *girl*-children. Particularly girl-children Amy's age . . ."

She glanced up quickly into George's face, covering the wedding ring with her right hand as she did so.

"They simply must be watched," she said. "They must be protected from their own immature impulses. Wouldn't you agree to that, George?"

"Amy is mature, Mrs. Wilson," he said. "More mature than most girls her age. I think I know that about her."

"Oh, I'm quite sure you know quite a bit about her, George," Gladys said. "Perhaps—well, may I suggest that perhaps you don't know all the right things. I mean to say—the things a mother might know, for example."

"What things, for example, Mrs. Wilson?"

"I'll be frank, George," she said. "Yes, I'll be very frank about it. I'm talking about the direction I want Amy's life to take. Her future. The whole beautiful, unfinished span of her life. It's all in front of her, George. I want nothing to spoil it. I should say, I want no *one* to spoil it."

She paused the barest of moments, breathed in, breathed out.

"You, for example, George," she said. "I wouldn't want you spoiling it."

He smiled and stared at his wrapped, bleeding hand. Then he looked back into Gladys' face.

"You are a bit older than Amy, you know, George," she said.

"But not enough that that would matter," he said, smiling still. "My age is not what would be wrong with Amy and me, is it, Mrs. Wilson?"

"You're certainly not making this easy for me, George," she said.

"Maybe I am," he said. "Maybe I'm just forcing you to come out and get it over with quick. To stop beating around the bush and tell me what's really on your mind."

"I'd rather just say that I don't want you to see my daughter any more—and leave it there, George. I'd rather just tell you that and not have anyone's feelings hurt," she said.

"Feelings!" he cried softly, leaning across the table a little. "How can you sit there and utter an order like that and in the same breath talk about feelings? What about Amy's feelings in this? Forget mine! What about hers? Doesn't she have any rights in this?"

"Amy's too young to understand her feelings, George," she said. "If she could really understand them—she'd know that I am right."

"It's *me* then," he said, struggling to hide his emotion. "Something about *me*. What is it, Mrs. Wilson? Have the courage to say what it is about me that makes it all wrong!"

"George, I wish you'd make it easier. If—"

"To hell with *easier*! Speak your mind to me, Mrs. Wilson. This isn't Amy you're talking to. I'm older—remember?"

"All right," she said, in a quieter, colder voice. "I don't think you're right for Amy. Let's leave it there. I have a right—"

"You have no right," he said bitterly. "Where two people in love—"

"I have all the rights," she interrupted softly, smiling now. "That's where you're wrong, young man. I have all the rights in this and you have none."

"Is it that I'm not good enough for her?" he whispered. "Isn't that what you're trying to say, Mrs. Wilson?"

She was still a moment, not smiling now.

"It's what I'm trying not to say," she said.

"What's wrong with me?" he said evenly. "Look at me, Mrs. Wilson. Tell me the things—"

"I'm looking," she said. "I'm looking at your bleeding hand,

for example—your hand bandaged in a napkin—I'm not finding it hard to imagine how you hurt it."

"How? How!"

"In a street fight," she said. "In a common street fight, I
should guess."

"All right," he said, wondering what she would think if he
bent to his sudden inclination to burst out laughing at her, at
Amy, at all of it. "All right," he said again, and covered his
mouth with his unhurt hand.

"Don't be bitter, George," she said. "Don't think unkindly of
me. I know you've had a hard life—raised in an orphanage as
you were. I'm only a mother trying to protect her daughter. I
mean to say—trying to see what's best for her daughter. That's
why I'm forbidding you to see Amy again."

"Forbidding, Mrs. Wilson?" he said, evenly. "Isn't that a little
strong, Mrs. Wilson?"

"You've forced me to talk strong, young man," she said.
"You've left me no 'out.' I've tried—"

"Because if you're forbidding me," he said, the knuckles of
his free hand whitening as he gripped the table edge. "If you're
forbidding me, then I'm afraid I'll have to ignore that entirely.
Because—"

"You can't ignore it, young man," she said suddenly, her eyes
hard as agate above the thinned, white resolution of her angry
mouth. "You cannot ignore it. And I'll have the courtesy to tell
you why you cannot ignore it—that's only fair, I think. If this
were a large city, young man, I could have my daughter's com-
ing-and-goings watched over by private detectives—"

"Private detectives!" he whispered. "Are you insane, woman!
As if I were trying to kidnap Amy—to harm her—"

"Listen to me, young man," she persisted. "Hear me out. I
think you had better, you know. I want no misunderstanding.
As I said, in a city I would have private detectives. I don't have
that here. I have something better."

"You have a castle with a cell in it and a small gold key," he
said.

"I have a husband," she said. "And my husband has friends. Two very good friends, indeed, young man. Yes, it's these two very good friends of whom I am speaking. I'm sure you've seen them around town. I would judge by your associates—your best friend—the boy you were in the Army with—who is a known dope fiend—I would judge that you know them very well."

"Who?" he breathed, and felt his own breath like a coldness, against his flesh.

"A Mister Stafford," she said. "A Mister Kelts."

He looked at her and fought back the urge to shudder. Then, somehow a long-lost image of Carmel came to haunt him.

"Two very capable police officers in town," she continued in her steely, iced manner. "Force my hand, young man, and I'll have you watched throughout your every waking moment. Am I making myself plain to you, young man? Remember, it was you who set the tone of this discussion, not I. Do I make myself utterly plain?"

"Go to hell, Mrs. Wilson," he said, rising and leaving the booth, yet still keeping his affrighted eyes on hers. "Go clean to hell, Mrs. Wilson."

Her mouth shaped the words; a breath was all the sound there was.

"Walk easy, white-trash orphan!" was her whisper.

And he turned at that, with a sob as if he had recoiled from a blow in the face and moved away, not running, not looking back either, but hurrying now down the steps of the place and up the calico, tree-shadowed sunlight on the brick sidewalk, his blurred eyes running all together, his pace quickening to a broken shamble, all the hurt and shame of the years stuck deep within his breast; seeking a where, an anywhere, in which, for a while—until that hallowed ninth hour when, despite Gladys, he would surely see his love—he might hide and be ashamed for a little time and then, pray God, be done with shame for a spell. It was late dusk. He moved toward the stone bridge which spanned the river from the town's clean sector onto the sprawling ghetto of poor who lived upon the far hill slopes.

"Go clean to hell, Mrs. Wilson!" he cried out to nobody, and then began to run.

Annie Love could always tell that it was five o'clock in the summertime when the corner of the yellow square of sunlight from her back door touched the edge of her Frigidaire. It was a few minutes off from September on into the fall, but it still beat getting up and going all the way to her bedroom to look at the alarm clock. In the winter months, of course, it was no good at all because, most of the time, the sun never got through to Baltimore Street and the back door to Annie Love's brothel was shut tight against the tomblike chill from the river mists and the sulfurous stink of the burning slag piles up on the hill at Paradise Slide. But in the sweet of the summer, when the wind was westering, and the jasmine drifted its ghostly sweetness through the patched screen door, Annie could tell the time just fine. Five o'clock. Time to send Sally or one of the other girls down to Big Brother's Market for a good big, thick slice of ham for supper and a shopping bag full of cold beer and maybe a little box of them good, thin mints with the chocolate on them. Saturday afternoon, to be sure, was the exception. That was the day Annie's three girls went over to the courthouse for their weekly tests at the County Health Office and it was generally five thirty before they got back. And every once in a while one of the girl's tests would come up positive and that would really throw the whole time schedule off good and proper with tears and wailing and Annie Love slippering in a gouty, shuffling rage through the rooms of her great gray house, naming on her strong, immaculate fingers the likeliest candidates of those foul men who had dared bring sickness and corruption into her spotless and orderly brothel.

"Stop bawling whilst I think a while, Betty June!" she would roar from the pulpit-like eminence of the fancy, bannistered staircase. "Hush that damned caterwauling whilst I think. Hah! Hah! I know now who it was!"

And on her swollen, aching ankles she would ease herself down into the parlor again and stagger to the juke box in arm-flailing, histrionic fury; stuffing quarters into the slot and stabbing her forefinger again and again on the button for Number 6B which always had been and always would be an old Vaughn Monroe recording called "When the Lights Go On Again All Over the World." It was Annie's own soul's comfort and cheer: that song. Because it was from the days during World War II when there had been an induction center in Elizabethtown and it reminded Annie of the years when there had been a true glory in her calling: those happy summer nights when she had helped soothe the lonely minds and bodies of the green young hill boys, torn away too soon from home.

"I know now who the son of a bitch was!" she would roar, beet-faced with fury, the ebony crucifix rising and falling on her neat black dress with the tumult of her heaving bosom. "Shut up that bawling, Betty June, whilst I think! Hah! Yes! It *was* him! That Polack bastard coal miner that come in late last Saturday night! I knowed it! I knowed it! Don't I always say I can tell when they got it? Don't it always show around their eyes?"

And her voice would rise, with the indignation of a high priestess whose temple has been defiled, and Betty June would cry the louder, and the record would shout its worn, sibilant melody thinly amid the din and uproar.

"There now! There, there now!" Annie would cry, cradling the grieving child in her great arms. "Hush, Betty June! It's not all that bad now! It's not the end of the world, honey! Why, you just go regular to Miss Moon for them penicillins for a week and you'll be good as ever! There now! Annie knows! It's a shame and abomination what them bastards brings amongst us! Annie knows! But don't take on this away, honey, for it'll all be gone in a week! Seven days, lamby! There, there now!"

And by the time the girl had been quieted and sent off to bed, Annie Love would be worked up until the whole Saturday night was spoiled for the rest of them and like as not would end up with Annie, bourbon-breathed and wrathful, rising from her rocker in the love-creaking stillness of the early morning and sending a giant, drunken miner pitching down the back steps into the honeysuckle, and for no other reason but that she had read something improper in his eyes: had remembered sensing it, vaguely, when he had come in and handed her his sweaty payday greenbacks and gone off with Ruby or Sally. And afterward she had sat there by her Frigidaire, rocking and sipping on a tumbler of raw rye and muttering to herself, building up the case against him with every measured pace of her chair, with every muffled love-cry from the jasmined dark, and rising at last, in righteous, cockeyed certainty that he was no less than a leper, had stormed off into the bedrooms with balled fists to curse and lash this diseased pariah back into the foggy, sullen streets. This had not been that sort of Saturday. This had been the best kind of Saturday Annie Love could ask for; with all three girls back from Miss Moon's clinic with clean bodies and happy hearts and they'd all had a good big fried chicken supper with lemon meringue pie for dessert and sat around laughing and joking while they waited for the night. When the sun went down over the slag piles at Paradise Slide and the dusky gold was gone from the river willows down the hill, the spirit changed in Annie Love's house. The girls grew quiet and waited for the folding down of night. And when the night had come among them they would wander out into the vine-sweet darkness of the long, wooden porch and wait restless in the swings and rockers for the coming of the strangers. With every nightfall there was a kind of solemn and nameless excitement stirring in their hearts. Even Annie Love would feel it.

George could not remember how he had come to be there in the brothel, could not recount the footsteps that had led him, numbed and dry-tongued and haunted throughout the dreadful afternoon and the panic of the sinking sun and nighttime's folding down. He had walked and he had crossed the gray stone

arch of the bridge, over the river and into the travesty of slum
streets that clutched the hill's bleak, eroded slopes and saw,
after nightfall, the fire rim of gold high up above Hunkie-town
where the slag piles burned by Paradise Slide and the big beer
joint neons snapping on-and-off and breathed the fried onion
and barbecued ribs in the breath of the street and wandered
on, past the stack of flashing motorcycles in front of the Ritzy
and up into the dusk and sleep of a street where the leaves bent
over the mist-damp bricks of the pavements and the wet boughs
of them brushed his head as he went wandering down the night.
And heard the creak of the rusty porch-swing chains and the
wooden, lazy rumor of rockers and heard them pause as his
own footsteps slowed upon the stones. And heard the voice,
hardly louder than the gray, soft wind that cooled his anguished
face, and wondered for a moment was it wind or women that
had leaned so softly into his mind and whispered there.

"Honey? Lonely, darlin'? Come on in!"

And then the dark shape against the dusky screen door and
the voice of Annie Love herself: whispering; harsh and warm
and lustrous like dark silk being torn.

"It's only two! That ain't a penny too much for any one of
my three, fine, healthy girls! Come on in off Baltimore Street,
honey, afore your two feet put down roots and turn you to a
tree!"

"I want a drink," he whispered, blinking into the gaudy Al-
pine landscape on the shade of the lamp in the parlor, feeling
it as the three girls stepped shyly in behind him and the screen
door softly closed.

"Why, sure! Sure, you do now!" cried Annie Love and
clapped her hard, clean fingers in her palm, "Ruby! Run yonder
to the kitchen and fetch down glasses and get out ice cubes.
We'll all have a snort!"

She breathed deeply, exultant in her calling, and feeling in
her heart that it was going to be one of the best Saturday nights
she had had all summer. She swiftly appraised him with a flick-

ering sweep of her shrewd, gray eyes and sniffed a breath of
good cologne demurely from the froth of her kerchief.

"You've got money?"

"Money?"

He turned to her and blinked again, as if he were desperately
trying to think something out and yet bear her question in mind
at the same time. He considered her politely and frowned as if
he were having trouble remembering what she had said.

"Yes!" she said, her eyes a little brighter. "Money! Whiskey
costs money and so does girls, young mister!"

"Money," he said. "Oh, yes! Yes, I have money."

And he fumbled his old wallet out of his hip pocket and
opened it, showing her, and then put it back and sat down very
carefully on the chair by the front door, his knees together and
his hands on his knees and stared at her feet.

"It's the custom" she said. "To ask first. It ain't nothing personal and it saves misunderstandings later. Sometimes one of
the girls—"

"I didn't come for that," he said. "I have a girl. I wanted a
drink if that'll be all right. I'll pay."

"Sure! Sure!" she crowed and listened to the three girls tinkling ice cubes and giggling in the kitchen. "I knowed you had
a girl when I first seen your face! And I said to myself: Annie,
there's a good clean young man who's got himself a girl friend—
a nice girl! And being as she's a nice girl, why, it's no monkey
business! That's the way of the world, I said to myself! But a
man is a man and when he's lonely . . ."

"I just want a drink," he said again and pressed his palms
harder onto the caps of his knees because they had begun to
tremble uncontrollably.

"First time you ever had a drink, ain't it?" said Annie Love.

"No, ma'am," he said and drank another shot down, straight,
and heard the ticking of the alarm clock away off in Annie
Love's bedroom as loud and clear as knuckles on a door panel.

"Well, here's to it!" cried Annie Love, downing a discreet

thimbleful and then dabbing primly at the corners of her lips with her hanky.

"I've got a girl," he said, looking slowly across the faces of Betty June and Ruby and Sally and taking a deep breath, smelling the explicit odor of the house: the composite scent of sleep and of woman-flesh.

"I'll bet she's pretty!" whispered Betty June, and pinched the lobe of his ear.

"Yes!" he said, smiling and feeling strong among them there and wanting suddenly to tell them of his love for Amy. "She's beautiful!" he said, pouring himself another drink, only this time he poured it in the tumbler. And before he scarcely knew what he was doing he had tugged the wallet out of his hip pocket and showed them all the snapshot of Amy when they had gone swimming at Lake Angel.

"That's her! Isn't she beautiful?"

"Lands' sakes!" cried Annie Love, elegantly. "She is a looker! And a body can see she's not the sort to put up with any monkey business neither! Just the same—a healthy young boy gets lonesome sometimes! That's the way of the world! Have another drink, boy! Or better yet—why not just let me keep out this here five dollars . . ."

She delicately edged the bank note from the lips of the wallet and then held it up for him to take back.

". . . and that'll pay for all that's left in the bottle! That's fair enough, ain't it?" cried Annie Love. "And then if you should want one of the girls later on . . ."

"Fair enough," he said, hiccupping gently. "Fare enough. Round trip fare."

He tilted back on the kitchen chair, smiling at Amy in her white bathing suit in the August of his billfold and winked at her very deliberately so she would not think he was going to be unfaithful to her that night.

"Please tell me, somebody," he said, making the words very carefully between his tingling tongue and mouth, "when it is nine o'clock. Remember that? Nine o'clock. Because I have a date with Amy at ten and I have to go get my car and be there on time. Will somebody please be sure and tell me when it's ten? I mean nine?"

"Sure!" said Annie Love. "Sure now! Don't you worry."

"Nine!" he repeated, scowling with concern. "I meant to say nine!"

"I've got a girl!" he exclaimed again, suddenly astonished, and trying hard to remember something of desperate importance about her. "But I've got a girl, I tell you!"

Gladys Wilson never drank when Loy was in town. This night, after dinner, she got comfortable in her red satin housecoat, fixed herself a good stiff highball, and when she had finished two inches of it, went to look at herself in the tall, genuine antique pier glass in the dining room. And she would stand before the unprejudiced silver of the glass, appraising the mark of time upon her flesh. First she reaches behind her and draws the red satin housecoat tight about her so that she can tell if her breasts still look firm and young. Then she lifts her chin and gently draws the skin down at the hollow of her throat to see if there are any new lines in her neck. Sometimes she lowers her eyes and allows a gentle smile to quiver in the corner of her lips.

"Not bad for thirty," said the voice that had sighed to the mirror through the years. "Not bad for thirty-three. Not bad for thirty-six. Not bad for thirty-seven, old dear!"

Gladys Simpson had been three months short of fifteen when Loy married her. She had lived all her childhood on her Scotch father's thousand-acre vegetable farm down in Danby County below the laurel of the mountains and she thought Loy was the handsomest man she had ever laid eyes on that night when she had seen his face at the Chautauqua meeting, under the tent, under the torches. Not only the handsomest man, but the first. She took him home one night while the sweet drifting brasses of the Chautauqua band played Victor Herbert behind the trees and her father, Ben Simpson, met them with a lantern under the pink-foaming plum tree blossoms in the yard and took one look at Loy Wilson and saw a thing in his face. Ben Simpson's eyes, in quivering, country sunlights, had learned to look into men and read them quickly, like horses. Ben immediately threw young Loy over the picket fence into the ditch below the blackberry bushes. Three nights later Gladys and Loy Wilson ran away to Choctaw and were married. Three years later Amy was born. Twenty-three years later Gladys stood here before the eternal glass, with tears in her eyes, and her fingers holding taut the skin at the hollow of her throat. Amy would never make that mistake; Amy was not going to marry any trash and waste her life, withering her beauty in neglect and sorrow. Amy was going to have college and a career to be free and be worshiped. Folks already said what a sweet, strong voice she had when she sang in the Presbyterian Choir. Amy was going to be an opera singer. Gladys was going to see to that and nothing could stand in her way or no one and she would see that it came to pass if it took every cent of money Loy Wilson could earn or steal to do it. Gladys drew her satin robe tight against her and went back into the front room and finished her highball at a single, long swallow. Then she got out the bottle from the bookcase and poured herself another one, a good deal darker this time. Gladys settled down in the big chair by the stairs and took a good gulp, quivering with resolution and sorrow and a tongueless rage; glaring at the stairway, listening to Amy up in her room, sobbing in the darkness.

"Amy!"

And the sobbing stopped and night took up its pulse, weaving its deep rhythm into the night sounds of cricket among the high, unstirring grasses; of green frogs down in the dark cattails of the river.

"Amy!"

"Yes—Yes, Mother."

"Amy, I want to talk to you."

"Mother, I don't feel like talking. You know I've been feeling bad all day. You know I didn't eat supper."

"Come down," said Gladys, evenly. "I'll fix you a hot toddy for your cramps."

"It's not cramps, Mother."

"Come down."

"Why, Mother? What for?"

Gladys kept her temper, gave Amy time to stop sobbing, to wash her face in cold water, to gather her spirits together.

"Coming, Amy?"

"Mother, why?"

"I want to talk to you is why. I want to talk to you about George Purdy is why. I want to talk to you about your future!"

There was no answer, but Gladys knew it was because Amy was in the bathroom getting her face back together. She drank some more of her second highball and began to feel sure of herself; knowing exactly how she would tell Amy that she wasn't going to be able to keep her date with George Purdy that night. Not that night, nor for that matter, any other night. Ever.

"Are *you* sore?"

"Me? Shoot, no!" she exclaimed with a toss of her hair in the brothel dark and knocked a cigarette out of a half empty pack and, of a sudden, the girl was all flame and shadow in the flare of the kitchen match. She blew smoke and the dark came back and he remembered for an instant the look she had thrown him in the light of that moment.

"Shoot!" she chuckled in the dark. "Why should I be sore? It's your money. You paid it to her. I reckon it all you want from me is to set here and talk and drink, then that's all. That's all. I ain't sore."

"Thanks," he said, and the bottle chattered on the tumbler's rim as he poured them both another inch.

"You ain't no queer, are you? No pansy?"

"No."

He could hear her easy, steady breathing in the dark and thought: Whores have night-eyes.

"You ain't runnin' from the Law, are you?" she said.

He got a little sore then, but he kept his teeth shut and felt round the table for her squashed pack of Camels and got one out and found a match and lighted it.

"No," he said, keeping his face steady and calm, in the flame-light, his eyes looking right into hers, for an instant before he blew back the dark again.

"I knowed you wasn't!" she laughed softly in the dark. "You're still just a boy! I don't reckon there's nothin' you could do that the Law'd want you for! You can tell," she murmured, and the coal of her cigarette came and went, a red speck in the darkness. "My sister Rose—she was a hustler. Went up north. Worked in a place called East Liverpool. One Saturday night— 'mongst all them steel-workin' Polacks and Hunkies—there come a stranger from the street. Rose hadn't never seen him before. Sweet Evening Breeze—the woman she was workin' for—she hadn't never seen him before. And Rose said she knowed the minute she laid eyes on him who he was and there wasn't a damned thing she could do but take his money and go on back in the room with him. And let him. And all the time her knowin' who he was. Damn if I could. Damn if I would. But my sister Rose—she had guts, I'll say that for her. Know who it was?"

"No," he said to the golden fire of his cigarette.

"John Dillinger is who it was!" she said. "John Dillinger, America's A-Number-One Public Enemy is who it was! And he'd killed a cop that very day. And Rose said it was just like she could smell the blood on him while he was pawin' her around there in the bed. That cop's blood. Just like it was still on him."

"Stop it," said his mouth without any air coming out, there-fore without sound, not even a whisper.

"I declare," she chattered on, heedless. "The way Rose's eyes used to light up when she was to tell that story you'd swear it was the best time she'd ever had with a man. Shoot! I'd be scared plumb to death in the bed with a man like that. But not old Rose. Not her! Though I'll swear it marked her life. She wrote my other sister, Jackie, about it the day after. And she wrote another letter from Gary, Indiana on the night they shot that John Dillinger to death and ever' letter we ever got from Rose she'd talk about that night—like it was the biggest, grandest thing that ever happened to her. But you could tell she got queer after that. Know what happened to her?"

"No," he sighed to the moon. "What happened to her?"

"She went crazy. Leastways, they said that's what it was, anyhow. Psycho. I was just a little, tiny girl then—the night she come home. I never even knowed who she was. I just mind the way she used to lie in the bed and holler in the pillow and scratch herself all over and I used to go and look at her lying there on her bed with Grandma's old quilt kicked off onto the floor and there was a light from a big blast furnace down the creek and Rose's face'd be all red and lit-up just like she was in hell from the light comin' in that bedroom window. And my Ma used to cry and try to get her to take some chicken soup and Rose'd throw the bowl at Ma and go to scratchin' and screamin' on the floor and hollerin' for fixes. And nobody knowed what she was talkin' about. Fixes. They said when she died it was the craziness and fear that done it. But sometimes I think it was the mark old John Dillinger left on her that night. All that scratchin' and screamin'. Sometimes I get to thinkin' about Rose and all that and her dyin' that night and I swear it was that. Him comin' into the house that night and her takin' him in the bedroom. And it wasn't the dope at all. It was that blood—all that meanness—that was what she was scratchin' herself about—trying to get his mark off her skin. Because—"

"Please don't talk about that anymore," he said, shutting his eyes to the stained moon in the patched, porch-door screen.

So she was still for a spell, and again he felt her appraisal there in the darkness.

"How come you so scared?" she whispered, with kindness, and her fingers ventured across the square of moon and took his own.

"Scared? I'm not scared of you! I told you I've got a girl."

"No," she said. "I don't mean scared of me. I mean just scared. Scared of somethin'. I know you ain't scared of me. I never meant that. But I know you're scared."

He took his hand away from hers long enough to pick up the glass and drink, but he put his hand back where her fingers could take hold of his again if they wanted to. And they did.

"It ain't none of my damned business," she said. "And if you don't want to talk about it, just plain say so. If you want me to shut my mouth, just plain say so. Miss Annie declares to everyone I'm the nosiest hustler on Baltimore Street. Always pokin' and pryin' into folk's souls. My daddy was that way, they say. Pay me no mind."

Near tears with the need to spill it out to her, he gulped down all of the whiskey in his glass and suddenly was deeply and wisely drunk.

"It's too late," he said, and dropped his cigarette and bent to pick it up elaborately between his thumb and forefinger; to put it back carefully between his lips. "It's too late. When I first came in I told you all to be sure to tell me when nine o'clock come. And you never did."

"It's not even eight-thirty yet," she said, gently.

"Yes it is. Oh, yes it is. I can tell. It looks like nine o'clock and it feels like nine o'clock. I can tell. But it doesn't make any difference. Don't worry about it. I wouldn't go get Amy anyway. Because I'm awful damned drunk and if I was to go to Amy's place drunk, I might slip and spill the whole thing. Her daddy might be there and I'd spill the whole thing. And you know what? If I ever was to spill that news around Amy's daddy— you know what?"

"What?" she whispered.

"*You* know what!" he chuckled, deeply amused at the way the moon moved its face whenever he moved his. "*You* know!"

And in the darkness the smile upon his face slowly faded and his eyes grew round as moons themselves.

"You *know* goddamned well what he'd do, Betty June."

"Can't you find no doctor for it?" she whispered. "Or is she too far gone? How far is she gone? I can write you down the phone number of a good one—a woman—she runs a clinic up state about thirty mile. And she don't charge but fifty."

And he laughed at this solemn, splendid joke that the night had given him, that his drunkenness had given him, and Betty June shuddered suddenly and took her fingers away and folded her arms under her breasts and felt something like a cold wind between them and something beyond the night, beyond the screen door, smelled suddenly like the wet hair of a dog.

He opened his eyes and it was as dark as when they had been lidded shut. He blinked and it was dark both ways. Sleeping with his mouth open had made his throat sore and dry and his tongue felt thick and cracked as an old shoe. His face was puckered and numb from slack-jawed, snoring sleep and his lips were fuzzy with bedlint and sticky with love. He flung an arm out to one side where there was no bed and then to the other side where the tangled sheets were still warm with her. But she was gone. His head was ringing but it didn't ache, and he lifted it carefully, blinking again and saw a crooked, golden streak where the bottom of the door was.

"Poor little Amy," he said softly with his big, dry tongue. "Sittin' there waitin'. Poor little darlin'."

He started to rise to go find his clothes but he didn't know the way, so he lay his head gently back on the pillow and thought a while more about poor little Amy. And thought how he had never meant to come to this house in the first place. Yes, he had meant to come here, but just to drink. Poor little Amy. He had gone and been faithless to her.

Lying here now and thinking: That Betty June and me got drunk in the kitchen and when that hollering music started in the juke box she said, "Let's go in the bedroom. Where we can drink and talk in peace." In peace. I meant to do what we did here in the bed. I even got out that picture of Amy again and showed it to her, and she made me close it up and put it back in my pocket because she said she didn't have any picture of a True Love to treasure like that. She kept on talking and her face was bright and happy with tears. And it made me remember Amy's face crying in Candyland this afternoon and I kissed Betty June and went over to finish the rest of my drink while she put away some things in the dresser drawer. When I looked up at her, though, she didn't have a stitch of clothes on except her shoes. I looked at her breasts and saw that she wasn't any older than Amy and here all the time me thinking she was older than me. She looked just like I always pictured Amy looking without any clothes. Round and rosy-nippled and slim and tears falling off her cheeks and dark curls tumbling down on her shivering shoulders like she was cold. She snapped out the light. And I kept trying to put it out of my mind that it was Amy beneath me in the dark—grieving and moaning against my mouth. Then I got mad at myself and ashamed. Because I was too drunk to do it and she stopped making that grieving sound and commenced to stroking my face and hugging me and kissing me and saying it didn't matter, that it was all right. I said you must think I'm queer, and she said, "No, no." "No, no," she said. "Sleep. Sleep a spell. Honey, you're just scared. Scared is all." And she lit a cigarette and laid there on her back blowing smoke up into the dark and I shut my eyes and tried to remember what I was scared of. I couldn't remember anything. Yes. Yes, I could! A little piece of it came back to me. It was about a nigger. Was he chasing me? Yes! Yes, that was what I was scared of. A little nigger kid. Negro. I mean Negro kid. He was chasing me. That's what I was scared of: that little Negro nigger kid.

He sat up in the bed now, the sweat streaming suddenly down his naked chest over his belly; starkly awake and listening sharply to the night. The streak of light beneath the door was the last light of earth. He felt his panic rise like a swelling bubble as the dark pressed down: the nigger dark all around him and the smear of light was blood.

"Betty June!"

His naked heels rung on the floor as he swung his legs down and dug his nails into the mattress. The door opened wide and she stood there, blinking at him under the naked bulb in the hallway. She had on her cheap little blue dress again.

"I went to get you some coffee."

He spilled most of it, scalding, onto his bare knees as he took the chattering cup and saucer from her and sucked a mouthful, bitter and black and burning, into his dried, sore throat.

"Got the shakes?"

He nodded fast and tried, clumsily, to steady the cup and saucer in his fingers.

"Rather have a drink?"

"Huh-uh. Thanks. Huh-uh. Not just now. Thanks."

She sat down beside him on the bedside, staring with kindly, wondering eyes.

"You sure are packing around a mess of misery."

"Yeah. Yeah. Be all right. Be fine."

She smiled and shook her head and took the cup and saucer gently from his hands.

"You don't want to leave," she said. "You don't want to go home tonight. Do you?"

"Home?"

"You don't have to. That's one thing that nobody could ever say about Miss Annie. There's never been anyone throwed out of Miss Annie's house to stagger and fall in the streets for the cops to grab."

"Cops?" he whispered. "I never did anything!"

Her grave gaze steadied and fixed on something in his eyes, seized something from his voice, and suddenly understood.

"Then," she said. "Maybe you saw somebody else do something . . ."

He sobbed and bit a knuckle till blood sprang between his teeth.

". . . and you're scared to tell."

She sighed and her eyes lighted with pride and defiance and a kind of maternal custody of him now.

"Screw the cops!" she said. "You don't have to tell."

He turned his anguished eyes to hers and made the lie again, bravely wondering how many more times he would have the strength to make it.

"No," he said. "It's not that way at all. It's not like you just said at all, Betty June. We—I never saw a thing!"

But she bit her lip and kept on thinking; determined not to relinquish this hard-won gem of insight.

"We! See? You started to say 'We.' That means it's you and someone else seen something!"

"No!"

She shrugged and let him be and put her arms around him instead, struggling her mouth around to his and kicking the door closed again with her bare left foot, then pushing him back she set forth upon a strange, fierce conquest of him: as if, having seized upon the secret of his sorrow, of his terror, she must now possess the flesh wherein it dwelt and in the violence of the act of love which now he wrought furiously in the dark upon her rich, welcoming loins, she might confirm the fact of fury and of death which hung round him like the smell of burned powder in an aftermath of gunfire.

Twice he woke, with the drunken spin of moon between his heavy lids, and twice he gasped her name in the terror of that solitude, and each time she murmured and pressed against him, lulling him back into troubled sleep.

"Hush, honey, hush. I'm here. Try and get some sleep. I'll not leave. I'm right here now."

"No," he said thickly to the wet pillow against his lips.

"Hush now. Hush."

"Nine o'clock yet?"

"Sleep now. Hush now."

"Right," he muttered through the pillow. "Right."

She waited, listening for his rapid snores and then got up and stole to the window and pulled the cracked blind down, saving him from the moon, and stood for an instant, listening to his swift, anguished breath as the shapeless murmur of words grew less and less.

"God love him," she whispered to the dark and clasped her fingers in the dark. "God love 'em all."

ISAIAH

Isaiah Wilson lay alone, counting the night as if its passage were the whisper of numbers. He listened to the old hound's grumpy bark, muffled beneath the back porch; barking without lifting his muzzle from the smooth earth, because he was heavy with supper and stiff with years and uncertain what needed barking at beyond the scrub-pine edge of darkness. Something. Isaiah felt it, too: a footfall that impended in a sensibility beyond hearing. His bearded, craggy face among the goosedown pillow turned to the lace of the drifting window. There was a moon come up and there was a wind come with it to blow soft lights among the linden leaves and beneath them, fluttering, upon the silvered slates of the porch. The wind was westerly, and it was Isaiah's fancy that it wandered clean from East Texas, smelling of that, and smelling, too, of all sprawled land asleep between: prairie and high pine, and the galloping rivers and the big, broken-backed mountains west of sunfall. When the dog stopped barking, the wind soughed upon sill.

I wish I could get up and go back out there, the man thought, as he had done so often in those nights. For I am a burden to her this way, old this way. I will get up and go back out there one night, he thought. One good night with a moon when the wind is westering. I will just get up out of this trash of worn-out flesh and go, to fret them all no more.

It was a shame upon him, like something soiled upon him, that he had come to a time of leaning, on any of them, and most particularly her: his daughter, Nell, who loved him so richly and with none of the thin, patronizing deceits of common daughters toward old fathers. He had been the big tree among their lives and some of them had thrust up on trunks of their own among his shelter, while some others had vined in weakness on his boughs and some had altogether gone to earth. Strong yet, something of him nonetheless had creaked and splintered, leaning his tallness into the dark and the burden of that was hers, his daughter Nell's, and he cringed from that more than from anything that he had known in life. It was that way with him because he had come ninety years and, through most of them, had been the one that others leaned on. And now this was all turned round and wrong: his days grown crooked and their needs awry. No, not dying: that was not the dread that came with age, it was this other. He could not, in fact, remember the time in his life when he had dreaded death; though many the stinging, sweet instants when, facing death, he had feared it— but that was such a different thing, that momentary, loving clutch of life. Nor had the abstract dread, the rocking-chair speculation of it ever fretted him a moment, because it would be a going out—a getting up and going back out there; up-camp and yonder to a Reckoning or to a noneness and he did not bother his soul about which. In the days, vigilant for something, he sat out of doors: a giant, snow-bearded and black-eyed, stiff-backed upon his cane chair, by the sunny place in the dooryard where windfall apples thumped alike time: six-foot-four and shoulders still spaced proud and sturdy as a mustang's, while every pound of all two hundred and fifty of bone and muscle of him seemed focused and pounced in personal affront upon the fist-clasped crook of his black stick. Furious to be half-lame and slowed-up and numb-shouldered by a stroke, now two years past, that would have brought a man of half his years to nursing bed and spoon-fed tending. Still and all, it was an outrage and a misery; for six months after, they had to help him: to bed, to table, and to bath; his wife Sabby, snickering beneath the one giant elbow and his daughter Nell, grave and loving, beneath the other—Nell, who would endure beyond his death and, alone among his two children, flourish with the kind of grace and strength that had been his. Sabby would endure, as well, but if only by stubbornness and perversity, subsisting within herself upon the sap of her own vindictive and malevolent fiber, surviving Isaiah for spite's sake if for no other. And in the nights he seemed to yearn at the edge of stars, wearied a little with them all, wearied most, indeed, with himself and with what often seemed to him to amount to a very treason of his flesh against its spirit. And, in the mornings, when he went to his stiff chair by the tree, he presented the angry aspect of a mountain eagle, clip-winged and brought down to mere pacing among hens in a fence dooryard. In the dark of nights such as this now he would lie considering the twin imponderables: life behind and life before, feeling the wind upon his eyes and upon his great, nesting hands, and smell in that wind something come all the way from the Brazos and all the lands between, and something from the blown-away years as well. In the bee-sweet drowse and stitch of summer noon, by the big tree in the dooryard, he would look up and see it in the eyes of old Toby, the Mexican Negro, who had been through it with him; would read it there, too: the call to break camp and be on as if in answer to some prairie spoor, drifting and sweet in his senses. The old hound, too: Harry, the fat hound, toothless and leaky on the porchboards his haunches had worn smooth there, eyeing in rheumy impotence, like a deposed king, the mocking jack rabbits, cocky now in the lost, weedy province of his meadows: him, too, the badger-gray dog; all old things, shamed now in that autumn time by their burden upon the strong, good young. And yet, beneath the disenchantment smoky in their eyes, life's paradox persisted: the yearning to go and the tug to stay; an unquenchable hunch that life might need them one more time, that someone loved might need them one more time, that something might go wrong, with them not there. And this sustaining them—Isaiah, black Mex Toby, and the blind hound—the fear that Death might quench them like candles in a false morning to leave their loved dears in darkness. Yes, tonight, feeling that. Hearing the old dog's troubled, incompetent bark beneath the porch again, Isaiah felt that hunch, that tug toward life, stronger in that night than it had felt in many moons. And Toby, feeling it, too; Isaiah could hear him up and wandering in the yard, sleepless over something in the night, his footfalls crashing softly in the dry leaves. Crutched-up on his arm, Isaiah glared down through the tossing boughs among the moon in his curtained window and saw suddenly the half-breed's face, tiny and vivid as the face upon a red-hot penny, as he struck a match and cupped flame to his pipe; the flare of it printing his grooved, leathered face in fire for an instant upon the air, by the smokehouse, under the plane tree's shadow. Isaiah lay back down and sighed, remembering in New Mexico, sixty years before, on the third night of a cattle drive he had been asleep in his roll and an old Mex vaquero—a man past eighty, they said—had wakened him and warned him, in Spanish, to rouse the others; that the long horns were going to stampede. It seemed to Isaiah a queer, senseless thing to be doing, with the black herds humped almost motionless in rest all around him in the cold moonshine as far to either side as he could see, and no sudden sound even imaginable in that desert stillness to send the black bulls and their cows exploding up in panic. The old Mex was sure, though, sensing something, though, and kept whispering to Isaiah to hurry in the Name of the Virgin, and Isaiah had gone sheepishly around to each man sleeping in the fireshine, rousing men for no good reason at all that he could feel, because he was young, yet, and Time and the silences had not taught him their lessons, yet, and while the men got up cursing softly, the old vaquero stood stiff and white-eyed by the fire, crossing himself and whispering little prayers, and within the count of sixty a stewpan fell clattering in the chuck wagon and the herd was up like a bomb. Isaiah remembering that now, thinking: But what event comes tonight? Who comes out there? he sorrowed, restively, and saw the smoke of Toby's pipe curdle like cream in the moonlight beyond the plane tree's shadow, shapeless as the answers which the night gave him back. Loy? his mind queried and the pale pipe smoke dwindled in the air and was only moonshine and he knew, No. No, Loy would come across that threshold no more, no matter how dire his need, and even the rumor of that desperate memory sickened Isaiah's mind, who had not spoken one word to his son in forty-five years, not seen his living face, and lay now, remembering with the fresh pain that time had not numbed, the years through which the two of them, father and son, had lived and eaten and slept beneath the same roof in hatred, moving stiffly past one another upon tiptoe fury like circling dogs in a pit. Forty-five years that autumn since the terrible morning when, finally, Loy had gone, and Isaiah had spent the better part of the winter- after stalking through room and hall and closet and cupboard of the house, gathering together all last living mementos of his son and, in grave and stoic ritual, burning them in the stone oven by the smokehouse: letters from school, snapshots from infancy, birth certificate and high-school diploma, straw hat and bamboo walking stick, a ukulele from a boyhood trip to Mobile, and a copy of Kipling's poems. All gone up at last to stain the pale, sea-faded sky for a twinkling and then wash out on the wind.

On the other side of the house, moonless, Nell slept. And in sleep alone—wherein, safely, the tintype dream silvers and darkens with its metaphors—in sleep alone, may Nell now witness her spirit then, in a season long gone down the rains and winds of over forty years; seeing her self then, and Loy then, and Luke: all, as they then had been. Nell Wilson's movement from child into womanhood had been as stunning and abrupt as if some voice, in the perfumed air of her infantile bedroom, had commanded it. Sabby would have forbade it, if ever she had found some wizard way to bind the swelling breasts and curse the seed's red rhythm. Nell was a woman overnight. And then had begun a desperate time, because, at the outset, at least, it did not seem to her that the change was in herself at all, but rather some alteration in her brother and in Luke. Nothing ever was the same: and so each, alone, moved irresolutely outward bound, like creature neither child nor man, stumbling and confounded amid a drugged smoke of burning toys. On the morning of her twelfth birthday Nell was milking in the stable and a wasp, dull-footed in the chill of autumn dawn, fell from his cluster of clay castles on the boards high above her, and fell into the open neck of her dress. She walked down to the house, in the mists, with the foaming milk still hot in the pail, and bit her lip in agony and shut her eyes against the tears that squeezed out of her dark lashes and scattered down her cheek. Luke stepped out of Toby's cabin with her birthday present in his hand.

"Nelly! Why, what's wrong?"

"Nothing, Luke. It's really nothing."

"You're crying! And it your birthday. Did the old cow kick . . . ?"

"A wasp," she sobbed gently. "It stung my chest. Oh, God, it just hurts something fierce, Luke."

"Here," he offered, manfully. "Lemme suck out the poison."

And she just stood there while he undid the twenty buttons of her dress, to the waist, and pulled down the straps of her shift over her hard, round shoulders and she had thought: No, he shouldn't. No, I shouldn't let him 'cause I'm different, I'm changed. But she felt her tongue too heavy to forbid him and her head was all swimmy and it couldn't be the wasp sting that made her blood pound so slow and thick in the muscles of her throat and she just stood there, her head a little upturned, lips a little opened, and eyes fallen closed as if upon a sensuous dream and Luke just stood there and dared not suck the poison out, dared not even touch her, because she was different and changed; it was not chest anymore, it was breast; it was not child, it was woman and the smell of the foaming milk in her pail was thick in the air and his own head got strange. For a spell neither moved. Luke just looked in wonder and was struck with something beautiful and at the same time shameful, rising in his blood. Nell, in the rosy morning, stood in a bath of light like mother-of-pearl and the first gold of sunup struck through the scrub pines and shone on the round and nippled aureoles and he could see the white welt between them where the wasp sting was. Then both wakened and Nell blushed and stammered something and fidgeted the straps back up over her shoulders and looked down, sucking her lip in shame and watched her fingers fumble the twenty buttons up again. Luke, scarlet, thrust the gift into her hands then and fled back into the lantern that Toby had lit to get their breakfast by. No, the old years were gone: never again could they run on summer dog days to the deep place in PawPaw River and strip and swim naked in innocence and grace. Nothing ever would be the same. And when the time of transition was itself complete and each of them altered almost beyond the others' recognition and forever more immutable, Luke drew more to himself and stayed alone in the cool, long summer dusks in the barn loft struggling for a means to announce his identity upon the earth, squinting and sweating and cursing among little pots of carriage paint he'd saved up and bought from Eck T. Wilfong in Goshen, and when, by late hour lampshine, he would see what his brushes had made upon the flat panel of white pine and curse and break it on his knee and weep alone a while into his big fingers, and Nell alone knew why.

"Why, he's just *queer*—that's why!" Sabby would say, stitching with a vicious, stabbing industry of needle at the party dress she was making for Nell. "Nigger—and still not-nigger! Just like his fool father! Neither white nor black! Fish or fowl! No wonder he's *queer*! Land sakes, that boy's not right in the head—spending all kinds of hours up in the barn loft. He's not been right since your father took you all on that trip to New Orleans! I declare, he'll burn that barn down one of these nights—mark my words. But just let me try to tell your father that and he snaps my head off. I declare, Nelly, in many ways I hope you never marry!"

"Mama, what an awful thing to say!"

"I mean it. Men! The nasty things! You'll know someday what I am saying is true, child! Only then it'll be too late! Too late! The nasty things. There's but one thing they want of a woman and when they've slaked their evil thirst upon her poor, tired body, she's put away to the kitchen and the nursery to slave."

"Mama!"

Oh, how she dreaded these conversations; and Nell would not soon forget the dreadful sickening morning when she was eleven and Sabby had taken her to the camphorous, shuttered dark of her own bedroom and there in sterile twilight had told the child about the matters of man and woman's conceiving, and of the thralldom of bearing the child in nausea and pain; nothing would ever be the same. She could not look Isaiah in the eyes for so long after that; could not bear to fancy that, looking there in those so long-loved eyes, she would read some awful confirmation of Sabby's accusal. In a winter dusk Isaiah had halted her in the parlor by the stained-glass lamp as she was on her way to the kitchen for an apple. He had reached his big hand to her chin, cupped it, and lifted her face to look him in the eye.

"No," he said gently. "It's not that way, my dear."

She made no pretense of not knowing what he meant and her eyes searched his face desperately for a truth and, at last, found it.

"She's told you," he said. "Sometime in the past six months about matters of the flesh, Nelly. And I know, just as sure as if I'd been standing by the door listening, how she told them to you. Why, my dear, if it was that way—if it was evil and dark and painful like she told you—do you reckon they'd write all the lovely songs and poems and plays about it?"

"No," she whispered and her eyelashes, thick as water-color brushes, fell close upon her cheek.

"No," he said, nudging her chin up a little with his hand. "No, look at me, Nelly. I don't want you going out crippled into the world—thinking it must be like that—like she told you it would be. It can be ugly and mean and painful, like she says. Nelly, you remember the morning you and me and Toby helped the ewe birth her baby lamb?"

"Yes, Papa."

"Down there in the stable in the lamplight and the rainy wind blowing outside and the ewe crying and then the little new lamb? Nelly, if it was all ugly and mean like she told you—do you believe the old ewe would have cried so when we took the little lamb away that spring night? Do you think the little lamb would have cried like it cried, too? Why, Nelly, if it was like she said—men and women and all the creatures of almighty God's creation would have stopped it long ago—and the towns would have fallen still and empty and the forests would just be leaves falling. Don't that stand to reason, daughter?"

"Yes, Papa."

She had been flushed and embarrassed when he began talking to her there, but as his strong, sure voice went on, her chin rested a little in the cradle of his big hand and her eyes gentled. And she went forth in peace and expectation. She felt like a silence, sometimes, waiting to be filled with sound. And other times that unfilled stillness frightened her. It was mostly Loy that made it frighten her. Sabby's dire warnings and vague, obscene predictions had ceased to trouble Nell. But now it was as if Loy had become in a way which she could not grasp, for motives which she dared hardly imagine and in a manner against which she was strangely defenseless, the emissary of Sabby's sinister policy. The first time she knew of this was an autumn night when she had gone to Goshen with a neighbor's boy named Coley Mayhew, and they had sat in the rockaway and watched the torchlight parade and heard the band and the speeches. They had held hands under the buffalo robe because it was frosty, and besides there was a chilled, steely fervor to the shouting speeches and the big banner with President Wilson's cold, spinsterish face with the weave and wash of torchlight

flickering over it. Well, maybe it had been the flush of that
excitement that he had seen on her face when she ran to the
top of the stairs that night, something male and animal in the
air, and Coley talking about running off to Canada and joining
the air force. She was quite breathless at the doorway to her
bedroom; her dark eyes flashing under her veil and her bitten
lips as red as if she had rouged them and, feeling as if she had
never been quite so alive in all her days, she leaned against the
doorway, smiling, and then gave a little breathless laugh at a
nameless happiness. She stood a moment, smiling, eyes closed,
catching her breath and heard Coley's buggy wheels go spi-
dering away into the road among the pecan trees and when she
reached up to draw the hat pin from her hair she saw Loy sitting
by the window, staring at her.

"Loy! I never! Scare a body half to—Loy, how dare you be
sitting here in my room—spying on me that way!"

He watched her, and she could see his face, cold in the moonlight through the bubbled panes, not even blinking, his lips thin
as a bloodless wound.

"Loy, you hear me? What right have you got to be waiting up
for me?"

She swept the wide hat off her head and crossed the room to
her vanity and lay the hat there and stood, trembling and furious and scared. Loy snapped his gold case-watch shut and
dropped it in his vest.

"Somebody's got to look out for you," he said, in a voice that
was both soft and strangulated, and he was still for a while and
she could hear his slow, hard breath and he swallowed two or
three times, audibly, and cracked his knuckles in his palms.

"And just what does that mean?" she cried. "Just what kind
of insinuation is that supposed to be, if you please?"

"Papa doesn't seem to care," he went on, as if something had
him by the throat. "Mama can't seem to get through to you—
and I know she's tried because we've talked about it."

"Talked about what? About what?"

"About you!" he cried suddenly.

"What right have you to talk to Mama about anything that
concerns my own personal life!"

"I'm your brother, Nelly. Remember that? Your brother. And
Mama's our mother! Does that mean anything to you? That
word—*mother!* Somebody who's the dearest and best love you'll
ever know—who tries to raise you up in decent, Christian—"

"Stop, Loy!"

But he was buoyant now with righteous fury; even his voice
had somehow softened in its consolation, though the edge of it
was more menacing now.

"Did he get fresh with you?"

"Who?"

"You know damned well who! Did Coley Mayhew try to get
flirty with you!"

He had her shoulders in the iron bite of his hands now and
she began to feel a little faint with a terror of something now
that pervaded the air between them.

"I can't see why he didn't!" he said, smiling with bright-eyed
outrage. "I know damned well I would have. Why not? The way
you dress! That sweet-smelling face powder! That veil and that
big wide hat a man might look for on a Beale Street yellow!"

She tore her shoulders free and slapped him across the mouth
so hard that her fingers came away wet from the spittle she had
struck from his lips. His eyes, unchanged, regarded her in the
deeps of their grave madness.

"Now strike the other cheek," he said softly, and turned his
face a little.

"Loy, let me alone! Go to bed!" she moaned.

"Strike the other cheek!" he whispered, with a sound like the
rip of silk.

"No, Loy!" she wailed, in a lost wind of grief, and leaned her
hips back against the vanity, and did not have the strength to
resist when his fingers reached down and took her limp wrist
and lifted her lifeless arm and struck himself across the other
cheek with her own senseless fingers.

"You can't have forgotten *all* the Christian decency and cus-

tom that Mama raised us in, Nelly," he said with terrible gentleness. "Even the simple matter of turning the other cheek,
Nelly!"

Nell faltered backwards across the rag rug to her bed and sat
down awkwardly in the feathertick, staring in stunned dum-
found at the fingers of her hand with which he had struck
himself. They seemed no longer parts of her body, weightless
and involuntary, as if they had grown numb in a frostbite of
dread. He was not done, either, although now he did not look
into her live face as he spoke, but in the image of it in the long
mirror of her vanity; and that seemed to her the essence of a
malediction: Loy addressing not the fleshed fact of her, but her
cold, mercuried specter. In that spell of silence before he went
on, Sabby, nearby, sneezed in the lid of her silver snuffbox and
betrayed herself, eavesdropping at some doorway of the night.

"Nelly, I've been watching you," he said. "Oh, don't think I
haven't been keeping an eye on you, little sister. Because somebody has to if Papa don't care enough to. Just don't think I
haven't been keeping a close eye on you, little sister, because I
have. Ever since you started sprouting up into woman's clothes
about two years before it was even decent for you to be growing
that way! Even when you was thirteen! Back when you was
twelve! I told Mama then she ought to be more careful the way
she dressed you! I told her the way boys was starting to eye you
and the way them bastards along the walks in Goshen used to
wink and whisper on Saturday night when Papa's taken us to
town!"

She kept still, almost lulled by the horror of this, and searched
the dim face of him, moon-washed in the mirror of her vanity,
and saw that face was anguished and tortured: the tendons of
his throat sprung out in cords, and tears standing in his eyes.

"Listen!" he said. "Listen, Nelly! The only reason I care about
you at all is because you're my sister! Can't you reason enough
to understand that? The way Mama raised us you ought to
understand that, Nelly! Nelly, I know the way a man looks at a
woman! I hear the way they talk about a woman that just gives

out the littlest hint that she might be *easy*! Can't you *see* that, Nelly! Just one little hint can ruin a woman's pure name! Forever! Nelly, a man just can't be a true Christian gentleman and not care about his own sister's good name!"

"I haven't done anything," she whispered to the dark—not to him but to the dark—as if it need know this before it, in some cosmic rage of its own, closed around her.

"No," he said. "No, I know you haven't done anything. Well, I know you haven't. I don't intend you ever shall, Nelly. A woman is weak and a poor judge when it comes to things like this. A man can just sweet-talk the purest Christian girl in the world into *anything*, Nelly. That's why God put kinsmen round a girl—to protect her till she's got a husband to do the job of protecting. That's the job of a *father*! But when—sometimes it falls to a brother to do it. To *protect* her, I mean. Nelly, for God's sake, heed what I'm saying because I don't want—"

And to the dark again, her whispered psalm of innocence: "I haven't done anything!"

"—to have to kill anyone! Nelly, you hear me? I don't want to have to fetch Papa's pistol from the rolltop some night and have to go into Goshen—"

"—wouldn't do anything!"

"—and gun somebody down. Because, Nelly, don't ever make any mistake about that. Just as sure as God's good sun rises in the east every morning—any man ever lays so much as a dirty look on you and I know about it—"

And her whisper gone so still now that her lips did not even move with it, so that it was only a thought in her pulsing throat: He keeps on that way. His voice keeping on that way—talking about it—makes a body almost want it.

"—I'll kill him, Nelly," he said. "Just mind that and keep on minding it and don't ever forget it. I'll shoot him down like a mad dog in the road. So just think about that—"

"You'd like it to happen! Want it to happen!"

"—every time you go fancying yourself all up like Mademoiselle Modiste—veils and face powder and pompadour—and those tight-fitting suits that Papa lets you pick out in Memphis in the spring! Lord, you'd almost think Papa himself was setting you up for downfall! Mama picks you decent clothes—the kind of clothes that suit a Christian lady! But you just remember— everytime you go to Goshen—or a box social—or church—all dressed up like some kind of fancy coquette—just mind well that you're tempting some poor, simple-minded man to go and get himself shot!"

She ran past him, out of her room, and heard her mother's door click softly to, and fled down the stairs into the amber oceans of the night hall, and out the front door and into the cold night air; fresh as water against her face, beneath the livid silver of the moon. She heard the hoofs of the bay on the Goshen road and the whisper of Isaiah's buggy, homeward from the Wilson rally, and knew she could not face him in that night. She ran, stumbling up the yard, and heard the window of her bedroom go rocketing up and Loy's voice persisting, pursuing.

"Just remember, Nelly! Remember real good what I told you!"

She ran toward the stable, toward the quivering line of lantern shine from the loft where Luke would be. To Sabby this was another proof of his mongrel madness: Luke had decided that he was going to become a painter, and Isaiah had let him have the loft for his studio. In the barn, in the dark where the cattle moaned and the air was fumed with the ammonia of animal fact, she felt a rush of terror at this reminder of flesh. She went up the loft ladder toward light sifting in the cracks, her hobbled skirts held knee-high so her toes could take the rungs.

"Luke!" she whispered. "Luke!"

And drummed on the boards till the skin of her knuckles broke and bled and she burst down in tears as if this simple outer wound had epitomized all the ones within. Luke blinked down in the square of yellow and helped her up, into his light. He looked at her and then kindly turned away, his big hands slowly wiping a brush on a rainbow rag. He had shed tears enough in his life to know, with a fine, sharp wince of instinct, when tears should be let alone: to gush out like a spring flash flood and wash a way for words. She sat on a wooden box, bruised knuckles in her mouth, sobbing, knees clenched together in the long, tight sheath of her good, gray serge, and rocked a little back and forth on the tips of her tan kid shoes. Luke went on cleaning the brush. Sometimes in the rests of sobs he cast a grave glance sidelong and then looked away again, quickly, as if he had no right to see her in a sorrow so personal; it seemed an embarrassment as keen as if he had come upon her bathing. And presently she stopped, hiccupped gently in a breath of resolution, and dried her eyes, childlike, on either sleeve.

"Luke, I'm awful sorry!"

"No cause to be, Nelly. No cause to be sorry at all."

He put the brush and the gay rag down and turned to her, smiling and trying to tell her with his lonely, deepset eyes that she didn't have to explain at all and maybe it would be better in the long haul if things like that weren't explained at all.

Her blue-gray eyes drifted to the window that Luke kept wiped clean always to frame the light of sun or moon in this barn-loft room that he had made into a way of seeing things.

"Luke, why do things have to change always!"

He fetched the brush up slowly and began wiping it again.

"Everything changes, Nelly. Trees change. Grass changes. Flowers. Even the light changes—when the moon stands here—or there or yonder. Or the sun—"

"No! I mean why do people have to—to grow—and change—and get full of ugliness and—meanness, Luke! Lately I've gotten awful—just perfectly dreadful! I just wish things were like they used to be, Luke! Like they were when we were little—you and—me—and—"

"And Loy?" he said gently.

She bit her knuckle and her lashes closed softly, against more tears, and nodded quickly.

"I just think—tonight I was just thinking!" she cried out presently. "The way we used to be. The three of us. You and him and me. Fishing and—swimming—and killing snakes together! We even—always seemed to catch the croup together! Luke, I wish those good, old times hadn't gone! We might just as well have been three boys, Luke—three brothers! Why, it didn't even matter about Loy and me being white and—"

She stopped then and stood up and went to the window, and looked out, struck tongueless with shame and remorse, and watched the stars' faint flutter in the cold autumn sky.

"Now you see?" she whispered, in dread of this spider that had gone scuttling out of her mind, without her ever knowing that it lived and webbed there. "You see what's happened? How I've changed? You see now, don't you? That I could ever say such a thing as that—to *you*, Luke! God forgive me! God forgive me! If Papa had heard me say that he'd have just died!"

"For saying what, Nelly? That you and Loy is white? That my Papa is half nigger—"

"Luke, don't make me curl up and die for shame, too!"

"—and half Mex? Lord, Nelly, you're not to blame for that! Lord, Nelly, I'm not so thin-skinned that a thing like that could hurt me anymore. Shoot! I guess I've spent half my life or more trying to figure out just what color I really am! I guess I must be about half a paint-box full—any way you look at it! Papa—half nigger—half Mex. Mama—full-blood Comanche! Why, Nelly, if I was to set over yonder there and paint my own picture—I don't believe I'd know just how to get the color right. I know one thing though! I'd know the shape though! I'd sure get that right! Man shape, Nelly! I'd paint that right!"

She listened intently, watching him, though still she could not face him; staring at him now as Loy had stared at her, imaged in the glass: his lean, sad boy's face golded on cheek and jaw by the lip of yellow flame above the lantern's wick.

"Nelly, you're right though," he said. "We three changed—you and Loy and me. Yes, that's so. But the color never changed. There's not a one of the three of us that's gotten a shade lighter—or a shade darker—since the days when we fished and swam and killed snakes together up on the PawPaw. Nelly, that was children then. Nelly, you know well and good what's really changed. We've grown up—all three!"

"But does that mean . . . ? Luke, we've got to keep on being friends! Just because we've grown up—does that mean . . . ? Luke, we've all three got to keep on loving each other! I just can't bear it—thinking that would *ever* change!"

"Well, Nelly, it couldn't ever change for me," he said. "I don't reckon it's needed for me to say that—how I feel—how I'd always feel—about you and Loy. You remember that August afternoon in the deep place up on PawPaw and I took and knotted up with green-apple cramps. Loy saved my life that time, Nelly. I'd not ever forget that soon. But it's more—it's more—it's deeper than that, Nelly. Has Loy . . . Did Loy and you have some kind of fuss tonight?"

"No!"

"No. Well, and I shouldn't have asked that either. That's none of my business."

"It is! I mean, it would be—if we had! Oh, Luke, I want us all three to share everything like we always did! I don't want— I just can't stand it—us all three shooting out into life—alone— going different ways—alone!"

He looked down, smiling softly, into the palms of his hands smeared and mottled with paint.

"I—I better get back to the house," she said. "Papa's home. Luke, I'm sorry—coming up here and carrying on like this!"

"That's all right, Nelly," he said, and frowned a little, still staring at the paints on his palms, and seemed almost at the point of making out some meaningful design among their random rainbow when he rubbed them hard along the denim of his trousers and looked up at her.

"Don't let growing scare you so, Nelly. It hurts. No one knows that better than me. It hurts. But it's a glory, Nelly. Don't let

anyone meddle with it or try to keep you from it! That's one
sin I can't remember them mentioning in the Scriptures and I
think it's the worst. Be real proud of being a woman, Nelly."

She reddened to the roots of her hair, and looked quickly to
the floor, more desperately ashamed than ever, and feeling
inexplicably naked: the ghost of a wasp's sting scalding the flesh
between her breasts, as if in remonstrance to their presence.
And, without a breath of goodnight or of thanks, fled down the
ladder and up through the cold grass to the house, where some
few late lamps ominously glittered in the cracks of latched,
listening bedroom doors. Bolting her own against all the house,
Nell stood in her room, watching the spill of moon shift slowly
across her rug. She fetched from the clothespress the gray-
flannel sack of a nightgown that Sabby made her wear and
stared at its bunched drabness in her hand and threw it into
the corner and went to bed naked and lay in the dark, with a
softly growing wonder and joy, letting her fingers discover the
round richness of her change. And fell asleep thinking: Yes!
Yes! It's a glory! Luke is right! It hurts. But it's a glory! Growing!

And yet, in dreams, she fell to wondering why it should be
so strange and hard for all of them: Luke working out the queer
dream of his motley blood in the cow-smelling stable room; Loy
acting out a dark drama in her room that night that neither of
them dared understand; and her mother: almost lustful in her
very lustlessness. And even Isaiah. And his own father, dead
now since 1910: Major Wilson. They were a strange family,
living and dying there in Kingdom County. There was nothing
about any of them indigenous to the parched, mean cotton-
patch and scrub-pine landscape of that place: each of them
stood in bright contrast to the yellow clay, like flowers from
another, alien world. The people of Kingdom County eyed
them with troubled speculation, and never came away with any
reasonable answer to the family's enigma. They were Virginians. And that was something queer and unpredictable. Nell
never forgot a conversation she had overheard the week after
her grandfather's death: two Kingdom County tenant farmers

talking about the Major and not knowing she was listening, squatting down in her black-cotton stockings behind a prune barrel while Isaiah stood in the back arguing with Jonah Martin about Bryan.

"I 'low he was okay—old Major Wilson. Just like you, I never cottoned to some of the fancy notions he had about niggers, but he leastways wasn't no Yankee. No sir. He never told much about it but he was in the States War and that's a fact! My old pappy was in the same Yankee prison with him and he said he was one fightin' man, that old Major. Them old ones that just sets and studies over the past—them there's the ones that seen it thickest. Old Noah Tatum can rant and holler all he pleases about his hard times in the States War. Everybody in Kingdom County knows he never fit nothin' no bigger nor meaner than a middle-aged regiment of Tennessee Home Guards. Old Major Wilson—he seen it all right. He seen it thick and hard. He wouldn't never talk about it much, but he seen it all right. He was queer—I'll grant ye! He won't have nothin' to do with the Klan. Like that time he whupped Jase Burley the whole length of the gallery of his house with a snake-whip—the second time Jase come to talk him into the Klan. Queer. Yes, he was. But he was a Southerner—through to his marrow!"

And the other mumbled something, soft and gently contentious, and she could smell the quid of apple tobacco in his jaw.

"I know! I know! I don't neither. But them Virginians is all cut that way—them tired-water gentlemen! My pappy declares they was worse than Yankees sometimes. A man just couldn't never tell when one of them would take and stand up for a nigger like he'd throwed in with every Yankee, nigger-lovin' Carpetbagger south of Saint Louis! Old Major was like that. His boy Isaiah? Well now, he's cut about the same! He come back from the West in nineteen-and-one with that mongrel Toby ridin' right beside him like he was his own flesh brother and there's never been a man in Kingdom County yet who could make his mind up just *what* that Toby is! Some says nigger— some says Mexican. Some says Indian. Jake Lowther declares he knows for a fact he is some special breed of a Jew. I sure figure he's got nigger blood in him. His woman was Indian—that flashy baggage name of Judith he brought with him when he come to Kingdom County with Isaiah. She died of the purple fever when the boy, Luke, was born. Anyways—nobody has come right out and raised the question. Isaiah come riding back from Texas in nineteen-and-one with Toby there and the woman Judith—riding right along beside of him—like they was all kin. I be dammed if I know how the Klan stood by and swallered that. And old Major seen to it that Toby got a cabin and five acres of Kingdom County land to farm just like they was kin. And nobody never said a word. I reckon maybe—at the first, at least—they was scared to—bluffed down by the Old Major and Isaiah. That Isaiah's no man to get cute with. I watched him whup Jess Blake and his brother Mark right out yonder in front of this store and never shifted his boots more than three foot from where the fight commenced."

And the other mumbled again, some lazy comment in the drowsy quiet of the summer forenoon.

"What? Yes! Now come to think of it—you're right. That was over Toby, too. Jess passed some kind of smart crack about Toby's boy Luke playing with Isaiah's own two as if there wasn't no difference. Lord, ain't it all messed up anymore? I declare, a man can't tell a nigger no more unless he's got a card hung round his neck. I just wished I knowed—I sure do—about that Toby. If it was mine to say, I'd say nigger. And that boy Luke, too. Nigger, I'd say and let it rest there. Well, we'll see. I reckon Isaiah knows. Maybe time will prove it. Maybe Isaiah won't countenance that Luke and his own two running together in a year or two. That gal Nelly—she's growing up fast. 'Gainst she starts into hairin' and tittin'—well, we'll see. I declare, it's only forty-five years since the States War and it seems like the niggers is taking over stronger every day. If it wasn't for a little night ride every six months or so, it's no telling how far they'd have run out of hand. Sometimes I purely doubt if them tired-water Virginians really knowed what the States War was about.

Though they surely was fighting men. That's what my old pappy says—and he knows. Fought shoulder to shoulder with them at Wilderness and Vicksburg, too—and that's what he says."

Toby confounded them all the more when they would see him with the buckboard in Goshen, come to town for supplies. It was the only time they ever saw him there. The tight skin of his wide face was dark as sage honey and nobody had ever seen the lips under his big, chestnut mustache. So he was that enigma. You couldn't tell from the palms of his hands, either, or from the color of his nails. None of the sure nigger-signs. Nor kinky hair. Nothing you could pin down for sure. His irises were dark as little glowing cups of communion wine but the whites weren't yellowed. It was his comportment that itched and maddened them to the iteration of the question. He wore the good, serviceable leather boots of a cowhand but he kept them spotless of mud and polished till the hide shone lustrous and hard as horn. He wore a sombrero, too, without any band and with the sweat mark staining up from the brim like a dark insinuation of mixed blood, but he kept it brushed and wore it straight and sober upon his head, as a rabbi might or a venerable Navajo, and not with the raffish, twisted brim of the vaqueros hats in Remington prints. His manner was cold and the effect of it, as far as they were concerned, lofty, and all that more offensive because there was nothing in it which would justify challenge. Sometimes one of them would meet his gaze angrily on the boardwalk in front of Martin's Store and search it for the insolence that the searcher imagined to be there and see, with impotent astonishment, that it was not insolence at all, but a deep, inner absorption: as if his mind were involved in a soliloquy in a foreign tongue, and therefore wholly unaccountable to anything within their range of ethnic impeachment. When he had bought what he needed at Martin's counter he would pay and take his goods and go courteously somehow, indeed, more courtly than courteous, as if he were rooted within the memory of a culture more infuriatingly cavalier than old

Major's Virginia. In all those years since he had come back to
Kingdom County, with the Comanche, Judith and Isaiah Wilson, Toby had become the village conundrum: as baffling, as
exquisitely enraging as the jar of beans whose number was to
be guessed in the drug-store window. And as emotionless. When
the face of Judith, lithic and aboriginal in its masked passion,
had been coffined and buried on Isaiah's own burial plot, Toby's
pace had hardly changed at all, and then not slowed down at
all, but perhaps even quickened a little, because Death had put
its little silver spur into him, reminding him of what he owed
to Life. And to Luke, who was all the life of her that endured
now. Isaiah kept aloof from Toby's remorseless, unremitting,
and sometimes terrible toil to shape Luke into what he thought
he should be. Toby's tenderness with his son was like a woman's
and his discipline was like an inquisition. They talked little in
those long, odd evenings in the years after Judith's death. Summer dusks, winter dusks; the sifting brown downfall of autumn
nights and the green Priapean blood-rise of spring evenings:
Toby would sit in their cabin, by lamplight, darning his son's
cheap black stockings on a gourd, squinting and pinch-eyed
over the business that fumbled and labored awkwardly under
his big fingers; his face beaded with the chilled sweat of frustra-
tion, but otherwise impassive until it was done and then he
would sit a while with the black, limp tatters of a book across
his brushed alpaca knees and read till the faraway clock in
Isaiah's parlor struck eight, and nobody knew if it was a Christian English Bible or a Mexican Bible or whether it was a Bible,
at all, or perhaps some black, damned book of heresy he read
there: some tract of nigger, Mexican, Indian, or whatever, because nobody ever got that near. No matter that, though, for
on Sunday mornings he and the boy followed Isaiah and Nell
and Loy and Sabby, in that order, up the road a half mile to
the church that Major Wilson had built in the time when he
had built the house itself, in a decade when the war-stunted
land still steamed from the blood of Sherman's butcheries: that
church, neat as a plaything among the pecan trees; its sweet,

foolish bronze bell speaking out in those morning mists like a Swiss watch chiming in a thick vest, and the preacher himself, who rode down PawPaw River every Sabbath to preach just for them, in their private family chapel, and not so much because they were better than the rest of Kingdom County, but because there wasn't any Episcopalian Church for fifty miles in that thick Baptist land. Though that, too, seemed part of the Virginia queerness of them all, and whoever was offended by that snub still kept still if only out of a natural, countryman's fascination to see how it would all turn out, this familial oddity among them that seemed sometimes almost like a very old sampler fashioned by a long-dead and idiot adolescent girl: stitched and embroidered finely in red and black pictures and words that nobody had figured out the key to yet. Nor ever would until Loy, in a tight-jawed rage, years later, had come to the Baptist Church and never walked that quiet Sunday road with his kinsman again. And not until then had anyone in Kingdom County ever really cared; it never had seemed, until then, worth doing anything about—even a thing as simple as sending six night-riders to put the little chapel to the torch. In a strange, back-country way the people of Kingdom County discovered, if not a pride, at least a proud novelty, in watching the family in their midst: like a town which boasted a two-headed calf or a gardener who has discovered a harmless, intricate tropism among his nasturtiums. Nell had been perhaps the first to sense at the almost simultaneous maturation of the three of them how they had, as if at some warning within the earshot only of blood-pulse and gland-flow, scattered and each gone off a separate, desperate way, like bolting sheep. The last time they had any of them really been together had been the week that Isaiah took the three of them on a long-promised trip to New Orleans to an exposition fair. Like Christmas night's last, most dazzling, most beautifully blinding firework, that week had been the brilliant, dreamlike climax to infancy. Toby drove them to Goshen depot in the phaeton and they rode away in the fat and plush and polished mahogany of the train coach and waved goodbye to Toby, saw him diminish slowly through the smoke and grit, clash and bell, and all the steam and stained-glass dazzle of the train's bugling departure; and then a day and a night aboard a steamboat in staterooms whose wedding-cake paint peeled and blistered in proximity to the hot, perilous boilers and the drive shafts of the paddle wheels hurled stampeding past, inches from their heads, and it was as wonderful and dangerous as a dream of flying; and the hotel in New Orleans that none could quite believe real until they had screamed and bounced in its feather ticks and heard, for the first time, the hot, soft murmur of Southern city night across the sills of a hotel. Nell thought that night that she would like to stay in that city, in that room, perhaps forever and never go back to Kingdom County at all, and she and Luke and Loy would never part. She would go out into the city and make a great fortune and they would live in the hotel forever and Isaiah, but not Sabby, should come and visit them every week and she would cook him dinner. Loy found her by the window sill, breathing in the city night. She made the error of confiding in him her fancy.

"Shoot! That's a crazy idea! Stay here—and never—never see Mama again!"

"It's only a pretend!"

He stood, bemused and pouting; knobby-kneed in his short nightshirt.

"All right," he said. "It's only a pretend. What would we do for money?"

"I'd earn it," she sang softly. "Just hundreds and hundreds of dollars! We'd have so much I—I could give Papa some!"

"Girls don't earn money! What could you do?"

"I'd . . . I'd . . . !" she gasped, clutching the dream, and tried to think of a word and remembered the one with the most elegant ring to it: a word she had read once in one of the illicit, carved-leather volumes of Dumas in Grandfather Wilson's locked bookcase.

"I'd be a *paramour*!"

He had no more definition of the word in his mind than she

did, but was as sensitive to its remotely voluptuous sound as she was and he never forgot it, remembering it carefully until the time when that night's wicked spark of suspicion could be fanned up to flame. On the second night of their trip Loy got sick eating pralines and threw up most of the night and cried for Sabby. But for Luke, at least, and for Nell it was the most perfect week of their lives. Isaiah took them to a show with real velvet in the seats where they saw an operetta called *The Fortune Teller* and a diamond chandelier as big as the peach tree above the smokehouse. He took them to an art gallery, too, where Loy didn't want to go, but hollered that Isaiah had promised to take them to the docks to see the boats.

"That'll do, Loy," said Isaiah, in his quiet way, against which no mortal, man nor boy, had ever discovered a successful counter-objection, and they went to the art gallery. It was no more wonderful to Nell than all the rest of it and to Loy it was an obscure adult joke that his father had chosen to perpetrate against them, in the always unaccountable name of discipline and, much worse, of culture: to be led into this glum and lin-seed-smelling mausoleum of vaguely improper pictures in the cracked gilt of their mildewed frames; watery, crepuscular land-scapes sinister with those misgivings Loy always felt in dusk's real presence, when the nagging, insomniac misery of his child-hood nights impended; or shameless French Venuses tussling indecently with their Cupids in a godless and un-Episcopal out-of-doors.

"Beautiful! Beautiful!" Nell's voice sang, and her black slip-pers ran, tapping back and forth across the marble, from frame to frame. "Look, Papa. This one! Oh, this! The little spaniel and the fruit! Oh, all the beautiful fruit in the beautiful basket! Oh, Papa! Luke! Loy! Come look! This one!"

Isaiah murmured and nodded, smiling and blowing long curls of stogie smoke through his dark beard, his eyes smiling too and loving, under the dark brows, under the pearl brim of his brushed dress Stetson.

"Loy, you're not looking!" she squealed and dragged him by

the sleeve, tallow-faced and furious. "Luke! Looky at this one! Oh, the lady and the lambs and the pearly, big moon!"

Luke, indeed, did nothing else but look; could look no more intently; had never looked at any things with more of himself: his whole body had turned eyes. He was dry-mouthed and shivering a little deep inside his flesh and bones, though all the outside skin of him was still and only his eyes, beneath the cap brim, and his bone-bright knuckles where he clutched the hem of his ragged, brushed and threadbare linsey jacket; only these showed any of what was happening, like a man stupored under the first tongue-tying turmoil of first love or of drunkenness. Nell skipped away to find another treasure and squealed to them to come and see it, too, while Luke looked slowly all the way up Isaiah, up the blade of pants-crease to vest, and up vest buttons, past the golden, thick links of watch chain, up to beard and then to eyes.

"Are they *real*, sir?"

"Well, lad, yes. Yes, I suppose, a man should rightly say they're real. They're pictures. Real pictures, I mean to say. And first-rate ones, too, I'd say! First-rate!"

"Beautiful! Beautiful!" Nell sang, skipping away among a host of stone gods in the dusk of the tall, barred windows.

"Hand-painted?" whispered Luke.

"Every one!" said Isaiah. "Painted by hand."

Luke kept still then for a spell, chewing all that over; clamped his teeth shut and decided to ask no more questions to show what a fool he was, and it would take him a while to chew all that over. It might take him years, he knew, to understand those short answers to so much and stole to one of the pictures in an awe in which heart, breath, and pulse all seemed, for an instant, postponed, until there was nothing left in him but a glowing cup of wonder. He dared not reach his finger up to touch the luminous crust of paint upon the canvas because he did not wish to know just yet that it was only that, only paint, only canvas, unreal. Isaiah had told him it was real and Isaiah never lied. His father never lied either and, if it came to a time when he might lie, he would keep still but he would not lie. And Isaiah had told him that this picture had been made by a hand. He looked down, with scared child-eyes, to his bony hands that jutted from short, frayed cuffs. He could scarcely endure his excitement. I have hands! he thought, astonished. Well, I have hands! And it seemed as if he had never known that fact before. He looked again at the painting and, child there, knew he stood before a reality that could stretch its light into the remotest reaches of his life. That riddle of pigmentation which was, whether he dared so soon admit it, always to be the stamp upon him, as it had been upon his father Toby—hide and heart forever—seemed now less shadowy and insoluble. Here was a hint of something he, who had never been quite anything, could be. No, not now. But someday. Somehow. He might do it. Yes, he could do it if ever he got learning enough. Yes, he thought, because I have hands. And he said they were painted by hands. And so, upon the spot, he swore it to himself: that he would be that someday, vowed it in unalterable contract with the future: the way a child swears in love and fury that he will someday be a sheriff or a fireman or a balloonist. He knew the way Loy was always swearing he was going to be this or that, and a gypsy on the Goshen road with a collared brown bear dancing on his chain was enough to change his mind. Luke knew he would never change. It was the first time in his life he had sworn he would be anything. It was the first day it had ever occurred to him that there was anything worth being. Isaiah called after Nelly and gathered glaring Loy under his hand.

"Come now, my dears, it's time to go back to the hotel and wash up for supper!"

Luke searched desperately among the stone crowds: the marble, the alabaster, and the bronze, the plaster of Paris and the granite: full-figure and torso, and the bearded, visored bust heroes on their fluted pedestals: Beauregard, Lee, Jackson, Stuart. Luke looked furiously among them for God. Because if there was ever a time it was now: to pray to Him for That. Where?

"Come along, Luke. Nelly?"

No, He was not among them, and now Isaiah herded the three children gently down the marble steps, among the blind stone eyes.

"Someday I will!" Luke said suddenly, aloud, to the moon in the Spanish moss above him, as they walked back to the hotel.

"Will what, Luke?" said Nelly happily.

"Be a hand-painter of things!" Luke exclaimed in a voice that for all its soprano reediness was dauntless as a grenadier's.

"Shoot!" cried Loy, at that. "You hear what Luke say, Papa?"

"No, Loy. Come along, children. Come!"

"Luke says—" Loy gasped. "Luke says—he's going to be a hand-painter of—of pictures, Papa! Hah, don't that beat the Dutch, Papa? Old Luke yonder thinking he could ever learn how!"

"Hush your teasing of Luke, boy! He may be! He may be. God alone knows what we will be, boy!"

That week in New Orleans, that trip, that moment in the burning room was the fuse of Luke's life; it was never to be quite the same again. Toby, uneasy with his sense of the change in Luke, thought at first it was something his boy had caught from the drinking water in New Orleans or from a poisonous whiff from the swamps that he might have breathed on the boat deck: not yellowjack nor blackwater nor cholera, not malaria nor breakbone fever, but something incipient, more cunningly debilitative than any of those, and, troubled at heart, Toby watched Luke where he would sit a-staring on the stoop, when supper was over, and moon, calf-eyed over the colors of the delta sundown as if it tore at his heart like the face of a girl.

"Luke? Hey, boy! Hah, there! Luke? Boy—you sick?"

"Sick? What? Oh no, Papa! No, I feel good, Papa!"

"Good, eh? You act like a sick horse, Luke!"

"Sick? Hoh, no, Papa!" Luke would cry softly. "I feel good. It's nice when the work's done—when supper's done—just to sit and look at the sky. You want me to do something else, Papa? Fetch stove wood, Papa?"

"No, Luke. There's plenty wood."

"I washed them supper plates at the pump, Papa! That sure was a good supper, Papa! You sure can cook good! Did I miss any dirty dishes, Papa?"

"No, Luke. Dishes all washed."

"Papa, you want me to run to Goshen and get you a poke of Bright Chance Tobacco?"

"No, Luke. I got plenty!" cried Toby, his dark eyes shining with concern and his face finely furrowed with lines of difficulty over the manner with which he should explain his thoughts to his son and searched Luke's face, yearning for some clue. But there was nothing to read in Luke's eyes, liquid and sleepy with their dream. Toby felt vaguely uneasy.

"Someday," he would say to Luke in the evenings, "this little piece of land will be yours, my Luke. Someday this two acres that the Cap'n gave me will be yours. Sometimes I don't think you give enough thought to that, my Luke. It is no small blessing to have a piece of land. Luke, you're restless! Sometimes I hear things in your voice that frighten me."

"Papa, I'm awful tired tonight! You just imagine things, Papa!"

"No. No, my Luke. I know your heart like I knew your mother's. I can't always read what is there, but I can see writing."

"Papa, it's just that sometimes a son can't always be just what his father thinks he should!" Luke cried. "I mean, maybe I just wasn't ever meant to be a farmer, Papa!"

"What?"

"Papa, I been worryin' myself sick ever since last spring— wondering how I could tell you how I feel about my life—what I want to be, Papa!"

Toby sat down stiffly in the chair by the door and stared at Luke with the eyes of an old and frightened child.

"And what is that, my Luke?"

"Papa, I sure bet you're gonna get mad at me when I tell you!"

"No. No, because there is only one thing you can be. And you

will be that. When a man is born to the land—when he has
deeds—that is what he must do."

"No, Papa. I thought it all out. And I've got to talk to you
about it, Papa. You'll get mad but I can't help that. You'll think
I'm shiftless and ornery but I can't help that, Papa."

"No," Toby said. "A man when he is young is entitled to
commit errors of judgment. Go on."

"Papa, I thought it out hard and long. Papa, I've got to be a
painter when I'm a man."

"A painter? This is a joke, my Luke?"

"No! No, Papa! No joke!"

"A painter? What kind of painter? A man with a ladder painting barns? No, my Luke! It *is* a joke!"

"No joke, Papa!"

"Painting barns—houses—fences?"

"No, Papa. Pictures!"

"Pictures? A painter of pictures? Luke! Luke, that is no work
for a man's hands—for a man's life! That is a game for little
children—with the little crayons in school, Luke!"

"No, Papa!"

"Don't tell me 'no'! I have seen the world! I know what is
work for a man's hands and what is work for a child's! Pictures?
Pictures! My Luke, please tell me this *is* a joke!"

"No, Papa. Ever since that trip to New Orleans, Papa! The
Captain took us all to a place full of pictures men had painted!
Papa, it was like in a church!"

"Don't say that! I know these pictures and they are not the
pictures I have seen in churches! Don't mock God, my Luke,
and you *do* mock Him when you say that, for I have seen the
pictures in the churches! Long ago, little one! Yes, long ago!
And I have no one to blame but myself if you don't know them,
too! I have no one to blame that I did not raise you in the light
of His pictures—none but myself! But don't ever say that!"

"But, Papa, it was like that feeling in a church!"

"Ah, God help me, I have raised you bad, my Luke!"

"Papa, I got to say it. It was better—it was bigger than that feeling—than *any* feeling I ever had up at their church!"

And he stood wild-eyed in the doorway, like a shaggy-haired child-hermit and pointed a shaking finger up the dusk to the Captain's salt-box chapel, under the cool and godly dusk of first moonrise. Toby struck him with the flat of his hand and, though it was Luke who went sprawling across the boards, it was Toby who shook as if his hand had struck some proxy of himself. He leaned a little on his hands, flat-palmed on their single table and looked softly at Luke across the smoking lamp.

"Now we each have something to forgive the other, my Luke," he said. "Now we can talk at the beginning. If you will forgive my blow of anger, I will forgive your bad words, and we can talk at the beginning."

"Yes, Papa."

"With no sobbing. That is for women. Stop sobbing. There have been things in this talk that could have made me sob, too, and my breath is not sobbing and my eye is dry. No sobbing, my Luke."

"Yes, Papa."

Toby sat down at the table and began to stroke the wood with flat outward motions of his hands as he might, within those hands' memory, have seen a woman stroke a linen cloth on a table less harsh, in a time of fuller fortune; and so began, painfully and carefully, to explain to Luke why he must put this childishness out of his mind. He talked of land as if it were a god in his blood and in the blood of his father, who had been a black slave sold on the block in Galveston in a time even before Austin or General Sam, and in the blood of his mother who had been a Mexican which was half as poor and twice as bad in that time, in that place, than blackness which, at least, had the dignity of dollar worth. Then he talked to Luke a while about Luke's dead mother Judith who, in some places where they had ridden, was worse than either Mex or nigger and landless beyond the most improbable political pretext or speculation;

and how, despite all this confluence of earthless and nomadic race they had come at last, through the loving kindness of a man named Isaiah Wilson, to own land. Land. Land. And he said the word again like it was honey to his tongue.

"Down at the Goshen Courthouse, my Luke," he said. "The deed. The first week we came here—your mother—him and me—we rode to Goshen Courthouse with his father—the Major—and he made the deed. Two acres. Land, my Luke. For my seed and yours forever."

"Yes, Papa," Luke kept saying, but it seemed to him, in sorrow, that all that Toby was saying was making him more sure of what he knew best about himself: that Toby's voice was like a sad music to the words in Luke's own heart.

"You see now, Luke?"

"No, Papa. I won't lie to you, Papa."

"Luke! My Luke! In the name of your mother! In the name of God's mother, too! Think what we owe the Captain!"

"Owe, Papa? Yes. Yes, I know that."

"Luke! My Luke! God forgive me, I have raised you bad! Luke! Forgive me, Laddy! Captain gave us that land! *Gave*, Luke! Do you think for a man to own land means nothing? Luke, how do you think the Captain will feel when he sees my boy—my seed's own child—grow up and say: Land? Land! Hah, I spit on land, Captain Isaiah! Hah, Captain! Piss on land! I am going to be a painter of pictures!"

"Papa, I wish I could be—what you think I should be!"

Toby searched the boy-man eyes for a weakness, for a splintering, for a shift but could not see it; seeing instead with a grief that had the bloody taste of pride in its mouth, a stubbornness that Toby could never horsewhip out nor shame out nor pray away: something of himself and he sighed and shivered because, for an instant that made him groan softly in his belly, he saw the eyes of his wife Judith again, and that had been something of himself there, too.

"My Luke," he mumbled and shrugged. "I would rather—"

"You would rather see me dead, Papa?" said Luke.

"No. No. Not dead. I know what dead is. I would rather—I would rather you be—But what good is it to say what I would rather you be? You will be what God knows you will be!"

And he held the boy, awkwardly, rocking a little to and fro, and patting the shoulder under the gingham of the shirt that he had mended last week with that same huge and fumbling hand.

"Someday, Papa, you might change your mind!" cried Luke. "Someday you might be proud when I grow up and be a famous painter of pictures!"

"God knows," whispered Toby, in a voice that Luke seemed to be hearing from another throat, in another time, in another place. "God knows that you will be what you will be! That is all I know for sure, my Luke!"

On an April night in 1915 Jess Willard, white, knocked out Jack Johnson, Negro, in the twenty-sixth round of a world's championship bout in Havana, Cuba. Perhaps it was the least of reasons Loy would always have for remembering that night: it was his seventeenth birthday and Isaiah had taken him into town that night and there had been a ten-dollar gold piece to spend as he pleased. He would more likely remember that night for a moment when, seated by his father in the buggy, he had seen men come stumbling out of the newspaper office, hollering and cursing.

"Is it a war, Papa?"

"Why, no, Loy. I think not."

The men who had come hollering and cursing out now went in through the snapping, gingerbread doors of Bracey's Saloon without saying at all what they had been so aroused about. Tom Drum, town editor, came out of his office and spit between the boards of the sidewalk and stared at three young Negroes who loafed on the other side of Chinaberry Street in the shadows of the big elms and out of the street lamp's circle. Tom Drum's muscles twitched steady, like fish gills beneath the weathered skin, and he kept his fists shoved down hard in the pockets of his baggy, homespun coat. The three Negroes whispered together. They were like one dark creature making a soft sound to itself. One of them kicked the dust with his naked toe in the dark and the three moved wordlessly away. When they had gone perhaps ten feet they separated into three and turning, stopped and stared back across the breadth of Chinaberry Street as if it were a clearing in the jungle between themselves and Tom Drum and the two in the buggy. One of them laughed and arched his hips and did a cakewalk through a diminished ray of street light that filtered through the tree boughs overhead. Another laughed and smacked his knees, watching, and bent and laughed again at his companion, while the third figure, silent and bemused, fetched a bottle from his rags and threw his head back, drinking. He threw his bottle tinkling among the hardened mud ruts of the street then, and the three men together, roared with laughter, smacking one another's backs, and cakewalked a space beneath the trees and then moved off: three struggling to impute through laughter and an intricate casualness their indifference to the event which had, a moment before, come out of the newspaper office, announcing itself, cursing and unclenched, at last. The man on the boardwalk watched the Negroes diminish in the distance and when they had gone he looked up at Isaiah and Loy. Somebody broke something small and glass in Bracey's Saloon.

"What's the ruckus about, Tom?"

Tom Drum's bright eyes, not blinking and not unkind, looked at Isaiah from beneath the bowler hat. He spat again as if he were not at all sure whether or not it was worth while answering a white man who might not be as judiciously concerned about the answer to that question as the Christian, and only, God might count on him to be.

"The nigger finally got whipped," Tom Drum said presently. "Jess Willard done it in twenty-six rounds. It just come over on the wire."

He glanced up Chinaberry Street again, at that, to see if the three had really disappeared, or if they might not be hidden in the shadows of stores or beneath trees to hear him confirm in words that probably they had already sensed or smelled on the international wind, or even in the ether of earth around them, without need of telegraph wire or cable nor even of three Goshen cotton farmers hollering and cussing, unintelligibly, out of the office of the Goshen *Echo*: leaving behind them, in the wake of that apostrophe, a sense of ozone on the air as in the aftermath of lightning. Tom Drum looked up at Isaiah and the boy again. His face seemed waiting for some word of approval or its opposite from the older man. Then, with a shrugging movement that seemed almost a sneer of his shoulders, he turned and moved back into the office and bent, uneasy in the lemony light, listening to the chatter of the telegraph bug as if there might now come a revision of the first report.

"Well, Loy, what's it to be?" cried Isaiah, smiling at the livid, quiet face beside him, and holding up between his big fingers a winking ten-dollar eagle. "What's it to be, my boy? Will you tuck it away and save it? Or do you want to spend it on some nonsense down at Jamieson's? Mind now—you may do as you want with it!"

In a flash Loy had the buggy whip out of his father's hand and had struck the bay mare's rump till she sprang and threw them both back hard into the dimpled, black leather of the seat, while the wheels spun, biting road earth for purchase, and in the split-instant after, the carriage seemed to gather and hurtle itself forward into the mad mare's wake, as if itself had become more animate than horse was, while Isaiah yelled and fought for the reins in Loy's cold, furious fists. It had been a quarter mile beyond town in a pitching, breakneck career down the moonless spring road before Isaiah had brought the shocked mare to standstill. Loy sat silent, his thin fingers pressed into the round of either knee, staring stiff ahead into dark. Isaiah felt more confused than angry, and a little more frightened than either; peering around, breathless in his beard, trying to see Loy's features in the deeper night shadow of the buggy's bonnet.

"Now what in Jupiter's name did you ever do a fool thing like that for, boy? You know this mare is spooky!"

"I wanted to get home!"

"But you know this mare's spirit, Loy! And if you wanted to get home—all you had to do was say so!"

"I wanted to get home quick, Papa!"

"Quick! Why?"

"Because—because it's coming up to rain! Papa, you know spring cloudbursts in Kingdom County this time of year! I wanted—I wanted to get home, Papa!"

"Yes. Yes, and you pretty near took us both there! To a home a sight longer than the one you were born in! Look at me, boy! There's more to it than this! More than just . . . Here! Look at me!"

Isaiah fetched a kitchen match from his vest and struck it on the whipcord of his britches and held it up to see, and yet on the same instant, dreading what might be there; what, indeed, seemed, through some poetry of smell, to be insinuated in the phosphorus fume of the match's flare.

"Son, are you sick? Here! No, don't turn your face away! Are you sick, I say?"

"Let me alone. Papa, let's just—just get home! Home!"

"No. There's something here that wants understanding! You *are* sick! Was it something . . . Something . . . ? Here, boy. Let me see your face!"

And the match flame, which died then suddenly in a gust of rain-rich air, had shown him the face of someone whom he had not, it seemed, met until that hideous, momentary illumination: a mask white as coffin pine and eyes dark as wet bricks which stared as if astonished at their own pitiless indignation: a face childlike still in shape and essence, yet, at the same time, stitched through with marks of a sudden and contemptuous maturity, like the infantile, arrogant faces of midgets sometimes seem,

and despite all this, despite that proud and self-possessed malev-
olence, tears streamed down its cold cheeks like sap from
wounded wood, as if something behind the awful mask of Loy's
face mourned the death of the child it had been and the whole
man it could never be. It might have been that face and not the
wind that had swept the flame in cold fright from the match.
Isaiah sat very still, felt the stick break in his fingers, and decided
that he would rather continue that conversation in the mercy
of darkness, and it had been Loy who had resumed and Isaiah
who now could but sit and listen, cringing in upon himself at
the sound: child-voice still and yet cold and old as the measured
scrape of a razor against a two-days' beard; Isaiah feeling very
old in a twinkling, and very afraid, as well, though not of the
boy, nor even of himself, so much as afraid in the presence of
some dark inquisition of the general family of his species: himself, his seed, his kin, unkin, and the world at large that night.

"Yes, that's correct. Yes," Loy was saying. "It was something
back there, Papa, and maybe it's just as well it all came to a head
so that we can talk. No, it wasn't because of rain that I wanted
that—to get home. No, it wasn't really that at all, Papa, but
something that's been festering in me, you might say. Yes, festering is the word for it, Papa, and then when Mister Drum
came out of the *Echo* and told us about—"

"About the fight. Yes, I thought it might be that. But still—
why? Why? You never showed any care or interest about pugilism? If—"

"Papa, let me finish this. You asked me what I felt so let me
finish, kindly. You did ask me!"

"Yes! Yes!"

"It's hard to put in a way. Hard to put in words. What I mean
to say—hard to put in words a feeling like this so's it won't come
to you as too big of a hurt. If I could just come out plain and
say it, then it would be easy but—"

"Speak plain, Loy! No man, least of all my own flesh, has ever
had to talk around things in my presence!"

"Yes. Yes, I know that about you, Papa. Yes. You're a great

one for—what do you call it? Reason. Fairness and reason. You and Grandpap! He was—"

"Leave my father out of this discussion if you please."

"Well, now that's a little hard, Papa. That's a little hard—don't you think? After all, Grandpap did fight in the States War and gave up four brothers so's that *they* wouldn't take over the land and the women and all the rest of it that so many good, decent white—"

"They? So that who?"

"Grandpap did. And brothers dead so's that—"

"No. No, I mean so that *who* couldn't take over!"

"Why, Papa, that's why it's so plagued hard to talk to you about this. I know how you hate that word! Or have I maybe got all that backwards, Papa? Is it that you really *love* that word—that name which—?"

"Nigras! That's it isn't it? Nigras! Is that what all this palaver is heading into?"

"Well, Papa, other folks around Kingdom County call them—"

"Nigras!" Isaiah interrupted, in a kind of shouting whisper to the moonless night, and felt the first drop of rain strike his clenched hands as if the dark, too, wept.

"Yes. Yes. Well, all right. However you want to pronounce it. I never was that much of a stickler for pronunciation, Papa. However you want it. You heard how Mister Drum said it when he came out of the *Echo* and told us about the fight. And you saw—you *saw*, Papa, how hard he looked at you for a little spell before he even told you at all. Papa, how can I say this to you without it hurting you! God, a son likes to feel *proud* of his Pa!"

"And you felt reason to be ashamed of me. Is that about the length and breadth of it, Loy? Ashamed because—"

"No. Well, no, Papa, not—not ashamed. I—I don't know how to say it!"

"—Ashamed because I didn't stand up and shout and curse for joy because a white man beat a colored man in a prize-fight

fifteen hundred, maybe two thousand miles away, on an island
where—"

"Ashamed!" Loy sobbed suddenly. "Yes. Yes, I might as well
own up to it! Ashamed! Papa, you asked me! You said for me
to speak up! Papa, it's just that—well, it's not that I'm ashamed
of you! It's that I'm ashamed of that—in your mind! I couldn't
ever be ashamed of you, Papa! Why, everybody in Kingdom
County knows you're a *man*! In most things you . . . !"

"A man? And what precisely does it mean to you, Loy?—to
be a man?"

"Papa, back there in Goshen—Papa, there are good white
men gathering in Bracey's Saloon tonight—getting ready for
anything—anything, Papa, when the niggers hear about their
Jack Johnson finally getting his come-uppance after seven long
years of—"

"I never knew you were interested in fists and contests like—"

"It's not that! It's not *that*!"

"And these—these good men you mention, Loy, who are in
Bracey's getting ready for anything. They must discover how
good they are as men only after they've had four or five glasses
of corn whiskey?"

"You know I don't mean that, Papa! You're trying to twist
my words when all I'm trying to say is something that's just
been—festering inside me for years—since before I can even
remember, Papa! And then tonight when Mister Drum come
out of the *Echo* and told us about the nigger being whipped at
last and waited, and you didn't say anything—didn't smile—
Papa, I just felt like I wanted to crawl into something and hide!
And the way Mister Drum looked at you then, Papa, when you
didn't smile or say anything at all, and all those men in Bracey's
shouting and celebrating because the white race had—"

"White race! White! Loy, it was two men—two men on an
island fifteen hundred—two thousand miles—"

"You know what I mean! Papa, you do know what I mean!
When I saw that look in Mister Drum's face and you didn't say

anything—Papa, I wanted to just get home quick and hide.
Hide, Papa! Like I was—well, ashamed of certain things in my
family. I mean, Papa, I don't think folks in Kingdom County
have ever gotten it quite clear how you *feel* about certain things
that it's awful important for a good, white, Christian, American
man to be right-thinking about, Papa. Well, sure! Sure, they
know about your being a man—I mean, they know how if ever
it came to protecting Mama or Nelly. Or any white woman, for
that matter—when it come to that you'd be as good a man as
ever walked the earth but—"

"What has our women folks to do with this—this prizefight
miles and miles away?"

"Papa, how can I say it? Papa, folks in Kingdom County know
how Grandpa gave Toby land!"

"Toby is my friend, boy!"

"How it was Grandpap who fought and gave up brothers to
make sure the niggers wouldn't—"

"No! That is not so! I will not sit here and listen to you make
a lynch party out of that sacred struggle!"

"Papa, it's so! Kingdom County folks know Toby is half nigger!"

"He is my friend!"

"—And once you give a nigger land he wants more, Papa.
Deny that if you can, Papa! More!"

"When has Toby ever asked?"

"And pretty soon—pretty soon, Papa, he's cakewalkin'
around all uppity with notions that he's as good as you! And if
he's as good as you, Papa—"

"He is my friend, young man!"

"—if he's as good as you, Papa, why then, it's plain as black
Bible print that he's got the right to sit beside you! And if he's
got the right to sit beside you, then why not the right to sit by
Mama or Nelly? And if . . . ?"

Isaiah's hand lashed out, in the reflex before thought, to
strike Loy's mouth, and though some angel of sweet reason
stayed bone and muscle, halting them in mid-air, palm still

cupped for the blow, he knew he might as well have let it fall unchecked, for Loy heard it—the uncoiling of a spring of outrage, the furious fabric rustle of sleeve—and had, victorious, felt the palm's hurtling onrush and then its jolting halt in the air, against nothing, as if it had come up hard against a wall of prudence, and then he had felt its radiant, angry warmth, inches from his cheek. While Isaiah, in a quaking shame, felt against that hand, Loy's smirking mouth.

"It would matter then," that mouth said presently, softly. "The notion that one of them might ever dare—even Toby. It does make a difference. Papa? Doesn't it? You wouldn't have started to hit me if it didn't! Papa? Beneath it all, you feel the same as me!"

In a twinkling, rain descended in vast sheets across the dark land and round the buggy, wrapping them both within a pure, prisoning crystal: men held close captive within the penitentiary of an understanding so dreadful and so mutual that neither need ever speak of those matters again, although the time would rise when they would: Loy now, stiff and smiling and yet a little faint after so sweet a spasm of winning, and Isaiah, eyes aglare, swimming with rain, searched blindly for the road beyond the mare as if that were the ultimate truth of things lost suddenly between obscured fences and the rain-swarming trenches of mud. Wiser than either, the mare led them homeward, while Isaiah, slumped above the fisted reins, closed his eyes, wondering whether God does not, in certain agonies, pray to man for strength.

Back up PawPaw River seven miles where the marching rain had not yet come to quench their torches, Tom Drum and twelve others rode out that midnight and burned alive in his cabin a man named Lonny Jackson, because in the impromptu saloon census they had all taken of Kingdom County Negroes, Jackson was the nearest any of them could come to the name of the nigger Willard had whipped at last and nobody was sober enough at that point to remember exactly where Havana was, so it didn't matter anyway. Whipped at last, and now they could talk about it: the sepia anathema which had hung above them since 1908 and the downfall of Tommy Burns. Most of them didn't even remember his name, nor where it had happened; it was half a world away, in Australia, but if you thought about it a minute, if you thought about it right, it was no farther off than the wife's bedroom. Even the ones who had had, heretofore, only the dimmest interest in pugilism, even the ones who had stopped being concerned about the sport since the good, forty-round epoch of Jeffries, since Sullivan who, at least, and even if he was a damned Yankee mick, had the delicacy never to soil his bare fists with nigger blood at all. No one ever talked about prizefighting in those seven years, in those parts, though every one knew that it was a black man who reigned. Until that night. And all of a sudden all of it unclenched and the sweaty glove tugged off the community hand and the tape unwound from their common fist so that the fingers, at last, could flex and reach for a revolver. One nigger, at least, was lying down that night, but you could pretty well reckon that the rest wouldn't take it that way. Their gesture was instructed by that dark contingency, the unreconstructable logic of genital fear. The Negro world's champion was whipped, at last. But that fact, however corroborated by newsprint and word of mouth, was but rumor printed on the air that needed a kind of extempore, sanguine, civic notarization with gun and rope and something flammable as the oil of Druid immolations, before it would be, to them, real in any safe, sound sense. The Negroes of Kingdom County had to be made to believe it. But, more, they themselves had to be made to believe it. Tom Drum, in Bracey's Saloon, had told of the three Negroes in the shadows across from his office under the elms of Chinaberry Street: strutting black cocks, cakewalking off in impudent refutation of a fact whose verbal confirmation had not even reached them: they had known by the shouts and curses of the others who had come out first, signaling the news, had known like the old ones were supposed to have known by the pulse of drums in the green stone age of their childer past, or perhaps by the pulse of something else that no white man could or would even want to hear and understand. Everyone in Kingdom County, black and white, everyone around the world knew Johnson was to fight in Havana that night. And when the news came, those three, those million dark listeners, knew. Without a word of white mouth to tell them. And knowing, denied it: cakewalked off, arrogant and denying. Something must be done. And anyone would do. Tom Drum himself recalled, in Bracey's Saloon, as they stood swaying and the torches of their resolution caught, one by one, and flared reflected like blood in the mahogany bar patina, how he had said when he picked out a new Stetson that afternoon at Jamieson's: "Any one will do, Jason, just so long as the color is right." So everybody stopped trying to figure out through the whiskeyed stogie smoke of their wits where they could, in Kingdom County, find a nigger named, appropriately, Johnson: as if they had needed to, if only in self-defense, pay some dim homage to civilized process, if only through an indemnifying rickety logic of namesake. Jackson came close enough. And so they tumulted into the street and rallied for the night ride.

The Negro, Lonny Jackson, never enjoyed the satisfaction of knowing why he was being murdered. And perhaps this was an ignorance which he shared in common with his murderers. It would not, in the long run of such accountings, much matter. It had been a simple case of no one man being sober enough that night in Bracey's Saloon to remember anything more about Havana except the sinking of the *Maine* and, for some few of them, the honey-dark nipples of a girl who had kissed them there once, in a war. It was the place where Jess Willard, white, finally whipped Jack Johnson, Negro. It was an island with a nigger on it. And so was that night. And that would make it do.

LOY

And at Annie Love's, George was suddenly wakened, drunk yet, but the night, already notorious with rumor, murmured its own obscure chronicles in the remotest reaches of Annie Love's big house, where lights burned late and feet creaked and glasses chinked and chimed among the ebb and wane of other voices: a warp and woof of sound with a threat, almost indistinguishable, but yet as dark and doomful as the drip of knife-loosed blood.

"That voice!" he gasped, trying to get up. "Gotta go, Betty June! Heard that voice! Gotta get out!" And she was awake in an instant and her hand was pressing his wild, hot face back into the damp pillow.

"Hush, now! Hush! Wait! Lie right there whilst I fetch us both a drink!"

He lay still and glared into the luminous furies that webbed his hot eyes. And listened to her scratching matches and clinking glasses in the dark and then the splash of liquor. She came back to the bed, holding a glass to him in the dark.

"You hear voices yonder?" he whispered, shivering suddenly

with a thought that these might be the fancies of delirium. "You hear him out yonder talkin', don't you?"

"Sure now! Sure I do! Now bottoms up! And then it's back to sleep!"

"Sleep!" He seized her wrist suddenly and held it in a stinging grip.

"You do hear a man's voice?" he cried softly to her.

"Him? Don't pay him no mind! He don't come around but once a month! That sonofabitch," she whispered, through breathed-out smoke. "Bastard cop. Bastard Lowdy Kelts."

"Home," he murmured and twisted in the sheets as the knife of that name pricked his sleep. "Home!"

"Hush now! Lie still and sleep! Get to hollerin' and he'll like as not come back here and pinch you just for the show! And if you're in any sort of trouble with the Law you'll not want that, I reckon. If you done something. If you seen something. Whatever. So be still."

"Never done nothin'. Never saw nothin'."

"Don't matter none. Just be still. Every now and then the Law pulls a raid among the houses. That's to make a good show of their selves in the newspaper. Every now and then. It just don't look right—a man goin' fishin' all the time and never comin' home with nothing but the bait he set out with. So hush up now and he'll not hear. Sleep now."

"Won't tell. Swear won't tell."

"Won't tell what? See there now! It's on your mind so it's not just my fancy! I declare! *You!* If you ain't a caution. Just be still, that's all! He'll light out directly. When she pays him he stays for a few drinks and then he lights out. Won't look at none of us girls. Stares through me like I was made of glass. So hush. Sleep now."

"Home," he breathed desperately and struggled in his flesh. But no muscle on any bone of him would obey and so, subsiding, he fell back in darkness.

* * *

And remembering how he had wondered before, so many times, in the years after those twelve seasons in the Children's Home on the bleak hill above Goshen, if he had not really met Amy there: in that troubled house, and then: in those troubled days. However sharply he might remind himself that this could not have been: that through those three years of his exile from the kiss or care of kin other than his sister Carmel, Amy had been growing up somewhere far off in another town, another house. Then he would suppose that it was the dream of her that had begun in him there; then. That it was the face of her that he had begun to seek there; then. Before the Children's Home, before memory of Time, that face had been there waiting for him. And he was to know, instantly and jubilantly, on a star-crossed night a full decade later that the face which he had learned to call Amy, was the face that he had desperately imagined: a living girl-face of flesh and of liquor of tongue and fragile bone that fit to the very lashes of its eyes the mask that he had long ago molded out of starshine and shadow and need, in that strange house on the hill above Goshen, with the harsh charity of the county blanket against his nose and the whole world's night stuffed into that democratic bedroom whose stale air whispered nightlong with the snores and flatulence and gasps of its orphaned wards, among whom he had, under the whipcrack of need, made friends. In that house George was given a bed with quilts and windows shut against the legions of winter rain, and plain, hot, country food, and clocks to chime him to his rising and clocks to strike him to his chores and to his meals and gaslights promptly quenched at eight to admit him to the solaces of his improbable dreams. Mister Fish and Missus Fish. He thought of running rivers and dark sea deeps. Missus Fish and Mister Fish. And dreamed sometimes of the cold and lipless mouth of Missus Fish impaled upon a hook and pulling up the trotline in the dark had seen another mouth, awry and bleeding upon another barb: the mouth of Mister Fish. Neither kind nor unkind, neither warm nor cold: Master and Mistress of the County Children's Home, they seen to it

that everyone was done justly by and seen that malefactor was
quick to taste the switch upon his butt. They took their picayune
pay from the County and said thank you and got along and
kept shut-mouthed and knew that they had earned ten times
that sum for what they endured. Sore throats got soup-spoons-
ful of honey and lemon juice, and impious spirits were banished
to the black, shuttered room where God sat frowning and his
rats skittered and squeaked through the heart-thundering
blackness.

"Rats?" said Clegg, the handyman, to George, pale and
shaken after an afternoon's incarceration there. "Hell, they ain't
rats in that room, boy! Them's ghosts! Shore now! You never
thought them was rats did ye? Them ain't rats! Them's *brats*!
Ghosts of ornery, mean, impudent brats that got sent to the
room—and *died*! Skeert dead! Shore you didn't die o' fright up
there today, boy? Better give yourself a pinch! Better feel and
see if your bones still has meat on 'em! Mebbe *you're* a ghost,
too."

George tottered off bravely, on shaky legs, to the kitchen
where a peck of potatoes waited to be peeled; and took up the
honed and twinkling paring knife to prick his knee until his red
blood gleamed, gloriously, in a single bead, confirming his life.
Then squatting on a stool he began peeling the potatoes for
their evening meal. Hannah, the cook, black and tall, a Nigerian
princess, glared baldy-eyed at him throughout, her fists on her
hips.

"What you done to yourself, boy!"

"Nothin'."

"Ain't *nothin'*. You taken that peelin' knife and brung the
blood with it! I seen you! How come?"

"I slipped!"

"Ain't slipped! I seed you! I seed you plain! You taken the
knife and you cut you' knee! I war lookin' all durin' and
throughout!"

She glared, studying him ravenously, while furiously he
slashed at the peel of the potato in his trembling fingers.

"I know what you up to! You 'low if you leg is hurt Miz Fish won't give you no chores!"

He said nothing and the gray peels flew under his frantic, panicky industry. Hannah folded her fine black arms and turned her eyes to the window where flakes of first snow came shaking down from the dusk.

"I'll not tell," she said distinctly and his hands froze for an instant in the idiot iteration of their wasteful, chopping task, and he looked at her, wondering, almost affronted by her gratuitous, unaccountable kindness, blinking behind the steamy lenses of his spectacles. And suddenly he both loved and feared her within the same space of feeling. For there was a ritual complicity between them now: his taking of his own blood within her witnessing had become their common secret and he was her favorite among all the forty after that day. From her kitchen window she watched him in the winter yard, or in summer, from her screen door, her eyes strangely stirred with a light that might have been pity, a smile's ghost playing in the corners of her proud, dark mouth while she wiped grainy sugar from her pale palms when the pies were laid to bake. All forty of the children adored her, with her pretending withering scorn of them, and her shouted rage when they came up the hill from the school at Goshen to beg an evening apple or some jelly-bread to hide in their beds against the hour when the lights went down. The girls in the home wore the common blue dress, scissored and stitched by the poor in the County sewing rooms and rimmed with the lacy, five-and-ten rickrack which was the monstrous and terrible finishing touch to Charity's notion of beauty. The boys wore cotton sweaters and Levi's. So that, yearn as they might, be as different as they might, beneath the cloth, beneath the skin, within the bone contained within their genesis and the unripened seeds of their loins the varied riffraff and glory and felony of all the world's kingdoms—they were the same; they could not be different from one another.

And there was his older sister Carmel. Carmel Purdy and her younger brother George had been summarily deposited on the doorstoop of the Children's Home by the County Sheriff one winter's morning. Carmel: fine-faced and high-boned and stiff-shouldered, with icy Asias of grief and unregenerate anger in her eyes; George: snuffling and defeated. Carmel, eleven, and George, five, had kept apart from the other children from that outset; thin-lipped and silent and furious with an air of stunned pride that sprang not so much from their present mean straits as from their past, lost glories. It came into common knowledge that their father had been a Marine Corps veteran of five Pacific campaigns, but that was later. It appeared that their mother was a waitress who had died of tuberculosis, but that was later. It appeared that their father had done his best to keep them all together on his pay from the box factory and his check from the government, but what with a nine-hour shift and darning their socks and getting them breakfast and supper, it was all too much. He had taught Carmel how to get lunch and take care of George who was then always pale, poorly, and coughing; instructed her how to sew up torn things. He had taught her something else, but that came later. It grew to be, for a while, everybody's game to try and draw these two strange creatures out of their snug-chambered nautilus of thought, and out into the arena of testing: to win or to lose. And it was darkly reassuring for the other children to hang around them, to look at them and know that here was someone you were better than: however same your blue dress might be, however common your County sweater. And the taunter steps back to take the measure of his teasing. Yet always, when he would be tempted to punctuate his tirade with a finger flipped against the cold, proud, steady nostrils, or poked into the ribbed-flesh beneath the drab blue County dress, he would hold back—and wonder why he held back—sensing a coiled and clenched ferocity. And feel ashamed to admit that reservation. Carmel Purdy was only a girl. Gene, who was seventeen, and who did more bullying than any of the other children; even Gene had never gone too far with Carmel. Not with Carmel. But one day he went too far with George and that was worse. Gene had found George alone in the cellar where Missus Fish had sent him to fetch up a half-dozen two-quart Mason jars of tomatoes for supper. The cellar door was open, and Gene, passing through the cold yard in the evening dusk had heard George's cough and sneaked down into the funky cellar. George was lifting a heavy Mason jar down from the high, dusty shelf and struggling to keep from dropping it while coughs racked him and snot ran down his lips and over his chin. Gene pushed him and the jar fell and burst and hardly had George stooped, wailing, to pick the wet tomatoes and shivers of glass from his soaked and ugly shoes, than Carmel appeared in the cellar doorway. And Missus Fish came running. And Gene stood back, triumphant and blushing with having brought down at last a fraction of that invincible brother-and-sister union from its high horse.

"You, George! Can't you even fetch a jar of tomatoes upstairs and do it right! Wipe your nose, boy! And stop that sniveling!"

Carmel looked gravely into the old woman's face. "George never dropped them tomatoes, Missus Fish. It was Gene that pushed him!"

"You now! Just keep your nose out of this, missy! I'll ask for your opinions when the time comes that I've need of 'em!"

"I'll swear to it," Carmel said softly, terribly. "On the memory of my dead dad I'll swear to it."

Missus Fish gawped and whirled on Gene; mad because she had irrevocably lost all authority in the situation and it was too late to grope it back.

"Gene?"

"She's a goddamn liar!"

"Boy, I'll not abide profanity in this house!"

"—A goddamn liar!"

"Not another word! Mister Fish! Mister Fish!"

And Mister Fish fetched Gene off by the scruff of his scarlet-speckled, shaved neck and gave him twelve good licks with the brass buckle of his heavy belt while Fish's brother Clegg held him down and then they banished him to the shuttered black room till the evening meal was done and he was sent to bed with an empty, growling stomach to a night of hungry, vengeful dreams. In the morning, after breakfast, on the cold, dawn road to school Gene came up behind Carmel and George, passed them, white-lipped and raging with the night's accumulated intentions, and planted himself, feet apart, before them so they could not pass. But it was Carmel who spoke even before Gene's mean mouth had even gotten all the way open.

"Get out of the way."

Gene made a mean, sneering grin.

"Get out of the way," Carmel said again. "I'm warnin' you," Carmel said evenly. "Don't never pick on him again. If you do, you'll be sorry."

Suddenly the school bell came stammering up the frosty wind and Gene hawked and spat elaborately on the frozen road and turned his back, swaggering off down the ruts for Goshen, loud and cursing among the older boys.

"Don't pay her no goddamn mind, Gene!"

"She hain't nothin' but a girl, Gene!"

"Stuck-up old girl! She hain't no better'n us!"

Carmel's face maintained its composure. But everyone had seen how far Gene had gone with Carmel and gotten away with it. Carmel was only an eleven-year-old girl. And a skinny girl. An unforgivable girl, each child might have added in the confessional of his heart, where secrets cannot sting, where the only shame is loneliness. Yet Carmel stood out: a flame among their faceless, gray shapes. Carmel was Carmel, sufficient unto herself; sufficient unto God—and to the Fishes, handservants by His throne. What touchstone did she hide? What had she smuggled among them there that kept her warm in the always winter of that never Home? Gene was to discover the answer first.

None of the children was surprised at the tumult in the kitchen that day: the slam of the heavy door and the shaggy head of George trying to run the giant, aproned gauntlet of Hannah and Missus Fish. And blood. Blood on Hannah's clean blue apron and blood streaming from George's nose and his croupy, hoarse voice raised in outcry.

"Who done it? Who done it, I say? Answer me, boy! If it's a lad your own size you'll just march right back out of doors and stand up to him! Was it John? Was it one of the older lads?"

He stopped crying then; subsiding to a clenched, occasional rhythm of hiccuped sobs, and fixed his strong teeth hard in his lower lip, not looking at her, feeling the fateful ebbing of the seconds, and knowing that he would not tell.

"Ten seconds, boy!"

Hanging from his bunched shirt-collar in the fist of her free hand, George kept silent, eyes closed and calm, like a butcher's slaughtered lamb in Easter week, the cold blood jelling on his lip.

"Time's up, mister! Off to the room with you!"

And scarcely had she uttered the words, when the kitchen door, slowly opening, showed them the face of Carmel, pale as a pearl, but otherwise unchanged.

"I know who done it," she said. "It was Gene that done it."

"Hah! Too late! Too late! It was him I asked—not you! Shut your mouth now or you'll be up in the room with him!"

"You want to be fair," she said quietly. "You want to be just, Missus Fish. It was Gene that bloodied George's nose, for I saw it happen!"

"One more word, Carmel! One more!"

A smile faintly stirred the corners of Carmel's mouth. Then boldly she cast her fortune in with that of her brother.

"I don't care what you do, Missus Fish."

Well, a body had to admire her: that Carmel. A body just had to take his hat off to that Carmel: choosing black hours in the shuttered room and a supperless night just for the spend thrift gallantry of eight words. Her and him. Carmel and George. And while the dusk of that day folded like a wing upon the winter windows, while supper smells coiled sharp and pungent through the stale, darkening rooms of the Children's Home, while Carmel and George whispered reassurances to one another in the squeaking, rat-tailed blackness of the room, Clegg and Mister Fish and Missus Fish called and searched about the

grounds for Gene. He was nowhere. They set the children all
to searching, too. But Gene was nowhere. It was nine that night
when they found him. Mister Fish had notified the Goshen
police at sundown, before they all sat down to their supper table
with its sinister empty chair. Gene's chair. At eight that night,
just before Mister Fish began his rounds of screwing out the
cold gas flames along the peeling walls, the police car came up
the road from Goshen, its red light flickering through the low
elms of the yard. They had Gene.

"We got your boy, Fish."

"Where was he?"

"Runnin' off. We caught him on the tracks behind the freight
depot. We'd had him back up here sooner but Doc Shumacker
had to set his arm. Fish, you and your missus must treat these
kids pretty rough up here. Well, I guess they got it comin'.'"

"Arm? Set his arm?"

"It was busted."

"Well, I never laid a hand on him, O. T.! I swear to God! You
say his arm is busted! Well, now ain't that terrible! I swear to
God, O. T., neither me nor the missus laid a hand on that boy
today! Now and then I've taken a strap to him, but nothing like
this!"

"Don't explain, Fish. Nobody's askin' you to explain, Fish.
How you and your ol' woman handle him is business between
you and the County. I reckon once and a while some of these
little bastards gits ornery enough to rate a busted arm!"

Gene got out of the police car, his right arm thickly bandaged
and in a sling. He swayed a little in the sudden light of winter
moon that flooded from the ragged clouds. His face was the
color of whey.

"I fell down!" he whispered, staring into the dark grain of
the kitchen table, after the police had gone and Mister and
Missus Fish stood above him, sharp-eyed and purse-mouthed
with quizzing.

The children knew better. They knew nothing else, but they

knew better. They did not know the truth, but they knew the lie. And Gene's dominion upon them was done. Skulking through their midst, his bully voice shrunk to a whine among their ringing queries. But Missus Fish persisted.

"Carmel, how did Gene's arm git busted? You taken and hit him with something! A spade mebbe—or a mattock! You tripped him! That's it—hain't it? You pushed him! Answer me, girl! Which was it?"

But the old woman would have had the answer no sooner with a hot poker scorching the child's naked soles; or had she pressed the lids back from those dreaming, gray eyes and tried, with all her motherwit, to read their slumbering cipher.

Gene ran away again, on a clear, cold October night nearly two years later; this time for good. George saw him go: George and one other, though neither ever told that they had seen. George woke suddenly in the dark room full of sleeping boys and kept very still, listening until he heard it again, the faint chatter of the window being raised and, fainter still, the swift, hushed sobbing of Gene's desperate breath. Turning his head very slowly on the pillow, George could see him plain, at last, and watched him climb over the sill and clutch the rainpipe, thrusting his foot among the vines for purchase; over the sill and into the luminous infinity of moon, the face in that final instant still fisted and knotted into a fury and beneath the fury something else: wounded and confounded, as if it were as perplexed by the inexact nature of its grievance as outraged by it. Then Gene's face was gone. In a whisper of movement George was out of bed and across the floor, silently, to the window sill, to see Gene stood in the mists by the barn staring up at the house for a last moment. No one had heard. No one had seen. Just George and the other: above him, at the window of the room where the girls lay sleeping: all but one, and George knew that when her fingers broke a chip of wood from the rotting sill and it landed in George's hair and he had looked up. Looked up and seen her face: Carmel. Looked and knew that she had been there watching it all along; had perhaps lain awake for many nights harking for the footfalls and rumors of that exodus. George looked up and Carmel looked down, her eyes bright and calm and her mouth curled in a rare smile and her gaze meeting George's gaze in honest and unwavering exchange. *We seen him run away. But we'll not tell we seen him. It's a secret that we'll share.*

And so it had come to pass: their growing even closer. That Christmas at the Children's Home, George found the curious gift beneath his pillow and somehow knew who had put it there. Though he could not think what it was nor what it was meant for, except just that: a gift from his sister. And tore it open and a medal fell out of the paper, cold and chilly on his bare chest. Nor any word upon the paper of the gift to tell its meaning. And still he knew instantly that it was from her. And the cold disk of bronze warmed in his fist. Carmel. And his heart beat thuds of warmness in his ribs that sent their good cheer clean to his chilled toe-tips. Their father's Marine Corps medal. She told him that in the autumn dusk of another year and there was something deep and welling behind her strange gray eyes.

"He's dead," she said to him one November afternoon when George had mentioned their father.

"Dead?" he whispered. "Did Missus Fish tell you that?"

"No!" she scolded softly. "*Them!* I wouldn't pay no mind to anything *they* said anyways! I just know—that's all. Don't you ever just know things? George? *I* do! 'Specially when it come to Daddy! He's dead and I know it. He had the tuberculosis. And he died. I know. Our Ma had it, and they taken her away, and me and Daddy used to go see her at Hope Hill. And then—after a spell—they wouldn't let me go—just Daddy—he went to see her. And then a while later they wouldn't let Daddy go. And one evening—right during supper—me and Daddy stopped eating and laid down our spoons—and looked at each other across the plates—and it was just like somebody had blowed out the lamp—only it was still light—just like that—we knowed. I reckon that's where he catched it—from Ma. And now—he's dead, too."

George looked at her in a queer wonder; watching the shadows of November sunlight in her candid, quiet eyes.

"Ain't you sad? Don't it make you—feel like cryin' Carmel? It does me. It sure does."

And as he began weeping, she stood up and picked up a pebble and threw it into the face of the mackerel sky; into the Goliath brow of glowering winter; pitching it overhand, easy and casual, like a boy, and walked off alone.

And George saw that, knew that. Carmel was nearly fourteen now, nearly grown, and the hoydenish fury that, through her tomboy-hood coiled like a steel spring in every bone and tendon of her contended now with something new: some yielding thing, some soft and swelling and opening-out thing; however doomed it might be, like an autumn wildflower in the misapprehension that the sunlight was April's. George searched for her one cold Saturday afternoon and found her, back to the wall, splay fingered, the shoulder of her blue dress ripped, and Clegg was standing a few yards away, eyes downcast and looking like a sheep-killing dog while Fish confronted him; whispering in furious undertone.

"I warned you before! You may be my own brother but I'll not have it! I've given you chance after chance and I want it known here and now that you'll not get another! Brother or not! Me and Nevada has worked ourselves half into the grave to keep this place goin'—to keep body and soul together—and I'll not have you wreckin' it! You hear!"

Clegg mumbled something and his eyes wandered between Fish's big, broken shoes.

"You hear! Goddamn it, Ira, I'll not have it!"

Carmel inched along the wall, something furious and dangerous, something almost laughing in her eyes, and ran off toward the barn.

George went to the fence afterwards and searched the long fields until he found her, distant and small, walking up the brown slopes beyond the north field. He caught up with her in the dusk of that day.

"What'd he do to you?"

"Nothin'."

"Listen!" George shouted, manfully kicking through the dry leaves. "Don't you worry none, Carmel! I'll keep him from you! I'll protect you!"

She turned her eyes on him, and for a glimmering so brief that it might have been the stir and drift of vagrant sunlight among the leaves above her head, she looked at George with a warmth that he would remember until his dying; her face becoming, in that look's revelation, the dream-face of his nights' yearnings.

"You never worry about little old Carmel, buddy," she said sweetly with a queer, high edge to her voice that he remembered from the day she had stood facing Gene on the cold road to Goshen school. "Don't you ever lose any sleep about little old Carmel," she said, and broke the stick in her hands and then broke the two halves and then, in her quick, strong fingers, breaking the quarters, again.

"But he's mean—and sneaky—and dirty!" said George. "And he's bigger than you."

"Bigger?" she said, without looking at him. "Bigger don't mean shit. Pardon my French, but bigger don't mean shit! Gene was bigger, too!"

He remembered that; took it to dreams with him; remembered it on the day when George was passing the square barn door and saw the floor of the barn, and now there was a shadow there, and he waited and the shadow became Carmel's black stockinged little leg stepping carefully backwards until she stood in full view. He could not see her face, but something in the posture of her body made him know that she was facing someone. She backed more, stepping carefully, delicately, upon the balls of her feet, and then the other shadow came. And he watched and saw that it was Clegg and the man was crouched, with fingers outstretched toward the frail and now motionless figure of the little girl. George opened his mouth to shout something. He could not speak, could not move, seeing them both now in full figure, facing one another across a shaft of dusty light beneath the haymow. Clegg's face had dissolved to complete madness.

"Missus Fish! Mister Fish! Oh God, go help her! Please! Missus Fish! Mister Fish!"

Carmel surely heard him and Clegg heard, too, but it didn't matter now: what he had begun must be done because it didn't matter now, whether he did or didn't—she'd tell. She'd tell and that would be the end of old Clegg at the Home. He was in too far now to stop. George hollered and hollered and Carmel never looked up; she seemed curiously balancing herself on the soles of her ragged shoes and her eyes seemed intent upon where Clegg's feet would go next. He made a grab for her, and in the years to come when George would remember the image of the man and the child in that moment it would never seem quite real; it would always seem a dream. Clegg closed in upon her, arms out, and suddenly she had stepped sideways in a movement as frail and elegant as a curtsey. Clegg had suddenly gone pitching heels over head among the stacked rakes and hoes and shovels, and when he had stumbled up and turned to face her, his eyes were stunned and bugged-out with something of the disbelieving horror that George remembered in the moonlit face of Gene. She stood, feet apart, her bright eyes watching Clegg's big, quaking shoes as he staggered to his legs and made for her again. For the last time. He screamed something that the wind obscured and struck at her, furiously and brutally, with his fist, and with that same dancing-school lightness, with a mincing gesture of lightning swiftness, she seemed to bend mincingly again and Clegg's body went clean over her and pitched head first among the rakes and into a box of field corn. The children came pouring out the back door at that instant, gathering in a half-moon around the barn door to watch and Missus Fish came screaming in their wake and Mister Fish followed and Hannah watched, silent and bald-eyed from the kitchen window. Someone began the chant and the others picked it up and soon it was louder than the shouting of the elders.

"Kill him! Kill him! Kill him! Kill him!"

Missus Fish was struggling, flailing her big, freckled arms to get through the ringing children, and Mister Fish was lashing at their red ears with the big flat of his hand. Carmel looked down at still Clegg, humped queer and breathless over a hay rake with two prongs showing and two prongs not, while from beneath him in the scattered corn, some new autumn redness crawled between the boards. She stood a long, daring moment looking down at him surveying the justice of it. Then she turned and looked at all the ringed children, face by face, and at the faces of Missus Fish and Mister Fish as if she wanted them to see her good and see Clegg good, for the last time, and see who had won, after all, if only so's they could carry into the years ahead a memory of that justice: of it and of her there, and of the knowing that Big ain't always Strong and Little ain't always Weak. Then she turned, not hurriedly, and ran in a long, leisured gait down the barnyard to the fence and over it and into the burning. George shouted. And his shout became a scream. Fish and his missus broke, finally, through the cordon of clasped child hands, pursuing. And suddenly, with the same voice starting as before, the children commenced a chant and the choir of them quickened as Carmel fled: "Run! Run! Run! Run! Run! Run! Run!" Their voices rose with it and rang with it until it was louder than the Fishes' shouting, louder than the wind, louder than the burning brush and dry grass: "Run! Run! Run! Run!" Heroine; deathless queen of their legends: she fled before Fish, before flame, into the orange and smudge of sweet and burning autumn, while they chanted their psalm and saw her blue dress pick the yellow flower of fire and bear it with her, running still, in flames, her clothes wholly on fire now, phoenix, seeming to survive her very flaming death; her figure diminishing, like a burning blue butterfly among the blossoms of the flame.

"A child has been murdered."

"Come on now, honey, open your eyes. Come on now—git up! Nobody been murdered here, sweety! Come on! Git—"

"A child—"

"It's ten o'clock. Can't leave you sleep no more; can't honey! Miss Annie Love's fixin' to start her Jesus Chat and I gotta git you up and dressed and outa my doggoned bed! And that's all there is to it! Now open your eyes 'gainst I throw cold water in your face. Come on now."

George's lids flinched before the rumor of flame: quivering, striving to dare open; to confront the flame and define it. The flame, he knew next, was cold; it was his eyeballs that held that heat; that scorching, scalding throb that seem to be cindering the brain behind them. Open. Open. Not flame at all. Not flame but the sun in a strange window and the light on the face of a strange girl.

"There now! That's half of it! Gittin' your eyes open is half the battle! Now—up—up!"

And the strange girl's fingers stopped slapping him lightly across his cheek and found their way to his shoulders and tugged at him. He sat up suddenly, remembering Betty June, and blinked in rhythm to the throb in his head, working his dry tongue back and forth in his dry mouth so that he could repeat what he had been trying to articulate in the limbo of his drunken awakening. When his mouth was wet inside, enough to speak better, he couldn't remember what it was he had wanted so badly to say. He scratched his head and yawned, tasting whiskey in his breath.

"I got drunk."

"You sure as hell did. But that don't matter. That was what you come here for and that's your business. But now you gotta git up and git your clothes on and git on home!"

"Is it morning?"

"It is! It's Sunday morning! And it's ten o'clock. And ten thirty's when Miss Annie Love starts her Jesus Chat."

"What?"

He got out of bed unsteadily, holding his shorts in front of him in a sudden, unaccountable mood of shyness and turned around to pull them on, half-hearing what the girl was babbling about as he dressed and tried to piece together the terror of some lost memory.

"Was you ever drunk last night!" she cried. "Honey, I've seen some drinkin' in my little ol' life but you sure won the medal last night!"

The medal. The medal. The meddling voice of her buzzed against him like a fly. He felt sick, but it seemed like it was more from what he could not remember than from the liquor he had drunk. Something stood waiting behind a big closed door in his mind waiting and dangerous with impatience.

"It's seldom enough that Miss Annie lets a customer stay the whole night!" she exclaimed, bright-eyed and fresh from sleep. "But I don't mind her never lettin' any man stay on Sunday mornin' for her Jesus Chat. That's just for us girls!"

He paused, in the middle of pulling on his shirt and stared at her.

"What's this Jesus Chat stuff?"

"You'd laugh," she said. "You'd holler and laugh. You'd mock it. Gee, it's quarter past now! Miss Annie'll be ding-dongin' her big bell directly!"

"What big bell? I wish you'd tell me what's goin' on!"

"Nothin'! Nothin'! Just hurry and git dressed! Lordamighty, there 'tis now!"

While to George's astonished ears there came the shouting of a bell in quavering reveille through the house: the voice of it shifting and rising through kitchen and parlor and hallway, and with it the imperious voice of Miss Annie Love calling her girls by name. George sat back down on the bed, resting his forehead delicately in his hands while, with a gasp and a final, sudden

brush of fingers across the starched, prim bosom of her good
Sunday dress, Betty June gave a last approving glance in her
looking glass and was gone. George sat very still, keeping his
eyes in his palms, and tried to think why a bell should make its
incongruous outcry to the astonished Sabbath air: that brothel
air, stale and tired out with its testament of night-doings:
breathed-out payday whiskey smell and the ghosts of spent
flesh and cigarettes. He tried remembering again all the grave
parable of his dream; tried auguring its sinister relevance to the
bell's sharp alarm and the voice of Annie Love, calling her
harlots like Gabriel gathering his dead, fetching them up by the
nape of their dreams and bustling them out blinking into the
bright Sunday parlor. Then the bell in her hand stopped as
suddenly as it had begun, but down in the morning the churches
of the town chimed bright, small echoes of it like clocks all
striking in a jewelry store. Annie Love appeared in the doorway,
nun-black in her Sabbath best, the bell still in her fist while with
the fingers of her fat right hand she kept its brass tongue quiet.
She scowled at George and pressed her lips thinly together in
a kind of wrathy beatitude. He looked at her from between his
fingers and then slowly lifted his face.

"You, now!" she cried out. "I reckon you're sobered up
enough to know what day it is!"

"Yes'm. Sunday."

"And what does folks do on Sunday? Don't bother to answer
that for you're likely too hung-over to remember! But mind
this! *He* remembers!"

And she stabbed a forefinger toward the heaven of mildewed
bedroom ceiling.

"*He* remembers!" she exclaimed again, the jowls of her face
quivering with emotion. "The same Him that marks the spar-
row's fall! Don't you think *He* don't remember what Jesus-loving
folks is supposed to do on His day!"

She studied him hard, searching his face for something she
had thought her words would rouse there, but saw instead only
weariness and sickness and fear.

"Pray is what!" she cried. "Pray and sing His praises is what is expected! Hear them bells? Hah, ring them bells!"

He listened and heard them: the drifting, broken carillons down in the town.

"Ain't one of them calling you?" she inquired.

"No'm," he sighed. "I—wouldn't have much business being in church this morning."

"That's what you think!" she snorted. "You've got a sight more reason for bein' in a church this mornin' than me or the girls!"

"What do you mean?"

"I reckon you know better than I do what I mean!" she said, and behind the anger in her eyes he thought he glimpsed the faintest flash of fear. "Prayin' would suit your needs right well this mornin', young mister!"

He stood up, shakey-legged and pale and reached for his jacket.

"I'll be goin'," he said.

Annie Love looked again; staring hard at the floor, at his feet shaking an angry tear from her eye.

"Howsomeever!" she growled. "If you're of a mind to pray— and I'd say you was from the looks of you—you can stay! Mind you! It'd be the first time! The first outsider that was ever here! May He strike me dead if that ain't the truth!"

She turned away then, with the bell still muted in her hands and then turned, back, her face gentled oddly, and looked at him a moment more.

"For a boy that carries on and hollers in his sleep about the things you do," she said solemnly. "You could stand a little in the need of prayer!"

And before he could ask her what she had meant by it, what she had heard from him in the drunken babble of his sleep, or who had been there to hear it, too, she had squared her shoulders and gone from the doorway. George stood up and pulled his jacket on slowly, listening to it all in a kind of stunned fascination, as if it were part of the strange chronicle of his dreams. He walked down the musty hallway toward the parlor, softly so as not to be heard. There stood Miss Annie Love: livid-faced and yet, somehow, fiery in her fisted evocation and her three whores, pale-faced in unrouged Sabbath innocence, sat before the staircase in three straight-backed chairs, with their nail-bitten hands resting limp and upright in their laps, like sleeping doves. For a moment George paused among the shadows, against the wall.

"Now then! We're here together again, Lord! It's been a rough week as per usual but we made it!" roared Miss Annie in a voice of rib-poking, Rotary-Club familiarity. "Lord, you stuck by us for another seven days! And we're all mighty grateful! Ain't that so, girls!"

"Amen!" choired the three in a single, fervid cheer.

"Wow!" cried Miss Annie Love, slapping her plump palms together. "Reckon You heard *that* Amen loud enough, Lord! Reckon there'll not be another Amen down in them hypocritical churches this Sunday mornin' that'll top that one! Don't worry, Lord! We're hip to all them phonies down there—just like You are! Sanctimonious preachers and two-faced thinkers and three-faced doers! Women that points their scornin' fingers up yonder at us girls on Baltimore Street whilst their men folks comes sheep-eyed and horny to our door! How about that, Lord! Don't it beat them Pharisees to hell and gone! And when you git right down to the nub of it, Lord—who done You the mostest harm—Mary Magdalene—and everybody knows she was a hustler!—or Judas Iscariot—and all you got to do is set Thine eye upon any pew of any church in this town this Sunday mornin' to know what *he* was; sure, Lord! Hustlin' is a sin! You don't need to tell us that for it is writ plain in the Book! Hustlin' is a sin! And don't think there hain't one of the girls on the street that don't know it and hain't lookin' and scroungin' her pennies for the day she can git out of it and settle down somewheres decent with a home and a TV and a washing machine! We're hip, Lord! We get high ever' Sunday on You! We git our joy-pops from Jesus' love! Hain't that so, girls!"

"Amen! Amen! Amen!"

"Turn on with prayers, sinners! Git hip to Jesus' love! 'Cause when you *meet* Him—when you get to *know* Him—you find out he's a walkin', livin' *doll*!"

George felt his way along the wall throughout the streaming storm of exhortation and found his way to a split-bottom chair. Miss Annie Love paused, wheezing for breath, her eyes wild in the peeling chiaroscuro of flowers in the wallpaper; her fists still lifted in the middle of her dark and terrible psalm, in a half crouching pose of desperation in the toils of her furious, maddened logic; seeming as if about to spring upon the Lord, if, at last, it came to that, to wrest His mercy from Him with her very hands. The still moving lights of the juke box beneath the stair rail, which she gripped now, was like some perversion of stained glass as it sent drifting across her contorted brow the yellows and purples and scarlets of a tortured theology. George's mouth had fallen slightly open as he listened and stared in chilled fascination.

"Amen! Amen! Amen!" cried Betty June and Sally and Ruby in one voice and licked their lips with quivering tongue-tips. So absorbed were they in Annie Love's dark psalm that none turned her eyes, none sensed, nor heard a movement in the vines that framed the parlor window. The breeze might have made it, but there was no air moving in the morning of that breathless Sunday. Only George sensed it, heard it, and turning his eyes, saw it—the face above the sill beside the empty beer glass, a head, it first seemed, unattached, like Baptist John or Cheshire Cat. Negro-face, child-face, ghost-face: George saw it without astonishment, as if he had known that it would pursue him to that house, to that window, to the Now moment. No. No, hold on to yourself. No, because it can't be him, because you saw him killed. It's another. But wishing just the same that the boy would go away, would take away from the window that face, that head that did not seem to belong to a body. George moved his eyes back to Annie Love. He heard a freight-train wail faint, and grieve behind the shimmering heat. I'll run off,

George thought. Away from here. Away from the place where it happened. I'll forget what I saw, forget Amy, forget them all, forget the Me I have made here, forget this place and this Now and this earth.

"Hyep! Hyep, Lord!" cried Annie Love. "Hyep! Ever'body's praisin' you good and loud this Sunday morning! Hyep, Lord! Even them African Baptists down on Sweet River Lane! Hear 'em, Lord? Ever'body's hollerin' and shoutin' about Jesus' love! Black niggers! Sneaky black rascals just itchin' to shack up with white women! Hyep! Hyep! You know, don't You, Lord! Niggers runnin' the land! Sneakin' and spyin'! Just waitin' their chance! Mixin' in the schools! Mixin' in the mills! Mixin' in the beds! Hah, Hyep, Lord! *You* know! *You* see it!"

She stopped short, gripping the stair rail, breathless, a lank rope of gray hair fallen across her ruddy face, and the heads of the three girls turned slowly, as if her thoughts had commanded them, and saw the face of the Negro boy in the window. Absorbed in the amazing performance of this crazy old white woman, he apparently felt nothing personal about her tirade, watching it, hearing it as he would witness a drunk throwing a fit in the street and even if it were, he could turn and run back into the street before any one of them could make a move to lay hands on him. "Nigger!" screamed Miss Annie Love and, almost as if her explosive shriek had been a signal, the face of the black child assumed for a split second an expression of utmost consternation and then, as if jerked up by the hand of some puppet master, disappeared from the frame.

"Got him! Hah, got him!" bawled a voice, possibly God's from beyond the vines. "Hah, got him, Miss Annie!"

And at a muffled thrashing sound in the shrubs and the caterwauling of a child, Miss Annie rushed to her front door, the girls babbling in her wake.

"Got him! Hold—still—you—bastard! Got him, Miss Annie Love!"

It was the one-eyed, half-wit peddler Doggy Brennan who sold shoe strings in the streets of the town. Now, proud-eyed as a prize retriever, Doggy dragged the struggling, screaming child up the steps to Miss Annie Love's screen door.

"Doggy's got him! Hyere he is, Miss Annie! Doggy catched the little nigger peepin' in the parlor window! Hain't that naughty now!"

"Give him here!"

Something like a bell began clanging in George's head; something that swelled irresistibly and grew louder and louder. And he watched the girls ringing themselves behind Miss Annie Love as the old peddler, holding the child's arms behind its writhing body, bore him wailing into the parlor.

"Whatcha gonna do with him, Miss Annie? Cut him up for cat-bait?"

She held the child's arms now in the twin rings of her fists and Doggy watched, giggling and waiting for her to thank him.

"Now then!" cried Miss Annie Love with her face thrown back in the thralldom of a vision. "Lord, you plain outdone yourself this time! It's just like a sign! Ever'thing I been sayin' here this mornin'—all rolled up into one black nigger ball!"

"Gwan then!" cried Betty June, moving toward Doggy. "Shoo. Scat. Miss Annie's talkin' to the Lord!"

"Doggy's goin'!" he cried and then leaned a little toward her, cozening and squinty. "But I don't 'low," he whispered, "as how my favors'd be worth a shot of rye, now would they?"

"Later!" cried Betty June. "Gwan! Come back at sundown! You'll get it! Gwan now! Scat outa here! Gwan, Doggy Brennan!"

Miss Annie Love seemed as unaware of Doggy's departure as she had been of his presence. All her messianic emotion was focused on the propped-up figure of the frightened child on the steps. He lay back, breathing slowly and heavily, his mouth open, his eyes looking down his face at her in abject horror.

"Lord, you sent him as a sign! Lord, you sure come through this mornin'! A livin' proof, Lord, of what I been sayin' hyer! Hain't that so, Lord!"

And now she bent, addressing not God but the child.

"Hain't that right, boy! Hain't it? Well answer me! *Hain't it!* You niggers start young don't ye! Word gets round, don't it, about that nice young white poontang, don't it! Well, don't it? Speak out! Don't just lie there makin' squishy sounds like a dyin' frog! Hain't that why you came peepin'! Hain't it! Goddamn your black nigger soul, hain't it!"

She backed up, without turning, until she stood beside the chair where Ruby sat.

"Ruby, stand up!"

Ruby took her finger out of her mouth and stood up. Miss Annie Love reached down to the hem of Ruby's plain dress and dragged it up.

"Get a good look, nigger!" cried Miss Annie Love.

Ruby's big, nail-bit fingers covered her eyes for fear and shame.

"Miss Annie, I hain't wearin' no panties; Miss Annie—"

"Get ye a good eyeful, nigger, because you never know when an eyeful of young, white poontang like this is gonna be your last! Know what I mean, boy?"

George's pulse, like a bell getting louder and louder in his ears, and it was getting so loud he couldn't stand it much more and something left over from the night's dark journey whispering over and over in his pulses: A child has been murdered. Yes, but. Yes, but. Yes, but a child has been murdered. Yes, but. Yes, but! And he bit his lip until the blood sang red and stinging on his tongue.

Miss Annie Love dropped Ruby's skirt and Ruby collapsed in the chair, her whole body rag-doll limp like she had just endured the spasm of love.

"Did ye get an eyeful?" chanted Miss Annie Love, advancing again upon the dark child cowering on the stairs. "Did it look good, boy?"

George stood up.

"Leave him go!"

But she could hear nothing in that hush-breathed Sabbath but the many voices of the Lord, speaking judgments in her head.

"Leave him go!"

Slowly her face turned from the child to George.

"What was that, mister?" she whispered.

"I said, leave him go! He ain't done nothin'!"

"He—ain't—done—nothin'!" she repeated. "Well who the hell asked for your two-bits on the subject of what this nigger has or hain't done? You seen him spyin', didn't you? You seen him peepin' in the window, hopin' for a glimpse of white meat, didn't you? Weren't you the one that come in here drunk last night and raved in your sleep about nigger kids. The whole livelong night! Ravin' in your sleep like you was crazy with it! Hollerin' and mumblin' about this nigger kid bein' killed! And you didn't sound so damned particular about *that*!"

He turned his eyes to Betty June's face in sickly supplication.

"I never woulda thought it," Betty June was saying. "I never woulda pegged you—"

"Thought what?" he asked. "Thought what?"

"—for a nigger-lover," she went on. "I feel dirty you touched me! I feel dirty you done it to me! Like some of the nigger rubbed off on me!"

She darted forward, her face illumined with a passion and struck the child across the face. "Nigger! And you! You! A nigger-lover!"

"No!" he shouted and as he moved forward, it seemed that Betty June's still upraised palm might strike him, too. But she saw something, read something in his face and drew back against Miss Annie Love's apron and watched him as he gathered up the limp body of the Negro boy and held him upright, defying them. Miss Annie Love glared but did not lift a finger, nor did Betty June, nor Sally, nor Ruby. Their eyes followed him as he backed across the parlor toward the screen door, the child dangling in his grip. When he got to the door he leaned against the jamb, breathing hard and shook the body. The fear-stunned eyes of the boy rolled to the light.

"Get a hold now! Get a hold of yourself!"

With a free hand he reached to the window sill and, picking up the half-empty glass of stale beer he threw it in the child's face.

"Get a hold! You'll be all right! Go along!"

He pulled the screen door open behind him and flung it wide with the toe of his shoe.

"Now, run home!"

Like a dark shadow the boy sprang alive and fled into the calico sunshine. George leaned in the doorway, breathing hard, looking at them through a lock of fallen hair.

"It's not involved!" he roared. "*Nigger* is not involved in this! A child is a child!"

He moved down the steps, gripping the railing, and shook his head as if to loosen something from his eyes.

"*A child!*" he explained again to the sun.

Miss Annie Love hurled the empty beer glass from the parlor window. He heard it burst and tinkle on the paving stones.

He walked down Baltimore Street under the summer trees: right foot, left foot, right foot, carefully. So no one would notice him and stop him and ask him anything. Because if they did he would have to tell. He was not sure yet just why, but he knew that he wouldn't be able to keep it in anymore. Remotely, like the muffled bark of a cellared dog, the cursing voice of Miss Annie Love followed him. Right foot, left foot, carefully. Because he knew now that he would tell. No matter what they would do to him for it afterwards, he would have to tell. He turned at the corner and started down the steep stones of Sugar Street, towards the town, walking very carefully.

The room. And the bulb hanging in the middle of it. And the two men. "What time last night you say this was?"

"Oh, I left there around two. Around two, I'd say it was."

"And you didn't take any pains to go in that room and get him up out of bed and find out who he was and whether he really seen anything Friday night?"

"Loy, I just never attached no importance at the time."

"You didn't?"

"Well, Loy—"

"You never attached no importance."

"Well, no, Loy."

"You know why, don't you?"

"Well, Loy, I—"

"The reason is because you're an ignorant, illiterate, mother-humpin' son of a bitch."

"Well, Loy, what was I to have did if I hadda got him up outa the bed."

"You'd have run him in, is what you'd have done. You'd have run him in and he would have been booked for drunkenness and immoral congress. He'd have been out pickin' cucumbers on the Farm for the next thirty days. So's we could ask him. So's we could find out whether he seen anything Friday night."

"Well, Loy, what do you reckon we can do?"

"Call Verge."

"I done that. He'll be in here directly."

"Where is he now?"

"He was down at the Coroner's when I talked to him. That's where I called him at. Look, Loy, it may not be nothin' at all."

"Shut up."

"Shall I call Verge again? Tell him hurry up?"

"Negative."

The white bulb in the middle of the air, the moon on a dirty cord, began suddenly to sing thinly. In that shabby, windowless room of the courthouse it burned eternally, night and day. It hung above the men's heads like the slashed, sole, dangling and dying testicle of a lynched municipal conscience.

"What time did they find the nigger?"

"Sunup, Loy."

"Who found it?"

"Coley Pipes seen it. Him and his Missus was walkin' to town on their way to church."

"Where was it?"

"Stuck down under a branch on a log. At the dam. Loy, I think—"

"You think what? Ain't it a little late for you to start thinkin', mister?"

"Well, I just think it might have been nothin' at all. Just some drunk talkin' in his sleep about a murdered nigger. Loy, there wasn't nobody on the river road Friday night when we done it."

"When we done what, Lowdy?"

"When we shot—"

"When we done what, Lowdy?"

"Well, Loy, it's just you and me here now talkin'. I know what to say if someone else was to—"

"When we done what, Lowdy?"

"Nothin', Loy."

"Nothin' is right. Now tell me again about this drunk you heard at Annie's."

"Well, I was in the kitchen havin' a sociable drink with Annie."

"You poor dumb bastard. You're so dumb it smells on you."

"Well, Loy, if you want me to tell you how it was."

"You were conducting an investigation as a police officer in a known house of prostitution."

"Well, yes, Loy. Godamighty."

"Remember that if you can. Do you think you can remember that if anything should come out of this? If a reporter should ask you?"

"Sure, Loy. But this is just you and me talkin'."

"It's just you and me talkin'. Now it is. But if someone else was out there on the river road Friday night. Someone besides us. Besides us and the dead nigger. If someone was up at Annie's house last night hollerin' drunk about it. If someone was to blab his mouth off and get you and me and Verge in trouble. Think about those 'ifs' for a spell, Lowdy, if it don't strain your pea-size brain!"

"Wouldn't nobody dare, Loy!"

"No. Shit no. Wouldn't nobody dare."

"Not one of *our* folks, Loy! Why, who ever heard tell of such a thing!"

"*Our* folks! Our *which* folks!"

"White folks, Loy. Wouldn't no white man ever think of such a thing. Not in *this* country!"

"Maybe not here. Maybe not in Augusta County. But there's other parts of the country, mister. And there's snoopers. There's wrong-minded folks. Suppose it was one of them wrong-minded folks that seen what we done?"

"Well, Loy, I can always go back to Annie's and git a description. And then I can hunt him down."

"That's right brilliant, Lowdy. You'll go huntin' down a drunk on a madam's description. You'll go through all the beer joints till you come up with a feller with a hangover and a sore pecker."

"Well, Loy, I'm just tryin', that's all. Tryin'."

"Well stop tryin'. You make me sick to listen to you. Let me do the thinking from now on since you plainly don't know how."

"Okay, Loy. Okay."

"Jesus, I don't dare leave town for twenty-four hours without something like this happening."

"I called your number first thing this mornin', Loy. Your missus said you'd be back sometime 'fore noon."

"You never said nothin' to the Chief about him? About the drunk?"

"No. Hell, no."

"Nor the Sheriff?"

"Loy, I ain't that dumb."

"You're that dumb."

"Well, I never said nothin'."

"Did you say anythin' to Verge?"

"No. I barely spoken to Verge at all this mornin', what with all the ruckus over them finding the dead nigger."

"Nobody knows, then. Just you and me."

"Well, Miss Annie Love. And the girls."

"Nobody else."

"No."

"Then it's between us to find him."

"I can get the Chief on it."

"Negative! You dumb bastard! Negative! That's just it. The Chief of Police ain't in on this! Nor the Sheriff! I'm the power in this County!"

"Right, Loy. I guess ever'body in this courthouse knows that."

"And everybody in the County knows it. Remember that!"

"I'll not forget it, Loy."

"And you and Verge—you take your orders from me! Not the Chief! Nor anybody else! Get that through your head, too! If you value your ass. Because if and when this all should come to trial—"

"Trial! What—all? Trial!"

"Trial for shootin' the nigger! It could well come to that! There was witnesses in my store the mornin' he insulted my wife! Word spread that day. There'd hardly be a white man in the County that didn't expect me to shoot the nigger. There'll be plenty to say who done it. They'll like as not charge me with it. The point is—provin' it. The point is—who saw? Not should-be nor hearsay nor dead-reckoning! Who saw? That's all!"

"Loy, they couldn't hang us on whispers!"

"No, but they could on a witness! They could even drag in the Feds! You know all that fuss about voting! You know how the wind blows!"

"My God, Loy, if a white man can't even kill a nigger that insults his wife!"

"Keep your head, dummy! Don't start whimperin' now!"

"There wasn't no witnesses, Loy! My God, there wasn't no-body but us down on the river road that night!"

"You hope! You pray and hope!"

"Well, you reckon—there was, Loy?"

"I'll know. Before sundown tonight, I'll know. Stir your ass up, mister! Find me that man that was up at Annie's last night!"

"Loy, how? I don't even know what he looks like."

"No, but Annie Love knows."

"Annie?"

"Or the whore."

"You mean, Loy, for me to drive one or the other of them up and down past all the beer joints till they spot him?"

"Affirmative."

"Maybe they won't."

"Maybe they better."

"Couldn't me an Verge just go around all them joints our ownselves?"

"Negative."

"Verge is terr'ble smart, Loy. He—"

"Verge couldn't locate Sunday morning on the butt end of Saturday midnight."

"Well, don't it look funny, Loy? I mean folks seein' her—a madam—ridin' around of a Sunday afternoon in a red car with two officers of the law?"

"It will look a hell of a sight funnier me and two officers of the law ridin' on our asses up to State Prison!"

"My God, Loy. Couldn't never happen here! Not *here*! Wouldn't no white man dare to tell an Augusta County court he seen such of a thing!"

"Find him."

"Well, all right, Loy. If I can get old Annie to co-operate."

"Find him."

"I'll have her to start out with that café at the bus depot. He just might—"

"Find him."

"I'll have Verge to come along, too."

"Find him!"

The light bulb, singing thin as a mosquito, flashes brilliant and goes out. In total darkness the two men curse among scraping chairs.

   None of the men looked at each other. Yet they all talked to each other. Everybody in Smiley Deep's Green Moon Café had been talking about it all that morning. Everybody in Augusta County. The story had even made the news services. Smiley Deep could hardly remember ever doing such a brisk beer business of a Sunday. Smiley and his brother Marl had been drawing beers hand over fist since ten A.M. and had hardly time to wash out the glasses. One after the other they had been putting beers before the men, but neither Smiley nor Marl looked at a man's eyes nor he at theirs. Hardly any man in Augusta County was home with his family that Sunday. No man wanted to be around women that Sunday. Nearly every man or grown-enough boy in the whole county was knotted together that day: in beer joints, in pool rooms, in country stores and filling stations, on street corners, and under the courthouse elms. They were all busy talking about the lynching, and spitting and not looking at each other. George sat staring at the mark his beer glass made on the countertop and waited for Hawk to come back from the men's washroom. Hawk hadn't said anything after George had got done telling him the whole story. He had just sat there, not even nodding, listening, and when George was done he got up quietly and went into the men's toilet. George felt that if he hadn't found his roommate and spilled it all out to him, he would have just split open with it and gone yelling it to someone, anyone, maybe even the town cops. George had known, without thinking twice, that it was safe to talk to Hawk about it; he knew how Hawk felt about most things.
   Hawk came out of the men's toilet after a while. He took his leather jacket off a coat hook and put it back on. He sat down on the bar stool beside George. On the back of Hawk's leather

jacket there were three words carefully lettered with stencils
and white auto store paint. The words said: "There Goes
Hawk." Hawk didn't say anything for a while.

George said, "Well, that's the way it was. That's how me and
Amy happened to see it happen."

"You got trouble," Hawk said softly. "Oh, you got big trouble."

"I know it," George said calmly.

"Even if you don't do anything—don't say a word about it to
anybody—you're in a bag. And nobody can tell you what to do
about that but your own self, boy."

"I've already decided what I've got to do," George said.

"Well," Hawk said. "I wouldn't never try to tell you. You
know how I feel about things like that. But I don't know just
exactly what I'd do if I was in your shoes. I think I know what
I would do—or what I would have done once. But I ain't even
sure about that. When you come up to a thing face to face—
yourself—that's something again. Something else. I learned
that good a long while back. Before Vietnam. I learned that
good back when I was a baby, I reckon."

"I know what to do," George said. "I'm scared. But I know
what to do. And the funny thing is—I was a whole lot scareder
before I made up my mind what to do. That's a queer thing
when you think about it. Scareder before I decided."

"No, it's not," Hawk said. "No. Lemme explain you something. All the kinds of scared a man can feel is like—Christ,
how can I picture it for you. It's like *colors*! Like the *spectrum*.
What I mean is, boy—there's this spectrum of human scaredness and in it—way up at the end of it—there's Fear. Then
comes Terror. And then Terror Unutterable. And beyond
that—well, there's this queer kind of *calm*—a sort of ultra-violet
awe! And I think maybe this might be what the Old Men used
to mean by the Fear of God. Because, boy it's out there in that
calm—out there in that queer, quiet awe—that a man makes
his mind up about things."

Hawk sat on the bar stool, shivering a very little bit and

sweating a very little bit and rubbing with a broken fingernail at the skin under the leather on the inside of his left forearm.

"That's something," Hawk said, "I used to know about."

He shut his eyes and a little trickle of sweat crept down his cheek along the edge of his dark sideburns.

"A way long whiles back," he said. "Way long back there. Before we was in the Army together. I mean, back when I was a man."

"You're a man, Hawk," George said. "You're a good man, Hawk."

Hawk swung suddenly off the bar stool and went over to the juke box and took a dime out of his pocket. His shaking hand chattered the coin all up and down around the slot before it could make it go in. Hawk waited till the jazz started. Then he came back on the beat, walking carefully back to the bar and climbed the high stool and sat with his eyes shut and his fists knotted; tensed, like he was waiting for something to happen, for good news like a letter from home or something.

"Your trouble and my trouble," Hawk said. "Your trouble is bad trouble, but my trouble is still worse trouble, George. Much worse trouble, George baby."

George turned his face slowly and stared. Hawk patted the tips of his fingers on the edge of the bar like it was a drum; with a driving, gentle fury Hawk drummed. George stopped the left hand and held Hawk's wrist.

"You on that again, Hawk?"

Hawk shook his wrist free and went on playing his drum and waiting for the letter from home.

"Ah, Christ, Hawk! Not again!"

Hawk heard the grave and splendid thunder in his fingers. The jazz that streamed through him was already years ago.

"Ah, Christ, Hawk! You said you'd kicked it."

George leaned around to stare into Hawk's sweating face. Hawk's eyes were squint-tight shut and his two front teeth were biting his lower lip until the red letter came.

"You had one of those things in there," George whispered,

trying to stop Hawk's left hand. "In the men's room! Hawk! You crazy? Didn't you get in enough trouble in the Army with that stuff?"

Hawk got the good news like a sweet, cool sundown in his parched pulse. Hawk turned his head to George on the arc of a century and when his eyes got to George he smiled with unutterable delight to discover that all that time ago was still now. He looked at George through a hundred miles of inches, reasoning with a mad and exquisite clarity.

"Hawk! You crazy? Somebody goes in that toilet. Somebody catches you—you're finished!"

"Finished," Hawk said in a soft whisper. "Sure. Finished. Any way you slice it, I'm finished. Except over here—when it's like this—finished is all turned inside out. And it's beginning."

George stared at his empty beer glass.

"I know what you're thinking. You're thinking you come to me with trouble today and I let you down. George, if cops walked in that door right now and grabbed you—I couldn't help. George, even if I hadn't shot up that fix—I couldn't have helped. I'd only do you more harm trying. Baby, I'm not clean."

"It's all right, Hawk."

Hawk frowned and tried to concentrate but it was so difficult talking across so much time and space to George: he seemed so long-away and far-ago.

"Dig? I mean, you *really* dig, boy?"

"It's all right, Hawk," George said again.

"I'm not clean," Hawk said with terrible and precise slowness. "I'd help if I was clean. So I'm no good to you today, baby. I'm no good to myself. Any day. I'm high, is why."

"It's my trouble," George said. "Even if you could help, it would still be my trouble. I'm the one who had to decide what to do. And I know what to do. I just wanted somebody to talk to. Until it comes time to do it."

"Then talk to me, boy. It's not like I was drunk. Christ, my mind is clear! Clear! Talk like we used to talk in the Army."

"Amy," George said to the wet circle.

"Amy!" Hawk whispered. "Amy! My God, name like a song! Like a song!"

"Amy," George said, eyes closed, and still talking to the wet circle. "I got no right to make up anybody's mind but my own mind. I got no right to make up Amy's mind."

Hawk looked down at George and saw everything so clearly. He saw how reasonable and clear everything really was. He was anxious to show George how fine he was thinking.

"You talk to Amy about what to do?" he said.

"Yes. Yesterday. Yes."

"I mean sound her?"

"Christ, Hawk! How do you reckon she'd feel? It's her own daddy!"

"Careful!" Hawk said. "If you're not careful with thoughts, sometimes it's like dimes and nickels slipping through your fingers. Careful, baby. Don't never reckon how a person feels until they say! And sometimes not even then! Christ, I know Amy. I don't love her and know her like you! But I know her. And I'm wise she'll do what's right! Christ, I wish you could see how clear I can see all of it from out here! From clean way out here, George!"

George sat with his eyes shut, his head still throbbing, and listened to the men all talking about what had happened.

"What the hell!" cried Hawk suddenly. "Was she *proud* of it? Her big, brave daddy killin' a nigger kid with the help of two fine other citizens!"

Some of the eyes in the bar turned suddenly in Hawk's direction and thought about what he had said, but they decided directly that they had heard it wrong and looked away again.

"She wasn't proud!" George whispered. "She was scared— mixed up and scared. She was cryin'! We was both—swearin' we would never tell! Swearin' to each other how we had never seen it! Christ, I finally had myself half-believing it, Hawk! That I hadn't seen it happen at all! That it was just a nightmare!"

Hawk rocked on his bar stool and whispered with his eyes closed.

"Listen, George baby! Listen!" Hawk whispered solemnly. "Your nightmare, I can hear it! The whole length of the bar— the whole length of America. They're whisperin' about it!"

"Come on, Hawk!"

"I can even hear Loy Wilson whisperin' about it!" Hawk sang softly from his little trance. "I served under a sweet son-of-a-bitch like him for six months in Vietnam and I'd know his mother-lovin' whisper anywhere! In any alley—at God's blackest hour of midnight—I'd know his whisper, boy!"

Hawk opened his eyes, and turned them to George: all careful and cautious and reasonable again.

"No," Hawk whispered. "You never dreamed it. It's a nightmare, but you never dreamed it. It's real. And I'm not saying that to make it worse for you! You think I'm high and flying and that's why I'm saying this. I'm very quiet, George."

"I called her this morning," George said to Hawk because he had to talk to somebody and even Hawk like this was better than nobody.

"When?"

"Noon."

"What'd she say?"

"Her mother answered."

"What'd *she* say?"

"She said Amy wasn't home. She told me yesterday I wasn't to see her anymore. She called me white trash."

"Where was Amy? Did she say?"

"She didn't say. She hung up."

Hawk swung suddenly off the bar stool and went to bend over the juke box as if he were picking out a selection. George saw his face and felt his feet chill in his socks.

"What's wrong, Hawk?" George whispered.

"Nothing. Nothing. Just get the hell quietly up and go walking slowly back to the john and stay there till I come for you."

"Hawk, what's. . . ?"

"One of the hardest things to learn," said Hawk, "is when an Army buddy says do something it's always better to do it and ask why after. You think 'cause I'm high that means I'm not clear! Christ, I'm clear! I can see everything! Now do what I tell you! Will you?"

"Yes."

"It's too late now. Now don't move. Just keep your face turned towards me. Maybe they won't spot you."

"Who?"

"Cops. The one they call Lowdy and that other one— Stafford. They're going past the place real slow. In a prowl car. And there's a woman. In the back seat. Christ, boy, if I hadn't been turned on I wouldn't have noticed! See?"

"An old woman?"

"Yes. Light a cigarette. Do it casual."

"Annie," said George to himself and lighted a cigarette.

It's amazing, he thought. My hand has stopped shaking since I made up my mind. It's amazing how quiet everything has gotten since I made up my mind.

"What are they doing now?" he whispered, breathing out blue smoke.

Hawk said, "Now the old woman is getting out of the red car. She's lookin' in the window at the bar!"

"She see me?"

"I don't think."

"Hawk, get out now. Hawk, you can't get mixed up in this."

Hawk stared at his eyes in the mirror away in the back of the juke box, behind the stacks of records.

"I'm not clean," he said. "It's lousy, goddamn it! It wouldn't do any good. I'm not clean. See, I'm no good to you or anybody, boy!"

Hawk slipped the dime into the slot and pressed the red button and watched the silver fingers reaching for the record and lifting it carefully out from all the others.

"Because if you wanted to," Hawk said. "You couldn't tell them it was really just a drunk nightmare you was hollering about in Annie Love's house last night. That you never seen a thing. That you wasn't anywheres on earth but at the picture show Friday night."

"No," George said.

"No," Hawk said.

George said, "What are they doing now? The cops?"

Hawk said, "Getting out of the red car. And coming across the sidewalk toward the door."

He clenched his fists and shut his eyes and leaned into the plastic light, into the hammering jazz and big tears began squeezing out of his tightened lids like sap oozing out of something wooden.

"Say the word, baby!" he shouted. "Say it, George, and I'll stick with you!"

"No," George said and got off the bar stool. "Stay out of it. They're going to pick me up and if you start swinging they'll pick us both up. I need you outside of this. I need you to help Amy."

He looked for their faces in the swirling fume of stogie smoke.

"Will you help her, Hawk?" he asked.

Hawk nodded fast and straightened up, eyes still closed, weeping and moved sadly away toward the side door beyond the men's toilet. The words on his leather jacket said: "There Goes Hawk." Lowdy and Verge moved in upon George so swiftly that none of the men at the bar even noticed. Cops were in and out of Smiley Deep's Green Moon Café all day long anyway. And everybody was busy talking about what had happened. Nobody noticed George being swept cleanly back into the empty corner booth, with a cop under each arm pit, shoving up.

"You're under arrest, felluh."

"For what?"

"For drunkenness, felluh."

"I'm not drunk."

"Sure you are, felluh."

And their clenched, furious faces disappeared in his vision when Verge threw the water glass of whiskey into his face.

Bone-dry her cheeks and bone-dry her heart, for there were no tears left in either. It was the peace after rain's downbeating and not even her mother beyond the bolted bedroom door could shake her: coming every fifteen minutes, as she had been doing, to threaten and cajole by turns. Amy combed out her dark hair and, sitting by the window, felt nothing much at all, knowing nothing else for sure but that she could no longer stand it there: dreading the nearness of Gladys somehow more than her father's because of that in Gladys which was now violated and public by what Loy had done, so seeming, to keep it from being either. As if what he had done had not, on the contrary, been to keep this thing in Gladys chaste and inviolate but to assure its not being so. Made naked and exhibited: something of her mother, in the reflex ritual of what he had done.

"Will you open that door, Amy?"

"No, Mother. I've told you I want to be alone this morning. That's little enough to ask, Mother!"

"Amy!"

"Please go way from the door."

"I suppose it's too much to ask you to think a little of my feelings. Is that too much, Amy?"

"I know what you want to talk about, Mother. I just don't feel up to it this morning—talking about it."

"You know what's happening back there in town?"

"Yes, Mother. Yes. I know what's happening in town. I heard it on the nine o'clock news."

And something almost celebrant, almost gay, in the furious, cadenced click of Gladys' high heels up and down the boards beyond the bolted door.

"And you mean to say you're not worried, Amy?" Gladys cried, her voice now thin and clarion with anger and with that blood-dark other thing; that primitive and joyous thing.

"I think it's awful, Mother. Awful! Awful!"

Gladys sobbed and through the painted wood, horribly, Amy could fancy her smiling through her tears.

"Amy, open the door. Amy, my God, open the door! I need you! Don't you understand? Daddy's in trouble, Amy!"

Amy unbolted the door and opened it and stared at Gladys.

"I know, Mother. Daddy's in trouble."

Gladys had on her good blue silk dress: the one that brought out her eyes.

"That's all you can say?" she whispered. " 'Daddy's in trouble. I know mother.' That's all you can say! Dear God, Amy, you should be down on your knees with me praying for him!"

"I prayed for him, Mother."

Gladys had on her cultured-pearl earrings: the ones Loy bought her that Christmas in Chicago.

"You prayed for him. Well, pray more, Amy! Keep praying, Amy!"

Gladys had done her nails the night before and they looked neat and tasteful as she pressed her fingers in horror across her cheek and stared at Amy, shaking her head in a gesture of disbelief.

"You just stand there, Amy! You just stand there! Like it was nothing! You act like it was nothing! Amy, do you know there's rumors your father's going to be arrested! Arrested, Amy! Do you know I had to close up the store this morning because of all the snooping, pop-eyed crackers just come in to stare at *me*! Just like I was some kind of a sideshow girl, Amy! Just like they was all pointing their dirty fingers at me and snickering: She's the one! She's the lady the nigger insulted!"

"Well, aren't you, Mother?"

"Sure! Sure I am! Collie Moon heard it! And saw it! And the beer-man. They both did. How could it stay a secret in Augusta County with the both of them knowing it!"

"And they knew what Daddy would do," breathed Amy numbly to the billowing curtains above her hope chest.

"Yes! Yes! They knew!" cried Gladys, and Amy's eyes widened but dared not turn to see the dark victory in Gladys' face: that glory which sounded its passionate chord in her throat. "They knew! And there's not a man of them that wouldn't have done the same! Not a mortal one that doesn't wish this very Monday morning that he had had the chance your daddy did."

"But now—"

"But now what?" asked Gladys. "Amy. Amy, there's something not right-minded about you this morning! My God, I don't think you know! I don't think you appreciate what Daddy's going through for us!"

"Not us! No! No, Mother!"

"Not us? My God, Amy. What do you mean 'Not us! No, Mother!'?"

"I meant—I meant I don't *know*, Mother!"

"What do you mean you don't know!"

"Mother, I mean it wasn't *me* that it was done because of!"

Gladys stepped back in the manner of a silent-movie actress and pressed both hands to her cheeks.

"Almighty God, what sort of child have I raised up! What kind of woman!"

"Mother, stop! Stop it, Mother!"

"But what kind of—"

"Mother just let me be! I know they're all saying Daddy did it. I know! And they'll probably arrest him and there'll probably be a trial!"

"Well, doesn't that *matter* to you?"

"Mother, Daddy'll *get off*! He'll go *free*! You know that!"

Gladys sat down on the edge of the candlewick bedspread and took Amy's cold hand.

"Of course he'll go free!" she said. "That's not the point! You don't seem to realize what he'll be going through! And me! The humiliation of a public trial!"

"Don't touch me, Mother!"

"What? My God, what?"

"I don't want to be touched! I just want to be left alone. Mother, I'm sick and I'm ashamed and I feel dirty! Dirty!"

"Dirty from the insult of a nigger! Amy, that insult was meant as much for you as for me! For any decent white woman!"

"If that's what you want me to say," Amy said. "I'll say that, Mother!"

"Would there be anything else," whispered Gladys furiously, "that you would feel dirtied from?"

"Mother, it's not anything."

"Maybe you feel dirtied by having a daddy who was decent and manly and American enough—"

"He'll go free, Mother! This is Augusta County! He'll go free! That's all you—all we care about!"

"—to kill an uppity nigger who'd just as much as peeked under the skirts of—"

"Mother! Get out of my bedroom! I can't stand any more!"

Gladys burst suddenly into honest tears and in a twinkling her face was weathered and gaunt with a decade of secret passions that she had nightly oiled and creamed and painted over. Stark she stood, fists clenched, crying, with her eyes shut and her mouth ugly with weeping. Amy stood, wanting to touch her, wanting to stop the things from showing in Gladys' face, and not knowing how, not knowing what the things even were. Knowing only that they were things she had never known were there behind her mother's face and what she felt now was pity hand-in-hand with terror. Terror that things like that could hide behind a mother-face. Bone-dry, her eyes could shed no tears for Gladys, her hands could not reach up to help. She stood watching and knowing how much more surely that she had to get away. Gladys hurled herself sobbing upon Amy and clutched her, and Amy stood. She felt her mother's tears dropping on her naked neck, blood-warm, and her mother's fingers digging in her shoulders. Amy just stood. There was not a word for any of it. Because her terror was bigger than her pity.

"There!" Gladys murmured after the storm of sobs had passed. "I'm a fool! God, I'm a fool! Letting myself go like that. Honey baby, I'm sorry. Honest to God I'm sorry."

"It's all right."

"A good cry sometimes helps," Gladys said. "Well, *you* know! But I'm sorry, Amy baby! Lordy! We oughtn't to be hollering at each other at a time like this! The good Lord knows we'll need to stand together!"

"Mother, I—I can't help."

"Baby! Amy baby! Just your being here helps! You know that!"

"Mother, if Daddy should—"

"If Daddy should go up for trial? Amy baby, that's when I'd need you most of all!"

"Mother, maybe I wouldn't be any help!"

"Amy baby, just your being there—with me—would help."

"Maybe it wouldn't, Mother!"

"Amy, what does that mean?"

"Maybe I'd say—*something wrong*!"

"What?"

"People make *slips*! They say things wrong sometimes, Mother!"

"Amy honey, you're tired and you're nervous from all this! Hell, I guess I'm a fine one to be telling you about being tired and nervous. The way I taken on!"

Gladys took one of Amy's cigarettes, lighted it with trembling fingers, and sat down on the bed again.

"That lace was just right for your good Sunday black," she said, staring at the dress hanging in Amy's clothespress and blowing blue smoke into the air.

"*What*, Mother?"

"Your dress. The good Sunday black."

"Dress?"

"Amy! The good black I got the lace for!"

"Dress! Dress! Mother, how can you talk about dresses now!"

"Well, Amy baby, I was only trying to think ahead. You'll want to look nice. And still genteel. Conservative and genteel but still nice for such an occasion. I mean, should it—"

"What, Mother? For such a what occasion?"

"Why, for the trial!" Gladys said. "It could mean a lot. I mean, the right impression can shorten things like that."

"My God," Amy whispered and looked out the window through the billowing curtains at the black asphalt highway beyond the apple tree. "My God. My God."

But Gladys did not hear. She was repairing her face in Amy's vanity mirror, lost in dreams of the future, beyond whatever sinister inconveniences the trial of Loy might bring.

"Most folks that know me," Gladys said, "folks that see me every day would say, 'There's a wife whose first and foremost thought in life is looking out for her man.' Well, they're wrong. Most folks would guess that, Amy, but they're wrong. It's being a good mother! That's my first and foremost thought! My big aim in life is to see my little girl make something of herself! Have a good college education! A career!"

Amy thinking: Because if I stay even one more night under this roof I will go crazy. I have to get away before I go crazy and they start asking me the question. Because if I am crazy, I will tell the truth.

"Even with all this trouble," Gladys declared, "staring me right in the face. Even now that's all I'm thinking about. If it all should come to a humiliating public display, all I'm thinking about right now is my little baby Amy. Looking right. I mean looking decent and genteel in front of all that courtroom rabble. Lord, sometimes things look the worst when they're just fixin' to work out for the best, Amy! I mean if it *should* by chance come to that—a trial—and you and me have to get up there in front of all that rabble—we might just as well make the best of it. I mean look the part of what we are—a mother and daughter that any white, God-fearing American would be proud to defend with his life! Why, Amy, we're all likely as not to come out of all this better off as a family than ever!

That's why it's so important—thinking ahead! Even to little things like what to wear! After all they'd have our pictures in all the newspapers—There! I don't look like I'd been cryin' do I, honey?"

"No, Mother. You look just fine."

"We mustn't be mopin' around here with long, sad faces when Daddy comes home tonight."

"No, Mother. We mustn't do that."

"And in the store. If folks should stare. If anyone should come from the newspapers. We've got to look right. We've got to know what to say."

"Yes. We've got to know that. What to say," said Amy, and lay face down on the bed.

Now in those three days something in her had grown to woman swifter than breasts had come; more sudden than the unbidden, tumultuous teen-time budding of the flower in her flesh had been. Halfway down the staircase it came suddenly into her mind that she was running not from fear of Loy, but for love of George. And now in the whispering, dangerous dusk of that Monday she knew that she must find him and then, together, knew what must be together done. Gladys had taken a sleeping pill and lay huddled, snoring and murmuring in fitful afternoon sleep on her bed. Amy stood a spell, listening, and then put her suitcase on the carpeted stair and stole softly back to her mother's door. Gladys Wilson would not have wanted Amy to see her face right then. Gladys always wanted a chance to fix her face, to cautiously adjust its expression before anybody looked at it. Especially Amy. But now Amy looked and saw her mother's face with sorrow and pity in her heart: a face without pride and therefore vain. Amy felt old, grown-up and alone and old; as if she were woman now looking at child, a child that somehow improperly inhabited the flesh and aspect of a woman's body.

"My poor dear," Amy whispered. "My poor, poor dear."

She wanted to go over and take her mother in her arms and comfort her for all the lost years; she wanted to tell her mother over and over again that it would be all right: that she was not going to let that happen to her life. Gladys hunched up a little in her sleep, smiling at a dream of genteel dresses. Her lips worked, yearning in sleep.

"Goodbye," Amy whispered and ran softly down the muffled stairs. Goodbye, goodbye, her mouth, without breath, shaping the word over and over. Goodbye, and swept the light suitcase up in her fingers; goodbye, and shut the screen door gently in her wake. Goodbye, goodbye, and saw the orchard, gold-green under the seas of August dusk; like that drowned once-world of man beneath the flood of His chastising astonishment. And the fruit stood; yellow moons among their leaves. She thought: Eden. And I have eaten one of them and for that I must go running. Her eyes moved among the gnarled arms of the trees, among the smokey, dusk-green leaves and saw the cabins where the pickers of the harvest lived. Thinking: Must go a-running. I must get to Grandpa and Aunt Nell for help. The only ones. God, the only hope I have of saving him.

Remembering. The first time they had met; the first time she had laid eyes on him: it was at Merry's Dreamland on a sweet spring night when the air was like a wild flower. Mister Merry held a rock'n'roll dance contest every Friday night in the ballroom of his place, and George was with a plain, pleasant-faced little blonde girl named Elly Matthews. Amy was with a boy from high school named Jake Booth, and they were sitting watching George and his date and another couple doing a fast, complicated dance in the middle of the floor. Amy watched George with mild interest; she had the vaguest of feelings that she had seen him somewhere before, and that was, indeed, possible in a town the size of theirs. But it was somehow more than that; it was as if she had known him somewhere, some place else, in another time perhaps, and they had had different names and been creatures of wholly different fortunes. Jake felt a little irritated.

"You want to dance, Amy?"

She shook her head quickly, still watching George, frowning and still filled with that unanswerable and curious questioning. Then George stopped suddenly in the middle of a perfectly sensational split, his face filled with consternation, and he rose slowly to his feet, backing modestly away from the onlookers. Someone behind him set up a ruckus of uproarious laughter and George whirled, furious, and it was then that Amy saw that he had completely split open the seat of his trousers.

"Hey!" called out the astonished Jake Booth. "Where are you going?"

And she hadn't even answered him; it hadn't really seemed important to, somehow. She followed George into the shadows by the stacked cases of soft drinks.

"Can I help?" she asked.

"I guess that's supposed to be funny," he said. "Why don't you just go on back out there and laugh with the rest of them."

"No," she said. "I'm not laughing. And I can sew."

"You can what?"

"I can sew," she said. "I can very easily fix your pants for you. I take Home Ec in school and I know about these things."

He was silent for a spell, frowning at her through the shadows.

"That's nice of you," he said. "I didn't mean to shout at you. Can you really sew? I mean—could you fix them up?"

"Sure," she said. "Easy."

"Where you going to get needle and thread in a placc like this?"

"I got it," she said brightly. "In my pocketbook. It just so happens. By sheer chance."

"You do?"

"Yep," she said. "If you don't mind white. I mean white isn't the color of your pants and white's the only color thread I happen by chance to have with me."

"These old Army chinos," he said, with a wave of his hand. "You couldn't make them look any worse."

He looked so pathetic and helpless that her eyes grew a little moist and her heart was beating so fast she could hardly get her breath and she found herself thinking to herself: What a crazy world this one is. A perfectly strange boy splits his pants at a dance and you see it and take one look at his poor, embarrassed face and you know right off—certain as sunrise—that he's the man you're going to marry.

"Well," she said, practical-minded. "You'll have to take them off."

"What?"

"Your pants," she said. "Trousers, that is. You'll have to take them off."

"Oh, sure," he said. "Sure. I wasn't thinking. Sure. Would you mind—I mean, could you turn around, please?"

She turned around but not quickly enough not to notice that he was even more embarrassed because he was wearing a perfectly ridiculous pair of shorts with big green and red polka dots all over them. She took the trousers out to the kitchen where there was light and sewed solemnly and gravely by the big black stove and it seemed as if it were the lightest-hearted task she had ever been given to do; there seemed, indeed, something majestic and noble about those trousers.

"These are Army pants," she said to him somewhere behind the stove.

"Yep," he said. "I served my year."

She waited a moment, heart in her mouth, the quick needle trembling a little in her fingers.

"My," she said. "Goodness."

"What's your name?" he asked.

"Amy," she said. "Amy Wilson. What—what's yours?"

"George Purdy," he said.

"Pleased to meet you, George."

"Glad to know you, Amy."

And he forgot completely then and came marching around

the stove in his silly underpants with his hand held out to be shaken.

She remembered. And she would always remember it with wonder that was close to fear: that she had known so surely and so certainly in such a ridiculous situation that he was the one for her. Someone else took Elly Matthews home from Merry's Dreamland that night and Jake Booth sulked and loitered around till the place closed and then went home alone. George took Amy out for the first time in his souped-up car and they didn't do a thing but park and sit and stare at the moon above the river.

"Well," he said presently. "You sure can sew. Anybody ever ask me anything about Amy Wilson, I'd have to tell them she was sure some sewing fool."

"Thank you," she said. "It was nothing."

"What do you mean nothing!" he cried. "I was in a spot back there."

"I was honored," she said. "Really I was. I was honored to be of some usefulness to you. Any time."

"Well," he said. "I sure hope it never happens again."

"It's strange, isn't it," she said presently.

"What's that?"

"Oh," she said. "Strange how things happen—something rips and well—there you are."

"I don't think I follow you," he said.

But she knew that he followed her perfectly; he was just making her do all the work of getting things said between them.

"Just by sheer chance," she said. "I happened to have that white thread and a needle in my pocketbook. Isn't that the darndest kind of fate in the world. I mean, isn't it wonderful?"

"Yes," he said. "It's sure wonderful."

"I guess you might call that a lucky rip," she said boldly. "We mightn't not have ever met at all without it's happening."

That was when he kissed her and she moaned at the feelings of it and rolled and pushed in his arms but not in resistance. And now she remembered it; remembered how it had been one

another from that night on and nothing had ever come between
them to change it: their lives immutably bound forever together
by a simple but noble little length of mercerized cotton thread.

She leaned now against the shingles of the house of her childhood, eyes closed, her straw hat tilted back against the cracking
yellow paint. Trembling: the suitcase clutched dangling before
her. Breathless, but not from body's running, but some furious
exertion of decision.

She looked at her wrist watch. It was six thirty. The south-
bound bus came by the crossroads at six forty-five. She looked
up at her mother's bedroom window with a last sorrow from
which all longing had bled and went down off the porch and
up the grass toward the highway.

She leaned against the pole at the crossroads and turned her
eyes back once more to the yellow house and the store in the
front of it and the orchard behind, its green fire washing now
indistinguishably into the skies beyond. It was six forty. And
thought: Please, God. Don't let there be anybody on the bus
that knows me. Please, God. Let me get to Grandpa's.

Her head turned and her eyes darkened and widened. The
far yellow lights on the evening highway swayed and lurched
like the distant eyes of some furious and fleeing small animal.
It wasn't the bus for town. Because it was coming from town
and it was coming fast, tires thinly crying in the distance and
the spray of gravel like buckshot as it took the winding turns.
Without panic, without hurrying, Amy made her way up
through the high grass above the road and moved for the orchard. She stood in the green sea deeps of the orchard and
watched Loy's apple truck go careening past and skid almost
half-circle round in the gravel in front of the store. She could
hear Loy shouting Gladys' name all the way to the door and
through the darkened, silent house thinking: Poor Daddy. How
frightened he must be to be yelling so. She put her suitcase in
the grass, sitting on it, folding her hands and watching the

house through the apples and the leaves and the dusk, watching
the lights flash on in every room and hearing Gladys' thin and
nervous voice mingling with Loy's shouts. She waited, grieving
and solemn, but unafraid, watching and listening. In that
stillness of country dusk the voices from the house carried like
talk across water.

"Where's Amy? Goddamn it, Gladys, will you waken up and
tell me where Amy has gone to!"

"Loy, my God! Why she was in her room! Did you look?"

"Course I looked! Course I did! What the hell do you think
I'd do!"

The voices of them drifting random to her there, across the
oceans of the dusk, vagrant and nocturnal, like the bark of
waking hound-dogs beneath an evening porch. Doors slammed
remotely. She listened. Her mother calling her name; her father
calling her name. She sat among the low leaves, among the
apples, with lap-folded fingers and watched and listened for the
time when they should reconcile themselves to her being gone,
forever gone, and close the doors against her, forever against
her, and go to bed.

Gladys hollered: "I'll bet *he* came for her while I was napping."

"No, he never! I'll attest to that! He *couldn't* have!"

Leaning a little now, her ear cupped against the voice of her
father, diminished now to a mummur, thick with secrecy, with
catastrophe.

Gladys crying: "Oh, my God, no! Oh, he *never*! He *saw*? No!"

And that maddening silence again in which she knew Loy
whispered and the apple leaves flurried suddenly downward in
a dusk wind.

"And you made sure of that? How, Loy! In the name of God,
were you sure?"

"He shouted it in my face! That's how," bawled Loy suddenly,
and the leaves fell still. "Me and Verge and Lowdy had him in
the room for an hour before we took him away! He said he had
seen us kill the nigger Charley!"

"Loy, hush! My God, someone might hear out on the road!"

And that susurration like the pulse of dark's own heart; her father's whispering, and Amy rose, thinking somehow that the terror in her flesh must surely be luminous, cupping her ear beneath the brim of her straw, and running soundlessly through the grass toward the house, thinking: No. He wouldn't. No. He wouldn't dare. Oh God, no! He wouldn't dare hurt George! Even if he said he had seen! Even if he said he was going to tell! He wouldn't! My daddy wouldn't! They wouldn't hurt George. And half fell among the aura of thick jasmine against the yellow shingles by the kitchen window; flattened with arms outspread among the vines and moon-roused blossoms listening in horror for what her father was whispering.

"She'd never! Amy wouldn't never! Good God in heaven, Loy, what kind of child do you think we've spawned?"

"But she was with him Friday!" Loy's hoarse whisper like the panting of a dog. "Wasn't she! Well, wasn't she?"

"Oh Lord, let me think! Oh Lord! Well, yes! I reckon she was, Loy!"

"And you stand there and tell me it don't matter!—her not being here! You tell me that don't mean she's run off! And for all we know run off to the Law—to the Sheriff—to tell! To bear witness against her own father!"

"Shut up, Loy! Amy wouldn't never—"

And heard the flat wet sound of his hand across her mother's mouth, still moving in the midst of words shut off.

"Don't never tell me shut up, Gladys!"

Who wept now; gasped in long and strangled sobs: Gladys, face down upon the kitchen table.

"We've got to find her!" he said. "No matter what you think she would say or wouldn't say, would tell or wouldn't tell! There's no goddamned time for that kind of guessing, Gladys."

Amy pressed herself closer to the house, eyes closed, heart pounding behind her tongue, thinking how she must not get sick, must not faint and fall down because they would hear that and he would come out and find her.

Listening while Loy paced the furious yards between stove and Frigidaire and back again, beating his fist in a thick, cracking rhythm within his palm.

"Listen to me, goddamn you, Gladys, and listen good! It's time you wise up a little to some of the things that goes on around you! It's time you got wise to the things that's been happening in your own house—to your own daughter!"

"Loy, Amy wouldn't never . . . !"

"Shack up with him! Is that what you mean, Gladys! Well, don't be too damned sure! He got into her mind! Into her soul! What makes you think she'd be so all-fired hard to get into!"

"Loy!"

"Listen! Let me do the talking for a while! You know how Amy has changed these past few months! Restless and moony! Reading and thinking and spending all her time alone, when she's not been in town with him! Full of wild notions!"

"What—notions?"

"Queer notions! Radical notions! Rotten, filthy, un-American notions! There, goddamn it! There on the kitchen table—beside the butter dish—that book of poetry! Look at it! That's some of his crap, I'll wager."

"She wouldn't, Loy! My baby! No, Loy!" Gladys chanted, in a kind of crooning song. "No, Loy! Amy wouldn't never do that! Even—even if she was with him! Even if she *saw*! She adores her daddy!"

"I'll take no chances!"

"Well, dear God, you wouldn't hurt her like you and the boys hurt *him*! Dear God, Loy! Not your own daughter!"

"Christ, Gladys, why can't you shut up! No! Not hurt her! Just keep her locked in—nailed up! Just keep her home until the trial is over!"

"What trial? Loy, what . . . ?"

"The trial of me! The trial of Lowdy Kelts! The trial of Verge Stafford!"

"They'll—arrest *you*?"

"Yes! Yes, you fool woman!"

"H-how?"

"They know!"

"Who? Who told?"

"The nigger's mother seen us! When we come for him! She was on the street by the alley!"

"She told?"

"Christ, yes! She told!"

"Where's she at now, Loy?"

"In the jail! After she told the Chief she begged him to lock her up so's we couldn't get at her!"

"Can't Lowdy or Verge help?"

"Verge is under arrest! Lowdy is under arrest!"

"In jail!"

"The Chief let 'em go home! He told them to stick around!"

"And you, Loy?"

"I'm in it, too!"

"Arrested?"

"Yes! Yes!"

Gladys' voice trailed thinly out through the moon rise in a nasal wail of travail. Amy heard the chair scrape as Loy grabbed her up bodily and lashed her against the mouth.

"Hold yourself together, you fool woman! We've got to find our daughter!"

"Amy wouldn't tell! Loy, she wouldn't tell!" said Gladys like a child saying a lesson. "Them other two niggers might tell, Loy! Them's the ones you should be worryin' about!"

"They'll not tell!"

"They stayed shut in all day," Gladys said. "I went up to the door of the shack three times today and I could see them sitting 'longside of the stove. Just sitting and staring out from the dark—like cats. Them's the ones that might tell. Didn't the mother tell them?"

"She did," Loy said. "But they'll not tell!"

Amy felt her spirit drifting out of her flesh, born upon the sick scent of the jasmine fume:like a fog enveloping her, and thought she would faint with it, listening while Loy threw the screen door open with a raspy cry and glared up the moon-blasted orchard to the lanternless, blinded cabins of the Negro pickers.

"Would you tell, niggers?" he roared up into the green and distant blur of apple trees against the night. "You wouldn't tell—would you, niggers? You want to live—don't you, niggers? One little dead nigger ain't worth two more dead niggers, is it?"

The night prevailed, and dogs rallied behind the moon to speak safe answers among the patchwork distances of summer farms.

Loy strode back into the lighted kitchen.

"But Amy might tell," he said in a low voice.

"No, Loy!"

"But Amy might tell, Gladys," he said, his voice rising. "With her mind all—"

"Never, Loy. God, never!"

"—with her mind all twisted up and wrong-thinking—"

"Never, Loy!"

"—from that boy! That scum of the earth—that white trash!"

And then he went to the kitchen closet and was throwing things around in search for his big Delco electric torch, and when he found it went to the kitchen door and cast a quivering finger of light among the night yard and Amy ran out and up the yard toward the orchard, toward the moon that now, without passion, was enveloped in a slow-drifting rag of cloud. Running silently toward the orchard, among the silly white shapes of Monday's hung-out wash, standing like child's scissored fancies in the black, stunned air; cried a quick, faint cry when the clothesline caught her beneath the chin and held her for a moment imprisoned on a shadow-line, with the faint taste of blood from her aching throat.

"Amy!"

And she was still, mortal still, finger still, and eyelid silent, pulse and heart-beat still, and saw Loy's big black shape against the yellow of the door and the white column of his torch, like God's seeking eye, fingering the night; did not move, did not

breathe, standing with the rope still beneath her chin, against
her windpipe, doomstill, timestill, and hearing with a dread that
chilled her soul, the shrill, betraying chatter of her wrist watch.

"Amy?"

"Loy, is she . . . ?"

"Hush! I thought I heard—"

"Loy, you think she's out there—"

"Shut up! Shut up!"

While she froze, motionless in her pale coat among the white
laundry, standing in the dark.

"Amy? You yonder? Amy?"

He came down from the back porch now, swinging the torch
in wide arcs round him and went down the yard, away from
her, toward the road, calling her name. Her fingers went up to
the clothesline and took it from her aching throat and bent
slowly and darted off among the Monday wash, foot-silent and
breathless, toward the orchard.

"Amy?"

Gladys calling now, and following behind Loy and the searching light, toward the road and Amy running among the low
branches, among the apples, among the dark, without sound,
because she knew those mazed branches like the veins in her
flesh.

"Do you think it could have been her? Loy, you reckon she
could just be hidin' out here in the yard all this time?"

"How do I know! Amy?"

"Or yonder in the orchard, Loy?"

"Amy?"

And the moonlight sprang around her of a sudden in a leap
among the apples and the leaves and she froze again. Before
her, in the smoking mists, among the silvered, lunar leaves,
among the apple boughs, stood the black shapes of the Negro
shacks.

"Loy! Listen, Loy, she might have run up in the orchard!"

"Yes, I'll give a look around up yonder! Yes. She might."

Now the torch swung, stuttering light, spraying light, among bedsheets and leaves and shirts and Loy was coming up through the tall grass now, to the wash, towards the orchard and she thought: But there's nowhere else. I can't go in there. But there's nowhere else. And sweeping swiftly over the threshold, stared at the gleaming black faces in the ruddy lantern dusk. They said no word and seemed not to see, not to hear her, nor to know even her presence there, huddled back against the doorframe, away from the eyes of them, away from the eyes of him.

The old Negro man and woman sat in broken chairs on either end of the pine coffin which rested upon a child's wooden wagon. The young Negro girl sat in the little rocking chair that was too small for her, the chair that had been Amy's in her own childhood. On the floor beneath the window was an ancient and useless battery radio with a huge trumpet loud-speaker: a dusty, petrified flower, and from its throat there issued neither voice nor music but the grating, rushing comment of wordless static. The lamp bloomed up among the greasy litter of the meager supper. The child rocked and chewed gum with quick white teeth, eyes on Amy. She looked away to the face of the old man; thinking: No. I can't ask him either. For I haven't got the right. Why should he? Why should any of them hide me? And then to the face of the old woman; thinking: Nor her. Jesus God, nor her. None of them. And suddenly there was no one in that room from whom to beg asylum; no one of them whose eyes seemed to stare at her unseeing, uncaring, beyond every feeling, even grief.

"Hide me!" she whispered. "Don't let him find me! Please!"

The little girl rocked her chair and hugged her skirts round her knees and kept on staring. The old man rose suddenly and shuffled across the room to the lamp. He cupped his hand round the hot glass chimney and huffed a breath through his toothless gums and the night rolled in; and moonlight sprang through the broken, dusty window. Loy's boots squeaked in the high, wet grass beyond the open door. Amy flattened against the wall and held her breath and saw the torch beam flash across the floor boards and up the far wall and zigzag round the room till it found the old man. The spotlight gripped his face.

"Please, Mister Loy? What's wrong now, Mister Loy?"

"You hear anybody in the orchard tonight, Mose?"

"Not just lately, Mister Loy."

"What do you mean—not just lately? You hear anybody— any time—tonight?"

"Round sundown, Mister Loy. They was—"

"Speak out, nigger!"

"—a young girl!"

"Where! Where!"

The old man blinked in the fierce glare of Loy's torch and seemed to ponder.

"Me and Aunt Vashti," he said. "We seen her running down the highway. Towards town."

"When!"

"Well, it were just after sundown, Mister Loy."

"Was it my girl Amy?"

" 'Deed I couldn't no ways swear to that, Mister Loy, sir!"

"Well, did it *look* like her?"

"Come to think of it now, Mister Loy—"

"Yes or no, damn you!"

"Yessir! Yes, sir, Mister Loy! It surely did!"

"You ain't lyin' to me, Mose?"

" 'Fore God, Mister Loy!"

"Your family had enough trouble, Mose!—foolin' around with me and mine! You better not be lyin'!"

" 'Fore God! Reckon I'd be plumb crazy to lie to you, Mister Loy. No, sir!"

Loy spat a sound and the torch beam dashed away and in the simple dark Amy breathed out the thunder of her heartbeats in an outpour of inheld breath.

"Gladys!"

He was running down through the orchard again now towards the house. "Gladys! Mose says he saw Amy walking to town!—What? About an hour ago!—What?—Hell, get in the truck! We'll catch her on the road!—*What!*—Hell, I can't hear you! Just shut up and do like I say!"

The truck motor cursed and caught and thundered and the tires spun and threw gravel and skidded away up onto the asphalt and boomed off into the night.

Mose lighted the lamp with the kitchen match and looked at Amy and the little girl rocked and the old woman turned her eyes to the ashes in the old iron stove. The little girl grinned and ran over to the radio and hit it with the heel of her hand.

"This radio!" she said in a bright singsong."It don't get no shows! It just gets sounds!"

"Hush up, Nancy!" the old woman grumbled, without turning.

"You don't run me, Granny! Ma runs me. And Ma's in the town to tell the Law!"

"Young'uns!" moaned the old woman. "God's mercy on us! Young'uns!"

"Come night," Nancy sang right on, heedless, "it's a comfort, like Ma says, just to hear it crackle and buzz."

Her eyes widened to ivory moons and her lips paled and her gaze drifted to the long pine box.

"Charley used to fool with it," she said. "Charley claim he fix it someday. But Charley never fixed it," she whispered. "That fool radio."

Amy covered her face and began weeping in long, strong waves of silent gasping; cupping her bowed face into the nest of her fingers. She fell down on her knees on top of her suitcase and her straw hat tumbled off on the floor.

"I'm sorry. Oh, God! I'm sorry! Sorry! Oh, God, forgive . . . !"

"It wasn't your hand that done it," said the old man, lifted for a moment from the pit of his sorrow by Amy's need.

"Lean on King Jesus's arm!" cried the old woman suddenly to the ashes in the cold iron stove, and stirred among her shawl as if roused by a revelation in the dead cinders.

He sighed and turned his tired eyes to the night beyond the door.

"Jessie never should have gone to town to tell the Law."

"Lean on the Lord!" cried the old woman, as if growing closer to a fact.

"Jessie never should have gone," he said again to the wind that fingered the grass beyond the threshold. "It won't do nothin' but bring down more trouble. It won't bring Charley back! If her going to town to tell the Law would bring Charley back, then I'd have said go. But it won't."

"Your daddy sure would be put out!" the old man said softly. "You up here in a nigger house, Miss Amy."

"There wasn't any place else," she said numbly.

"I wasn't scolding you, Miss Amy," he said. "And it don't matter none. I don't reckon much more could fall on this family. He was a good boy. Charley was a good boy."

"The Lord called him!" cried Aunt Vashti.

"No," said the old man. "No, Vashti. Don't go shovin' this off on the Lord. The Lord gets enough shoved off on Him as it is."

"It—was—my—father," breathed Amy to herself.

"She seen it!" cried Aunt Vashti. "She seen her daddy and them two others kill Charley!"

"Hush, Vashti!"

"I'd never tell!" Amy cried, and glared around the room at the living and the dead. "Wouldn't any of you expect that of me!"

"Lord, no!" chuckled Mose. "Lord, no, child."

"Well, why are you smilin' at me like that then? It's my father! My own flesh and blood! You wouldn't expect a daughter to testify in court against her own father!"

"No, Miss Amy, Lord, no."

"But that—that doesn't mean that I think—what he did was right! You don't think that—do you?"

"Folks do what they has to do," he said. "Folks best be what they has to be. There's something big that runs through us all, Miss Amy, and when it comes the time to do somethin'—it gets done—right or wrong. And there's no way of tellin' whichever it'll be until you gets up to it."

"I just want to get to my grandpa. To my Aunt Nell," she whispered, as if in reply to some speaking in herself. "That's all, to get help for George! And then forget all the rest!"

And she looked then with sidelong, stealthy brightness to the pine box on the wagon, as if she half-fancied someone might be listening there, sleeping there and hearing her voice there, though through a mist of dreams.

She got up off her knees and pulled the suitcase up and held it before her in quivering fingers as if it were a shield against the dreadfulness of their mercy: both quick and dead.

"If it would bring him back!" she cried, her voice thin with terror of something that seemed now to find increase within her heart. "But—it wouldn't! It wouldn't! So—you've got no right—expecting that!"

And she backed slowly through the doorway, into the night, and the fragrance of the orchard windfall, into the shapes of moon among the apple boughs.

"You've got no right!" she cried. "No right at all—expecting that! Because it wouldn't bring him back! It wouldn't! Can't you see?"

And ran stumbling into the fields, into the tided oceans of the moon that rose and drifted among the corn.

ISAIAH

And Loy would have to smile. Sometimes, years later, he would even have to chuckle out loud, thinking back to that night when they had got home, that night of the lynching, drenched to the skin and dripping puddles on the carpet in the lampshine of the hallway, panting a little and glaring with curious brilliance into one another's eyes, like straining wrestlers, and he had known that night, for the first time, that he would be stronger, that he would win.

"I don't know you," Isaiah said, with a queer, defeated light of gentle grief shining in his eyes. "You see—I don't know you at all. My own boy—and I don't know you."

Loy smiled, and it was all out now, and he didn't care if Isaiah thrashed him for it, he was going to say it all now, that had festered and burned in him so long.

"No—you don't know me, Papa. But you know Toby—don't you, Papa. And you know Luke. Maybe you'd have got to know your own children, Papa, if you'd tried—if you hadn't been so busy minding after ones that weren't even your own kin—your own color! Niggers," Loy went on, gathering impetus like a runaway wheel. "You know all about them—don't you, Papa!"

"You want me to strike you," Isaiah said softly. "But I won't. That's what you want me to do—to raise my hand against you—but I won't."

But Loy didn't even seem to hear him, nor anything now, except his own furious, high adolescent voice running on with it, in one of those tempests of self-absorption that were to rise, raging, like summer squalls, throughout all his life. And all Isaiah could, in good conscience, do was to stand headlong into that tirade, with grace and honesty, because, after all, he had given Loy leave to speak his mind that night.

"The meek, Papa! The meek, you always told me, will inherit the earth! Yes, Papa! I reckon that's so! Your kind—and Grandpa's kind—the meek! But who do you reckon will be the ones to help them keep it? My kind, Papa! The kind I'm going to be!"

That was the night that Isaiah had decided to send Loy to military school. Because he knew now, in the presence of this terrifying tropism of his lineage, that it couldn't matter much, one way or the other, what military school made of him, except that perhaps it might make something of him that could be defined and defended against, perhaps even fought. It was, perhaps, the only instance in Isaiah's life when he had really been afraid. And utterly confounded. Because Loy loved military school. Isaiah never understood that. They were such fools: these strong, meek men. Loy loved the regimen at Gainesville. He was immensely popular. Illicitly, by candleshine, in the black dormitory, he read Marx and Engels and Henry George and Debs, and whispered just enough of these dilettante seditions around among the other plebes to create about himself an atmosphere of admirable iconoclasm and daring. Overcoming his almost dainty aloofness from sex he managed to sneak into a tar-paper whore house one Saturday night and lose his virginity. He was relieved to discover how little the experience meant to him: it was one thing out of the way and something that would never impede the singlemindedness of his life-plan, and because it had been with a Negress, it hadn't really counted at all that he had promised his mother Sabby that he would never have anything to do with a woman until his wedding. This blackness had not been woman, since she had not actually counted, in his ethos, as even human. At military school everyone, including his instructors, liked Loy. He took the bit of discipline in his teeth like a man, even joyfully, perhaps even with the flushed fervor of a flagellant, and as if he knew how wisely the hand which forced his head back was teaching him to grow iron hands of his own. He was sure of himself, sure of everything. Isaiah, never sure of anything except that what defiled human beings was evil, was therefore never sure of anything at all, but roamed his time on earth as if it were an uncharted sea and he a mariner, without compass or sextant, upon it: reckoning by star of night and heart of man and the wetted thumb of mercy held to the wind of each day's needs. Loy, on the contrary, was sure of everything. Iron-bound, at eighteen, with a virtual genius for safe platitudes and popular conformities, he drew others to him with the illusion of the exact opposite of these: the dazzling impression of boldness, originality, and respectable social rebellion. His blood, men sensed, was black with every dark drum of that nature to which few who were drawn to him ever permitted themselves to wholly succumb. His face, after those two years in Georgia, had coagulated into essence, revealing what he wanted it to show, masking the rest. As men of Kingdom County said when Loy came home: "It's made a man of him." And, when Isaiah saw that man his son was, he knew that it wouldn't have mattered anyway, that the mold of Loy had been shaped too long before those two school years to make them matter either way.

At Miss Darlington's Seminary, Nell Wilson learned Chaminade, Old Bible, and china painting. There was no Course in Life. There was a book called *Don'ts for Girls* which warned that warm baths in the evening before her young man called might dangerously lower her resistance to him in the hours to come.

It was, with obscene gentility, vague with a spinsterish, covert snicker about what there might be to resist. But afterwards, in that autumn, Nell knew there had been nothing there, book nor teacher, that might ever have told her what to do about Loy. And there was no one in the rooms of home. From that first night when she had found him waiting in her bedroom, his obsession persisted, redoubled, tripled, fed upon itself, grew heads like a luminous, imperishable hydra in her nightmared dark. She used to run to Coley, and could never tell him quite why she clung, trembling and weeping in his arms. Loy was everywhere in those nights of the fall before the war.

"Where you going, Nelly?"

"Loy! Is that you!"

He would move softly from the vined shadows by the gallery, and lay steel fingers gently on her wrist.

"Where you going, Nelly? It's past nine, Nelly."

"Goddamn you, Loy! Will you stop this sneaking up on me! Spying on me!"

"That's pretty speech for a nice young lady from Miss Darlington's! Papa would love hearing his sweet little gal cursing and profaning in the shadow of his house! And Mama—"

"I don't care! I don't care, Loy! For God's sake, what do you want of me? Do you want me to sit and crochet in my bedroom all night?"

"I'm your brother, Nelly. I never can seem to impress on you enough the importance of a brother when it comes to flirty, emotional little sisters!"

"Loy, I'm a woman! Will you please remember that!"

"You're seventeen, Nelly!"

"Yes, seventeen! And quite able to make my own decisions—to choose my own friends!"

"Where are you going, Nelly?"

"I'm going for a buggy ride if you must know!"

"Who with, Nelly?"

"With Coley Mayhew! I declare, Loy! I'm going for a buggy ride with Coley Mayhew and I don't care whether that meets

with your approval or not! And Thursday night I'm going to a
ball with Coley Mayhew! And for your information, Loy Wilson,
I've got Coley Mayhew's name marked for every dance on my
program!"

"Coley's a slacker. Everyone in Kingdom County knows that!
I'm in uniform, Nelly. Every *man* is! Even old Luke is!"

"Coley's not a slacker! His pa's dead and he's got an old, sick
mother to keep! Now—let—go—of—my—wrist!"

And she would tear away from him, taking away in her eyes
the silvered photographic print of his tight, smiling face above
its khaki collar; tearing away from him in a perfect convulsion
of dread and run to Coley's buggy, which waited for her in
those chilled, thrilling nights of war's eve in the shadow of the
pecan trees beyond the barn: Loy had already threatened him
if he called for Nelly at the house. She was giddy all that autumn
with her terror; as much a terror of what Loy seemed driving
her towards, as of himself and the unspeakable, unthinkable
inference of his attention; dizzy in the nights of war's eve when
the very air upon her flesh seemed tingling with the excitement
of the last, sweet waltz, and it always was Three O'Clock in the
Morning in those racing autumn months no matter what tock-
ing clocks might strike. Yet suddenly Nell stopped going out
with Coley Mayhew and she had told him he would have to
forget her. He couldn't understand anything that last night; she
had wanted him to be sensitive and understanding and know
that it was something she couldn't talk about and yet hoped he
would know just the same and either forgive that and forget
about her altogether or suddenly throw her back in the buggy
cushions and kidnap her or something: he was so stupid, stupid!
and she finally told him it was because she hated him because
he was so stupid and had burst out crying. She had to do it that
way because she knew if she told Coley that business about Loy's
threats he would face up to Loy and be killed and sometimes
in her dreams she had seen that: Coley lying dead on the lawn
by the summerhouse, and someone over him with a smoking
pistol and a smile, and then she wasn't sure sometimes that it

was Coley lying there at all. So she had to stop seeing him. And Coley, promptly and from that night on, fell wildly in love with Nell. Dressed up in the evenings she kept to her room so that what would have seemed, among lights and flowers and music, the studied, tasteful costume of a happy and beautiful woman seemed, among those sterile, shuttered walls, with its single and sardonic iteration of vanity mirror, the uniform of useless and cruel tragedy. She would smoke a cigarette: watching the rise and fall, the glow and ebb of the gold coal in her glass as she sat before it in the dark, choking sometimes against the smoke and wondering what was so evil in it that Sabby and the other queens of distaff virtue railed against it so; and wondered, conversely, what they found so nice about it: the harlots who smoked it on the sweet, leafy streets of bad towns, and yet she smoked one cigarette, every evening, with a ritualistic persistence, as if she might, by that strange imprisonment of so small a coal of hell-fire framed yonder in the dark oblong of her vanity, keep all the flammable frippery of her soul and body quarantined, so to speak, from total conflagration. And then sometimes, choking on the smoke, she would inhale some and a dying, lovely faint would sweep through her and she would lean forward, perceptibly, in the dark, and smile as if to shyly rebuke some whispered impropriety. And then her room would seem close, insufferable, and her body beneath its sad, unseen finery would grow choked and hot and she would get rid of this small, burning immolation to the thwarted god she had waked, and run down and sit, out-of-doors for a cold hour, on the gallery stoop. Sometimes she would find a note there, hidden in the fall-chilled leaves of the jasmine bush, and wonder, crushing the paper in her hand to be read later, if Coley himself had stolen up to hide it there or if he had sent a Negro, shadowing and making up through the pecan trees, across the dark lawn, to leave it for him. If there was no note she would sit there longer, shivering a little in the cool night, stroking the fur of the fox around her shoulders, and sometimes with cold fingertips lifting up its wizened, pinched face to stare back into the glass-eyed, dead, fixed astonishment of its mask: seeing in it with a little laugh of pity in her throat some of the murdered beauty of her own skin's forest promise.

Loy, busying himself in readiness for the war which seemed just made for him, neglected Nelly for a week or so. Once or twice, at meals, he would lower his glass and lick the milk from his upper lip and ask her what ever became of her slacker friend, and Sabby would titter and Isaiah, so intently averted from Loy's obsessions, would glare into his gravy and keep still and seem then almost as if he had become, by his silence, Loy's implicit and sinister advocate. She ate and kept silent to that, with eyes lowered. And all the while something whispered in her: Wait! Wait! It is not over! And yet, she knew, it could only be over; she had sent him away and even if she wanted to see him again Loy would be there, all iron and smiles. And Death. Perhaps it had been Death that had wakened Life in her. Coley's last note among the cold leaves told her that he had enlisted. She sat in her room that night a good long while after the kitchen match had gone out, stunned, and her blood gone thumping in her throat, and then she struck another match and held the flame, shaking, and read the note again through the cold and rain of tears, with her heart fairly choking the breath from her throat, that maybe now she wouldn't be ashamed to be seen with him any more, and if she would come to the old place on the road, beyond the grove, he'd be there with the buggy at eight. Lord love him, Lord love him, my darling, my dear! she sang in her heart, in the dark, thinking: You didn't have to! Oh, it wasn't that! It wasn't that at all and I still can't ever tell you what it was but I'll be there!

It was Loy struck the third match then. Nell whirled, first scared, then mad, then both, and mad-angry and mad-crazy both, too, and watched as Loy lifted the chimney of her little desk lamp and touched the flame to the wick's lip, then settled the chimney back and turned the wick-wheel up till the lamp was full brilliance: violating her room with its full brilliance, or perhaps that light was radiant from some unholy pallor in Loy's smiling face.

"Little sister's up to tricks!"

"Get—out!"

"Little sister Nelly is getting billy dooz! Gets them almost every night—hid down in the leaves of the jasmine bush. Ve-ery romantic, I must say! Not very *brave*—just romantic! Little sister's Lover don't hide the notes there himself! Sends one of his cousin's niggers up to hide it there for him! Wouldn't *dare* step a foot on his lady-love's doorstoop! And little sister Nelly gets all dressed up every night and sits there so's he can see— tricked out like a whore on a porch!"

"Yes!" she whispered. "Yes! Yes! Yes! Yes! Oh, you're right, Loy! I do! I have! I've done it all!"

"No," he said softly. "I'd know it if you had. No, you're still virtuous, little sister! I'd know."

"I'm not! I'm not! I've done—everything—all the things— they do—with *lots* of men!"

"No, you haven't, Nelly," he said. "You'd like to, maybe. That's something else again. That's the thing brothers are around for. To see you don't!"

"They've—kissed me!" she gasped, and rushed to her vanity drawer and held up a half-gone pack of Lucky Strikes. "See? I smoke cigarettes! I'm *bad*, Loy! Just like you say!"

"Sure you're bad. All girls are bad when there's not a right-thinking relative around to keep them good!"

"No! No! Loy, I *have*! I let them *kiss* me! I let them *feel* me! Everything, Loy!"

He smiled, sitting on the trunk before her window, menac-ingly good-humored, slouchy with assurance, and yet almost foppishly immaculate in his khaki and lieutenant's bars; he stretched his putted legs out to study the cold toes of his pol-ished Army shoes.

"Don't carry it too far, Nelly," he said softly. "Or I'm liable to take a notion to believe you—and somebody'll be lying dead tonight."

"He's in the Army! He enlisted!"

"I know!" Loy laughed. "Sure he did. After me and Wiley Peace and Jim Loudermilk and Polk Crowthers faced him this morning on the courthouse steps in front of half the folk in Kingdom County!"

"He'd have anyway! You *filth!*"

"Faced him and told him to his face he was a dirty slacker and Wiley Peace spit in his face and the yellow belly never lifted so much as a knuckle to defend himself when Polk smacked him across the cheek with the back of his hand—real easy—not enough to jar him—just enough to sort of grind Wiley's spit in a little—"

"Filth! Filth!"

"Nelly, your words don't hurt me any. When a man is a Christian and white and American he knows where God stands on family matters!"

He closed his eyes, a reverent moment, and heard the fading trumpets of his militant faith which had just, in full parade-dress, gone riding through his mind. Presently he opened his eyes and looked at Nelly, temperately, and fetched a briar pipe from his pocket and, biting it in his even, white teeth, sucked the stem and felt for a match.

"Let me see the note, Nelly."

"I will not."

"Yes, you will, Nelly. Come. Hand it over."

"No!"

It was still balled in her hand, and with a quick movement she had it spread flat and ran to the lamp with it and held it in the top of the smoking chimney. In a rush Loy's fingers were around her wrist, and the paper blackened and flamed and she could not let it go and Loy's pupils widened, watching it burn, and he seemed content with that, smiling a little and holding her black-gloved fingers there until the flame wrapped round

them and the pain raced in her arm and she closed her eyes,
knowing only her moan and the smell of burning kid. Yes, that
served as well as having the note would have served: punishing
her ungrateful hand for its insubordinance. He flung her wrist
away and turned his back to her as she nursed her scorched
fingers against her colorless, trembling mouth.

"You're better off," he observed, finding a match, at last. "Far
better off, Nelly, having a taste of hell-fire now than when it's
too late."

He struck the match and sucked flame to the black bowl and
puffed thoughtfully.

"I'll show you!" Nell cried. "Damn you Loy, I'll show you!"
and went flying down the stairwell just as the parlor clock's eight
strokes began. Far behind her the last stroke died in the dusk
as she moved, running, stumbling, through the shadows of the
pecan trees, toward the road. She saw Coley's roan and buggy
by the fence and her heart began to ache with such a wildness
that the pain forgot her fingers and all she could think was: "I
must! I must! Tonight! Because once I've given then I'll be safe!
Once I've given then I'll belong and he can't hurt me ever, ever
again!"

Making her, it seemed, ride forever and ever on the ching-
chang, hurly-burly dazzle of the merry-go-round at the carnival
where he had taken her that night Coley, scared fool-eyed and
tongue-tied with love for her enough as it was, felt now a new
fear to be alone with her because of the way she looked tonight,
the way she felt and sounded, smelled, perhaps, even, tonight:
her dark eyes soft and her mouth with something childish
stripped from it suddenly and her arm beneath his touch, soft
and yielding with assent. He was afraid in the presence of such
a strong and feminine Yes and kept her there among the jostling
ham-armed crowds with the butter-freckled faces of their girls
and the breath of them all sweet with Sen Sen and gin and
FanTan gum still could not mask the drifting scent of Nell's

soft, unuttered affirmation. And he held her waist in the pumping rise and fall of the painted horse's pistoned, frolicking circus and her red mouth opened to take the webbed, white cotton candy sweetness from her cone and her eyes shone like opening flowers as the carnival flames went wheeling round them there. He remembered how her mouth had shuddered softly when it rose to his in the buggy and he had been scared enough as it was with all his love for her and now this Yes was suddenly there and scared him more, and the darling, inept brush of her tongue upon his lips was fire, and away he had whisked her to the inane insurance of the milling carnival where there were people around them and not the persuasive, shut-eyed dark; and where nothing could happen that might happen if they were alone together in the buggy in the buffalo rug with the cool wind whispering. Something had happened inside Nell was all he knew and he wanted some time, a little time to study and guess whatever it might be, and so they kept laughing and pumping up and down on the plunging, wheeling carousel: and he kept feeling in his vest pocket every few nervous minutes to see if it was still there: the engagement ring he had bought at Jamieson's that morning, and after some time he knew that something had happened inside him as well as in Nell and his scaredness came to a strong, soft jolt and stopped when he knew that this, too, was Yes. They grew grave. They moved silent among the corny crowds, not looking into each other's eyes because of what each had last seen there that each wanted to keep in his eyes a while longer like wine's recent sweetness on the tongue. By the lemonade stand Nell gave Coley a sidelong, searching look, through her veil, wondering if Loy had lied about it all.

"Why did you join up, Coley?" she whispered, with a little rise in her voice to show indifference.

"Why? Why, honey, it's kind of hard to say! It just seems like a fellow can only stand it so long! I mean—bands playing!—everybody talking about the Belgian atrocities!—buying Liberty Bonds! Gee, Nelly, a fellow has just got to go when every other man is going! And, Nelly, you know something? Nelly, I just never could forget that girl they killed—that nurse! Edith Cavell! I could never get it out of my mind—the idea of them shooting that beautiful woman! You remember? The ones the Huns shot in nineteen-fifteen! Nelly, I still dream about that! A beautiful girl like that! Every time I think about her, darling, I think—what if it was *you* they had done it to!"

"Coley, you didn't have to do it! You didn't have to enlist!"

"Nelly, I would have anyway—sooner or later—"

"But your mother—"

"A real American can't—"

"Real American! I just feel sometimes—when they say it like that—they don't mean anything of the kind but just want a slogan as an excuse to go out and rush somebody or kill something!"

"Nelly, you better never let Loy hear you talking that way. Loy called Tom Shackelford an anarchist for just saying—"

"Loy calls lots of people lots of things!"

He took her shoulders and looked her gently in the eyes.

"Nelly, Loy and three of his friends whipped me on the courthouse steps this morning! I know he's told you that much, although—"

"Stop. Please, Coley!"

"—I can guess the way he made it sound! Nelly, if he's made you think that's why I joined—that him and the others shamed me—"

"It doesn't matter. You didn't *have* to!"

"—into joining—he's wrong! Nelly, I joined yesterday! You can go down and ask the recruiting sergeant yourself!"

"Oh, Coley, God, Coley, don't you know it doesn't matter to me whether you're in the Army or not!"

"And whatever Loy told you—I don't know *how* he told you! It was him and Wiley Peace and Jim Loudermilk held my arms so I couldn't fight back! And then Polk Crowthers whipped me! I'm not yellow and I'm not a slacker, either!"

"Coley, oh my poor darling, I know you're not! I can't bear your thinking I ever felt that! Please! Don't look away! Listen—"

"I—I thought it *did* matter to you. I—thought that's why you quit seeing me!"

"Oh, God!"

"Not—not that it had anything to do with my deciding one way or the other. But I did think you felt that way. Nelly—aren't you prouder of me now?"

"No."

"Then—ashamed?"

"Ashamed—only that you couldn't understand that I might have better reasons than that—for not seeing you."

"Nelly, I went wild. I don't think I'd known up till then how much I love you!"

"Ah, Coley."

"Anyway!" he cried suddenly. "I'll make a jim-dandy looking doughboy—don't you think?"

"I—guess. Yes, dear—"

"Nelly, it's a bully time to be living in! Can't you feel it in the air?"

"Yes, I feel it in the air," she said softly.

"Like the carnival here! Bands playing! Horses! Everybody stepping! And flags! A *feeling* in the air!"

"Death."

"What?"

"Nothing," she said. "I—I don't think I like it here anymore. Coley, I want to go. I'm cold."

After the carnival it was very still, and moonless. And because she was cold he had tucked the buffalo robe to her chin and put his arms around her to make her warm again. On the mile-long wind from the carnival they had heard, at last, the chiming dwindle and the bands run down, and saw the necklace of the Ferris wheel halt and wink out in the black, flat sky, and she couldn't seem to get warm enough against him, beneath the musky robe, and kept on shivering even after she knew it wasn't cold at all but something else that kept her teeth still chattering faintly: perhaps the image of that blacked-out midway and the stilled, empty swings and the dark, painted horses of the carousel hushed and halted in their midnight, and the jokers gone home and the band dumbed and packed off and there, central to that deserted, counterfeit city of human revelry, lay a dead man in an irreverently gilt black coffin, nameless, memoryless, immemorable; cheated out of human flesh's final prerogative of chemical dissolution, even, and yet, despite this joke by his living heirs to the earth, presiding ironically over the black, abandoned village of the fairgrounds like a dead king whose time to play his joke had not yet come.

"What are you thinking, Nelly?"

"Oh, Coley, I'm still cold."

"I've got the robe up, dear. I'm holding you as close—"

"Not close enough! Oh, Coley, I never want to die!"

"Well, who's talking about dying, honey? Gee, I never felt so alive in my life as I do now!"

"Hold me close, Coley."

"Nelly, I want to marry you," he said and laughed, against her lips, and the already widowed ring in the pocket of his vest shone in his mind like all the moonlight they would miss. She burst into tears.

"Nelly, don't. Don't cry. Lord, if you don't want me—"

"I do! Oh, God, I do!"

She was whispering to him, almost choking, her breath on his throat, above the high collar, and her hand stroking his cheek with a desperate tenderness as if she feared it might vanish, there and then, from beneath her fingers.

"Oh, love me, Coley!" she moaned softly. "Love me!"

"Yes, Nelly. It's just—I just want to do what's right!"

"Then *do* what's right! Love me!"

"I—do, Nelly. Lord knows I do!"

"But you treat me like a child," she said, bitterly. "You treat me like something frail and brittle and—and sacred and, Coley, I am not! I am not like that at all! I'm in the world, Coley, just like you! God I'm real!"

"Nelly, you're all excited—"

"Yes! Yes, I am! All excited! And that's shocking and nasty and awful to you, isn't it? You're just like . . ."

"Nelly, no. Don't say that. I know what you mean. I just—"

"No, you don't. You don't dare know what I mean! You don't love me, Coley, because you don't dare! You love the dream I got to be those weeks when I didn't see you—you love me as soon as I stopped being a woman of flesh and blood to you, and became a dream! And I'm not that! Coley, I won't be! When—someone tries to make something like that of me I feel like I'm being smothered—killed!—like there's no more *me*, at all—like a stuffed bird under a glass bell gathering dust in somebody's parlor! No! God, no! I won't be that! If—"

He fetched the little engagement ring frantically from his vest and held it up, winking, as if it were a touchstone against the storm of her unreason.

"Here," he said. "I've got the ring, at least."

"I don't want a ring! I want a *man*!"

"Nelly, you're the dearest, strangest creature I've ever known! Nelly, don't you reckon the man goes with the ring? Now, here—"

"Oh, of course! But the ring comes first—doesn't it? Would you want me if *I* came first? Before the ring? Before wedding—before church vows, God, conscience, or anything? Would you still want me, Coley? I don't think you would! Because I wouldn't be rare and nice and—and beautiful to you anymore!"

"Nelly! That's not so!"

"It is, too! You're just like my brother Loy! You think Nell Wilson is pure and innocent and—and *dead*! Well she's not, Coley! God, she's not! You quiver and get all thrilled talking about war and killing and that's just fine! It's fine and—and Christian and moral to let your flesh be thrilled by Death! But the minute Life comes near you—you cringe and pull away!

Oh, no! That's not Christian or manly—to let Life thrill you.
Unless it's with some harlot in a brothel, and that's not Life at
all! Not you—not my brother Loy—not anybody is ever going
to stamp out my heart!—my feelings! And yet—"

"Nelly, you don't know how I feel. You're not giving me any
chance at all!"

"—and yet, God help me, there must be some of that sickness
in me, too, or else I wouldn't know how you think about me
and still be in love with you. And I am in love with you, Coley. I
just need you to understand me and maybe help me understand
myself, that's all! I just feel all—all choky and suffocating sometimes—at home! I feel like I'm just being smothered with lies
and Virtue and things I'm not! God, I'm a *woman* just like my
father is a *man*!"

"Nelly, if you'd listen to me a minute. Nelly, I'd still want
you—"

"If you knew I was *free*? If you knew I—I smoked cigarettes?
Would you, Coley, really? What if you knew I carried on at Sem
for two whole years in a perfectly scandalous way! I—I nearly
got expelled, too! Except I was smart! I never got caught!"

"I still wouldn't—"

"Suppose I told you I'm not—not a *virgin*? Hah! You should
just see the expression on your face! Suppose I said I had gone
to bed with three—no *four* different men?"

"Have you, Nelly?" he said softly, smiling. "Who were they,
dear?"

"Oh," she cried airily. "I can't remember their names. Tr-
traveling men at the Commercial Hotel! With red galluses and
garters on their sleeves and yellow, shiny shoes! And—and lots
and lots of *gin*!" And she burst out, face-down, in tears at that,
but he pulled her fingers from her face and the dark between
them burned away and the veil before his mouth was torn away
and, away, afar, she heard her own voice crying in his mouth:
"Coley, now! Oh, Coley—do—do whatever it is—they do!" and
he was carrying her, still swaddled in the harsh, hair robe up
into the piney woods above the road-berm, and she wasn't shiv-

ering any more because her gift to him, waiting, was making
her all warm, all fire and a softness opening to be taken, and
the chilled dark poured round her naked thighs like light, and
now it seemed her body was all-enveloping him in a thundering,
tender faint: keeping him safe from the death inside of her: he
could not, would not leave her ever now! Once in her childhood's Christmas dreams she had wondered how the tender,
velvet sky must feel when roman candles pulsed their breaking
gold within it: those cold stars blowing with a soundless, sweet
boom and now Nell felt herself all such sky, and deep in the
midnight of her came this fulfillment, this pulse of lights blow
on and off within her until her very finger tips seemed shining
with that undulant illumination. Then, presently, she felt him
leave her body and she was all alone up there among her stars
and she stirred, sadly, hearing a train cry, grieving, somewhere
down the wind. She lay still, gathering breath again, rising from
the sweet, slack swoon to find herself again, astonished and
aglow with still loving him, forgiving him for leaving her body
which had thought he had come inside it to stay there forever,
and found, even in that act of forgiving, a new dimension of
her love. Because, oh, he had let her give! and no one ever had
done that: let her *give*, and she was safe now from whatever
faceless, family specter it was who had once lurked, menacing,
above them in the woods; and now, in a gasping catch of wonder
she felt the warmness of his seed ebb from her body, between
her thighs, and that seemed to her a curious, beautiful paradox,
and however well her mind might know the answer she loved
its riddle like a child. For it had seemed that all the giving had
been hers and now it astonished her that, in an act, in which
the gift had seemed wholly hers, that anything of him should
remain in her. He had cruelly left her, who had given him
everything, and now it seemed so strange that there could be
anything of him left in her to flow out now.

His face above her gathered into focus, anxious and pale, and
she had murmured a sound of love, watching him gravely, her
eyes smoky with quiet.

"It still wouldn't have mattered," he said.

"What wouldn't, Coley?"

"You told me a lie," he said gently. "That you'd done it before. I could tell you never had. But it still wouldn't have mattered. I just want you to know that, dear."

"Are you *sure*?" she whispered. "Are you *sure*?"

"I'm sure! I *love* you, Nelly!"

"*Me*, Coley! Are you sure? It's Nelly—*me*—you love?"

"By God, I'm sure, Nelly!"

She shivered, hugging him closer to her in the buggy again, under the robe again, because now the night wind had chilled still more and seemed to bear, even yet, the whim and scent of the deserted carnival and the painted breath of its carved carousel nostrils. So again she touched his cheek with her lips in swift, desperate gentleness lest that cheek might still somehow vanish beneath her mouth in the moving, dark air.

"Oh, Coley! Coley!" she whispered softly. "Coley, let's don't ever ever die!"

That was the autumn they got the movies in Goshen and those months seemed to her like the way the pictures flickered, always too fast for life, with the stiff, panic quickness like that to the figures of all she saw around her; everything but her was going too fast, and sleep was when the film broke. She could not ever remember dreaming much in that time of her life; sleep was the unlighted screen, while waking was the dream and everybody in it going too fast, everyone but her. Everything inside of her seemed moving with a delicious slowed ecstasy in that November so that all her life till then seemed now to her, in retrospection, birdlike, twitchy, and she would wonder, quietly, how she had ever lived so long without breaking through that wispy gauze wall that had separated her from silly girlhood and her Now. No, she had never really loved at all till Now, she knew, had never suspected how rich and lovely and terrifying it is to be a human being. Slow: her smile; slow: the illumined liquid eyes in her glowing face. And, oh, if they would only stop moving so fast: the ones all round her, even Coley: that was the only thing about her paradise that made her feel fear: light and shadow of that November stuttering fast and jerky before her eyes; ratcheting swiftly past its giant, projecting arc-lit lens, spinning inexorably off the thinning reel, and she would think in a hurt spasm of love: Wait! Wait! There mustn't be such haste! Oh, wait! I have so much more to give!

Isaiah read all this in her face and thought how long he had watched her through that autumn, hesitant on the scared threshold of that choice, remembering how he had wondered and prayed, biting back his counsel in the awful knowledge that only she could choose, that only she could move. Isaiah had seen, sensed, and known what Loy's dogging, unremitting persecution of Nell spelled out, and he knew that his intervention would only lure her yearning fatherwards and make of his gesture a crippling, sinister complicity. No, Nelly was a child no more in that house and that was good. For Loy, in the long measure of things, could hurt only children.

And he thought: The only hurts that can touch my Nelly now are the hurts of being a woman, and that's as God meant, I judge. I just pray to Him that she doesn't get hurt in loving. No. No. Whatever is the sense in praying that? Who can be man or woman alive in this world, loving, and not get somehow hurt.

"Why?" said Luke that night when she came to his loft, his hand cupping up her face to look him in the eye. "Why shouldn't you come to me to tell your troubles to?"

"I should be—*strong* though!" she said. "I shouldn't even have to come whimpering up to you this way!—Christmas night!—your last night!—last leave! I've just kept this corked up in me these weeks—since Coley went away, Luke! Telling Papa made it worse somehow!—the way he stood there quiet and strong while I told him, crying, and he looked so brave and his eyes never changed and it just seemed like his strength about it was just sapping all my own away! God, I wish I could be brave like Papa! I guess maybe I wanted him to get mad! to make him whip me or drive me out of his house the way they do in the tales! Well, I guess I never really thought he'd do that but I just somehow couldn't stand his being so strong about it, it made *me* feel weak, and I asked him if he was ashamed of me and he said he wasn't, and I asked him if he was glad or sorry and he said he was both glad and sorry, and he said something I couldn't somehow understand—about flowers not always grow-ing the way you'd laid the seeds, but that that didn't mean they weren't a fragrance and a joy, that a man shouldn't cut his flowers down because of that! And then he laid his hand on my head, Luke, and he said a thing I won't ever, ever forget. He said, 'Nell, there's nothing you could ever do that would make me ashamed of you!' Luke, how can I ever live up to that!"

"Why, Nelly, just by living up to yourself, I guess. Don't you figure that's what he meant to say?"

"Yes. Oh, I don't know. Sometimes I think Loy's the strong one in this family after all, Luke!"

"No. No, Nelly."

"I don't know. Loy always seems so *sure* of things! Life just seems cut like a road for Loy! He just seems like he moves on rails, Luke!"

"Better nobody ever get caught napping on those rails, Nelly," he said with a soft laugh after. "Lord, no."

"So I've—I've just kept it corked up since then," she went on. "There's nothing more to tell Papa. That's why I wanted to come up here tonight, Luke, and tell you all of it—everything I've done and everything that's happened—Coley and all of it. The smell of paints up here, Luke. It's the smell of braveness— of breaking away and wanting something more than just being born and being here a while and then going away to dark again! Luke, that day in New Orleans when Papa took us three to the museum I saw your face begin to *be born!* When you asked Papa about the pictures and he told you men's fingers had made them and you knew you could be a man and make them, too!

You chose a hard, lonely way because it was your way of moving toward light! It would have been easy to stay back here always in the land—in the dark where your Papa always wanted you to be!"

"The land was light to Papa, Nelly."

"Yes. I know, Luke! But not for you! Paintings were your light!"

"Other people's light, Nelly. I thought once it was mine."

"But, Luke, it's the trying that counts! It's the way you turned your face to the light and *tried*!"

"But to someone," he went on, heedless, "those pictures might be—beautiful. Maybe just two people."

"Luke, I haven't ever seen one of them and I already know!"

"No, wait. Let me finish. Papa thinks so. That's one."

"He's seen them, Luke?"

"Every last one."

"I thought he never wanted you to—"

"To be a fool, idiot thing like a painter? Yes, that's so. He never did. Lord, how that tribulation has made him suffer. But just the same there was always something—something in him that believed that a man had to decide for himself. Yes, that's so, I reckon. And when he'd wrestled it all out in his mind and within the sight of God, he did something I never wanted nor intended for him to do, Jesus only knows, and it's been almost more than I could bear just thinking about it at nights. Nelly, he wanted me to have painting lessons! Lord, Nelly, you've got to swear you'll never tell your father what I'm telling you tonight!"

"I swear! What, Luke?"

"That my crazy old Mex-nigger daddy mortgaged his two acres of land to buy me painting lessons, Nelly. That's what! You're wondering why nobody ever told your daddy about that mortgage in the Goshen Courthouse. Well, maybe it's because they haven't stopped laughing about it yet! No. Not about what he needed the money for! He never told them that! It was just such a rare, rich joke—him coming down there after all those

years and selling that land at all! After it had been such a puzzle
in their heads and a thorn in their sides all these years—that a
man who was a nigger and yet really wasn't even a nigger hundred percent that could *dare* own land that a white Southern
Christian had *dared* will and deed over to him! You see, Nelly,
that's the rich part of it to *them*! For all they know my Papa took
the cash—fifty silver dollars, Nelly—took it and went off to a
Memphis sporting house for the kind of evening an old colored
widower would—"

"No one would think that, Luke!"

"Well, whatever! It didn't matter. Crazy old Mex-nigger Toby
had sold the land right out from under his benefactor's nose
and that could be a rich secret they could sit on till it was warm
and hatched and the mortgage would be due! Then they could
laugh in Isaiah's face and show him you couldn't ever trust a
nigger anyways—even if he—*especially* if he was even a hundred
percent *that*! And so—"

"Papa would understand!"

"—and so once a week last summer I went every Thursday
night—after sundown, of course, so nobody would see me
sneaking to a white woman's house—and got my lessons from
Miss Tibby Cobbloy—"

"She's a good soul! She'd never tell, Luke!"

"She's a saint-on-earth is putting it better, Nelly. She didn't
want to take the money at all, at first, and then one night Papa
put on his good coat and brushed his hat and polished up his
boots and went to her house and told her all about how it was
with me and what I'd chosen."

"And she agreed?"

"Yes. And she tutored me. And nights—I'd stay up here
struggling and fighting to understand it all—nights till when it
was sunup and time to go work with Papa; I was so worn-out I
could hardly chew bacon, and then up here again at night and,
Nelly, I'd get to thinking about what Papa had given up for
my—painting lessons, I'd cry till the colors run together in my
eyes—and then I'd tackle it again and, Nelly, I swear it never

came out at all like I used to dream it would! Nelly, I used to think: I'll run off! That's what I'll do! I'll jump a freight some night when there's no moon and go up North and work hard—work at anything!—work and save and paint and study it in a real college and be a big famous success and come back then! But, Nelly, he'd have been dead by then! So, I kept on going to Miss Cobbloy's parlor and she taught me all she could, and then there was pictures on her walls for me to copy. You've seen them!

"Yes, Nelly. Yes, I chose. I learned to paint. Yes. Yes. Very carefully, Nelly!"

"Show me one, Luke."

"Why, Nelly? You've seen most all of them! One hangs down in Miss Tibby Cobbloy's dining room, Nelly—it's called 'The Angelus' by Millet. Maybe there's some you haven't seen, but somewhere, sometime you will! Landseer, Constable, Turner, Nelly! There's hardly a great picture in all those books of his— or hanging in her hall or dining room or parlor—hardly a one I didn't copy, Nelly! Littler, of course—but careful, Nelly!— every stroke as near as I could make it! Not as good, of course, but careful! You see—there had to be something beautiful to show Papa! I took them to him one by one after dark and I mind how he would sit at the table after supper and study my latest one in the lamplight and he wouldn't say much, but I mind the way his eyes shone and after a while he'd say: My crazy Luke! and I could tell he was proud. Constable, Landseer, Millet! He never heard of *them*—he'd never *seen* these pictures until now! So he thought they were all mine! Periods, styles, epochs of painting separated by five hundred years maybe—it was all the same to him—they were all mine!"

"But you—you showed him some pictures of your own, Luke!"

"No. No! Nelly, that's what I've been trying to tell you!"

"Well—why not, Luke?"

"Because they weren't fit, Nelly! They weren't worthy! Lord, can't you see how it made me feel—her being that kind to

me!—Papa being that kind! Kind, Nelly, kind! Till all that
kindness just pressed down on me till I couldn't . . . Nelly, I
just kept thinking about Papa's little piece of land and what it
had meant to him—what his giving it up for me had meant!
Not just that it was land, Nelly, but some dream *he* had, Nelly,
that was just as strong as mine has been! Nelly, I just kept
thinking: I've got to make good! There's just got to be something beautiful to show for all the sacrificing that's been going
on around here!"

"But didn't Miss Cobbloy ever say: 'Luke, paint something
beautiful that *you* see?' Didn't she ever?"

"Yes!"

"Well, didn't you ever?"

"Yes! Twice!"

"And was it how you wanted it to be?"

"No! I burned them!"

"Luke, why?"

"Because they were ugly is why!"

"Luke, they were *yours*! *That's* beauty!"

"No! They were ugly and sad! I couldn't show him *that*! He
knows that!"

"Oh, Luke, they couldn't have been ugly!"

"Yes, ugly! Sad and ugly! And *crazy*!"

"Luke, how? Can you tell me about them?"

"One was—one was a picture of my own damned face!"

"It's a good face, Luke. A strong, kind face."

"What colors, Nelly? What colors! Pick the tubes out!—mix
them!—show me!"

"I guess I've known your face so long I never looked that
hard, Luke."

"Well, I looked, Nelly. Hours of looking! Squinting and staring at it in my shaving mirror yonder on the nail! And trying
to get it right—the light right—and the shadows right—and
the damned colors right! Nelly, I stared and painted and stared
until I think I must have stared the skin right off my face and

painted the way my face felt the first time I heard him call Papa
a nigger!"

"Loy?"

"It doesn't matter *who!*"

"It was Loy."

"Yes! It was Loy! And it was my face the way it felt that night!
Nelly, I couldn't show Papa that! He *knows* that!"

"And you—burned it?"

"Nelly, yes! I had to have something *beautiful* to show!"

"And the other one?"

"Worse!"

"Can you tell me?"

"One night—one night—last spring—I knew what had happened that night—one night last spring I hid down by the barn
and watched the men ride past after they'd gone up PawPaw
River and killed that nigger boy, and it was the hour just before
sunup and they were on their way home to Goshen. I watched—
and a couple of them still had their torches burning and when
they come riding past—when they came out of the pecan grove
and rode past the house—I saw their faces. I saw their faces
and something—something made me look up toward the house
and I saw his face in his bedroom window—"

"Loy's?" she breathed.

"—Loy's face just above the sill—watching the men ride home
and his face was washed yellow with that torchlight and he was
smiling a little and his eyes were cold and bright and the lids
underneath them were puckered a little!"

"So you painted—that," she said.

"Yes."

"And burned it?"

"Oh, God Almighty, yes! Yes!"

"Luke, maybe—"

"No maybe, Nell! No maybe! You don't *know* how terrible
that picture was! I couldn't show that to *her!*"

"Why, Luke?"

"Because there was two of her cousins riding that night! That's why! And I couldn't show Papa! Because I'd always told him that if ever I learned to paint pictures, they'd be beautiful things!

"Well, they're gone. At least, they're gone. And all he'll ever see are the pictures I copied—yonder against the wall—with their faces turned away. Like children who weren't good enough in school."

"Can I see them, Luke?"

"Yes. No, wait. Not now. I want you to be the only other one to see them—but not now. Wait till I'm gone a spell. I want him to have them. They mean something to him because he doesn't know. And I want you to see them—all of them. And I want you to have one for yourself—I mean if you'd want one."

"Luke! You know I do!"

"Well, don't be too sure. They're pretty poor things. But you might want one—for friendship's sake. Only I want Papa to pick it out for you. He'll know by your eyes which one you want the most. Mind, Nelly, it's just a sentimental thing—they're none of them worth the paints and cloth they cost."

He stopped then, hearing some voice cry faint, drunk and malicious, behind the hissing lash of hail upon the glass.

"It's someone out in the road," she said. "Some drunkard from Goshen."

And then in an instant when the wind and hail subsided; as if in a moment the night had, sensing something amiss, held its wild breath, too, they heard the shout again, more clearly, before the sleet came flailing back against the glass, like whips.

"No," Luke said. "Not some drunkard from Goshen. It's Loy."

"Loy? Loy wouldn't be out on a Christmas night like this— *hollering* that way!"

"It's Loy," Luke said.

And now she knew, too, as they heard it again: that adamant, furious voice was stronger than the tumult of any storm. It was Loy and he was laughing and he was singing phrases of "Tipperary" and he was shouting Luke's name.

"He's—gone—crazy," she whispered.

"No," Luke said. "He hasn't gone crazy. His mind's too neat for that, Nelly. Loy'd never go crazy."

"Oh, Luke, I'm scared."

"Yes."

"Luke, I'll run up to the house. I'll wake up Papa!"

"Sit still, Nelly. Please, Nelly."

"I won't, Luke! This is outrageous! Papa's the only one to handle Loy! He'll thrash him if he finds out!"

"Nelly, you don't want me to die just yet—do you? Without a chance?"

"I don't know what you mean, Luke!"

"Loy's down there in the yard—in front of the barn—between here and the house. He's drunk, Nelly, and he's got a gun. It's late, Nelly. He thinks you're sound asleep up yonder in your spool-bed like every other decent, Christian, American white girl on earth! Nelly, Loy's got drunk tonight so's he'll have an excuse to come up here and pick some bone with me! Nelly, he's mad and he's drunk and what he's got to say to me's been waiting for years now—"

"Luke, you're fancying things!"

"Nelly, think! Think how *he* thinks! He's mad and he's drunk and he sees his sister come clambering down the ladder from this room—at this hour! Nelly, don't you know his mind *that* well yet?"

"Luke, where can I go? Where can I hide?"

They heard Loy's half-full bottle chink against the ladder rung in the barn below the floorboards and when, this time, his voice called out it was soft and involved with its mischievous, chuckling speculations; they could, for that softness, fairly feel the sound against their soles, like the vibration upon rails of a hurtling, inexorable calamity; a whispering hum of iron: "Hoh, Luke? Luke? It's Christmas night and company has come to call!"

"Where, Luke?" she cried in a whisper.

"Yonder, Nelly. In the closet for the hay rakes! There's room there!"

Before she fled away on tiptoe she glimpsed in the smile and droop of Luke's whole face such a certainty of Loy's deadliness that she almost screamed, till she cowered at last among the rakes in the dark that smelled of timothy and mice. Luke stood a moment, hearing Loy labor up the ladder with the fisted whiskey bottle ringing on each rung at every rise; stood staring down at the trap door at his boot-toes as a man might, strapped and doomed in the twinkling before noose and bag black all and the hangman trips him into history.

"Luke? Good old Brother Luke!"

Luke stood, biting his lip, then stooped, hooking the iron ring in his fingers, and pulled the trap door open. Foreshortened on the ladder in the quavering lampglow, Loy looked dwarfed beneath him: his face, swollen and sweat-streaked was rouged with blotches of a drunken flush like berry-stained pie crust, and his mussed hair gave his back-thrust head a twice-outsized distortion. His mouth was smiling but his eyes were something else.

"Welcome, Luke!" Loy said through his hard and careful smile. "No, that's all wrong! All wrong! That's what *you're* supposed to say, Luke! After all—after all it's *me* visiting *you*. That's right. I got it right now."

"Come on up, Loy."

"*Thank* you, Luke!"

The slack, weaving body of him at the top of the ladder seemed to sober suddenly; to gather some furious reserve of energy and he swung stiffly up into the room and got to his feet so coolly that Luke imagined for an instant that he was not drunk at all: he moved that easily, back and forth, between sodden, thick-tongued joviality and that crisp, official poise.

"Luke, I'm drunk. Bet you never saw me drunk before! Did you, Brother Luke?"

"No, Loy."

"Know something? Nobody has. You know why, Brother Luke? Because this is the first time I ever done it! That's very interesting—isn't it? Well, aren't you going to ask me to sit down?"

"That chair—the leg's busted a little. It's the best I can offer, Loy. Unless you'd care to sit yonder on the cot."

"Is it all right if I sit on this salt box, Brother Luke?"

"Well, sure, Loy. Anywhere."

"Thank you. I'll just sit here, thank you. I wouldn't want to break anything. This plain, old box will do nicely. Thank you."

He squatted on the box: a huge, old, red-faced child: eyeing Luke from that slitted mask of fierce, spurious affability and put the bottle between the glistening toes of his shoes.

"Never saw me drunk before—did you, Luke. *Excuse* me! *Brother* Luke!"

"No, Loy."

"Nobody has! *Nobody*, Brother Luke! Know something? Nobody ever *will*! Because now that I know what it's like—I don't have to ever do it again! Think that over, Brother Luke. It's pretty *deep*! If a man—look at it this way—if a man *knows* all the weaknesses . . . You listenin' to me, Brother Luke?"

"I'm listening, Loy."

"*Thank* you. If a man knows *all* the weaknesses of his *brother* men—I mean all of them—liquor, women! Well, that just about covers it! Liquor and women! If a man gets inside those weaknesses just *once*—and keeps his eyes open! Just once! Just long enough to look around real good inside and find out what there is that keeps most men chained up to one or the other—why, I figure a man who does that gets to be a pretty good authority on *chains*, so to speak! You following me, Brother Luke? I mean if a man wants to develop a gentle but stern hand over his fellow brothers, it just stands to reason he's got to know their weaknesses. I mean to say that if a man wants to see a good Christian, American world for *his* kind of people he's got to know—*other* ways, *other* kind of people. It's pretty deep. You following me, Brother Luke?"

"Yes, Loy."

"No, you're not. You're not following me at all. If I thought you was, I wouldn't be telling you this. This is between me and God and certain great, dead Americans who let this land slip away! How's the song go? No, that's not right! Slip away, slip away, slip away down South in Dixie! You never saw me drunk before! Did you, Luke?"

"No, Loy."

"You gonna tell Papa on me, Brother Luke?"

"Loy, what you do is your own affair."

"Really? Well, gosh that's good news! I've been living around this house—this farm—this land for so damned long wondering how long it'd be before you people—Aw, listen to me! Ain't that awful of me! Christmas night and all! You and me ol' lifelong *brothers* and me startin' to lose my temper on the eve of us going off to fight the Kaiser! Will you excuse me, *massuh*? Sure you will! Have a drink on me, Massuh Luke!"

He snatched up the bottle by its neck and thrust it toward Luke in a weaponing gesture.

"Loy, I don't much care for liquor."

Loy's eyes swelled under their tight lids and the irises bloomed out dark. Beneath the floor, in the grained, muffled quiet of the barn a rat trap snapped softly, inaccurately, and something unkilled dragged it off clattering to the dwindle of a piercing squeal which, at last, ceased in a silence which glazed like eyes. Luke took the bottle from Loy's fist, pulled out the cork, and raised it beading and sloshing toward his mouth.

"Well, haven't you got a *cup*?"

Luke lowered the bottle and went over to the littered window sill. He came back presently with a china cup without a handle.

"Boy, you sure got a lot to learn."

Luke poured a quarter inch of whiskey in the cup and held the bottle back to Loy.

"Well, aren't you gonna put the cork back in?"

And he waited, watching Luke, his eyes white-shining as the bowls of silver spoons. Luke put the cork carefully in the bottle and gave it back, with a smile as faint as the feathering crack in the bone-china cup his fingers gripped.

"What's funny? Something funny, Massuh Luke? You don't *think* you got a lot to learn?"

He whipped the cork out, flipped it into the shadows and threw his throat back in a long drink.

"Well, you *have*, boy!" he gasped presently, tears yellowing his glare. He thumped the frothing bottle back to the boards beneath his shoes again, wiped his cheeks on his khaki sleeve and belched softly. Then his mouth smiled again.

"A lot to learn! The Army is gonna do you a lot of good, boy. In fact, it's gonna do all you people a lot of good. Sometimes I think the good God of our Fathers invented wars just to teach people how to behave. You know that's—You know something? America needs a good war every so often to get everybody *sorted* out! Summer patriots—and some ain't! Say, that's pretty cute! Manners! That's all it ... You know what rank really means in the Army? Just manners, that's all! Keeping in line, that's all! In *place*! *Place*, by God! Everybody *sorted* out—in his by God *place*! The he-men from the sissies! The Americans from the anarchists! The—you people! Ah, Luke, hell! Don't let me go sounding off tonight like this! Tonight's Christmas night and tomorrow and the days after that is God-knows-what and hell, Luke, let's don't stand on ceremony tonight! Tonight we're just two lifelong friends, Luke! *Equals* tonight. Call me Loy. Let me hear you call me Loy, old Brother Luke! I *mean* it! I want to hear your voice tonight calling me Loy! Because you see—"

And he bent forward, shutting one eye to underscore his words, while the other eye widened and thrust up his brow in dramatic emphasis of brotherly confidence.

"—because you see, Luke, tomorrow is a different thing! Tonight we're just old Loy and old Luke! See? But tomorrow—Luke, you gonna have to start calling me *sir*."

Luke watched him gently and coldly, still nursing the little whiskey in his cup and wondered how soon it would start: his being afraid.

"Luke, you know I *worry* about you! I been thinking and worrying about you a long while! I *mean* it, boy! The way you been raised—I mean, the kind of ideas you may have caught from my father! Luke, you could be in real *danger*! There's men out there in that army that don't *know* you like I do, Luke—I mean make allowances for notions you may have got growing up the way you have. Luke, I swear to Christ and on the honor of my mother's good name—I got your good interests at heart, boy! I just can't stand thinking of what'd happen to you if you was to go out into that man's army and start acting like you was here! I mean, Luke, there are men who wouldn't understand! Am I clear?"

"You're clear."

"Well, you won't mind if I get a little clearer?"

"I hear you."

"That's good. Because this doesn't call for beating around the bush. When the safety of my old, lifelong *brother* Luke is involved—I reckon I—it's my duty to speak plain and not mince words! See, Luke? I'm talking to you in a real, Christian spirit of brotherhood and *love*! Our people always have the good interests of your people at heart, Luke! See?"

He gestured with a jabbing finger toward the general earth.

"Now it's this way! There are lines out yonder!" he said. "I didn't draw 'em! God drew 'em, Luke! And when certain people step over those lines. . . ! Listen! Look at it this way! What would—would happen say if dogs and cats started breeding up together! Or—or horses and cows! Suppose stallions and bulls should start breeding . . . What? I mean—stallions and *cows*, goddamn it! You see. You see? Well, you get my drift anyways! Things all just—the whole world just gone to. . . !"

And stopped, his head turning slightly, bobbing like a toy's head on a spring, staring nowhere waveringly, but listening acutely as if to confirm by its iteration a sob from somewhere behind the wood wall to his blurred left, dead-reckoning that

maybe it might have come from among the cold tines of the hay
rakes ranked, steel teeth in the closet where once they had
played as children hide-and-go-seek in its black, wheaty mouth
but thought: No, it wouldn't be anyone there, thought No, that
it was some older wind, sky-breathed, or the whimper of his own
offended righteousness, and decided he would have himself
another drink of the whiskey, and did that.

"Whoo! Hakah! Whoo!"

Choking on this last one; he had gone about one-half ounce
of alcohol too far now and even when his eyes were knuckled
clear of tears nothing looked quite the same: Luke was two now
and that indeed constituted a conspiracy to be observed with all
acuity: he was ready for that, even. He was suddenly drunker
than he had meant to be and yet, queerly, it was as if, in that
excess when things beyond his eyes lost their reality, he had
sobered into the abstraction of what those things and persons
meant within his mind, and that loosened his tongue to his
darkest dreams. Still it had been a long while before he said
anything more at all because it had taken him all this time to
think that he had not said anything more for a while and to
know that the wetness on the back of the hand that lay across
his knee was from a thin string of his own slobber, so long there
that it was cold already.

"Wh—khp—what?"

"I never said anything, Loy."

"Din' you? Well, whad I say?"

"Nothing, Loy."

"Mama knows."

"What, Loy?"

"I said Mama knows!" he roared, rising with his head back as
if he were trying to thrust his eyes upward through obscuring,
webbed untruths, and stood with desperate steadiness, glaring
across at the two-Luke plot in the whirling lie of the world.

"Knows what, Loy?" said the now many-Lukes, with that faint
smile that Loy knew someday he was going to have to smash
from off its faces.

Loy smiled back, keeping his secret for a while in the puffed cheeks of a silent giggle and felt behind him for the box to sit on again. He thought: I can say anything I want now. I can say it all now. I can say what I want now to him or to her or any of them because I have got them all locked up in my mind where they have to listen to me now and even if they don't like it they can't get out to do anything about it. I bet if I had another drink it would all be clearer to me, he thought, and he did, but he couldn't remember putting the bottle back between his shoes because there wasn't any time to it anymore. But it did clear up his thick tongue: he talked good now. But what man's voice was that which sobbed somewhere like his? He got up very carefully, like a construction of stacked glassware, walking slowly over to where Luke's canvases leaned their borrowed faces to the wall, and opening the fly of his khaki britches, he urinated upon them thoroughly: all of them, directing the stream from one to the other, precisely, like a boy pissing out the coals of a small campfire. It was an act so personal that it was done without a rage, anger, or even malice toward the fact of Luke there in the room with him, because that Luke was not, at that moment of his mind, even there: he pissed upon the footprints of a Luke gone somewhere else.

"Mama knows," he said softly to his eyes, which sometimes in the obscure latitudes of that drunkenness turned in to stare upon themselves. "Because her and I even discussed it. Where you, Luke?"

"I'm over here, Loy."

"Where? Oh. Well, no. Lemme set down again and we'll see about that. No, you ain't there. You wouldn't dare be there, Luke. Not and me like this, Luke! Hee! Lemme set—right— down—Hoh! You *really* there, Luke? You got spunk, boy! Naw, you ain't there! Listen! I know! And Mama knows! Because her and I even discussed it many's the time and it accounts for a who' lot of your wrong-thinking, Lukey brother! Because— Maybe, it wasn't you started the tale—I damned if I don't be fair about it! Did you? Was you the one, oh brother black, who spread the tale all round or was it somewhere's other—I mean else?"

"What tale?"

"You know what you always believed, Luke! Don't sit there and pretend like you're there and say you didn't because then I'll have to call you a lying, nigger sonofabitch and get mad! Listen! Din' I say we was going to be brothers tonight! Tomorrow something different but tonight brothers! Din' I? Sure, I did. And now you act like it wasn't! Come on, Lukey! We *talk* tonight! Awright? Awright! Then *talk*!"

"What do you want me to say, Loy?"

"Admit that you . . . Shit, you even want me to have to say it for you! You want to hear me say it so's it'll be just like you had the upper hand and it was true after all. All right! By God and merry Christmas—I'll say it! If it does your black heart good— I will! Go on, Lukey brother! *Admit* it! Goddamn, you admit it!"

"Admit what?"

"That you believed—and spread the tale from the time you was old enough to talk—that you—that *we was really brothers*! That's what! *I'll* say it! That once upon a while ago Papa got a half-breed nigger Indian girl knocked-up out there in West Texas and ol' Papa's conscience got to eatin' on him and ol' Papa's idealism got to bitin' on him and directly ol' Papa figgered he owed it to his soul's salvation that he fetch that poor knocked-up half-breed nigger redskin Hiawatha Liza Jane home and see that her and the quarter-blooded bastard never wanted for a roof and bacon. On'y Papa didn't face Grandpa or Kingdom County men with a nigger wife, so he hired a half-starved Mex named Toby to marry her and come along for show. Luke, you *know* that's what you always believed. Luke, you wouldn't! Luke, you know you always figgered: Why would any white man be so generous if it wasn' to ease his guilty soul. You know! Listen, Luke, and listen good 'cause your life may hang on it! It ain't true, Luke! Because if it was true—if it was *true* then you and your Ol' Black Joe Pappy Toby would have been stretched up long, long time ago. No, by God. In fact—In fact, where in hell

did you ever happen to dream up such a crazy notion as that,
Luke! That Isaiah Wilson was really your blood father? Did you
. . . I mean, boy, that takes some real imagination! Did he—did
he ever *say* that to you? Did he ever once *tell* you he was? Christ,
why can't you people ever just—just stay to yourselves and
stop—stop trying to sneak into *our* blood—*our* family. God
never meant. . . !"

"It's your notion, Loy. Before God, I never once thought
that."

"It's *my* notion! You son-of-a-bitch. I ought to kill you for
denying it!"

"I know my father's face. Toby is my father, Loy."

"Of *course* he's your father! But you think otherwise! You
think Isaiah Wilson is your father, you thief nigger bastard!
You want to believe that white, Christian, Wilson blood runs in
your niggered veins. Don't you?"

"No, Loy."

"*No, Loy! No, Loy!* Oh, you'd never own up to it! Because you
know I'd kill you for even whisperin' it aloud! But don't think
you fooled me! Don't think I don't know you've always believed
it! This white man don't fool as easy as some, Lukey *brother*! I'm
not like that wide-eyed, bearded Idealist up yonder asleep! By
God, *I bet you even think there's some of you in Nelly!* Own up to it!
Go ahead! I'll not hurt you! Not tonight! Remember I said
tonight was different—tonight we talk equal! Tomorrow is
something else! But tonight—Aw, Luke, own up! I know your
simple mind from cover to cover like the third reader! I bet—
I bet you even told Nelly you thought you was really her half-
brother—just so's you could get closer to her! And she's like
him—simple-headed and soft-minded and she'd feel sorry—
sorry—and that way you could get closer to her! Closer, by God,
than *me* even! Closer than her *own*! Her *own*!"

He staggered up, one hand flung out as if to strike away some
luminous specter printed in the air before his phantomed vision
and fell sprawling on hands and knees at Luke's feet, toppling
his bottle and spilling half the whiskey left. When Luke helped

him back to his legs, Loy wrenched away, and crouched with
his back averted, clutching his knees with his cracking fingers,
gasping and choking in a struggle to strangle back that humiliating deluge of tears; to overpower an inexcusable emotion which
now wrung his face like hands twisting a gray rag: No, no one
must ever see that. So he pretended he was sick. And Luke,
wisely and gravely, stood away, thinking it would be foolish to
throw away his life just yet: stood away, knowing how certainly
Loy would snap out his Army Colt and kill him if he knew he
had seen those tears, that naked loneliness for which cruelty
and coldness had been and must always be his shield. Though
Luke, in that moment, was himself lonelier than he in the terror
of his pity for the species of them all.

"I choked," Loy said directly, having straightened up and
turned around: his face all composed and rearranged again:
though like the face of someone who has died in agony, it looked
puffed and stretched with a ravaged and grotesque composure,
as if it had been clumsily embalmed by an apprentice mortician.
His smile made it worse. He sat down again on the box and
cracked his knuckles, kneading them in his palms, his gaze
swimming on the floorboards and the puddled whiskey he had
spilled.

"What are you, boy? Some kind of *nigger Christ*! Don't you
have any blood in you? Don't you get *mad*? You just—sit there—
taking all this! Why don't you hit me or something, huh?"

"I'm not mad at you, Loy."

"Well, why ain't you! Don't the things I been saying even get
under your skin? 'Bout your mama? Huh? You think you're
some kind of of nigger Jesus, don't you! Turn the other
cheek! That it? Or don't you people think about things like
mothers the way a white man does? Huh? Or sisters? Huh?
That it?"

His lolling face, slack-jawed and turgid, blinked and pouted
and tilted itself in the sidelong gaze of puzzlement, his eyes
winking and opening again, focusing and refocusing upon
those unfathomable Lukes.

"You 'fraid of me, Luke?"

His neck muscles caught his head before it fell and bobbed it up again.

"Huh, Luke? You 'fraid? It's because I got this gun on me! Hah! Tha's it! 'F I take off? Here! Take it off! I'll . . ."

He fumbled the snap of his holster open, yanked out the heavy blue .45 and threw it spinning across the floor.

"Now. You still afraid of me, Luke? You wanna hit me? Huh, Luke?"

"I don't want to hit you, Loy."

"Why? I mean—why not, Luke? You still 'fraid of me, Luke? Go ahead. Hit me, Luke. I swear to God you can hit me and I won't lift a finger back. Tonight's *special*! Tonight's your chance. Go ahead—punch me in the mouth as hard as you can! I won't raise a finger! You can brag about that, Luke! You can tell all the coons that you is the only one of 'em in Kingdom County ever hit a white man and lived long enough to tell it! Huh? Ain't that worth it? A'right then. Gotta better idea!"

He swung up, rickety, to his feet, swaying like a toppling derrick, and thrust his fists up, in the classic stance of the boxers printed on the little cards they gave away with groceries at Gallagher's Store.

"Come on, Luke. Le's find out which of us is the better—me drunk—or you sober! Jus' friendly, understan'? Jus' couple little frien'ly rounds, Lukey brother! 'Course you ain't no Jack Johnson and then, 'course, I ain't Jess Willard! But come on anyways!" And then, as if he had suddenly recalled his weariness he sat abruptly on the floor, beside the chair, his eyes searching uselessly for the bottle. And Luke saw his legs and arms slacken.

"Loy, I got no cause to fight with you."

"Boy, if you only knew. If you only knew."

"No cause at all, Loy."

"Boy, if you had any idea you'd start runnin' tonight and you wouldn' stop till you got clean to Africa! Boy, you'd run right across that ocean water and your feet wouldn' even get wet you'd be runnin' so fast. Come on, up! Jus' friendly like! Tell you what! I'll let you hit me first! Hard as you want."

"I don't want to fight, Loy."

"Not really fight, Boy! You lookin' at this all wrong-minded again! Now if we *hated* each other—if we *really hated* each other—then it'd be fightin'! This is just what you might think of as a little test of *manliness*!"

"My manliness doesn't stand in any need of testing, Loy."

"And mine *does*?" Loy whispered, his head lowered, his eyes sagging, a little muscle twitching beneath the flushed flesh of his jaw like something struggling to get out. "'S that it? 'S that what you mean, Lukey?"

"No. I don't mean anything, Loy. It's pretty late, Loy. Why don't we go to bed?"

"Why don't we go to bed? Wha's *that* mean? Why don't we. . . ? What kind of talk is that?"

"I mean why don't you go on up home, Loy."

"Oh, excuse me! I din' get the drift! Oh, you mean you're dismissing me? You mean I have your permission to go to bed? Well now, Luke, that's awful white of you! I was afraid maybe you planned to make me sleep down yonder in the wagon! Come on, Luke!—Come on, boy!"

"Loy, this is craziness."

Loy moved through the imperfect amber light, his face coming closer and closer to Luke's above the absurd perspective of his fists, and as it moved closer the veins beneath the forehead skin swelled out like ropes tightening round his skull: not vessels filled with blood at all, they seemed, but conduits of cold, black bile, or as if they were only clenched tendons and not arteries carrying any humor known to man at all: Luke, watching that face approach his, thought how it had been more than a decade and a half spanning that spare, few feet of distance between them, and now saw it so close that he could feel its breath along the line of his own cheekbone and smell the sourness of its drunken, dribbling lips: "*Fight* me, Luke!"

And when Loy's arm hooked up Luke feinted, thinking it was

a blow intended, and not ready when the arm came back up and wrapped round his neck in a grip of murderous, strangling attachment. Struggling, they staggered out together across the boards, their four feet chopping the floor for purchase as if they were one beast turned upon itself in suicidal compulsion. Then, again, Luke glimpsed the face, halved by shadow, the one illumined eye almost gentle, almost soft with something; the lips writhing back from their teeth in a grimace of an unspeakable, exquisite emotion; and Luke's breath went rattling while the wrist bone pressed deeper in his windpipe, and watched Loy's face, Loy's mouth grow closer, and felt some fresh terror rising in his mind, thinking: But, my God! But, what is he. . . ? My God, it's like he was *loving* me! and Loy's eyes bulged in a sudden vision, seeing no Luke at all there now in the tender fury of his grip.

"Nelly!" he groaned, searching Luke's eyes. "*Nelly*, don't keep pushing me away! I'll—kill—you—if you don't let me!"

In the instant that Luke's own arms flung Loy's away as if they were the soft limbs of a child, Loy's eyes glazed, jaw fell, joints jellied as the last of the liquor seized his brain and tilted it off into darkness; he slumped snoring to the floor at Luke's feet, murmuring half-words wetly, whimpering some small throat sound like a child grieving; his knees pulled up and his face wincing as if beneath the red frail bombardment of pulse upon his brain. Luke wiped his cheek where the kiss had nearly been, heard the closet door cry softly, saw Nell's chalky face in the black crack, staring. He sank back downwards on his cot, his face in his hands, shivering and rubbing his elbows upon his knees.

"Did he hurt you, Luke?"

"What? No. No, he didn't hurt me."

"Are you sure? You look like he hurt you, Luke."

"No, Nelly. I'm all right."

He got up and moved across the room to his kit, shuffling his feet as if moving suddenly under the heavy awareness of a fear long overdue.

"Tonight, Luke?"

"Yes. Tonight. I can't stand any more of it. I got train tickets for tomorrow but I got to go now. Tonight. I'll walk. Hop freights. Steal a horse. Anything to get back to camp—away from here, Nelly. Because I can't stand any more of it. I guess I'd never know how much I could stand if it hadn't been for tonight. Well, you heard him, Nelly!"

"Yes."

"Nelly, what—what did he want from me?"

"I don't know."

"Does *he* know, Nelly?"

"No, Luke. I don't think he knows."

"Well, maybe God knows. He made him. I don't think I want to know. Let God keep it to Himself if He knows. I just want to go away."

"Luke, what could I ever say—what could I ever do—to make you know that those things he said to you tonight were *him* talking and not. . . ?"

"And not you. Not your daddy. Well, I know that. You know I do. You didn't need to say that."

"What a way for us all to be saying goodbye!" she cried softly.

"One goodbye's the same as another," he said, and sat down again on the cot, his legs quaking and jerking in the full spasm of a terror he had kept long at bay. He stared at her with a foolish smile at his mouth as if shamed to be showing fear before her.

"Don't let him hurt you, Nelly," he said.

She shook her head, shaking the thought away, and scowled at Loy on the floor.

"I'll stay up here with him tonight," she said. "Keep him still. Keep him here. So Papa won't know. Christmas. This last night. I suppose it sounds foolish—I just don't want Papa to know. Oh, I know. There's not much he doesn't know about Loy. I mean, he wouldn't be surprised—at this, I guess. He'd take him up and put him to bed. Maybe that's what Loy'd want. Papa carrying him drunk up to bed and Mama shrieking down the hallway that it was Papa who had driven him to this. I can't stand that."

"Yes, it would be that way."

"Luke, my mind's all full of a terrible thought. It came to me in there—listening to him. I've got to say it, Luke."

"What, Nelly?"

"Luke, I kept thinking—you should have killed him tonight. Oh, God, how can I be saying such a thing and yet—and yet it kept coming into my mind in the closet—while I listened to him! Luke, my own brother and yet—and yet I couldn't help thinking of him—making it dangerous in the world for things I love!"

"You think I didn't think it, Nelly? You think there isn't something right now in my two hands that makes them want to go over there right now and choke him dead while he snores and bubbles there helpless?"

"Yes. Yes. That's the worst of it, Luke. Like he'd somehow made us over in his own image!"

"But the difference is this: we couldn't."

"And he'd laugh at that. He'd call that weak!"

"Yes, and maybe he's right."

"No!"

"I'm not sure of it. Maybe he's right. All I know is I couldn't."

Loy turned convulsively on the floor, glared for an instant at the webbed, dusty rafters, then closed his eyes again.

"Does he hear us?" she said.

"I don't know. I don't care anymore. If he rose up right now and fetched his pistol out yonder from under my cot and tried to shoot me, I don't think I could raise a hand to stop him. I'd rather be dead than be his kind of strong. This isn't just something I thought through tonight, Nelly. This is something that's come through years of hard nights' thinking, Nelly. Maybe that's why I never had time to pray. Or maybe that's praying and I didn't know. I've grown up and I've watched Loy grow and saw this hate growing in him every mortal day and it scared me and I knew I'd have to live with it because I'm—'You people' he kept saying tonight. 'You people' he said, meaning 'you niggers.' "

"Luke, do you think *I* think that?"

"Yes. Because most of the time *I* think that! Yes, Nelly. I don't mind because with you there isn't hate—there isn't that awful twisted scaredness that makes him like he is. And if—if he was to die—If there'd been a fight up here tonight, and say I killed him. Nelly, if Loy died—would hate be dead? Would hate in the world be dead, Nelly, if Loy lay dead tonight. So you see— I just can't somehow see it as *personal*! Nelly, there's so many of him that's sick with what he's got. Wars don't end it. Wars, God knows, make it stronger and make it more. So maybe—maybe, it come to me one night, the only way left is to let them beat themselves to pieces against our gentleness. A man can be strong like rock—or strong like water. Rock breaks, Nelly. Water runs on and sings in the rivers and rises up in rain. That's our kind of strong, Nelly, and that's the good kind, Nelly. They can't smash the sea! They can't shatter the rain!"

"He could have killed you though, Luke!"

"Yes. I was scared."

"And no court would have hanged him in this state!"

"Yes. I'll not lie. I thought that to myself while I watched him."

"Luke, then how can you say that his kind doesn't win?"

"Nelly, because your kind would remember."

"It's not enough!"

"It's enough. Because you'd never keep still. You'd remember and you'd never keep still till someday someone would feel ashamed or feel afraid and something in the land would change. No, you'd never keep still. And there's no thing on earth can beat the power of people who can't keep still. Not even his kind of strong is stronger than that."

The wind blew, shouldering up the stable's eaves and hail flailed the glass again.

"And what about you?" Luke said. "Will he ever know?"

"About the baby?"

"Yes. You know how he'd be. A little madder—a little more deadly than anything this country's ever seen."

"Yes, I know that. He'll be gone when it's born."

"And when he comes home?"

"I—I won't be here. I'll go away. I've talked to Papa. It's all been planned for, Luke. I—I'll go away. North maybe to stay with Cousin Hannah Jane. A big town somewhere, maybe. I'll work. Papa will help. No one in Kingdom County will ever know. I won't even let it be born here—where they'd know. They'd write him—they'd get word somehow—he'd find out. I—I know how he'd be. It's not—not myself I'd fear for, Luke. You don't know how he's always been about me. It's almost as if—ever since I've grown up—he's—I can't even say it."

Luke glanced nervously at the face of the twitching sleeper.

"Don't go just yet," she pleaded. "Talk a while with me, Luke. It'll be so long before we can talk again."

"It—wouldn't be good if he was to hear, Nelly."

"He's sleeping, Luke. He won't hear."

"Does he ever sleep, Nelly? Even like this? Would you ever dare sleep if you was him?"

"And yet it's so strange," she said with a shadow of a smile on her mouth and lay her fingers on the gentle roundness of her waist. "I wouldn't have it any other way. If it hadn't been for that hate in him—there wouldn't be this love in me. It's a queer world when hate drives us to love."

She sighed and looked at Luke's uneasy face.

"Coley wanted to marry me," she said, "before he went. He asked me—pleaded."

"What did you say?"

"No. I said no."

"Why, Nelly? You loved him."

"Yes. I did! But I said no, Luke!"

"Why? Wouldn't it all have been better?—the way things are?"

"No!" she said, with crackling eyes. "I felt like it was these times pushing me into something—something that hurrying spoils! At least, I'll have my baby! And there'll be *time—time* to raise it! I felt—I felt like Coley was just asking me to marry him because I was—what do they always call it?—*in trouble!* And I didn't think of it as trouble, Luke! A child born of love could never be trouble! Oh, I couldn't stand him thinking about me like that!"

"You're stubborn as your Papa, Nelly," he said softly.

"And who should I be like?—*Mama?* Oh, no, Luke! I love life too much to let people shove me into marriage like it was some kind of a game at a child's party and no one would like me unless I played! I'll scrub floors in a hotel up North before I'll let that happen!"

She looked at her slender child hands that lay in her lap like the twined white limbs of lovers.

"So I told Coley," she said, "that when he came back—when he came back for his Christmas furlough—I'd tell him yes or no. And there never was a Christmas furlough for him so that was that—they sent him to France Thanksgiving Day. And I'm sorry—God, I am sorry he has gone but I am glad still that I said no and it would always have been no until I could be sure that he wasn't just—just marrying me to save my good name from the mouths of trash. Oh, Luke, I want to be loved but I want to be *free!* I won't have any man marry me because he's sorry for me! Luke, you aren't even listening to me!"

And he wasn't, to her, at least; his face turned to look, dry-mouthed and staring at a terror come full-circle now and him not ready for it this time: still shuddering innardly with the delayed-action shock of his first encounter with it: the sleeper on the floor who no longer slept, that head turned now toward Luke and the girl, watching them: the wide, blood-veined eyes flashing back and forth between them: a tiger's pace in the cage of his face.

Luke whispering: "I knew I should have gone running right away. I knew I shouldn't have sat and talked nor even been. Because he never misses anything. Not even drunk. Not even asleep. Not even unconscious. Loy, you sure are—"

"Shut up," the lips formed.

"—thinking the wrong thing, Loy. You couldn't be more—"

"Shut up."

"—wrong, Loy. Oh God, I knew I should have gone when—"

"You and Nelly," the slit mouth said. "I always knew."

Nell stood braced and still, while everything inside her screamed; looking at his face pressed on the floorboards: the eyes moving first from Luke to her and then to Luke again and, in that circuit, making between the two of them that act which he had always wanted to happen, if only in the moralless rumor of his dreams; proxied to that intimacy, shifting back and forth, like his epicene eyes, being first him doing it to her and her having it done to by him, while Nell breathed: "No!"

"You," the mouth made softly. "And Luke. Yes. You and him. I heard it."

Nothing moved about him but his lips and the eyes and the rise and sink of his bellying breath under the dun, soaked Army shirt. And his brain: that moving, too, with marvelous, sober agility. While all the rest of him endured the mutiny of its parts: too drunk now to bring itself yet to execute what now it knew it someday must do: to rally sinew, bone, muscle of manliness, stainless steel rectitude of cause to that orgasm of violence which was yet to be the entire sum, meaning, and destined expression of Loy Wilson.

"You thought I wasn' listenin'—din' you!"

Jellied as a squid on a wharf dock, with only brain, eyes, mouth at his command: eyes shuttling back and forth between his sister's body and the other's, making of that inference the fact that he had always known would come to be, that he had inside wanted to be: a dark child, long before that night conceived, now born, accused, tried, and doomed all in the twinkling of his thoughts.

"Din' you? Ol' simple-minded Loy drunk on the passed-out floor and not even listenin' to his baby sister and her nigger lover!"

Saw crystal sweat beaded on Luke's face like frost clouding the chilled, dark silver of a pewter pitcher.

"Don' you know I always listen—even in my sleep? Huh? You thought I wasn' listenin'. Don' you know I been waitin' to hear this for so long? Huh? Don' you think I always knew you'd fuck my sister, nigger boy?"

"Loy, you filth! Oh, you filth! You lying, rotten. . . !"

Heard her voice break and saw her lids drop down in tears: he giggled; saw Luke there, staring, his undenying making it all the truer, and that would be dealt with in its time: he was too drunk now: brain, mouth and eyes were all he could move just then, but there would be time; there was no hurry: it had all been so long in coming that there was no hurry now.

"Goin' away tomorrow, Nelly! Away to war! That makes you feel safe—don'it? Huh? Well, that's all wrong to feel safe, Nelly. You know why? Huh? 'Cause I'm comin' back, little sister! That's why! Maybe you and your black baby won' even be here—maybe not even in Kingdom County—maybe not in this state—maybe North somewhere in the nigger-lovin' cities where. . . ! Little sister, make no mistake about one thing: I'll find it and I'll do what's needed to be done. Nelly, I don' think you believe me! Tell her, Luke. *You* know me, Luke. You know when I've got done with you I'll find *it*! Right, Luke? Sweatin'—ain't you, Luke? How come you sweatin' so, boy! It's winter!"

Watching them: tigered eyes of him watching hunters from its pit, measuring himself for the leap, the mauling moment yet to come.

"I always knew it," said the mouth, smiling. "Always did. You two. Now how come I'm so smart? Always knew you two were up to it. You never guessed I'd know—did you?"

"Luke, fetch his pistol! Hit him! Do—do something. Make him stop it!"

"He's a scared nigger, Nelly. You know scared niggers can't move. Except to run. He'll go runnin' directly. I'll have to hunt him a spell. Maybe in France."

"I hope you die! Die! I hope you're killed!"

"Sure you do, Nelly. But I won't. I'll be back to tend to my family business. Oh, God, I got you both to rights! I got you good. I *heard!* Don't tell me what I *heard!* You and him havin' a little sweet, goodbye chat and ol' big brother Loy passed out on the floor but don't make no mistake about it, little sister, I *heard* and, Nelly, I was *ready* for it because I always *knew!* Even when I was a little kid I used to dream about a little nigger kid to come squeezing out of this family—somehow! I never knew quite how but I knew it would come! Luke? Own up! Come on now, little black sambo, you're safe from the tiger. See? I'm drunk! Too drunk to raise my hand, let alone—come on now, Luke! Speak the truth and shame the devil! Speak for yourself and speak for your race, boy! It's a fact known to God Almighty that every nigger's fondest wish is—"

"Shut up, Loy! You gone too far!"

"Hah! I like that! Look, Nelly. A little spunk showin' up. I do like that! Guts, Nelly! Was it his guts you liked, Nelly, or his—?"

"I could kill you Loy!" Luke cried. "I could fetch yonder pistol and kill you and you couldn't do a thing to save yourself!"

"But you wouldn't. Luke, I'm drunk but I know my Luke. You're not a killer, Luke, you're a lover! Ain't that right, Nelly? Ain't Luke a lover? Luke? Show me what a lover you are! Take out your black-snake whip and crack it a little! Let her see it for the last time, Luke, and—"

Springing to the floor, to her knees, cupping her hand hard over his working, cold mouth, she felt the soundless words persist upon her palm: wet, the bubbling blow of his breath struggling under it, still making the dumb shape of words.

"Luke, run! God, run! *Now,* Luke!"

Now the mouth beneath palm-flesh snickered, tittering, till her hand could endure no more and she snatched it off, wiping words on her skirt, and rose away from him, her face curling in a wince of incredulous dread; watching now while he struggled up on an elbow, hung a moment, faltered, and fell back again, his head bouncing like a melon on the drumming floor.

"See?" he giggled. "Too drunk. You're safe. *Now* you're safe, I mean. Luke, you sure better stop a Hun bullet over there 'cause if you live to come home, there's a bad night's business waitin' for you, boy! Huh? You think I'm kiddin'—don't you? Both of you think—Don't you think I *know*! I *heard*! Listen to me! Stop whisperin' together and listen to *me*! I got eyes! I got a brain! Nelly, listen! You *wanted* it! Lord, I knew that from the first year you starting swellin' out in them little-girl dresses! You started wantin' it then! I could tell! You never knew that I—I bet you never knew I used to watch you get undressed in your room of nights just to see what your mind was up to! Oh, God, I knew! I'd see you stand there by the long mirror pridin' your evil eyes in yourself by lampshine and thinkin' no one saw! *Two* saw, little sister: God and me! When your breasts come out round and the dark hair grew there and you'd look and look in the long mirror, I knew it was time some *man* kept an eye on little sister in this family! Running your fingers up and down your shivering skin like you was gettin' it used to the feel of hands! Well, I knew right away *whose* hands! Oh, you played it smart, little sister! You did your finest to make me think it was a *white* man you wanted!—Tomcattin' in the buggy every chance you got—every time my back was turned with that lily-skinned, milky-mouthed. . . ! Well I played along, Nelly! I knew who you wanted it with! Not Coley! He'd be scared! He'd never have dared! Ain't no man gonna throw his life away for a piece of poontang! I knew who you wanted it with, Nelly! I *always* knew! Even before it was *time*, I knew! Easy! It was easy! Him and you—living like sister and brother! Ain't it always easy and no one lookin' or thinkin' wrong things when it's brother and sister? Up here in the barn room in the evenin's! Or was it at Miss Tibby Cobbloy's? That's where you done it—now wasn't it? Sure! I knew what you wanted, Nelly! Because a white girl knows—*every* white girl knows even before she's even sure what those things are for that it's a known fact of medical science that niggers is made bigger down there! Nelly, Luke's *is* bigger!I—"

Luke and her watching him now as if he were some kind of machine, mesmerized by that mouth making words soft, fast and clear in that body too drunk to move other than in the breath-heave of effort to keep the words blowing smoothly out

of the thin, swift lips; making her think how once she had
been taken to a sunny, sick room and seen Mister Jo Lafourche
paralyzed from a stroke and in all that dribbling, abandoned
empire of body, like a vast pump-station on strike, nothing
obeying him now save the eyes, brain and mouth: three rats
made masters in an empty store.

   "—thinking he *wasn't* my brother no matter what Papa said
no matter what he tried to make us think! No nigger blood was
here nor ever would be if one of us was man enough to keep it
out! No, by God, Jesus no! No nigger child to go struttin' out
in the land with Mama's blood in him—with Wilson name—
with—A dark child! I always knew—dreamed! A dark, dark
child! And I'd be the one have to go out and stop it—kill it—
keep it from. . . ! Did you blow out the lamp! Nelly? Luke!
Damn you! No—s'all right! I had my eyes shut! Like when I
used to dream and see the dark child and know I'd have to stop
it! Nelly, you listening to me? I'm coming home, Nelly! Don't
bother hidin' your little dark bastard for I'll have my dreams to
guide me, little sister! If it takes me all my life! If it takes me
forty years of hunting, Nelly! You're not listenin' to me, damn
you!"

   He shut one eye, focusing the other in a flinty glare upon
them like the ray of a guttering bull's-eye lantern; his tired
tongue quit him and his wits, wearying, blurred, though not so
much that he could not see the two of them and know how
inevitable had always been their juncture there in the cross-
hairs of his sight: shamelessly, Nelly and her chocolate-soldier
hero even now in an intimacy, whispering and murmuring by
the foreshortened parallelogram of the floor's black mouth;
her weeping and Luke bound for gory glory; sober, towering,
beautiful and able-bodied on his way to Cain's carnival with his
kit and his doomed, shamed eyes looking into hers before he
dropped, hangdog, down the trap door for the last time. When
suddenly, like a judgment of the Lord, a cold rain felt its way
in blowing rivulets across the dark window. Loy shifting his
twirly head to turn it from the sight of those two, lay glaring,

cyclops, into the slobbered dust beneath his scuffed forehead, because he could not bear it when she had bent to kiss Luke's cheek goodbye; because he could not endure his own instant dream of brush of flesh against his own mouth's loveless lips: he choked, convulsing, in a spasm of weeping. But no one would have known that it was weeping, for there were no tears there, and nothing to bear witness but the dust, if there had been.

The winter to come was to be a melancholy one. Nelly was whisked away in Isaiah's rockaway buggy to a town far from there, to the home of his sister, Hannah Jane. There, in the autumn, Nelly had her child, a tiny baby girl which, in Hannah Jane's tidy, generous parlor, was christened Lucy. Yes, it was to be a melancholy winter. For it was late in the year nineteen-eighteen and the flu epidemic was already laying its gray, wet hands upon the land. Hannah Jane, with the staunchness of her hillborn spirit and physical energy, tended Nelly through the sapping sickness. And prayed. And prayed some more. And cradled the infant Lucy as if it had been her own that nuzzled weakly at her now-stilled breasts. And prayed yet some more. But it was to be, indeed, a melancholy winter and so upon a morning in January of nineteen-nineteen, the rhyming year, the year in which Hannah Jane had placed such hopes and trust, the baby perished silently in Nelly's feeble arms. Nelly sat by the kitchen window in that house and village so far from home, sat for days staring out upon the cheerless prairie snow-bind of the land, sat speechless and sometimes it seemed breath-less as well. At last she roused suddenly from her sorrow, as was

her nature, and revived and awaited her father's arrival to take
her home. He came on a rainy winter's night in February and
together he and Nelly drove homeward through the rain, talking in ragged intervals about what should be done now. For
talk was flickering again like tatters of wildfire; talk about her
and Luke, dark talk, dangerous talk. And yet that was indeed
to be expected. Loy had been home since New Year's Day. How,
asked Nelly, could they protect Luke? But to this Isaiah spurred
the mare onward through the rains and remained unanswering.

     After the supper of that first night home, Nelly went fussing
around her old bedroom like a girl again, picking up familiar
things and putting them back again where they had been and
would always be: hairbrush, comb, pincushion, Bible, and little
box with seashells stuck all over it like nutmeats in a cake;
picking things up nervously and putting them back again and
seeing the square of dusk on the rug lengthen and turn gently
as always it had turned there and would so turn till doomsdusk.
Trying to get back again the feel of that room in which she
had grown up and in which everything seemed now in subtle,
plotted, but furious re-array. Not a glass hatpin nor mote of
dust might have moved in all that time and yet nothing was the
same and Nelly knew nothing would ever be the same, yet felt
that somehow she should make it be, so that she could endure
it there in that room to which she had returned to spend the rest
of her life. For a few moments she felt the desperate yearning to
run headlong back into the safety of the face of the girl who
had long left the long mirror above the vanity and she went
back to that glass again and again, smiling at the young stranger
gravely come there to reassure an uneasy visitor. Everything
else was changed, so maybe there was comfort in that. Even Loy
was changed, so maybe there wasn't anything so menacing about
everything else feeling different. She picked up her silver-
chased hairbrush and put it back again carefully in the shape
dust had carved round it on the mahogany of her vanity. Well,
nearly everything had changed: Sabby had not changed, at least,

and there was an astringent reassurance in that. She had met Nelly and Isaiah at the door and Isaiah had gone on grimly into the house and Nelly had looked at her mother and whispered: "Mama?" and Sabby had stood an instant and then with a camphorous exhalation that might have been the essence and breath of her, she murmured one sentence and turned again to her shadows: "I excuse you," she had said, not "forgive": that far more generous and holy prerogative; she "excused" as one "excuses" ill-trained children who have spilled a cup at table, and went then to have her supper alone in her room. Loy had, indeed, changed, and Nelly kept lifting her eyes from her plate from time to time to examine his new face that had come back from the Army like silver melted and stamped again in the image of the new emperor: some of the old was still there but the new face was smoother, quieter, all the boy smelted out of the metal now, and Nelly kept looking up at the new face from time to time and running her eyes quickly over the dazzling, disciplined face, new-minted, as if her eyes were fingers conning its measure and wondered if that newness were the stamp of kindness and understanding or if, on the contrary, it were their treacherous counterfeit. Never once did she catch him watching her; maybe, she thought, he doesn't want to embarrass me, or maybe, she thought, he doesn't have to look at me: knowing all he needs to know of me. Isaiah seemed reining his feelings in like hot horses all during the meal; he said nothing, he cut his meat like a surgeon and looked at neither of the two of them; and said nothing until he told them he wanted to talk to them both in the parlor at eight o'clock. It struck that then, as she sat in her room, moving things around, putting things back, and she got up and hurried out into the hallway, testing the clasp of the little cameo brooch at her throat, and thinking nervously: It won't start again. Loy's changed. I know everything is going to be all right. Luke's coming home this week and we will all be friends again in that world that was like the Peaceable Kingdom Luke told me of once. Loy was just growing up. The Army's made a man of Loy and now things will be—no, nothing, nothing will ever be the same, but there is still time for things to be good, even if things are changed.

Isaiah had his back to the doorway when she came in the room on the last stroke of the clock and saw him sitting at his old rolltop desk with the pictures of Debs and Altgeld over it.

"Papa?"

"Sit down, Nelly."

"Where's Loy, Papa?"

And started when she felt him move up suddenly behind her and brush her elbow and turned to see his new face smiling with its as yet unmeasured amiability. He was holding something out in the shadows to her.

"Cigarette?"

Flushing, murmuring no, turning away all-colored up and a little breathless, with the little desperate refusal rising to her mind that he had meant that by offering her a cigarette; no, it wasn't going to start again; no, things would be good now.

"Sit down, Loy."

"What's this about, sir?"

"Sit down, Loy."

"All—right."

Breathing that out: that assent, with a controlled and practiced air of someone well-schooled in the tediums of dealing with social decorums of the antiquated. He lighted a cigarette.

"I'd prefer your not smoking, if you please."

The breathed assent again, but this time after an interval of bemused silence, so stunningly timed that it might have been scored on a staff of music: a laboriously patient rest before an ironic coda. The cigarette coal twitched in the shadows and flicked its arc out the window into the spiraea. Loy sighed. Isaiah closed his big hands into fists and opening them again laid his fingers on the claws of his chair-arms.

"What's this about, sir?" Loy said lazily again.

"It's about you, sir," Isaiah said. "It's about you, sir, and it's about your sister and it's about Luke, sir!"

"Well, now I think that's a good thing for us to be talking about, Father, Luke's coming home this week, and I think that's a very fit subject."

"Thank you. I'm glad you think it's fit."

"I do, Father. I do, but I think—I think Mama ought to be here. I think any conversation about such important family matters—"

"Your mother is not in this discussion."

"Why not? This conversation certainly seems—"

"Your mother has chosen not to be in this conversation. Your mother has not been in conversations regarding this family for nearly twenty years. She was probably quite sensible in her option not to be included in this one. She very likely wouldn't know what we were discussing."

"What are we discussing, Father?"

"You in the main, sir."

"Me, Father? What've Luke and Nelly to do with me?"

"Plainly and simply this: they are to be let alone."

"Haven't they always been—let alone, Father?"

"Choose your words cautiously in this room here tonight, boy."

"Well, I meant nothing *insinuating*, sir."

"Be very, very careful that you don't, boy."

"I just want everything to be *honest* and *aboveboard*, sir. I don't think this is any time to be beating around the bush about things. After all, everyone in Kingdom County knows that Nelly—"

"I'm glad you put it that way, Loy. Glad, indeed. Honest and aboveboard. Perhaps you won't mind telling me your whereabouts upon a Christmas night. The Christmas night before you left for camp. That would be honest and aboveboard—to tell me that—don't you agree?"

"Nelly's told you? Didn't—? Is that what she—?"

"Don't you agree?"

"Well, I don't think it's really fair, sir."

"You don't think it's fair?"

"No, sir, I don't. I went to Goshen that night. I came home

late, sir—a little under the weather, sir—I didn't want to upset Mama—"

"So you went up to Luke's room—above the barn!"

"Yes, sir. Luke was a fellow-soldier. I knew he'd understand. What nonsense has Nelly told you, sir?"

"Keep talking. Just keep talking. Nelly's told me nothing. This tale came to me from a dozen filthy mouths during the last year of the war! Keep on!"

"Well, sir, I can very plainly see that you've been prejudiced. Nothing I could say could possibly alter—"

"Your sister was sitting in Luke's room that night. They were talking. That's the rest of it, isn't it?"

"Sir, I was a little under the weather that night. It was the first time, sir, the only time—the last time, sir—that I ever touched anything alcoholic. Sir, Father, I find it very, very difficult to recollect much about that night."

"You do?"

"I do, sir. It's a kind of haze. We—we all talked. That's so, isn't it, Nelly? We talked and then Luke decided he had to get back to camp a little early and I—I remember his leaving—"

"In the early hours of a winter morning—in a cold and drizzling rain—*on foot?*"

"Sir, I don't recollect how he left. As I say, it's all very—very hazy to me."

"Upon the heels of that night's unspeakable events—the safety—the honor—the very lives of certain human beings whose lives I regard as precious have been put in hazard! I'm talking about something that has led to an assault upon my home!"

"Assault, Father?"

"Assault upon my home has been perpetrated in the form of a filth of gossip in Kingdom County this past year! Is that clear to you? Is that *news* to you, Loy?"

"No, Father. It's not. I heard it when I got back from the Army last month."

"That was the *first* you heard of it?"

"Well, Father, I knew about—about, well, about—Nelly's *condition*, Father, before I left for camp—I knew that she was—in a certain way, Father."

"*Pregnant!* Is that a dirty word in your little book of dirty words, Loy?"

"Not exactly, Father. I knew Nelly was—*pregnant.*"

"How did you know, sir?"

"She—well, sir, Nelly—"

"She *told* you?"

"Not exactly, sir. I—She and Luke were talking that night when I came up to the barn room. She and Luke were talking and I heard him say—"

"You heard *him* say? Luke? You heard Luke say what?"

"I mean I heard *her* say, Father, that she was in a—she was pregnant. Heard Nelly, that is."

"And did you hear Luke say any single thing that would lead you to believe that he was responsible?"

"Well, Father, we've all three grown up so close—it's hard to judge things. F-father, I was drunk that night. I get things mixed up when I try to remember that night, Father. We three—Luke, Nelly, me—we grew up so close—the way Luke might say something—"

"Did you hear Luke say that he got Nelly pregnant!"

"Well, no, Father. No, I didn't. Father, it's hard to talk like this. Wh-whatever I say you'll get angry and—and violent. Which is—"

"Violent, Loy? God help your soul if I ever get violent with you, Loy? Speak out."

"Father, you're not being fair. There are Christian, decent people in this country who think it's just as—as despicable for a colored boy and a white girl to mix as—as it would be for brother and sister or for—for two men! Father, there's decent, Christian niggers who feel the same way! Father, I've heard some grumbles from *them* about—about the gossip!"

"Now we come to the nub of it. The gossip. Which is—"

"That Luke and Nelly—Well, that Luke's the father of Nelly's boy. I'll not beat around the bush and say I haven't heard it."

"And you've no idea who started that talk?"

"Well, yes, Father. Yes, I have a notion I do!"

"*Who,* sir!"

"Father, it's only gossip I've heard whispered behind our backs. You'll blame me as if it—"

"*Who!*"

"Coley Mayhew."

Slipping the name out softly, he sighed and folded his hands, his amused, stone-cold eyes shuttling swiftly back and forth between Isaiah's face and Nelly's, appraising with quick craftiness how that name had staggered the two of them from balance for the instant he needed; then with steely, oiled precision began talking again, rapidly, with a conviction tinctured with just the proper diffident and wistful regret: "You see? I can tell it from the look on both your faces! Now by just repeating that ornery word of gossip I've made you both angry with me! As if it was *me* that had started it!"

"Go on!"

"May I go on, Father? Nelly? Have I your permission to tell you the rest of the awful things they. . . ?"

"Go on, sir!"

"Very well, Father. They're saying that Luke—that Luke was Nelly's lover—that it was Luke who got Nelly—well, pregnant! But they're saying that Coley Mayhew was the one she laid the blame on! And they're saying—mind you now this is what *they're* saying—that Coley wrote certain people back here in Kingdom County to clear his own good name!"

"Are you trying to be silly with me now, boy?"

"No, Father. Maybe Coley Mayhew wouldn't want to come right out with a letter like that to me. I mean, about a serious thing like that."

"You expect me to believe that?"

"No. I don't, Father."

"Then you *are* being silly with me?"

"No, Father. I'm not. I just don't—don't expect you to believe anything I could possibly say here tonight. You didn't ask me here tonight to hear my side of this. It's plain that Nelly's told you something about that night when Luke went running!"

"*You* tell me, Loy. What *did* happen that night, Loy?"

"Father, I've told you—I don't remember. I was—drinking, Father."

"And you had nothing to do with the rumors, the gossip?"

"Father, why would I start filthy gossip about my own sister?"

"Yes! Yes! In God's name why?"

"The answer is perfectly simple, Father. I didn't."

"Then—! If—!"

"The answer is perfectly simple, Father: someone else did."

"Nelly, you swear?" cried Isaiah, gripping his chair till the old wood groaned. "That wild tale you told me—Nelly, you *swear?*"

"I swear, Father," she whispered.

Loy shrugged and stared at each fingernail, one by one. "Then what's the use of this?" he said. "You believe her, Father. You don't believe me. We're both your own children and yet—"

"To be *just* is all I want here!"

"—yet you choose to believe Nelly's word against mine! Why her word should seem so much more *pure*, Father, is hard for me to guess. She went off and had a child—"

"She *loved* someone and that is more than you have ever done!"

"—behind your back, Father. And now she tells you some wild tale that. . . ! Father, you called it a wild tale yourself!"

"I think I would be rather dead than believe it."

"Still you plainly believe it! As if you'd seen it sheared from the whole cloth with your own eyes. And turn against me!"

"I'm against no one! I'm against only lies and treachery! A spew of vicious gossip against innocents! That's what I'm against!"

Loy's eyes thinned a little, shining with excitement at this new and desperate gambit: "Father, suppose it were true?"

"Suppose that what?"

"For sake of pure theory, Father. Suppose Luke had been Nelly's lover? Would that have been so dreadful? Haven't you always been the one to—"

"That is not under discussion now, Loy!"

"Well, don't you think it is—in a way? Haven't you always been the one to pound equality into us all—from the time we were babies?"

"That's not the issue now! The life of someone in this household has been threatened! What I'm trying to get out of you—"

"I know, Father. You've preached to us all our lives—and Grandpa before you—that old Toby and little Luke were just the same as us in the eyes of God!"

"As they are!"

"Well, Father, have I said any different here tonight? I'm just, frankly, a little surprised that you'd say you'd—*rather be dead than* believe Luke was the father of Nelly's baby!"

"Don't twist my words, boy! I said I'd rather be—"

"Father, be fair. I'm just quoting you."

"—dead than have a son who'd say the things you said that night—"

"According to Nelly's tale!"

"—and write the kind of things back here to Kingdom County—"

"According to God-knows-who's tale!"

"—about his own sister and his childhood friend!"

"Yes, Father. Luke. My childhood friend. And do you know who stands between that childhood friend and a howling lynch mob?"

"Be careful, Father. He's lying! Oh, God, Loy, how could you?"

Wounded, his shoulders slumped a little and he glanced from one to the other of them in turn.

"Father. Nelly. Please listen to me. It's very important. I heard men talking when first I came home in March. About Nelly. About Luke. Why, they were talking about dragging Luke right

out of the train-coach when it pulls in and hanging him right
there in the depot!"

"You, of course, protested."

"Of course, Father. Naturally, I had to use judgment—tact.
I tell you I had to really do some talking up for old Luke there
that night. Naturally—well, naturally, I had to put it to them in
language—well in words they'd understand, Father. I mean, it
wasn't quite the cultured, civilized kind of conversation we're
all three having here tonight. I mean, I told the boys that I
knew my sister Nelly's good, Christian character well enough—
I mean knowing all her weaknesses I still could swear she would
not possibly have been fooling around with anyone with nigger
blood in their veins. You understand, Father, this is not how
I'd explain it to you or Nelly—you have to talk to men like that
in their own language. Well, I'm proud and happy to say that
my arguments won out—it took me about an hour's talking,
Father, but my own good sense of Christian charity won out.
Luke is safe."

"Yes," Isaiah said, and swung around in the big chair and
pulled out the top drawer of the roll-top desk. "Yes, I know
Luke is safe."

"Well, I sure hope you realize, Father, what danger he was
in there for a while. Those hot-headed boys . . ."

"No," said Isaiah. "He was never in danger for a minute. Not
Luke. Nor Toby, either."

He reached in the drawer; he laid the long Navy pistol among
the papers in the lampshine yellow by his arm.

"Because I made up my mind about this many weeks ago:
That if ever again there is hand or weapon or phrase of gossip
raised against your sister or against Luke or his father—in my
presence—I will kill the man who makes it."

The night was flesh-damp with breathless heat: like the air-
less, close clasp of a mitten. Isaiah had saddled the mare and

gone off in a dust-cloud toward Goshen: gone anywhere, Nelly
guessed, to get them all from the sight of his eyes for awhile.
She made a pitcher of lemonade in the dark kitchen and
thought how sick of them he must surely be; he would ride for
miles in the hot, moonless dark to be alone and away from them
all for an hour in a willowed coolness up the PawPaw, with no
comment to his ears for that while but the mare's snuffling and
the good jeer of green frogs loving down in the cattails. She
made the pitcher of lemonade in the dark, and listening to Loy
in the parlor, she marveled and wondered at his mind: he was
playing "Dardanella" on the Victrola and whistling along with it
like there had never been any contention between them at all
that night, like there wasn't a care in the world. She stood in the
dark, by the pump, sipping lemonade and feeling the chinking
chill of the tumbler in her hand and listening to Loy whistling
while he cranked the Victrola up and got the record on again
and played "Dardanella" again. Things move round and over
him like a rock, she thought, like he was a rock with the rest of
us a river moving over him. He came whistling to the kitchen
door and stood an instant finding her in the dark with his eyes.

"What's that you're drinking?"

"Lemonade."

"Pour me a glass. That sounds good. Lemonade. Good. I
thought maybe you might be sneaking something a little
stronger. Wait'll I go start that record again."

She stood with the glass gripped in her hand, angry for the
first time she could remember that night: angrier at that than
she had been at any of the things he had said to Isaiah; she
listened while he started "Dardanella" again and came back to
the dark beside her.

"What was that supposed to mean?" she said carefully.

"What, Nelly? What was what supposed to mean?"

"That—what you said about 'something stronger'?"

"Why—well, I haven't seen my little sister since before I went
to war. How am I suppose to know what new habits she's picked
up since then? You always were full of surprises, Nelly."

She shut her eyes in the darkness, and it was red inside her lids; Loy had struck a match, but the red was more than that.

"Cigarette, Nelly?"

She turned suddenly in the instant before he blew the match out and struck the pack of cigarettes out of his hand; in the dark his smoke fumed from the ebb and glow as he breathed in, blew out.

"That wasn't nice, Nelly. I declare, nobody seems to be very nice to me around here anymore."

"You're going to keep on—aren't you?"

"Papa tonight," he said. "Papa certainly wasn't nice to me—waving that rusty old pistol around—talkin' wild."

He squatted in the shadows and groped for the pack and the spilled smokes by her shoe-tips.

"Loy, I've never seen Papa like he was tonight."

"Neither have I, Nelly."

"Loy, I think you'd better keep it in mind—what Papa said tonight."

"Oh, I will, Nelly. I certainly will."

"Because enough has been said, Loy. Enough has been done. And suffered, Loy. Papa meant what he said tonight, Loy. About letting people *be* now!"

"You mean Luke. That's who you mean by 'people.' "

"Loy, there is nothing you—nothing anyone else on earth could ever do to me that would hurt *me*. Yes, Loy, I mean Luke!"

"Well, you heard what I told Papa in there. Didn't you?"

"Yes, I heard."

"But you don't believe me? Is that it, Nelly? Nelly, you don't seem to understand human nature very well. At least, *my* human nature. Nelly, look out yonder window—there by the pump! See how dark it is out there in the yard. See? You can hardly make out the shape of the butternut tree—you can hardly make out the chimney top of old nigger Toby's shack."

"Loy, get out of the kitchen and let me be!"

"No, wait. I just want to make a little point. I'm showin' you how *dark* it is out there. Nelly, that proves something. You know

what it proves? It proves that Loy Wilson is a man of his word—
that's what it proves! You know why? Because if it wasn't for
me—Nelly, if it hadn't been for me standing and sweating
and pleading and arguing with fifty men for the better part of
three hours last night—you know what? Nelly, that yard out
yonder wouldn't be dark, Nelly! Nelly, that yard out yonder
would be all glimmering and shining and quivering with red
and yellow and scarlet from a great big flaming cross! Believe
me! For it's true, Nelly. Those boys—I swear it took me *more*
than three hours to talk Wiley and Polk and the others out of
it. You know I've been kept hopping busy this week looking out
for old Luke. He's due home tomorrow, ain't it? Tomorrow on
the six thirty eastbound and, Nelly, I've just had to talk myself
hoarse this past few weeks making sure that Luke got out of
that train station *alive*! You've got no notion how stubborn those
boys are and, after all, I'm just one among many. Wait'll I
go fix the talking-machine. And pour me some more of that
lemonade."

He went off into dark again, to the parlor, where the record
had finished and the big tulip panted like an enormous beast.
She stood gripping the pump handle and listening while he
whistled and cranked the machine and started "Dardanella"
again.

"I like that tune. Catchy tune. Like a whore-house tune!
Thought I'd play it again. You like 'Dardanella,' Nelly?"

"What?"

"Nothing. You never listen to half the things I say to you. I
declare, Nelly, your mind seems to be in as much of a fog
anymore as Papa's!"

"There's nothing foggy about Papa's mind."

"Well, maybe 'foggy' ain't the word. You'll have to admit
though, that he's not quite the strong, unshakable idealist he
used to be—or used to act like he was!"

"If he heard you say that, Loy Wilson, you'd soon find out
how strong Papa is!"

"Sure, I would. He'd knock me down. Maybe he'd get out his

old horse-pistol and wave it around and make some kind of a high-sounded speech!"

"He'd *thrash* you!"

"Exactly. That's my whole point, Nelly! He's turned to violence, Nelly! And for Papa's kind of man—that's defeat! Nelly, tonight—there at his desk tonight—well, you saw him! Nelly, did you ever see or hear a more undignified, uncertain, weak—*disgusting*, is the word—exhibition in your whole life? Nelly, Papa was scared tonight!"

"Not scared of you, Loy Wilson!"

"Well, maybe not of me—maybe not scared of me personally. I mean, maybe not scared that he couldn't still whip me if it came to that. Maybe he could—maybe not."

"Suppose—suppose I tell him you said that? Suppose I tell him when he gets in tonight?"

"Go ahead."

"You're afraid!"

"No. No, I'm not afraid. I used to be, Nelly. When I was little I was afraid all the time—all the time. That's why I had to make it my business to grow up knowing ways to study human nature. Ah, it's a fascinating thing, Nelly—human nature. The Army now. There was my school. Nelly, that Army did me more good than ten years in state college could have! First of all, it helped me to get the number of men like Papa—a man who coddles niggers. Well, like Grandpa was. You know—these big-talking, high-flying idealists with their holy notions about the Old South—about *everything*—about the New Freedom—about making the world safe for Democracy—about all such sorts of big-sounding, empty-headed propositions that when you get them all boiled down don't add up to anything more than Bolshevism or some other immoral, foreign kind of 'ism' in which right-thinking people don't have a chance! Peace and Pacifism and Rights for Labor and Rights for the Niggers. Oh, they all talk so big—so *big*! But once you get them scared—once you get them mad—why, they're no different from my kind of man, Nelly. Take Papa! Take that fool old-maid college professor we've got slopping things up now in Washington! Oh, *he's* a fine one! God, I used to be ashamed those first months in the Army that maybe the guys would think he was some kin of ours with the Wilson name and all. I remembered when I heard him make that speech at the train station way back in nineteen-twelve and all that idealistic crap about labor and peace and all, it made me—I swear, I could almost see Papa standing up there behind the iron fence on the rear end of that train saying those same things and I wanted to *puke!* Even then I guess I knew what kind of a man I'd—what kind of right-thinking people it takes to really run a country. Nelly, speak the truth—were you proud of Papa in there tonight—trying to make a fool out of me and ending up by making a fool out of himself—and you?"

"Didn't it mean anything to you, Loy, that Papa had heard my version of what you did—of the filth and rottenness you poured out on Luke—on me—that Christmas night? Listen! Doesn't it mean anything that he wanted to give you a chance, Loy, in all *fairness*. . . ?"

"Fairness! Fairness! Oh, yes, how well I know that word! How Papa loves to mouth that word—fairness! Why, his fairness would run this land to hell in a year! *Justice* is *my* word, Nelly! Not fairness—*justice!* You know the difference? I hope and pray to God you do! Fairness is—is uncertainty, temporizing, cringing from facts, from right-thinking! Justice is the step of a bold man forward in the Right that—"

"But if that *bold* man is *wrong*, Loy? God, if he's wrong—like *you're* wrong, Loy?"

"Wrong? Wrong! Can't be, little sister! Why, the good Lord needs Just Men so bad He don't dare *let* them think wrong! He needs the Just Men to keep the wrong-thinkers in line! See? No, you don't see! You couldn't see. Because you're cut from the same stuff as him and Grandpa!"

"I pray that," she whispered. "Yes, I pray that."

"Do you? Well, you may live to see times when you'll pray different, little sister! Lord, sometimes when I see what the mush-headed dreamers have done to this family—to this whole country—I wonder we ever come through as good as we have! You, for example! What did being that way ever get you but a bad name in Kingdom County and a bastard nigger baby?"

"Loy, listen!"

"No, you listen a spell! It's Loy speech-time now! Papa's had his speech-time tonight! I'm talking now!"

"Loy, Papa's not to blame for anything I ever did! No one is."

"Didn't he fill your mind with notions that was against every good thing Mama raised us to believe? Didn't he?"

"No! I am my own! I did what I felt—what I believed! I'd do it again!"

"Would you? Well, you won't. Because you won't have the chance!"

"Loy, I don't have to stand this! I don't have to take this from you! You—"

"Yes, you do!"

"—heard Papa tonight! You heard what he said he'd do to anyone who slandered and tortured—!"

"But you won't tell Papa about us talking tonight, Nelly. You won't tell Papa the things I've said to you tonight. In the first place, he thinks he's got me so scared that he wouldn't believe it. In the second place—"

"I'll kill you myself, Loy!"

"See? Just like him! When you're scared and mad you turn just like him! That's my whole point! This whole earth's split up into Dreamers and Doers, Nelly. The Dreamers go around like creeping-Jesus, slobbering mush-headed notions about peace and love and turning-the-other-cheek and there's nary one in the showdown that's got the guts to carry through. Wham! Someone pricks your hide and you ain't a Dreamer no more. Wham! Down on all fours! Dog! Wolf! And the truth comes out that you weren't any better than the Doers after all! See what I mean, little sister? It's a simple matter of human nature and a knowledge of the animal that's man! See? It's the Doers that keeps the old earth turning even! Me! My kind! And while we're investigating the subject here tonight, little sister, maybe you can tell me what is so damned beautiful and idealistic about having bastards? Huh? What's wrong with waiting and getting engaged and having a wedding and doing things in a normal, Christian way with someone of a race God intended? Huh? You can't explain that, can you? Oh, I know! Don't tell it to me! God, I can't stand hearing all that crap again about how Love is stronger than Conscience and Women has as much rights as Men and the rest of that atheistic, agnostic, Bolshevist. . . ! Listen? You know something? I went through all that kind of thinking for a while! Oh, God, I used to get so lonely sometimes I'd believe anything—anything! Socialism, Free-Love, Atheism! You name it, Nelly! And then—and then I saw that it was all part of a big, cheap, rotten lie cooked up by people like Papa and Grandpa and men like that old Doc Wilson—that fool, granny college teacher in the White House! Nigger-lovers and—"

"Loy, I'm going to tell Papa all this you're saying tonight."

"No. You won't. You won't because you know I'm the one man in Kingdom County that stands between your nigger boy friend and a lynch party."

"Loy. Loy, you promised nothing was going to happen—"

"Sure. I promised. Maybe things might get out of hand. Maybe those boys might get too stubborn for even me to handle. Nelly, I'd advise you to think about those things."

"Papa would protect Luke."

"Maybe Papa wouldn't. I have a funny kind of notion I got through to Papa a little bit tonight. Huh? You think maybe? I have a funny idea maybe Papa's got a sneaking suspicion in his poor, brooding, fuzzy, philosophical brain tonight that maybe I been right all along about it being Luke that knocked you up."

"Loy, you believe that? You really and truly believe it?"

"Nelly, as if I'd done it myself."

She was still at that, head spinning, nauseated.

"As—as if I'd *seen* it myself. You know—well, you won't believe this, maybe. You know I used to look at you when I was a boy, Nelly, and I used to say to myself: There—next to Mama—

goes the most beautiful lady in the world! That's what I used to think, Nelly. Nelly, it was—it was just like you were some kind of a god or goddess come to earth! But I always knew—I always *knew* that you'd go and do some—some rotten thing with Luke! And I know now—Nelly, I know now just as sure and certain as if Lord God come down and told me that you and him did it together and did it together and did it together—!"

"I'd not be ashamed if I had!" she breathed to the black, mad silhouette.

"—and did it together until there was conceived in you a child as black as Satan's own!"

"God help you, poor Loy."

"Keep your sticky pity off me, whore."

He leaned back, breathing slow and steady, and she knew what massive, bunched convulsions of effort were toiling within his pitiable flesh to keep it from her eyes that she had hurt him. He tore at his shirt pocket and fetched his cigarettes and matches. Presently he showed his face by match flame and it was the coined, metal smile again, and she shivered as he held out the pack to her again in the soiling gesture.

"Cigarette?"

"All right, Loy. Thank you. I'll smoke a cigarette."

She took one and he held the match up and she saw the jade-hard glitter of his eyes in the flame, watching her as she took the light and was the whore that now he had to think she was. And now in the whored and equaled dark she felt his fury go back; watched the ebb and shine of his cigarette go down to a slower pulse. He laughed softly.

"Lemme go put that Victrola tune on again," he said, and went and wound the coiled iron and set the blasphemed silence racketing with his fox trot. He came softly back to the kitchen.

"You know I think it was a good thing you and me had this little talk tonight, Nelly. I mean, you might have gotten off on the wrong foot again with Luke. That could have been a real bad thing. I got one colored bastard to hunt out somewheres as it is. I don't reckon I'd want the trouble of having to find two."

She closed her eyes and began speaking softly to him as if she were explaining death to a child: "Loy, will you please listen to me a minute. My baby died of the flu."

"Sure it did. S-u-ure it did. Oh, yes! You know I'll find it. I mean, sooner or later. It may take a few months scratching around—maybe a few years. But I'll find the black bastard child."

"Loy. Loy, you're mad," she said softly.

"Mad? You mean crazy?" he coughed softly, and turned, leaning his elbows on the sink beside the pump and floating his gaze softly in the darkness drifting back and forth beyond the open window; chuckled. "Well, all right. Think that. Somebody tells you you're crazy, there's no sense telling them back that you're not. But that means that every white man beyond that sill, beyond that fence, beyond the state line—this whole big Union over—this wide world over—is crazy, too! Every white Christian on this globe, Nelly—who has a sister—or a wife—or daughters—is crazy, too. You know that, don't you? You just called all white, Christian gentlemen crazy?"

"Loy, there are decent, good white men who'd never *think* the things you think! Loy, you *know*."

"I know there's not a living one of them who ain't scared *sweatless* from the day he finds out the sweet feel of sin that what happened to me won't happen to him—that what happened to my little sister won't happen to his sister—or his wife—or his daughter! All the men out yonder in Kingdom County tonight sleeping uneasy in their beds? It makes no never mind where they come from! Have you heard their voices, Nelly, or didn't you want to hear: 'Man, would you want your sister to marry one of 'em?' Or 'Man, would you like to find your little daughter layin' up with a nigger?' Foreigners, even. Nelly, listen! I seen a little bit of world in this war! I kept my ears and eyes open! I may be crazy, Nelly, but I've got some sense! Englishmen, too, Nelly. I mind a boy in London I met by the name of Jarvy Partridge and he was a damned stuck-up Limey, but I hung around with him just to study him, watch him, feel him out on

things. I may be crazy but I know men, Nelly. I told him one
night about you and Luke and the black bastard you'd both
brought into the family—I was so crazy mad that night I had
to talk to someone about it, so I told Jarvy and he laughed and
snickered and said that wouldn't bother him one little bit. And
it was all I could do to keep from hitting him right there on the
spot, but I kept studying, watching, feeling him out and I knew
down deep it wasn't just me—I knew down deep he had his
own right-mindedness even if he was a damned Limey. And
sure enough, Nelly, one night in a London theater it was me
and Jarvy and his sister Peggy, and the show was over and we
were on our way out to the street when some soldier whistled
at Jarvy's sister and Jarvy half killed him with his riding crop.
'Bloody nigger!' he was hollering. 'Bloody nigger!' and I
watched and like to died laughing because it was some kind of
Arabian or Punjab soldier with a turban and a beard and he
didn't look like any nigger I'd ever seen."

She felt the handlike heat of the thick dark press like damp,
whorled flesh against her mouth, her breath, her eyes and felt
behind her with shaking hands to lean against the kitchen table.
She felt as trees must feel at firesound or at the footfall of
impending woodsmen among their old leaves; because she
could not move hand nor tongue nor eye to make a brave or
even reasonably nay to his atrocious syllogism: to shout a warning No to all the white, mad Loy who lay that night's very
moment the wide earth round, clenched in a furious and fearful
sleep beside its girl.

"—despite that," he was saying in the black air. "No, you'd
think it would but it hasn't. I still respect decent women despite
that. A person would think that what has happened to me would
turn them against women altogether. No. Because I know that
once I shed of this house and get out in the world and on my
own, I'll find a decent Christian white girl who'll be clean like I
used to think—Well, I still have my ideals, Nelly. You haven't
spoiled them. I think—yes, you've even strengthened them. I
know the woman I'll meet. She'll be clean and she'll be un-

touched. I guess that would sound a little old-timey and religious to you—to Papa. Is that crazy, too, Nelly? To want a pure virgin for a bride? All right. Then the rest of the boys out yonder tonight are crazy on that score, too. She will be my woman! That's crazy, too? All right. There are certain things I shall expect of her and the question of her not living up to those standards will simply not ever come up. I will not expect her to touch spirits. I think there is nothing more disgusting than a lady with drink on her breath. As for niggers? Well, I know that weakness exists. You taught me that, Nelly, and for that, at least, I thank you. I'll always be watching for that. And may the great Jehovah have mercy on any of our little darkskinned *brothers,* as Papa would call them, who ever has the fatal bad judgment to so much as *think* about a wife of mine! Oh, Nelly, I *thank* you in some ways for the good education you gave me so early in life!"

He stopped, listening, leaning a little in the dark till the hoof-beats of a rider on the Goshen road dwindled away.

"Thought that might be Papa coming home?" he said. "Well, what if it had been? Suppose it had been Papa and he come in here and found us talking and he said, 'Nelly, has Loy been picking on you?' What then? What would you have said, Nelly?"

"I would have said, No. Because I think I would do anything on earth—say anything anyone wants me to say—if only there could be peace amongst us again, Loy."

"Well, I'm for that! Papa was the one talking pistols in there tonight—not me, Nelly! Dragging out that rusty old Confederate Colt that hasn't been fired since Chancellorsville! Christ, it was all I could do to keep from laughing in his face! He thought he had me *scared*—did you hear him, Nelly? *You* thought I was scared, too, didn't you, Nelly? I had you fooled, too! Well, you just stand right there a minute and directly you'll *see* how scared I am of Papa and his pistol!"

And she stood with the sweat chilling in her palms while he pell-melled away into the dark toward Isaiah's desk and she heard him laughing to himself as he fumbled out a match, struck it, and lit a lamp and came back presently to the kitchen holding it up so that she could see the big gun winking in his fist.

"Terrifying, ain't it? Papa's big pistol!"

"Loy. Loy, please don't hurt me, Loy . . ."

"*Hurt* you! With *this*? Christ, you're dumber than *he* is! With this old hunk of brass and iron?"

He set the lamp by the pump and lifted the pistol to his chin, pressing the muzzle deep into the plump flesh of his backthrust, grinning chin.

"Loy, *don't*!"

"Why not? Wouldn't you just love to see your brother blow his head off? See? You're just as soft-minded as he is! Now you watch close, Nelly, because I'm going to pull the trigger! What's wrong, little sister? Didn't you pray many and many's the night that I wouldn't come back from France? That would have been neat—wouldn't it, Nelly?"

She prayed that she would faint, but knew that she could not; she pressed her fist into her teeth and watched the knuckle whiten on the trigger and saw the hammer rise and click impotently upon the percussion-cap moldered and useless in the big gun's breech. Loy lowered it and threw it clattering on the table near her hand.

"Now I'll bet you thought I took an awful gamble when I did that, Nelly. I'll bet you thought I really risked my life. Nelly, you should know me better than that. I never gamble. Besides— history, in a manner of speaking, is on my side of things. When a man like Papa starts talking pistols he ought to make sure he knows pistols. You know—in a way, that old pistol is sort of like Papa. Big and mean and fierce-looking—with his linen powder cartridge all moldy and his percussion cap all mildewed with time. Time, Nelly. You see? Time and history is always on the side of my kind of man. You might almost say that old pistol just naturally wouldn't have the heart to hurt a man that stands for the things I do—the things that old pistol was *made* for! It's a justice, Nelly! Isn't it? Time and history, Nelly! They look after my kind of man! Just as they'll take good care of Luke!"

"What do you mean?"

"What I say. I always mean what I say. There's Papa in the stable. You can wait here for him if you want. I've had a bellyful of him for tonight. I'm going to bed. You can wait here for him if you want. Maybe you and him can hatch up some more plots against me."

"Loy, wait! What did you mean? Loy, you promised you wouldn't hurt Luke!"

"I don't have to hurt Luke!" he roared with laughter and went away with the lamp, dragging the shadows behind him down the long, dark hall while she pattered in his wake.

"Loy, listen! You swore! You said they wouldn't hurt Luke!"

"They couldn't hurt Luke!" he laughed softly, moving ahead of her up the stairs. "Anything like killing Luke would be a mercy now. He got chlorined in the Argonne. He's got one lung left, and he's got two months to live."

"No, God."

"Yes, God. Nelly, you think God is someone you can push this way and that like Papa, just to suit your willfulness? Luke's coming home tomorrow to die."

And he moved off to his room while she groped, stumbling, through the stifling dark toward her bed and fell across it and lay till nearly dayrise without undressing, without sleeping, without moving; long after Isaiah had come up the stairs and gone wearily to his bed; and, at last, the whole house lay in a sprawl of sicklied dreams, all sleeping but that one whom sleep had never loved; that one, horned orphan of the earth, stiff-kneed and sweatless on the hard hair trunk by his door, with his teeth in the bitter apple of his fist, shedding tears that no eyes but his own had ever seen, and whispering in a sibilant anguish that no ears but his own had ever heard: "You were so beautiful! Oh, God, you were so beautiful! Why did you have to go and be so rotten?"

LOY

"I think they killed him."

"But you don't know," she whispered to the man on the Army cot.

"But I think they done it. I figured they would do it. Wouldn' you ifn' you was them?"

"Listen to me. Please try. Where's Hawk?"

"What for? Why should I tell you where Hawk is? You want Hawk to get it, too?"

Hawk's ex-fight manager, Mister Vinnie, lay on the cot, keeping his eyes on the stained ceiling. He had not looked at Amy when she came in the room, nor since. He just lay there with his bare arm hanging over the edge of the dirty mattress and rolled a silver quarter back and forth between the secondjoints of the fingers of his hand. Amy sat on her suitcase, her eyes fixed upon him, thinking cautiously what words would move him; what fear might reach him. He seemed so cunningly absorbed in the stain upon the ceiling that he hardly knew she was there. The rolling coin in his fist seemed an action independent of the rest of him: like the winking on and off of a neon sign. He wore blue Levi's and a dirty T-shirt; and the faded blue and the dirty cotton and the buckwheat-batter skin seemed almost of a single color: the totality of him; he looked like a dirty string. Even the blue of the tattooed "Mother" in its heart seemed dingy beneath the sallow, bloodless skin of his half-bared chest.

"If you thought Hawk might be in danger, too—you'd tell me then, Mister Vinnie? Wouldn't you? If I could show you—"

"Hawk's in trouble as it is. In danger as it is. Your big-mouthed boy friend seen to that."

"Is Hawk hiding somewhere, Mister Vinnie?"

The man shut one eye and stared at the stain that way for a while. He had looked at that stain for too long with both eyes. With the one eye it took on a more complex dimension. He considered the myriad nights he had found within the shapes and mottled colors and hues and shifting expressions of that simple stain what others might have seen in a great painting. When he was turned-on real good the stain got better and better and ran on sometimes like a first-run movie. For weeks. And always different.

Amy got up and went to the frail table at the head of the cot. Standing by the table Amy looked down at the litter upon it: the spoon and the little folded papers and the hypodermic and the tumbler of water and she thought: His medicine. He is sick. But I mustn't be soft and sentimental. I've got to be strong and hard even if he is sick and maybe even crazy. He's got to be made to tell me. She lifted the tumbler of water and held it over the gray man's face. And uptilted it. And the water splashed down into his face, upon his eyes which did not even blink, did not even shut. Though the order of thoughts behind those eyes was now set clicking and shuttering into the fantastic new patterns of another logic; as if what she had done with the water were like twisting the kaleidoscope tube before the eye of an astonished child. Little pools of water stood in the hollows of his eyes now like rains gathered in the eyes of some stone god fallen in a forest.

"Where is Hawk, Mister Vinnie? I know you're sick and I'm sorry about that. But I've got to know."

He frowned a very little: she was the one dark cloud between him and all the sunshine of his night. He thought maybe that if he talked to her she might disappear. And so, in slow-motion, sat up on the bed: an elegant and somehow timeless gathering together of all the elements of himself for reassembly; upright, on the edge of the cot now and the water had run out of his eyes and down his face and onto the blue-hearted "Mother" of his chest, soaking into his gray T-shirt. He wrapped his hands carefully and closely around the clanging silver of the twenty-five cent piece so that it would be silent, and rubbed his burst tennis shoes slowly one against the other with voluptuous enjoyment.

"That time Hawk got busted," he said. "And they taken him off and put him up for the cure in Fort Worth—in the gov'ment hospital. And they done busted me, too. On account of me being Hawk's manager, I reckon, they 'lowed I better go along with him to the gov'ment hospital. Sho! But the Fight Commission—he taken away Hawk's license. Even so!—even so I was still Hawk's manager! So I am hip they 'lowed I better go along with him to the gov'ment hospital. Me'n Hawk been buddies a long, long time. Sho! Longer'n Hawk and your big-mouthed boy friend George was buddies! 'Fore Hawk even got shipped off to Vietnam! Sho he was! That's where Hawk taken to the Habit! In Vietnam! In the gov'ment hospital in Vietnam. That judge 'lowed it was me turned Hawk on the first time but it wasn't. Noways. It was the gov'ment its ownself. Then I reckon it was fair. The gov'ment turned him on. The gov'ment turned him off. Sho!"

"Mister Vinnie, where is Hawk?" she whispered, gentled with a deathly, steady calm, certain beyond shadow of doubt that she could bend him, make him tell where Hawk had gone and that Hawk alone in all the black, electric fury of that city night could tell her where George had gone.

"Where, Mister Vinnie?"

"Sweetie," said the gray man gently. "You are pretty as a fresh-iced cupcake. But you are sure one customer for hurrying things. You mustn't hurry everything up like that."

She backed away from him, from the table and sat again on her suitcase: persistent and righteous and immovable.

"Where is Hawk, Mister Vinnie?"

He rubbed his tennis shoes one against the other, slowly, and gathered her into his perspective again.

"Hawk may get clean one of these days," he said. "Hawk may kick it. Then Hawk and me is heading right up the sweet old comeback trail! You know something, Lady Cupcake? I refereed Hawk's first good bout. The American Legion Stadium. Atlanta. Nineteen and sixty. He taken a bad cut over his left eye and the nigger caught him with two mean left-hooks. And Hawk was down. I counted him up to nine and you know something, Lady Cupcake? My boy Hawk riz up like the Wrath of Jehovah and smote that black Pharisee down like Samson! For the count. And I knowed that night that this was my boy! Sho! Am hip I knowed that night that not me—not nobody else—not no one ever—would count to ten over that boy. Not my Hawk!"

He yawned at her through the gray veils of his dream.

"Is it daytime?" he whispered gravely. "Or is it nighttime?"

"It's nighttime," she breathed. "And Hawk's out there in trouble, Mister Vinnie. Where, Mister Vinnie? Where is he? Don't you even *care*?"

He leaned forward, rocking gently upon his haunches on the creaking cot, nursing his elbows in the gray cradles of his hands.

"Why, sho!" he said. "Sho. I care. I am hip ain't nary other soul cares."

But seemed not addressing his words to her at all, nor even to have heard her at all; but rather to be absorbed totally in the awareness of the ponderous and slowed-down avalanche of Time all round him; around him and beyond him and beyond her, as well; beyond even the thin, cheap walls, gaudy with tear marks of the rains of gone summers and crazy with plaster cracks from the shaking, clashing freight trains which, almost hourly through the nights, seemed to go rocketing beneath the very, quaking floors. Amy studied him gravely; saw him in his caged world beyond her own; she would go through his own hell, if need be, to find Hawk, to get to George. And so her wits circled him, keen-eyed and cunning.

"Where's Hawk, Mister Vinnie?" she said again softly.

And suddenly he began talking—"Never would have gotten in no trouble—none of the troubles he done got into ifn' it hadn't been for them! First it was her that worked in the bus terminal restaurant! Blonde, damned bitch! You take this mess now—this mean ruckus about the nigger-boy they lynched! Sho! Same damned jazz all over again! George wouldn't be in all this mess now if it wasn't for that! Yes, Christ, I am hip. I would rather be hooked on junk than on that. I am hip. I have seen a sight more men murdered for that than for junk! Sho! Even—even ifn' I had it all to start out clean-slate over again— all young again and dumb again and Jesus-pure again—I would sho pick gettin' hooked on white stuff than that! Sho! It's a pity and a wonder that the U.S.A. gov'ment don't set up hospitals to help a man kick the chick habit, too! 'Cause—! Now deny it if you can! Ifn' he hadn't been parked out in the car that night alongside of you he wouldn't have seen that nigger-boy get lynched! I mean George wouldn't! I mean ifn' he had to pick some gash why'n hell did he pick the very one whose daddy was going to be doing the lynchin'! And be there to see it! And then go blabbin' it all over this white man's town! Sho! And the fuzz leanin' in listenin' with their po-lice badges fairly scratching his cheek and him—poor, misguided son-of-a-bitch blabbin' it! And them listenin'! And then—and then!—as if that ain't bad enough—blabbin' it to that poor, dumb, misguided Hawk who is ever' bit as un-American and nigger-lovin' and wrong-thinkin' as him! I done preached him logically many's and many's the time about that, too! Sho! I preached him! Cool it, I say!"

He fell silent for a moment, not looking at her, his head cocked sideways a little, jerking it a little as if trying to shake

loose some memory, like he would shake free a coat hung high
upon some school-cloakroom hook. And then began again, his
speech lurching forward like a hot rod picking up again after
the pause in a curve. I tried to make that boy Hawk into Something Big! It was one of *them*—got in the way—ever' damn time!
Right between me and my boy Hawk right when his Big Chance
was ripe! Jes' when I'd have him ready! First time it was that
one in the bus-terminal restaurant got him all dosed up the very
night before a big ten-round event in Delta City! Sho! An' even
in the Army! Even in Vietnam! It was a damned G.I. nurse that
got him hooked on M! In the gov'ment hospital! Sho! They
taken a little piece of iron out of his shoulder and he hollered
and taken on with the pain so bad she mothered him and messed
him up with M ever' night till by the time he come home from
Vietnam he was totin' a monkey on his shoulders as big as King
Kong! Sho' Trouble! And now—and now—it's you!"

"Where is he?"

"Sho. I'll tell you. He's out hidin' somewheres in the freight
yards with the shakes. Sho. That's where Hawk is! And the fuzz
been up here twice tonight in the red cars huntin' him and come
up here and each time I had to grab up ever'thing and run
and hide down the hall in the blind lady's room. Huntin' him!
Because they know what George done tol' him! And I reckon
they know him for a nigger-lover, too—poor, dumb, misguided
son! Now, you see? You see what kind of trouble you brought
down on my boy? Now you see?"

He spoke it gently, without real anger. Amy sat on, her knees
so tight-pressed together that her thighs ached, and endured it
all, witnessing, and listening and stared, her dark woman's eyes
grave under the brim of the child's straw hat. Herself steady
now, on her two feet now, calm and couraged now, after four
days that had hurtled her out of infancy headlong, out of her
simpering, bobby-soxed non-age into a fierce and proud nubil-
ity.

"—then ifn' you was so anxious to know where Hawk was
at—how come you don't go runnin' out to find him—hidin'

behind a coal hopper somewheres out yonder in the freight yards? Sho! Why don't you go find him? You couldn't mess things up for him any worse than they are now, I reckon!"

He grinned at her, furious, patient.

"Or," he added softly. "Why don't you run tell the po-lice?"

And glanced sidelong at her and winked and clasped his fingers round his knee and rocked on the cot, giggling like a girl.

"Sho now!" he crowed. "I am the Secret Man! You know what they—you know what them cats up at the—up at the—up at the—American Legion Gymnasium at Delta City—you know what they used to call me? The Medic! Sho! That's what they used to call me! The Medic! 'Cause I am the Secret Man! I'm God's half-brother! Sho now! They hain't a secret on earth or in heaven that is beyond my power to reveal! Like maybe I might even tell you—"

That little art that she had learned in a split-second: pretending to be indifferent but not pretending too much: keeping her eyes casually on the tennis shoes that rubbed together, not looking at his face; pretending that she didn't really care anymore what he was saying.

"—might even tell you—where George is at!" he finished in a whisper. "Ask me that, Lady Cupcake! Ask me real nice and soft and ladylike: Medic, where is George Purdy at?"

Struggling with herself to keep still, she won, watching him, and thought: No, Mister Vinnie. No, because you hate me, Mister Vinnie, and you are just playing with me now—teasing me—with all that wound-up hate like a silk-leader on a reel and you figure you got me hooked and you'll play me out a little. No, Mister Vinnie.

"Go on!" he said, his fingernails making a swift, dry chatter as he scratched the twitching skin beneath his Adam's apple. You talkin' to the Medic, lady! The Secret Man! Go on! Ask me! Say: Medic, where's George Purdy at? Because—I *know!*"

Blinking at her, he kept on scratching and yawning and then chuckling, philosophically, shook his head.

"I swear to God—I don't know which of the two I pity him the most for—them huntin' him down—or you huntin' him down! Either way—he is booked to go! Either way! Them after him. You after him. Like a man caught out yonder in the freight yards with nothin' but a strip of cinders between him and two high-ballin' express trains bearin' down on him! Sho! It's awful to witness!"

Yawned again, and stopped smiling and the bright pinpoints of his gray, old-young eyes flashed and remembered something.

"Please," he said, almost whiney with coaxing, "ask me. Say: Medic, where is my baby-boy George Purdy at?"

He watched her face with fierce attention.

"I'll clue you one thing," he said. *"He's alive!"*

She sat stiff and dumb upon her suitcase, knees tight and lips tight and stared at him.

"Hawk told me," he said. "Ask him your ownself. That's him coming down Morning Alley now. He'll be up here in a second."

And covered his face with a forearm, lying with his eyes glazed, to the wall, but listening with ears keened-up as a cricket's to the sound that her ears could not hear yet: the faint, fast, slightly stiff-legged footfalls of Hawk coming down the wet paving stones of Morning Alley. When Amy slipped to the window she heard them, saw him: Hawk, at the far end of the alley, hugging the wall, beyond the betrayal of gas lamp which cast a glistening yellow triangle of light across the bricks at the corner. She kept back from sight, in the window, though she could see no one following him, though he ran as if there were. The neon sign at the Negro barbecue place down beyond the boarding house, in Morning Alley's deeps, imposed upon the darkness a stacatto, fluttering redness. Hawk stood one bare second before the house, looked up to the lighted window, saw Amy's face, looked behind him to see if they followed, and darted quickly into the hallway.

"Trouble," said the Medic to the wall. "Always trouble. Ever' damn one of 'em. Trouble."

And Hawk slipped through the door, in the echo of his footsteps on the stairs.

His face was damp but it was not from the mists in Morning Alley. He leaned against the wall and stared at Amy, learning to breathe again, the chest under his wet shirt finding a steadier rise and fall.

"Amy, you have got to get out of town."

"No!"

"Tonight, Amy! I don't know how—or by what means—"

"I'm not going anywhere till I know about George. Not leaving. No, Hawk. Not without—"

"Will you listen!"

"I won't listen!"

"You will listen!" he whispered, and had her shoulders in his big, scared hands, shaking her. "You've got to!"

She began to quake and thought she was going to cry but she didn't: that was last week when she might have cried. Now she just trembled and glared at Hawk.

"Because it's the only way you can help him," he said. "If you'll for Christ's sake let me finish. There is not one thing under heaven you can do for George in this town. Not tonight. You've got to get out, Amy. You've got to do that because it is the only last prayer we've any of us got of helping him ever!"

Her mouth fell slack; and Hawk thinking, from her eyes, that a scream might be gathering in her throat, cupped his hand, ready to stop it.

"George," he said again in a soft, strong voice, "is alive, Amy. Just get that in your head and try to hang on to that when all the rest of it seems too much to bear. Can you do that?"

"Yes. But—"

"But what? But you think you'll go running around Augusta County tonight till you find George. Is that it? Just go out that door downstairs and go runnin' up Morning Alley screaming his name? Run through Elizabethtown yellin' for George! Is that how? You reckon that's gonna find you George, Amy? And pretty soon your daddy sees you or hears you and picks you up like a nice little quiet-mouthed daughter and locks you up at home—or one of them cop buddies of his takes you to him! Is that how?"

"He needs me, Hawk," was all she could think to say. "That's all I know. George needs me."

"Then don't let him down. Keep out of their hands. For Christ's sake, Amy, don't you see? Once your daddy can get you out of town—can shut you up—then they could finish their job of shutting George up," he said. "Finish it for good. Because he'd be the only one left with a mouth to do any talking with."

"Him," murmured the Medic, gravely. "And Hawk."

"Shut up, Vinnie!" Hawk cried striding out into the room. "You're sure doing one hell of a lot to help!"

He began snatching up papers and spoon and hypodermic needle in a fury and glaring at the gray man on the cot.

"Leavin' your candy all spread out so that if they come by—"

"They been here," said the Medic. "I hid. Miz Ryder—down the hall—she's blind. I hid. I don't 'low she even knowed I was there. I hid behind her rocking chair both times. Twicet they was here. Them two. Lookin' for you, Hawk."

"They just wanted to sound me," he said, with a glance to the black window. "Just ask me—"

"Sure they did," said the Medic. "Sure. Sure they did."

"Well they know I couldn't testify against them!" cried Hawk in a kind of blind rage at something that had not yet been said. "I didn't see the nigger killed!"

"Sure," said the Medic. "I am hip. Sure, Hawk."

"They know?" Amy said. "They know George told you—what he saw?"

"Yes."

"How?"

"How? Christ, I don't know how! Someone saw us in the beer joint Sunday when—"

"Why didn't they take you, too, then?" she said.

"I don't know! Christ, Amy, I don't know. It's just been crazy

luck all round. Tonight. Tonight I knew they were hunting me.
I hid. Up in the empty store at the end of Morning Alley. I saw
them come up here twice. And each time they went away. And
then I saw you come in. And just when I was ready to come
down Morning Alley they came back and they turned their
lights off and sat there watching the place for an hour—maybe
longer. I thought any minute they'd see you at the window. I
just lay there on the floor of the empty store praying and watching them through the letter slot."

"Hawk, what if they took me in? I haven't done anything!
What if they took me to the courthouse!"

"Listen, Amy. Tonight it's their town—*their night!* Tomorrow—or the next day—when the whole state knows about it—
when maybe the whole country knows about it—it could be
different. Maybe it will be and maybe it won't be. Maybe the
rest of the country'll just figure—it's their mess—let them work
it out in their own way! They've been running it a long time
that way—and they've got to live with them—so let them run
it! Maybe. Maybe not. But tonight—it's their show! Can't you
understand that? They've thrown George into a labor gang ten
miles down the river at Big Possum Creek! They—"

"For what? For what, Hawk? They can't just—"

"For drunkenness! For bein' in a whore house! That's what?
It don't matter!"

"George wouldn't! Hawk, he—"

"It don't matter—would he—or wouldn't he! Amy, you don't
understand me yet! This town's gone a little bit crazy tonight!
The big sticks have taken over Augusta County tonight, Amy!
It's theirs! Their town! Their night! I know none of it makes
sense to you! Your pappy and them other two are under arrest
and at the same time they ain't under arrest! They're in custody
of the County Sheriff and they ain't in custody of the County
Sheriff. They're free and they're not free! At least, there's no jail
bars around 'em. It's cute! But it's a fact, Amy! And meanwhile
they're free enough to make tonight count—to mop up
things—to tie up things—to shut up things! And I mean every

last mortal being who might cause them trouble at the trial! Oh, hell yes! Hell, they'll be tried proper by a judge—and a jury of tried and true Augusta County men! Hell, yes! But tonight's the chance that the whole county's given them to do what needs to be done! Can you understand that, Amy? To mop it up—tie it up—shut it up! I mean like everyone who might be the slightest risk of testifyin'! Like George! Like you!"

"Hawk, don't they know? Don't they understand? I don't—I wouldn't tell!"

"Wouldn't tell what?"

"What I—what we saw that night! Hawk, I *couldn't* tell! Hawk, my own daddy was one—"

"But George would tell!"

"He wouldn't! Hawk, he wouldn't! Hawk, I know George's beliefs—his ideals! I know all that! But when it comes to—maybe comes to Daddy's life!"

"Or maybe his own!"

"Hawk, I still can't believe it! Hawk, you don't think I believe what Daddy and—what they did was right. You know I don't believe in lynching!"

"Neither does George, Amy! He disbelieves in it real strong, Amy! Strong enough to say what he saw if anyone ever gets him to the courtroom and still alive to talk!"

"No, Hawk, he wouldn't!"

"Why not? He told them he would! Shouted it in their faces—your daddy and Lowdy and the other one! He took a pretty good beatin' for that! Before they took him to the farm!"

"But, Hawk!"

"But he would! It's more than just ideals, Amy!"

"But he's a white man!" she screamed suddenly in his eyes and then suddenly fell silent and aghast and something else she had not known was hiding all that time behind the thickness of her jungle, in the bare and lonely solitude of her soul at the edge of the clearing.

"Oh, Hawk, God help us all!" she grieved in a gush of tears.

He nodded and stared bitterly at his upturned palms.

"I don't reckon I'm so much of an expert that I could say who'll help us. There'll be time to know, I reckon. Time to choose, Amy. Maybe right is just—just going off somewhere—to the farthest corner of nowhere and pretending for the rest of your days that it all never happened."

"Yes!" she whispered. "Yes! That it all never happened. But, Hawk, I couldn't do it alone. It's something between George and me and whatever forgetting—whatever pretending—we've got to do it together. I just don't think I could live with this—this memory for the rest of my life if I was alone. It needs two of us—the forgetting. That's why—"

"That's why you've got to go," he said. "That's why you've got to get out of Augusta County tonight. If you love George, Amy, you'll do that."

"I can't think it," she whispered. "I can't believe it."

"They'd kill him. You need money?" Hawk said.

In the stunned thralldom of her speculations she lifted her face, empty-eyed, and stared at Hawk who had asked her something and she couldn't remember what.

"Money," he said. "You need money. Is that a problem?"

Something whispered in the street like the thought-quick flash of a fish within the darks of a sea. Hawk glanced, uneasy, to the screen, to the window sill across which wisps of the white-haired fog curled out into the dumb, yellow lampshine.

"Money? No. No. I've got a little. Enough."

Hawk moved quickly into the middle of the room and took Amy's wrist in a hard grip and pulled her with him against the wall, beside the window. Beyond the screen, where the fog played through and moving across the sill, diminished instantly among the light, something was astir in the alley: something more than the random woman's laughter in the rib-joint.

"Hear that?" he said quietly. "They're comin' back. Don't be scared. Goddamn you, don't be scared! You've got no right to be now!" He glared at her and told her to stay flat against the wall, not to move before the window. And hunched down and moved out with incredible deftness, bent over and lightning quick, snatching up the Medic's needle and spoon and the papers of his dreams and stuffing his pockets with them, looking with a kind of frenzied quietude all round him in the room for any evidence that they might leave that could betray anyone's having been there in the ticking moments that were left to them before the big feet came announcing themselves upon the sagging stairboards. Think. And caught up the Medic from his cot, throwing him over his hunched shoulder like an out-sized, staring doll, and then motioned Amy frantically to the doorway to the hall.

"Quick! Quick!"

She obeyed, following him, hunched down, too, out of the yellow picture frame of window, and even as she crossed the threshold on Hawk's frenzied heels she heard the unintelligible cackle of police radio.

"Quick! Here! No. Not that door. Here!"

The door was open and Hawk, bearing the Medic, stumbled into the room, and tumbled him like a bag of sticks onto the linoleum. Turned then, poker-faced still except for a little twitch above his mouth's left corner: a fighter's mouth still except for that, and grabbing Amy in after him, held a finger against his lips in a command for silence, before he closed the door, cutting the hallway's lampshine from his face.

"Listen to me," he whispered, his mouth so close to her ear that his lips could scarcely move, as if in a kind of frenzied kiss: breathing the words into her ear and she listened and heard that and heard the sentried tread of a rocking chair and heard that, too, and the police radio was fainter now and the weary, brutal boots already laboring up the faraway stairs. "Listen to me. Don't breathe. Don't make a sound. She'll hide us. Hear me? She'll hide us. But don't breathe. She hates women. She'll not know. So keep your mouth—"

And the rocker spoke a voice among its wooden racket and she knew someone was there. Amy blinked into the blinding idiot abstraction of a television screen beyond the etched silhouette of potted ferns.

"That you, my boys?" cried the old, blind woman in a trumpet of croupy welcome. "Is that you, my young friends?"

Hawk went across the floor on all fours, Amy could see his dark shape scuttling across the bleak, cracked linoleum like a dog, toward the rocking lump within its sagging, bulging wicker: shawed and embalmed with habit before the little zigzag glare of television screen. He was hissing and shushing her to silence as he went and now she whispered, too; delighted that he was there: him and Mister Vinnie, her young friends, and they had come to her for help again, to hide themselves again, and she was whispering like a child in a game, in a perfect ecstasy of complicity.

"Them po-lice after you agin—them devils! Pshaw now! Ain't that a caution! Won't they never leave you poor young boys alone! Pshaw! Not botherin' a livin' soul and them devils—"

"Please, Miz Ryder, hush! They're out there in the hallway— if they hear you whisperin'—"

"I will!" she panted. "I will! And if they come huntin' you here—you can hide yonder in the broom closet! I will!"

And she fell still, breathing like a small and broken harmonica and rocking to its tune, and they hunched behind her chair, among the fragrant, prehistoric forests of her ferns and rubber-plants and listened to Verge and Lowdy out yonder somewhere going through things, moving the iron feet of their beds and stomping through the deserted room. Miz Ryder's round face shone with happy mischief in the dim illumination of the TV set. Them young boys was a caution. That Herbert and his friend George and Mister Vinnie. She had never known Hawk as anyone but Herbert; he was always Herbert to her and his nice friend, George and Mister Vinnie. The nice young men who lived down the hall.

Then, as if a knob had suddenly been twisted by some listener's hand, voices were suddenly clear and sharp, outside Hawk's room, coming down the hallway, slowly and half-decided, tossing that indecision indolently back and forth between them like a baseball.

SHADOW OF MY BROTHER

"Shall we bust in and take a look around? She might—"
"I don't give a goddamn, Verge. You and Loy runnin' this whole show. I don't see no chance of him or the other one bein' there!"

Miz Ryder's fat hand flew out, silhouetted against the TV screen, gesturing like a queen granting asylum: her plump thumb stabbing toward the kitchen door. Hawk, with a furious energy, made more terrible by its total soundlessness, swept up the scarecrow Medic and bore him off in a chaos of dangling arms and trouser-legs, like a man with all bones broken, with Amy fleeting silently in his wake. Miz Ryder was alone. She leaned forward with an outcry of rocker and turned the TV music up good and loud. She felt the hall light fall upon her even as the door flung wide and banged its knob into the plaster till the dusty teacups on the knickknack shelf chattered like cold teeth.

"Turn that damn TV down, old woman!"

She turned her head, as if startled, her head bobbing and weaving in the gesture of the blind feeling for sensation, and fetched her white cane upright with a thump.

"Who's that?" she bleated, child-faced and guileless.

Lowdy walked over and snapped the dial down to silence again, and stood wide-legged before the blind woman's chair, the bullets in his sagging belt sparking and twinkling in the antic flicker of the TV screen.

"Where's the boy named Hawk that lives down the hall!"

"Who asks!" she cried out now, half-risen, her white cane fingering the air like the antenna of moth. "Who comes bustin' into a poor, blind old woman's rooms in the middle of the night—hollerin' and shoutin' like drunken niggers!"

"Come on, Verge, she don't know."

"Shut your mouth, Lowdy. Come on now, old woman! Where's he at?"

"What right!" she yelled, her lips wet with wrath. "By what right! Comin' stompin' and hollerin' in here like drunken . . . I've a mind to holler for the po-lice!"

"This is the po-lice. Feel that!"

He grabbed her goose-plump wrist and pressed his cold star in the flesh of her palm.

"So shut up," he continued. "Just shut up your hollerin' and set right still and you'll not get hurt. Where's the one called Hawk?"

"Hawk? Hawk? I don't know no such of a name! Hawk! Hain't ary one of my roomers named Hawk! Come bustin' in here! I keep a respectable rooming house! I don't know no Hawk!"

"Pretty cute," Verge said. "I reckon you see a damned sight more than you let on, old blind woman."

"What do you want from me?"

"Where's that boy named Hawk? You wouldn't be hidin' no-body in here would you now, cute old woman?"

"Hidin'? Hidin'! I don't know what any of this means! What do you want? There's two young men has the second-floor front! Hain't they there? Did you knock?"

"Yeah, we knocked. We done more'n knock. We taken a look round."

"Then they're out! That's all. Hawk? Hain't nary one of them give me that name! Hawk? There's Herbert. And the other one George. Then there's Mister Vinnie. Nice, decent young men. What're you po-lice devilin' 'em about now! Speedin' again! Lord, it's a caution!"

"Sure," said Verge. "Speedin', old woman. Sure."

Verge snapped the switch and strange old lamps with stained-glass shades bloomed like the blossoms of a myth among the filagree of fern fronds all among them.

"Take a look round her kitchen, Lowdy, while me and cute-talkin' old woman here has some more cute talk together."

"Ah, God!" she blathered suddenly, in a gush of tears like freshets from two stones. "Ah, dear God have mercy! To be blind and have men stormin' and hollerin' into a body's room in the dead of night! Ah, God!"

Verge, shamed and sheepish, pinched his nose in a quick gesture: some shabby, sentimental nerve of propriety touched in the split-instant of her outcry, for he was the kind of man who, behind the blunt, blue pistol muzzle of his eyes, would wince and grieve at a tawdry claptrap death scene in a bad movie. But the moment passed and his face was iced; more furious now that she had made him feel anything like that.

"Hain't no sign of no one out here, Verge," cried Lowdy from the kitchen and came back into the broken light of the parlor.

"Just don't think you're puttin' nothing over on me nor Lowdy, cute old woman!" Verge said hoarsely, his voice near breaking with his fury of knowing that she was somehow thwarting him, and not knowing just how; something in his voice gone a half-tone higher like a dynamo with a hot axle, and Amy and Hawk, hearing him from their rusty hide-out on the fire-escape, both shivered for fear of the blind woman's safety.

He smiled suddenly, as if with the inspiration of a child whose mind has stumbled suddenly upon a brilliant and cunning prank and swung his revolver up out of its scuffed, greasy holster and his big thumb clicked it to half-cock; knowing she'd hear it, knowing how scared it would make her.

"Hey, Lowdy, how about me puttin' a bullet through ol' singin' cowboy yonder in the TV? How about that, Lowdy?"

"Come on, Verge. He ain't here. We're wastin' time! Loy said keep huntin' all night till we come back with him."

Verge swung on him, his eyelids curled queer with a sort of sad mastery of wrath, the gun hanging in his big hand, bouncing like a toy.

"Don't be tellin' me what Loy said. Don't be tellin' me what's right, you mother! What's sense and what ain't. You're the dumb-assed bastard in this foul-up affair!—not me! You ignorant cracker! It wasn't me that stood by the whore's bedroom Saturday night and heard Purdy hollerin' in his sleep about the poor, little, piti-ful, pathetic nigger that got his black ass lynched! Just mind that, you mother!"

"Put up your gun, Lowdy," Verge murmured, almost wearily, leaning lazy against the doorjamb and rubbing his lip with his finger so the twitch of it wouldn't show.

Lowdy glared like he was half of a mind to gun Verge himself down. It was Daisy Ryder and the wind stirring the billowing white curtains and the statement of thunder that broke that notion.

"Nigger," whispered the blind woman, working her mouth and rocking to and fro with a paced and anguished rhythm, heedless of gun or Lowdy or Verge or world beyond her thoughts. "That nigger. Hah! That's what they're wanted for! For that lynchin'! Hah! I heared it on the eleven o'clock news tonight! Hah!"

The thunder prowled the night and big drops of warm rain broke suddenly against the rattling screen in the window.

"Them two scamps! Praise God! Lord, ifn' I thought it was true—I'd not charge 'em room rent for a year!"

She rose suddenly from her rocker, gripping the white cane like a shepherd's crook and brandishing it furiously in the electric air.

"Get out! Damn cops! Get out! Guns or no guns! If them two boys done that lynchin' I say, 'Praise God!' You hear! Get out! Nigger-lovin' cops!"

Lowdy moved toward the door and elbowed Verge out into the gaslit hallway. He turned once to stare stonily at the old, blind fool.

"Git on back to the car, Verge."

Verge went off, big-booted and whistling, into the echoing hallway. Lowdy kept on a while, just staring.

"You ain't cute after all, blind, old woman. You just plain fuckin' dumb."

He disappeared and the thunder rolled like iron balls bouncing across an attic floor and Daisy Ryder, frothy with wrath, still flailed the air with her stick, addressing her outrage to the empty air which he had left behind.

"Devils!"

And the white stick struck a crack-feathered coffee cup from the table and sent its shards spinning and tinkling about the floor.

"Come bustin' in here! Devils! And poor me blind and help-less as a mole!"

And slashed a fern frond with her cane as if it were one of them and her cane a saber. And then with a great sigh sank, boneless as a pillow, in the basket of her chair and stomped her cane hard upon the fury in final utterance of her outrage.

"She thinks it was me and George," Hawk whispered as they crouched upon the rusted fire escape, sheltered by the high boughs of a tree, and watched the tumult of lightning slash white sheets beyond the silhouetted, slum buildings that tow-ered round Morning Alley. "Amy, you heard her. She thinks it was us! Thinks they was after us for the lynching! Amy, you heard a joke to beat that?"

"Don't, Hawk. It don't matter. They went. It's a blessing of God she thought that, maybe. Reckon we can go back in now," she said softly. "It's comin' up to rain."

"Not yet," he said. "Not yet. She'll tap on the sill when it's safe. She hears like a cricket. She'll know when they've gone."

The thunder brawled and bumbled its reverberations among the night shapes and suddenly in a puff of breeze they smelled the chyme-sweet green of country grass, like the breath of cows: it came among them suddenly, lifted from somnolent meadows far away and then set down solid among them by the wind before the storm: the free, sweet breath of countryside shoul-dering away the sad and greasy smell of those poor streets. Hawk lifted his eyes: defendant to the judgment of the moon, across which crawled now the dark, swelling tatters of thunder-head.

"Anyhow," he said. "You convinced now. Huh? I don't need to sell you anymore on it—do I? How bad they're after you? After me? After anyone that knows a whisper of the truth? Do I?"

"No."

"Well, that's good, at least. You heard them with your own ears."

"I knew," she sighed. "Before. I just couldn't let myself know out loud for a while. I knew—in the yard—in the orchard—when I heard Daddy."

"Then the thing now is to get you out of town."

"Yes. I know that."

"Where? You know where?"

"No," she said. "I've got this aunt lives up in the state beyond Goshen."

"That ain't far enough. Not near far enough. It ain't north enough to be safe, Amy. Think of somewheres else. You got kin anywhere's else?"

"Nowheres," she said. "Aunt Nelly. That's where. She just plain adores me and she'd never tell Daddy. He'd never guess."

"His sister?"

"Mmm."

"Your daddy's sister?"

"Yes. I said, yes."

"Christ, Amy! You sure?"

"Sure, Hawk. She's—good. My God, she's so good that when I was little and Mama took me to see her once I loved her so much I wished she was Mama and I lived there. I never forgot."

"How'll you get there?"

"Walk," she said. "Walk."

"With every road out of town watched? Fat chance."

"I'll walk the fields and meadows. I'll hide when I see car-lights—keep back from the roads—hide in bushes. I'll know how."

"But walking out that front door in a while. Walking up Morning Alley."

"I'll get there. Pray, maybe. You pray, too."

"Praying won't hide you from the flashlights of them two guns."

"Hah!" he cried and smacked his palm with his flat, square fist. "I know how! It's a better than even chance, Amy!"

"How?"

"Dress you like a boy. You're small. One of Vinnie's old jackets. His pants. You could likely thumb out of town in one of them produce trailer trucks. They don't start north till nigh dawn."

"Yes. I could."

"I'd have to learn you how to walk!" he smiled critically. "Christ, you walk so damn girl-easy-so damned hippy. Christ, Amy, you think you could walk right?"

"Hawk, I reckon I could grow wings and fly like a bird if I willed it hard enough—if it was the only way."

"It's the only way," he said, and the rain fell suddenly in deafening suddenness upon them. The lightning bloomed suddenly like a false, garish day and Hawk saw Amy's eyes wide with shock and her hand to her mouth, afraid he would say anything, or that she would cry out, for the blind woman was in the sill. Her cane rapped three hollow drums upon the rotting sill and she beckoned to them to come in, that the hunters had gone. Miz Ryder stood back from the window, her cane planted square between her swollen shoes. Amy had her shoes in her hand, and stole breathless and stiff in long tiptoes toward the green light of the blind woman's parlor, and stood for a moment looking back, till Hawk and the man in his arms were safely in.

"My lads!" cried Miz Ryder, shouting above the wind, above the jumping thunder. "My boys! If I'd ever have knowed! If I'd ever have guessed! I'm proud this night to have you 'neath my roof! Boys, I don't reckon I was even so proud when my own dear Clyde was here—may the Lord forgive his poor, cursed soul! George? Herbert? Come in, my boys! Come in—and tell me every word of it! Was there guns? Was there torches? Did you tie the black bastard tight to a good fat lighter pine with sharp barbed-wire! Hah! Tell me it all! Don't spare me, my lads! Don't keep a jot nor tittle of it from me! I love it! God, how I love it! Did you burn him?"

Hawk moved out into the jungled, hideous chamber of ferns, stumbling now, silent, toward the door, toward the hallway, while she shuffled, tapping, tapping, relentless, at his heels, squawling at him for the tale of it, of how he had done it, until the doubt like a hammer on his brain began again, the thinking that maybe in some queer twist of things, in the logic of his humanity and its blooded responsibility, that she was right. That he was. That he had. That they all had.

"You all right?" he said to Amy, at last.

"Yes."

"You sure? Can you make it?"

"I—Yes."

He rummaged in a closet, in a drawer, fetched up the scarecrow pants and shirt and the stained, pinched fedora with an old parlay stub stuck still in the frayed, disreputable band. The Medic lay straight like a man newly dead on his cot, his hands arranged so on the rise and fall of his chest.

"Get out of them clothes. Hurry."

She peeled out of her wet coat and pulled the wet dress over her head; stood looking at him then, teeth chattering in a sudden chill, her arms folded over her brassiered breasts and her stomach sucking in and out in the hiccup of her breath. He threw her the clothes. She stared at them dumbly for a spell and then began dressing, thinking: That's funny. Hawk is the second man ever saw me without nothing more on than that. George had been the first.

And now remembering. How it had been the first time. It was the day of a picnic—just the two of them—and they had found a spot by the river, under a vast, high willow tree and miles from any farmhouse, far down from the river road. Amy brought the lunch: things she had spent the evening before fixing: fried chicken and deviled eggs and buttermilk cornbread and two peach cobblers.

"Someday," she observed gravely as she laid things about on the tablecloth she had spread on the grass. "Someday I'll be setting table like this. In our own house."

"I can see you doing that," he said. "In our own kitchen."

"No," she said. "We'll be much fancier than that—we'll eat in our dining room."

He went over and kissed her lightly on the neck.

"I'm starved," he said.

"Me, too."

And they began to eat in a grave and furious energy, their appetites spurred by the softness of the spring day and their own emotions toward each other.

"Mother's been after me again," she said. "I hate to bring up an unpleasantness on a day like this—in a place like this. But it's on my mind!"

"About me," he said.

She nodded.

"In a way," she said. "Yes. I guess it's about you. George, she thinks it's awful that you room with Hawk."

"Did you explain to her?" he said, flushing. "Hawk is an Army buddy. Hawk is my friend. We've been through things together."

"I explained that," she said.

"Do you understand? That's more important."

"You know I do, George. I've always understood. I think Hawk is a fine person, really. Of course, I'm sorry he has this—this habit—this sickness. But I don't condemn him."

"Does your mother think that I use the stuff, too?" he asked.

"I don't know," she said. "No. I don't think so. I guess maybe. Oh, George, Mother wouldn't approve of anybody I went out seriously with. You know how she is."

"Yes. I guess that's some consolation. It's nothing personal."

"I'll tell you what is personal though," she said gently. "Very personal, George. It's personal what I feel about you. Very, very personal."

He smiled at her through a rueful expression.

"Ah, Amy."

And he went to her, kneeling in the grass beside her and holding her in his arms, kissing her hard on the mouth. After a breathless spell he pulled away and stared into her eyes, lightly glazed with passion and wide with a small and sudden fright.

"Does it scare you?" he said.

She nodded, hard and fast, three times.

"You want to know something," he said. "It scares me, too. It scares the living hell out of me. And I'm the brave Army boy."

"The brave Army boy," she laughed lightly.

"It scares me, Amy," he said. "Because I don't ever want to do anything to hurt you."

She swallowed hard and looked at him boldly.

"Sometimes," she said. "When boys are scared about things— well, girls have to be bold about them."

He blushed and lowered his gaze to her hands, working together nervously in her lap.

"No, look at me, George," she said, lifting a hand to his face and drawing it round to her sight.

"Listen," she said. "I know what you mean about—hurting me. George, sometimes people want to be hurt. A little."

"I don't understand," he said, honestly, and shook his head.

"About us," she said. "The only thing I wouldn't want is for anything we did together to be cheapened. Oh, I know. Nothing we could ever do together would be—*could* be cheap. What I'm trying to say is I don't want us fumbling around in a car somewhere or lying about our names in a motel. Oh, I can't explain it somehow. Hope you understand what I'm trying to explain, honey."

"Yes, I think I do."

"What I'm really trying to say is—well, I think you want me in that way."

"Yes," he said in an agony of blushing.

"And I know I want you in that way," she said. "I guess it doesn't matter too much that I don't know really what it is I want. I mean, I know, but I've never known it. Oh, God, I'm not telling you right. George, damn it, I'm a virgin. That's all. Somehow it's embarrassing to have to say a thing like that. I mean, in this day and age it's kind of backward for a girl to be a thing like that."

"Amy!"

"You don't mind it?" she said. "You know what it means. I

probably wouldn't be any good at it. Not at first. You'd have to
teach me. Wouldn't you? Well, yes. You don't even have to
answer. Maybe I'd catch on quick. Oh, God, I think we're talking
about it too much. Why do things have to be so—so—"

He kissed her again then and then pulled away, awed by her
boldness, awed by the largeness of his love for her.

"It's good to talk things over," he said. "I think that's a very
useful thing."

And he was thankful for talk that would postpone a thing of
such fire and beauty that awed him so.

"This picnic was my idea, you know," she said suddenly, even
more boldly. "So don't start feeling guilty that you lured me out
to this lonely spot to take advantage of me. If there was any
luring done, George Purdy, it was Amy Wilson that did it.
George, in some ways I don't think you're understanding what
it is I'm driving at."

"What?" he said stupidly, helplessly. "I mean—well, I think
I know."

"I want you to have what you want," she said softly. "And I
think what you want is for us—for me too. Oh," she said. "I
want it to be right and beautiful. I want it to be a more-than-
just-once thing. I want us to keep on doing it together and I
want it to get more beautiful each time. Maybe that's not how
it is, though. Can it be like that, George?"

"I don't know," he said honestly. "I've never—done that with
someone I was in love with."

"Haven't you, honey?" she said, her face glorious with en-
chantment. "Well, gee, that sort of makes you a virgin, too, in
a way. I mean, if the other times were just with girls. Any girls."

"I guess it does," he said. "I guess I am, Amy."

"I guess we're both pretty young and naïve," she said. "And
I know there are people—good and smart and kind people—
who would say we ought to wait. But, George, the way the world
is! Sometimes you can wait things away until they're dust. Dust!
I look at you sometimes and I love you so much and I feel this
absolute pang in my insides—this absolute pang, George, of

fear that something might happen—Mother or something—
that I'd never see you again. And that's when I really want you
the most."

She swallowed and stared hard at his chin.

"Like now," she said in a very small voice.

"Ah, Amy. My love. My love."

"I guess," she said, closing her eyes, and unbuttoning the top
button of her dress. "When boys are scared, then girls have to
be bold."

It triggered everything then; she was in his arms and with a
fury of infinite gentleness they were fumbling and undoing,
unfastening and loosening one another's clothing and then rose
and flung the garments from themselves till they lay about on
the grass like huge petaled flowers, and they were naked in a
moment and he was caressing her: she was moist clear to her
knees with excitement for him and all open and warm to him
when he went inside her. And she was more astonished than
he that even though it was the first time for her, there was no
pain except the ineffable pain of passion itself; she was as full
of want and need of him as if they had been married for a long
while. And now, with Hawk, remembering, it seemed to her,
indeed, that they had been.

Amy pulled the shirt tails up and tucked them in, her fingers
awkward at this man-dressing; something in her flesh cringing
at it, as if somehow, without skirt and hose and proper woman's
clothes she was subtly defenseless in a world of men. Amy pulled
the felt hat on over her bunched-up hair and turned to Hawk,
forlorn-eyed and hopeful. He groaned. She looked, in that
grotesque and pitiable disguise, more emphatically female than
she had in skirt and blouse. Beneath the cheap, sketched outline
of a man's remnant sale sports coat and the threadbare, creased
pants, the round line of loin and hip and breast-swell spoke her
lie.

"I feel silly," she said irrelevantly. "I look like a boy, Hawk?
Do I?"

He stared at her gloomily. With luck she would pass, in the

trickery of street lamp and pass in the indefinite illumination
of beer-joint neon; the night might help her keep her secret.

"Walk," he said, arms folded, staring critically. "Let me see
how you walk."

She minced to the door and back again, waiting then like a
child before a dancing master.

"Christ, no!" he said. "Oh, good Christ, no! Not that way!
Jesus no! Keep your—your hips—Go on. Walk again. And keep
your hips—you know! Don't—*swing* nothing, for Christ's sake!"

"I wasn't swinging anything," she said, a little piqued.
"Here—like this?"

"Oh, God, I reckon. I reckon that's the closest you'd ever
come to it if I was to teach you all night, and we ain't got all
night!"

He walked to her from behind and smacked her sharply on
the rump.

"Keep them—keep that—from swingin'! Stop swinging your
ass, goddamn it all!"

She had tears in her eyes then but he scattered them onto
her cheeks when he grabbed her shoulders.

"Sure," she said. "I'm all right, Hawk. I understand."

"I reckon you going to make it, Amy," he said, smiling at her.
"Anybody had all of God's holy luck you had tonight—nothing
could happen now. It could, but it sure won't. Not with all the
luck you've had. Looky there!"

He motioned to her suitcase, still standing at the edge of the
puddle of rain by the window. Even then, for an instant, she
did not grasp.

"See what I mean?" he said, fetching an automatic pistol out
of one of his shoes in the black clothes closet. "All the time. It
was standing right there."

"Hawk, you reckon they. . . ?"

" 'Course they didn't. If they'd have seen it—do you reckon
they'd have left without tearin' this house down shingle by shingle till they found you! The stars is with you tonight, Amy! All
the time we was hidin'! All the while they was in here pokin'

around for game as picayune as me and Vinnie—that there
suitcase was settin' right yonder on the floor—plain as a tomb-
stone with your name cut right in it. And they never noticed.
Now hurry."

"Hawk, my suitcase."

"With a suitcase they'd look at you closer!"

"Hawk, all my things!"

"There's other *things!*"

He pressed close to the door, listening for the old woman,
and heard nothing and inched the door open.

"She out there?"

"No. No. It's clear. Come on. Quick. Quick."

She ran like a child in his quick steps down stairs and when
they came to the door she stole ahead of him onto the threshold
and stood looking up the—glistening, silent stones. The storm
was gone. The winds had driven the rains away, and now the
glum street shone with a queer innocence after its washing; the
mean, narrow corridor which had looked punished and old like
the pinched, cunning face of a slum child, was now graced with
its instant of newness. The stars had come out in hot, southern
brilliance and little winds still whirled wandering down Morning
Alley, like the last squads of the storm's legions, shivering the
mirroring puddles into ruffles, scattering the light.

"It's clear," he whispered sharply.

He shoved her elbow with a nervous little jolt and they began
walking, with no look to either side of them. "Keep walking
along just like you doing, baby. You doing fine, baby. Just walk.
And keep thinking how—like I said. Don't swing! Hear? Just
walk like we was on our ways nowhere special—two men on
their way home somewheres maybe. All right?"

"All right," she whispered sharply, earnestly, setting her
whole flesh hard to the task of it.

She felt numbed with calm outside, but her whole soul roiled
with excitement within at what had become a sort of solemn
and awesome game.

"We're doing good. We're doing good," he said thinly from

the edge of his mouth, keeping his eyes hard on the wedge of lighted stone beneath the street lamp's gas flame at the mouth of Morning Alley.

"Goin' good," he whispered. "Just a ways now. Just a ways. You know where you're goin' now do you?"

"Yes. Yes, I know where."

"Cross Mole Street to the tracks—the freight yard—"

"Yes."

"The highway's up above the tracks," he said. "Up yonder on the side of the hill."

"No highway. I keep away from the highway. I stick to the meadows."

"Right! Now you're cooking. No matter what—keep off the roads—they might be patrolling it. Your daddy knows you're runnin' somewhere. Jesus! Jesus, will you try to walk right! I can feel your thigh bumping mine, you goddamn fool girl. Can't you learn it like I said?"

"Yes! I'm sorry. Yes!"

She whimpered that and stiffened, walking puppet-legged, her buttocks aching from the holding in so tight and remembered about first walking to the teacher's desk in first grade with all the boys' eyes upon her that she had loathed in the playground swings that last tomboy summer before school; and the other girls staring at her in her black ribbed stockings and Butterick-pattern blue-flower dress that Gladys had scissored out and stitched up on her Singer, and them thinking she was poor and she wasn't; her daddy was richer than any of theirs, smarter than any of theirs, only he lived plain, he lived humble. Poor Daddy, she thought, remembering him and the years that were goodbye now, the rare, sweet times upon his lap, the moments when she had searched his face and found something warm there that she could never remember, never summon back when he was gone. Daddy, she thought, and remembered the time she had been let come in the parlor when his company was there and she hadn't been able to say a word because it was the Governor and he had a gold tooth and smelled like nigger

gin and had a purry, soft, deep voice like the bee's song in a
hive and Daddy had been mad because she couldn't curtsey or
remember her company speech she was so scared. One Christmas he had kissed her on the nose and she had been so excited
she had gone off to the bathroom and cried and been sick to
her stomach yearning so that he would love her after all. Daddy,
she thought and remembered how she had used to wonder how
he ever got that power with Governors and State Senators and
all and them living so humble and seeming so poor and the
girls in school staring at her funny dress from the patterns in
Delineator and Gladys, Mommy, crying alone in the dark and
drinking that stuff whenever Daddy was away with his generals
and Senators and gold-toothed governors and all. And one
spring day in a rush of loathing, admiration, and shame all a-
mingling she had known the why, grasped the how: learned his
secret in sickening revelation. She had been sunning herself up
in the orchard, dozing on a quilt in the new grass, and Loy and
a Great Man were sitting down on the back porch, with drinks,
under the mango tree; speaking in voices hushed and hoarse
as the whisper of knives, and she had listened, out of their sight,
catching a word every here and then: Loy talking, low and hard,
and the other man: the god, making knotted, little sounds of
resistance that were not somehow words at all, and she had laid
there hearing, stiff in a gathering dread. Loy's voice had got
louder at something the other had whined and he was saying:
"But you don't. You just don't. Can't you see that? The sooner
you get that notion through your head the better off you're
gonna be. Maybe you used to, but you don't anymore. I do. Me.
I do. Understand? And that don't just go for the state capital—
that means D.C., too. Understand? Used-to-be ain't Now, and
the sooner you boys get that understood the better for you."
And the god's bumbling protest bubbled and broke like a
woman's sob, bleating it, something: a kind of apostrophe ad-
dressed more, by the sound of it, to the scudding summer clouds
than to Daddy, and yet Daddy answering quick: "How? I be
glad to tell you how. Sure. You ought to know. But since you

don't seem to—I'll oblige. How? I saved it up. Because nobody
was watching. And I saved it up. Because when you live Humble
and think Big—won't be anybody watching you. Like me. That's
why I still keep my goddamned store out front yonder—and
my orchard—that beat-up old pickup truck. That's why I dress
my women plain and me likewise. Plain. Folks trust a plain man
like me, Judge. They don't have to always be keeping their eye
on a plain man like me, Judge. Just like that hunchback, crippled Mister R. J. Tolley peddling newspapers all those years in
his dumpy little stand by the Chickasaw courthouse. Saved his
pennies—bought this—bought that—listened for tips and bought
some more. Big men talk loose around a man like that—drop
tips on big things. Tips, Judge. Buy this. Sell that. Buy some
more of the other. And when the pennies got to be dollars, it
was no time till the dollars got to be gilt-edged shares. And directly the shares got to be people. And they were the Right people. And it wasn't no time at all till he owned the news that went
into it. You see, nobody had been watching. Live Humble and
think Big, Judge, and folks'll leave you be to run your business
and theirs, too, and kiss your hand for it. It's American, ain't it?
Why, sure it is! Live like that, Judge, and a man wouldn't be
noticed snitching the satin cushion from off of God Almighty's
throne!" And heard the pirate honeybees go droning golden
dust-trails through the blossomed air for an instant's silence
after he had done and then that awful sound that she had never
heard before: a man's clotted, broken weeping; twice-terrible
because it was the same voice that she had heard so often before
on the P.A. system on the state capital steps and on the radio:
the voice of the face who hung framed and sacrosanct in all the
big, good places: school and courthouse hall and bank lobby
and once in high-school assembly on a day for dead heroes.
Daddy, she thought, grieving, because she was leaving him
alone to such a loneliness: a god who must die someday alone
on the stone, plundered pinnacle of all his thankless power.

　　Hawk beside her, and they did not slow when they came to
the alley's rise, but moved on out into the sullen light of the

corner lamp and on, Hawk's hand perking her elbow a little when her feet in faintness faltered in an instant's Gethsemane, and then sturdily walked on. No one was around anywhere; nor any car light. There were only the stars. And the dull lights of the freight depot shone like dirty glass beads strung in the ruddy mist of steam and smoke about the freight engines panting among themselves like chained dogs. The street sign under the gas lamp on the pole: Mole St. Molest. Molest. No, she thought, the worst of it was over and warmth for Hawk flowed through her like love, Hawk who had helped her to the frontier here of all her woman's life to be. She turned suddenly facing him and reached her small hands up and pulled down his mouth to be kissed in thanks, for nothing less would have served.

"Christ, that was smart! Jesus, if anyone had of seen that now!"

"I'm sorry, Hawk."

She dangled there: travesty of woman in the Medic's clothes.

"I didn't think, Hawk."

"Well, think. Because you've got to think. Every minute of it. From here on out, Amy. Every damned minute of it!"

"I just wanted to—Hawk, I had to thank you! Because you never had to do any of this—any of it, Hawk! You didn't have to be mixed up in it from the very first—for his sake—or mine either!"

He stared at her a moment, blushed, and turned away and spat, ridding his mouth of that taste of thanks which might make him ask himself that: Why he had done it, any of it.

"Now go on," he said gruffly. "Go on. Walk up the gravel berm yonder to the tracks. Cross over. Into that meadow. Below the state highway. Goshen is north. Where I'm pointing. That's north."

"I know north," she said, smiling a little.

She felt an itching pleasure that her womanness, tombed up in those awful tobacco-smelling man's clothes, had touched him so.

"Keep off the highway," he said, looking off north, and spitting again. "Mind now. Walk the meadows. Sleep in barns. Mind yourself now."

"I'll mind myself," she said softly, gravely old and wise-seeing. "It's yourself for you to take care of now, Hawk. Don't worry a bit about me, Hawk."

"Goodbye," he said and turned away.

And she was gone and he heard her scramble up the cinders and cross the steel ribbons to the meadow. He stood for a good spell till her sound was gone. And now, oddly, alone; himself alone to fear for, he was fearful more than then: with all her needing to sustain him. And she, too, fearful, watched; crouched in the high, wet timothy, determined not to go until her eyes had seen him safely back, her whole body tensed to his safe going to his door. By the fan of light upon the polished bricks of Mole Street, by the alley's mouth, he stopped and looked both ways, dreadful in that motion of contrived casualness, and then turned and ran away from the alley. Amy could see clear to the rooming house and the windows shining small, like a furnace door, above the murky light above the threshold, and beyond that to the neon, like a twitching golden snake, above the rib-joint; beyond that, Morning Alley's deeps were aqua-tint; dark clusters, speculations of shadow, and the indistinguishable flickerings of the nameless commerce of the nightfolk. She gasped when suddenly she saw Lowdy and Verge's police-car standing empty, purring by the roominghouse threshold. She somehow knew they were inside, upstairs, again in the room. They would be going through her suitcase now, thwarted and furious; they would be merciless in their inquisition of the puzzled and terrified blind woman.

Yes, it is time to be going, Amy thought now, rising. Yes, there is nothing more here now.

And, heedless of whether anyone saw her or not, she stood up in the wet, waist-high timothy of the meadow and walked away into the pale flutter of the morning star.

ISAIAH

At the first, the worst of it was that Luke did not need Nelly at all: that almost transluscent shell of a boy who came on the train that evening. The worst of it was her thinking that her coming back there, sore-wombed from the child's death, had been a coming back to a need. And there was no need. Because he was beyond needing anything but the Sleep that had slighted him in the dirty green gas cloud at Argonne Forest. Not her. Not even his father Toby. He lived nearly two months. Sometimes Nelly would go down to the chair by Toby's shack where Luke sat mornings, getting a little sun, and sit in the grass by his feet.

"Soon!" she would whisper with a dreadful gaiety. "Soon you'll be strong and well as ever, Luke! And you'll be up in the room again *painting*!"

The look he gave her, when his face turned, neither agreed nor disagreed. Sometimes he nodded when she said that, sometimes he merely looked down at her and gave no sign that he had even heard, that he had ever known her, at all. He smiled sometimes, but it would be at nothing she had said, and that would strike a little sharper pain in her: to think what awful joke his spirit told itself, too terrible for her sharing. He was as

thin as any human being she had ever seen: thin beyond the
mere dissipation of flesh upon its bone; thin in a way which
made it seem sometimes, when she came upon him with the
sun behind him, that his substance had gone to such a frail
integument that she could see light gleam through it from the
sun beyond.

Toby witnessed, with what might to some have seemed sto-
icism but which, to those who knew his measure, would be the
dumb, desperate tumult of a man busy with the business of
keeping feelings ordered within himself—it was not emotionless, perhaps not even heroic; it was simply that outer quietude
which, in some men, is the measure of the fury of the last-ditch
grief within them.

Loy watched Luke, too, through that summer's dying, and
said nothing; while Isaiah watched Loy, with the glister of savage watchfulness in his eyes: the two men passing together stiffly
in the house on elegant, infuriated tiptoe, like bristled pit-dogs
gathering their blood for the last bite and grapple in the saw-
dust.

She, watching Luke's face, searching his grave and still curious smile, tried with a timid, dreadful sympathy to fancy what
pictures those inturned eyes saw so she might share his grief;
hearing, even as she searched him, the pitiless effort of breath
in his lung: it was war Luke watched and it was men and it was
a thing that had broken his heart because he had learned that
it was endless and beginningless and frontiered only by the
human spirit; it was war in his mind, and it was war in places
with the falseface of peace where war had no right to be. His
face was like a meadow: it would, at some thought's passage
over it, darken, and then, in a spell, grow sunny again, and
presently be shadowed again. Luke was not mad; he was rather
driven inward to an unspeakable sanity: seeing them all with an
agony of mercy: doomed and hopeless before human loveless-
ness. Sometimes while she watched him his sunk eyes would
swiftly turn to her and focus and see her and come back: "Nelly?
Listen, Nelly!"

"Sit still, Luke. Whatever it is you want, I'll get it. Don't try to get up. You know what Doctor Chandler said! Rest, Luke!"

"Yes, but, Nelly, you don't understand! Someone's got to *help* them!"

"I know, Luke. Everything's going to be all right."

"No, damn it! It ain't! You don't understand me, Nelly! Somebody has got to *help* them!"

And he would go struggling up in the cane chair then, his face pale with worry and his dark eyes burning, while the breath fought thinly in his lung like a bee in a stoneware jug. "Listen, Nelly. There's not a great deal of time left, Nelly, and it's *so* important! Somebody has got to *help* them! Jesus, you can't *see*!"

"Tell me, Luke. Then tell me what my eyes can't see," she would say gentlingly and he would settle back slowly, almost drifting downward into the sagging wicker with the fragile insubstance of the sticks and skin that was left of him, and drag her hand into his and crush it for an instant in the grip of his vision.

"Somebody has got to help them!"

"Who, Luke? Help who?" she whispered.

He looked at her and she searched his face, dark now, and watched his pupils widening and pinpointing and widening again as his perspectives shuttled back and forth between his realities and the myth of her presence; he flung her hand away and scowled into the markless summer sky. "You're no help. Get away from me. Jesus, *you* don't understand."

"Luke, I *want* to understand."

"No one wants to understand. Just—just get away from me. I can get along. Go on up to the house."

But he let her stay just the same; let her stay there at his feet, among the old dandelions of their childhood, while Kingdom County neighbors buggying past would see her there, at his feet, and snicker upon this confirmation of the shameless rumor, and wonder what it was that held her there now, what she could see in him now who wasn't good for anything anymore, who wasn't set even to be alive more than a few weeks more. But he let her stay, while his eyes doomed in again upon themselves, upon his thoughts and she would search his face again, knowing that what she saw there was not madness but some specific distillation of human sanity and wanting, almost selfishly, to have it from him. Them. Who? He would not say. Not until the very August of his death and he had gotten Isaiah and Toby to carry him up the ladder to his old cot in the barn room, and that was when. Before the last week, when he had been too weak to move from the bed, he had wandered that room like some caged and inconsolable captive: she would come up the ladder and see him sitting on his chair staring at the caked brushes in his old paint cans as if in some furious, final effort at vital recollection. When she came into the stable and stood with her hand on the ladder before her strong arms swooped her up to the open trap door she would sometimes hear his grievous, slow tread upon the old floor above her, and the hard flutter of his rasping breath was like a sob of anger over something he must leave, soon and irrevocably, undone. In that last month Toby slept on an old quilt beside the cot. Luke wanted no such womanish solicitudes, but Toby was immovable. In the afternoons Isaiah came, late, wanting perhaps a kindness of early evening light upon his face that would not illuminate something there that he would not wish Luke to see: these encounters of the two men were painful and almost wordless. Nelly spent the mornings.

"You'll be well again by autumn!" she would cry, bringing him a cold custard she had made the night before. "Up and well again by the time the leaves turn, Luke!"

"What?" he would whisper, turning to her. "Oh, yes. Yes, I know I will. Don't worry about me, Nelly."

The hot wind blew from the open window. The sun-bathed countryside racketed monotonously with the grasshopper voice of its life. Everything protested a dying. Luke stirred, scowling toward the window, toward the quaking sunlight in the leaves of the plane tree.

"They're killing each other," he said softly.

"Luke," she said gently. "Don't excite yourself."

"They're killing each other, Nelly. And somebody has got to help them. I thought you'd understand. Nelly, I thought if anyone on earth could understand it would be you, Nelly."

This was in the last week he was able to sit up in the chair. His jade-pale knuckles whitened on the rubbed ends of the chair arms. His dark eyes blazed with his final anguished energy.

"Somebody has got to help them, Nelly," he whispered like a lash.

"Who, Luke dear?"

"All the Loys," he said. "Jesus, I thought when I came back and told you that you'd understand. You, Nelly. You always understood! Nelly, they're killing each other."

"Luke. Luke, who?" she whispered again with puzzled gentleness.

"The Loys! Can't you *understand*. Jesus, Nelly! Can't you *try*?"

"No," she lied softly, in the first terror of understanding.

"Listen," he gasped presently. "Ever since that night—that Christmas night in this very room, Nelly—I *knew*! I went running out of here that night—down the ladder—scared as a rabbit. I ran, Nelly. But I knew that it was more than just running from him. I knew I had to run out yonder in the world and find out the Why of how he was and how I was and why the world was what it was and why it had made us what it did!"

"No one—least of all me," she said, "blamed you for running that night, Luke."

"Yes. Yes. Be still. That doesn't matter. Be still and let me tell you. I know that. That doesn't matter. He could have killed me then and maybe it would have been better. Because maybe it is better to be dead than to know what I know now. Because it wasn't long," he continued, with wandering, wild eyes. "It wasn't long before I saw—before I knew—that some of him was everywhere—that some of him was everyone! The Loys are everywhere! Loy killing and Loy killed! Do you get me, Nelly? They were all Loy! See? The ones who pulled the trigger—Loy! And the ones who took the bullets—Loy! All Loy! So I thought—I thought: What can I do about a thing like that?—and I went crazy for a little while wondering—kept walking on slow through that woods and the little hail and kept shooting and shooting the Loys and trying to keep from laughing because I knew it wasn't doing any good, knew it wouldn't stop anything, and presently a tree was blown away like a big hand plucked it up and I opened my eyes and I was lying by the edge of a puddle of water with the sky in it, Nelly, and I looked at the man in the puddle staring back from my face and wearing my tin hat and his hate and horror in my eyes and that was Loy, too! Me! And I just lay there in the leaves and blood and began grabbing up little chunks of dirt and throwing it in the puddle so's the face couldn't see me and so's I couldn't see the Loy that was me. I lay there and heard them shouting 'gas' and watched the green cloud come and never cared at all. Nelly, I could easier got up and bayoneted that creeping green cloud than I could have gone on shooting that ghost of hate that was everywhere."

Subsiding then, shuddering, his hollow eyes resumed their vacant regard of the meadow; gold in the window and beyond, where only the ant soldiered down the jungle of his grass, and the bass blue fly thundered sunward, dazzling in his jets of shimmering light. A week later she would hold him in her arms, among the drenched, tortured sheets of his cot, while Isaiah stood by the window with his father's old Confederate scripture in his hand and Toby crouched, soundless, by Luke's pillow making the room dreadful with that soundlessness. Her holding Luke there at the last and thinking how right it was, at the last, that it should be so: them together, knitted together in a fatal parody of the physical embrace conjured upon their lives by the merciless myths of their people. Like all men, their ghostly testaments notwithstanding, he died hard and he died afraid. His eyes, in that last hour, were fingers tugging at the fabric of light which, at last, failing, tore in their grasp; though even then in the penumbra in which those three last faces came ringing round his mind, in that illumination whose rays traitored his wits at the last, he saw now as if in a black mirror, things and

Time and them with a dazzling and fantastic vividness; stiffening now with a last fevered alertness in Nelly's arms, his whole flesh suddenly possessed with a furious and final energy, he squeezed her hand, drowning, and his look flashed through his dark eyes' fading and their fear. "Nelly?"

"Yes, Luke my dear."

"Nelly, now listen! You got to watch out for him the best you know how! Nelly, are you there?"

"Yes. Yes."

"Nelly? You got to watch out for *him*! For *Loy*, Nelly!"

Her knuckles creaked in his wild grip and he swallowed then and she heard him mustering breath in his breast.

"Jesus, it's Loy hurting Loy—Loy killing Loy—what I mean, Nelly! Papa? Papa? Mister Wilson! Are you there? Listen now—listen, you got to *see*! Loy? Loy, have mercy on yourself! Man! Man, you still got *time*!"

Upon the failure of that breath's desperate summit, his mouth opened still with astonishment at something he felt broken softly like a snapped stem inside his chest, his lips, rounded to that moment's ultimate consternation, and she, clasping his face to hers with wild, strong fingers, pressed her mouth hard against his mouth confounding with a kiss, as though in the only woman reflex of life-giving love that her anguished senses could extemporize she would beat death. But he was gone. And then suddenly it got so much later. It was so much darker. Too late to save. Too dark to see. And he was gone. And the gentle hands upon her shoulders were too strong in their restraint.

Nelly sat in the buggy with veiled, bowed face while Toby and Isaiah, struggling and straining with the ropes like fishermen at nets in a dark brawl of oceans, lowered the long box into the grave. Afterwards, Toby stood staring at the folded banner in his hands as if he were wondering, for an awkward moment, what his hands should now do with it. Isaiah read some words from the Bible. He fetched two spades from the buckboard and

together he and Toby began filling the grave again. When the
last of the earth was heaped and rounded, Nelly descended
from the buggy with a flag smaller than the other was and stuck
it like a flower at the long mound's head. For a spell the three
stood looking at this bright, muslin emblem, puny on its candy
stick, rising and standing to the summer wind as if intimating
an intent within itself, huge with an honor disproportionate to
its littleness, insurgent to any dissent, positive as a whipping
tongue of flame. Isaiah helped Nelly back into the buggy and
climbed up beside her. Toby dark, bowed, big-hatted swung
up into the buckboard seat. Yet, a spell more, the three were
motionless, listening, as if struggling to remember something:
as if in danger of going away without something; as though
some precious intangible might yet be salvaged from the ruined
tangible which had, a moment before, involved them in its
dreadful necessities. Then the whips snapped on the sweating
horse-rumps. The wagon, dry-axled, groaned like wood speaking a grief which flesh had found unutterable. In a moment
they were gone, down the road, under the hill.

Later some children who had come there to play in the cemetery that summer, stared, wordless and uneasy, at this new
mound, rebellious in its earth-torn newness, among the older,
adjusted shapes beneath the rounded grass: nothing moved
there except the vivid, tiny flag: and this solitary, focused activ-
ity seemed to express some spirit of that earth and its recent
rearrangements—some woken and wrathful thing in that previ-
ous tranquility—the soft grass and the old flat stones speaking
their soundless legends out upon the light now seemed dis-
turbed, as if some animate anger had suddenly possessed these
inanimate things: Antietam, 1862, Fredericksburg, 1862, once
loved, once loving; numerals and names of men whose memory
was stone braille to be read by the blind fingers of the unjudging
wind, now wakened, now affronted. A boy shivered. His sister
saw him do that and giggled.

"You shivered, Tincum!" cried the girl. "That means someone just walked over your grave."

It was at this precise instant that the boy saw the bearded man walking back up the hill toward them.

The children stood their ground, though a little sheepish, as if they had been caught illicitly in a grown-up game beyond their comprehension; standing firm though with a kind of hangdog defiance, while the big man looked gently at them, each in turn, his strange eyes moving from one face to the other, and when he had done with that he shook his head and blinked as if he did not believe in them at all.

"Nelly and Loy and Luke?" he murmured. "No. No. Gone. Forever gone."

He sat down slowly on a gravestone and scratched his bearded cheek thoughtfully with his hatbrim and looked again at the children with the vacant madness of a grief: "Yes. That's it, after all. It's just that you've not learned to hate yet. You're not old enough for hate yet. None of you here knows Hate—do you?" said the big man.

The children flushed and bit their lips nervously before the crazy man.

"None of you here," said the big man again, "knows Hate? Do you?"

"Hate?" asked the boy.

Now the big hand holding the hat indicated one of the other children who was black.

"You, boy?" said the big man. "Do the others hate you yet for anything?"

"You leave Finch be!" piped the girl. "He ain't done a thing!"

"Then what I say is so," said the big man. "You've not learned Hate yet. God keep you so."

"Hate?" said Tincum, gathering spunk from the girl. "Well, who's to hate?"

"Oh, some shadow of yourself, I reckon," said the big man. "Just that. It's all it is in the end. Some shadow of yourself. It's never more than that," the big man went on, as if he were alone. "Shadow of boys running into men. Shadow of your brother, you see. That's all it ever is. Black shadow of you each that is only a trick of sun. Some shadow that is your own shadow, in the end. That in the end is *you*—each of you. You'll not let that happen—will you? Will you, Loy? Nelly? You, Luke? You'll not let Hate turn you against yourself?"

He sighed wearily and his eyes dropped away suddenly from the astonished faces of the children.

"Yes. You will," he groaned, engaging his vision in the motions of the wind-stirred grass. "Why, of course, you will. We always do."

The children studied the big man's face, enthralled, but there was no real madness in his face. And now he said no more to them, and did not even look up to see if they might have gone, or if they had ever really been there at all: ghost-children from another place, another afternoon. Presently, the children took deep breaths and began filing slowly away, stepping high-footed and flush-faced through the grass of the graves, toward the road to supper.

The moonlight was so brilliant when Isaiah woke and started up in his bed that he thought he had fallen asleep back up there in the grass, on the hill, that he had only dozed off for an instant and that it was still afternoon and if he looked down the road he would see the last of the children stringing toward the town. He kept slipping back that night, again and again, into the dream that he had stayed there to guard Luke's grave. He dreamed now that he was dreaming there and dreamed that he woke up there, shaken with a threat, glaring round him for a sign of marauders. But the dream road was empty and the dream wind was still. In his bed Isaiah dreamed that he woke and sat up in the grass among the moon-silvered stones, like a giant among the dwarfed buildings of an abandoned city, thinking: I'm a fool. I should know better than that. He wouldn't dare do that. There's no need for me staying up here all night, like a sentry, above that boy's grave.

Yet, in his bed now, he was there; in his dream he had gone

up into the high grass of a promontory above the Wilson plot and fallen asleep there to wake anxiously from time to time and look down the curve of hill toward the little flag still whipping on its stick in the wash of wind and moon. In time grass would come and make that fresh mound like the others; in time it would not seem so churned and new among those other settled eminences, come, at last, to truce with earth: Isaiah's Confederate father and the three dead Virginia Captains who had ridden with him up the Shenandoah Valley: them and their four wives with names shining there soft as old pewter: Jess and Patience, Silence and Tildy; and dead Luke's Indian mother, Judith; in time Isaiah and Toby would go to town together, to Clay Joyner's yard, and choose an honest, plain stone, like the rest, and have it cut with Luke's name and the numbers of his years. Muttering in his dream now, in the sweat-soaked bolster his head moving, dreaming he is there and dreaming what Loy had said that afternoon.

"Father, I suppose this may sound like a pretty mercenary thing to be bringing up when everybody seems to be in such a state of *mourning*!—well now you know how bad I feel about old Luke's departure from our mortal midst! I wish he could have been with us a little longer—you and Nelly both know that. Father, I think it's only my duty to pass along messages— things I've been told to tell you by people in town. Now Major Mott—he's Commander of the new veteran's group here in the County—he asked me if I'd be kind enough to remind you that just for that little piece of ground—that few square feet of earth on the Wilson family plot—well, he wanted to point out to you that if we'd *sold* it to the Cemetery Council instead of burying Luke there—they'd have given us Perpetual Care for the whole plot—you know: keep the grass mowed and all. Of course, I told the Major I thought that sounded a little mercenary, but I promised him I'd pass the thought along to you, Father. Well now what are you looking at me that way for, Father? I'm just passing along—Look, Father! You may as well know it now as later, Father—feelings in Kingdom County are a little higher about this than we had any idea they'd be. I mean, it was bad enough when Goshen's own undertaker refused Luke's body and you and poor old Toby had to make his coffin yourselves. Now, didn't I help you? Admit it, Father! I fetched nails from town! Well, what's got into Nelly?—storming out that way after throwing me a look mean enough to kill? What has everyone got their feathers up at me for? You'd think I personally had something to do with. . . ! *May* I speak? *May* I continue speaking man-to-man, Father, without these emotional flare-ups? I merely want to say that feelings—*public* feelings about Luke's being buried on our plot are running out of hand, Father! You know I couldn't do a thing about the stand the veterans took. And it's getting worse! It just seems like those boys in town are getting too damned headstrong for any arguing. Well, I guess you know how cocky veterans are after a war and all and—well, the way Major Mott put it, they sort of feel that certain *principles* are involved! I'm just *reporting* a frame of mind, Father, that's all! Polk Crowther's told me the minute he heard Luke was dead that he'd personally see to it that not a veteran in Kingdom County would stand honor guard at Luke's funeral! Well now, what could I do, Father? I'm just one among many and, besides, anything I'd say about it much would be taken as *personal*! I just thought you ought to know how much *worse* things have gotten since Luke's burial this afternoon. Some of the boys in town— well, I see no cause to mention any particular names—Father, I heard them swear they'd never let Luke's body lie among white, Christian dead. Well, now why do you glare at me that way for? *May* I speak my mind to you, Father, without those cursing looks every time I say anything you happen to disagree with? Now, think for a minute, sir! Would I be warning you about all these rumors if I was completely on their side of things? I'll not deny that I feel strange about anyone—*anyone* with an ounce of black blood in them, lying among men like Grandpa and Uncle Jake and the rest. Not to mention Grandma and Aunt Silence—our women! Well, I'll not deny it! You know my feelings, Father. But I spoke up to the boys in town this afternoon, sir! I told them I thought they were getting a little out of line. I mean, talking fool-talk about the Klan digging Luke's coffin up—I mean, and dragging it off somewhere on a buckboard and burying it in some cotton-patch ditch where. . . !"

Exhausted, Isaiah slept and dreamed sleep in mumbling intervals, snapping alert to every random nightsound, seeing in the dream sky how the moon had slipped to another willow in that space of time: another yard of sky; then slumping to that fitful sleep within a sleep again, dreaming that he waked, finally, witnessing what was taking place below him on the grass, among the stones of that place his mind had come there to sentry, seeing it happen for some long while before realizing that what he watched now was undreamed of reality: buckboard and the mare from home and Loy, alone, already waist-deep in the violated grave and the spade flashing bright in that admixture of cold moon-and hot lamp-light which seemed to stain texture and shape of things moving in the puddle of illumination with the devilish tinctures of myth: as if man moving, spade winking, and rhythmed fountaining of earth were the already discredited events of a diabolical legend. Dreamer, he went down slowly through the grass, among the other stones, staring harder as he drew close, staring and knuckling his hot eyes to stare the harder, thinking he would, at last, pierce the illusion of it; knowing all the while that it would stop as dreams must; stepping once upon a flag stick, not Luke's, the wood snapping like a fluted bone beneath his boot-heel as he strode closer, crouched a little, his eyes not believing what he saw even when Loy had heard him and looked up, open-faced at last, his earth-streaked cheeks glistening with sweat and defiance.

The curtain blowing across the pillow wisped his cheek and woke him to the hushed bedroom, to the too-stillness of the still house. He lay a minute tensed, listening, his muscles uncoiling from the dreamed conflict, and turned his eyes to see the morning light smoke pale in the window. Then he swung out of the bed and moved into the hallway. Sabby's bedroom door was

latched shut as always like the lid of a dusty hope chest. Isaiah
had gone to bed clothed, except for his boots; he walked down
the long upstairs hallway toward the high milky window at the
end of it, moving quietly in his stockinged feet. From twelve
foot's distance he could see Loy's bedroom door half-open. And
walked on slowly, his eyes hopeful in the far windowed morning
at the hall's end, thinking abstractedly: Morning light. Yes. I
remember from sunups long ago. Yes, I remember thinking
that, feeling that: that only at dawn does a man see that night
is not the presence of darkness but the absence of light. He
remembered seeing that, feeling that in the long cold winter
winds of Northern Mexico long ago when he blinked awake in
his blanket. At sundown night seems like the positive element:
drifting sediment: a palpable opaque pigmentation in the air.
At sundown night flows against windows like dark wine, evoking
lamps and cups and graces. But no. It is the passing of light,
which comes again at morning. Hope. Yes, he thought, that is
why dawn is always hope. It's morning again and the darkness
was a dream. Loy wouldn't be gone. Now he passed Nelly's open
bedroom door and saw her empty bed. He remembered she
had told him at bedtime that she and Toby were going to take
flowers to Luke's grave at sunrise. He glimpsed in the long glass
of Nelly's vanity mirror a section of his own face, blanched and
terrified with his own speculations. He moved to Loy's threshold
and stared in at the unslept-in bed. Well then, thinking, he has
run away from home. That's why he is not there. He wouldn't
do that: what his eyes said, what his mocking said; not what I
dreamed. No. Loy, no! He felt panic begin knotting cold in his
belly like it had once when Loy had nearly died from typhoid
in his infancy. Isaiah went back to his room and pulled his
boots over his stockinged feet, his eyes uneasy now at the light
brightening in the window. Was it only the rising of the sun?
Was there not some other flickering, ruddy flame of coal-oil
torches tinctured faintly in that strange, guttering dawn? The
pale light angled across the dusky flowers of the rugs in the
parlor. Isaiah opened the front door and looked down across

the lawn, the barn, Toby's shack, the trees at the road's bend misted and indefinite in the billowed, immovable bog. When he first heard the crying voices approaching on the road he imagined that in a moment he would see the riders and their horses, though some reflex in his mind shut tight in agony against the thought that Loy would be among them and then, suddenly, the two figures took shape in the curtains of the mists beyond the trees at road's bend: Toby and Nelly, running in the morning toward home. Nelly, sobbing, threw herself into his arms then, while he watched Toby who stood for a moment behind her looking at them both with something broken and quietly insane in his dark face before he turned, without a word, and went with a queer, stiff walk down the lawn toward his cabin, and Isaiah, stroking her shoulders and saying: "Get hold. Get hold, my girl. There. Get hold and tell me."

"We picked flowers. Toby. And we took them. Sunrise. They had been there. In the night. Horses. Their hooves had trampled and torn the lawn to pieces. Oh, my God, Father, we saw the cross burning even before we got there! Grandpa's—"

"Nelly, get hold."

"—Grandpa's gravestone smashed and kicked over—split in half!"

"You didn't see any of them. You don't know if—No. No."

"And Luke, Father! His—They've dug up his—!"

"You didn't *see* any of them," he prayed into her hair. "That's what I'm getting at. They'd gone when you got there?"

"You're blind! blind!" Nelly wailed, tearing loose from his strong arms, pulling herself away from him and falling back against the gallery wall. "Is Loy in his bed, Father? *Is* he? Is the mare in her stall, Father? Is the buckboard in the barn, Father? You *know* he's among them!"

"Nelly. Take hold."

"*Father,* take hold! Haven't you heard him threaten it? Haven't you seen it in his face? He's mocked you with it! You *know* he's among them tonight!"

"Nelly. Be still. Let me think."

"Yes, I know. Be fair! Fair! You're weak with your own fairness, Father! You're manacled with your own goodness! No—
don't touch me! Do what you please. I haven't the strength to
stand any more of it. Bless him—forgive him when he comes
riding home! Do what you will! I only know I can't stand any
more of it. It's yours to finish now however you will!"

"Nelly, my God, he's *ours*!"

"He's *us*!" she cried. "Maybe that's the heart of it! Maybe that's
why none of us can move! Just let me go! I don't care any more!
I just want to go to my room and stay there—and lock out
everything until I die! I don't feel fit to be in the world since I
saw that grave spaded open! Do what you *can* now! What you
must, Father! What *ever* it is—I'll know that it's no better nor
worse than what I would have done. Loy's split in two—but so
are we, I know that now, and God Himself only knows which
half will win the world or die trying. Loy thinks it's black and
white flesh that splits his world! Go reason with him if you've
breath enough to last a thousand years of talk! Change him! If
you made him love Negroes, he'd find something else to hate!
Jews! Eskimos! Catholics! Bolsheviks! Make everyone on earth
alike and he'd find some difference—some thing to hate! Do
what you can, Father. I won't care. Someday we'll each need
our own forgiveness—whether we forgive him now or ever."

And so he was alone, even before she had done talking, alone
even before she had run off down the gallery and into the
house and then gone very slowly up the stairs to her room, not
hurrying now because there was no hurry now, because she
knew now how predestined that room had always been in her
life: how many decades stretched out now from that morning
in whose light she could see, clearly illuminated, that bedroom
which would be the little, carpeted universe of her whole exis-
tence. Alone, he went down through the white bunting of mists
to the stable now to wait for Loy to come back with the mare
and buckboard, thinking: Well, at least, whatever else, he is not
a horse thief. At least, he'll come back for that and then I'll face

it out with him. God, give me strength. God, rein back my anger. Walking slowly toward the stable with his eyes closed, thinking: Lord, don't let me kill him because then he will have won it. And looked up then, without surprise, to see them ringing the yard; standing by the barn door he looked around the circle of them as if they were some natural, residual debris left in the retreat of night; among the white, indemnifying fog, the hoods upon their sheeted bodies made them seem as if they were, each, the spirit of fog itself with holes slashed in it for their anonymous, identical eyes to stare at him there, dispassionately: twenty Klansmen on horseback and two in the buckboard and they had come up quietly to encircle him there in the yard, by the barn door. Come there, perhaps, more than just out of the fundamentalist, quaint honesty which required them to return the buckboard and mare, to somehow ratify by their presence what business they had been about that night, and to impress upon him by a few moments of that sullen, insolent presence, their seriousness and their contempt for him. Or come there, perhaps, to kill him, he thought almost hopefully, wishing for an instant that if that was what they had come to do, that they would get it done. And I never heard them come, he marveled, feeling a strong, sure peace warm him in the mist's chill; twenty horses and the buckboard muffling softly behind my mare while my ears were stoppered with her words and the blood pounding in my head with prayer and rage and sorrow, stuffing up my ears. Loy? No, that doesn't matter. I don't know which one is Loy and I don't want to know. Because if I know and the minute I know it will be too much for me and I will pull him down from his mount and strangle him with my two hands long before any of their bullets could ever finish me. Loy? God, don't let me know which one. Which one? All. Yes, all Loy now. He looked at the feet beneath the two white-shrouded figures in the buckboard and saw, with relief, that neither was Loy: muddy boots and the clay-spattered leggings of the veterans. The horses nickered and stomped but the hooded riders were silent:

spectral around him like bandaged survivors of some nocturnal catastrophe: the black eyeholes floating in the chalky, anonymous drape of hoods like spiders fallen into milk.

"Here's your mare, Wilson. And your wagon."

And he recognized that voice as belonging to the one named Lowther and thought again, watching him and the other one climb down and unhitch the mare with arrogant slowness: Neither of them is Loy. And I thank God for that. Because if I knew which man among them was him it would be his death at my hands and he would have won it. Seeing the blue light glint fast along the barrels of the rifles resting on the tired flanks of the horses and waiting for them to get done with him, and wanting more than he had ever wanted to do anything to drag the nearest man from his mount and shred the hood off his shoulders so that he could get at the windpipe with thumbs and, at the same time, fearing more than he had ever feared anything that beneath the cheap muslin he would find that it was his son. And so he kept his big hands knotted and aching by his side, waiting for them to get done with him.

"Don't bury no more niggers in white graveyards, Wilson."

"Is that what you've come to say?"

"Yea, that's all Wilson."

"If there is any one man of you who'd care to climb down off his horse and say that to my face without a hood—without a gun—Any two men of you. Any three."

"We're one man, Wilson."

"Yes, God help us all, you're one man. And you make me ashamed to share the earth with you."

He stared round at them all again with slow and unfrightened loathing; knowing how much one of them, at least, wanted him to do what he would have done a month before: to run to the house, to the parlor for the old Confederate pistol and give them the provocation to kill, which would continue on and on beyond his mere dying in that ceaseless propagation of violence which, perhaps alone among them all, Luke had come to understand and left in a little legacy of last, bloody words. No, he thought, this is the stronger, harder way. And not to run amok among them was the greatest effort of spirit that he had ever known.

"My son Loy is among you," he said, steadily.

"That's right, Wilson."

"I don't want to know which one. Because if I knew which one there would not be enough bullets in all your rifles to keep my hands from strangling him before you killed me. Keep—covered. Don't let me know which one. Loy? Don't speak—just listen. God help you if you speak or show your face to me now. Listen, Loy. If ever you set foot upon the threshold of this house again you'd better come armed or praying. I am strong—but I would not be strong enough to keep from killing you."

He turned and walked up the lawn through the wisping fog toward the gallery and felt their eyes on his back and heard that one hoarse whisper like a gasp of fear among them: "Give it to him, Polk!"

"*You* give it to him! I'll not shoot any white man in the back!"

"Give it to him, Polk! Damn you, reach me the rifle then!"

"Shut up, Loy!"

Hearing that, his pace hesitant the barest second, every nerve of him yearning to whirl and search the slotted hoods to see which one stirred with the recent breath of speech, but kept on going his hard, sure way in slow, broadbacked contempt of them.

"Mister Wilson? Look around and pick out which one of us is Loy."

"Come on, Polk! Let's get t'hell on home!"

"Shut up, Jim."

"Hey, Mister Wilson? Don't appear like Loy here's too fond of his daddy. He wants me to shoot you in the back, Mister Wilson!"

"Come on, Polk! I don't like this."

"You didn't like digging the nigger's coffin up neither, you chicken-livered son-of-a-bitch. Now, shut up."

"Shoot him, Polk. He's nigh to the steps."

"Hold it! No shooting unless he commences it. Maybe one of us might just go up and give him a good whipping to remember."

"*You* go up and whip him. I done seen three stout boys try it one morning on Gallagher's porch. Let's get t'hell on home. We done what we set out to do, Polk!"

"Father?"

And even at Loy's unmistakable voice he did not turn around, but stood for a flash with his shoulders shuddering to its echo, every clenched ounce of his flesh and bone wanting to turn and pick it out from among the others and knowing now that it wouldn't matter if he knew; thinking that it wouldn't matter if he watched as every man of them stripped off his hood and let him search their faces until he found the face of his son among the twenty-two of them; that it wouldn't matter now because even flesh would be mask and each face Loy.

"Why don't you turn around, Father, and pick out which one is me!"

"Come on, Loy! We come back here like you and Polk wanted. You done seen his face. You done let him know you was with us when we rode to the graveyard tonight! That's enough! Now let's be off! He—"

"Shut up, Jim! I want to watch him a spell more! You don't know how I waited! Big, brave daddy crawling in his hole!"

"I don't like none of this, Polk. I declare, I just don't see the sense to it."

They stared restlessly at Isaiah's motionless, broad back in the frame of the gallery mocking them more with that expanse of wide blue denim than he could have with any contempt of face. Except for Loy and Polk, none of the men liked something that was happening suddenly among them: a thing seeded and sprouting in their bullying, united midst.

"By God, we done what was right tonight!" cried one in a high, hoarse voice as a man sometimes speaks aloud to himself in reassurance. "By God, the dead nigger had no right lying in a white man's graveyard. We done what was needful to be done about that. By God! But now I don't clearly see what's the sense in all this lolligagging around here for!"

"To watch him crawl, that's what for!"

"Loy, he ain't crawling! Loy, you think your daddy is scared of us, you better give another think."

"Well then, hell! Lemme try his nerve! Hey, Wilson?"

Polk chuckled then and threw his .30-.30 up, aimed well and fired. The bullet chopped into wood by Isaiah's left arm, scattering flakes of white paint across his motionless shoulder. Polk cursed softly and pumped his rifle, firing an inch closer this time and sent a two-inch splinter of wood flying into Isaiah's shoulder-length hair. Now two men flung themselves across Polk's gun and held it down: the three hooded figures hung, struggling almost motionless across the neck of Polk's rearing horse, panting and cursing thickly beneath the cloth.

"Stop it! We done enough!"

"Let him go, you bastards!"

"Enough, I said!"

"Kill him!"

"Loy, you're crazy!"

And still not a hair of him moved, nothing of him flinched nor even so much as admitted that he cared that they were there. Some men, cursing quietly, spurred their horses slowly down toward the road. The hoofs, bound in gunny sacks, struck dust up soundlessly as they rode away toward Goshen. The rest of the riders tarried a spell, restlessly, as if in an angry effort to salvage what was left of face; the eyes behind the cutouts of their hoods kept carefully averted from one another, like the faces of strange men in a public toilet.

"We done showed the son-of-a-bitch! Now let's get t'hell home!"

"That's right! Polk could just have easily shot him as not!"

Isaiah stood listening to their voices, angry at something that had stolen among them to unease them without reason; listened as they muttered, whispered, cursed, and singly rode away, the burlap-bandaged hoofs going off softly in the stealth of the dust.

"You coming, Loy?"

"You think I'd stay here?"

"If I was your doctor, I'd not prescribe it."

"Christ, you don't think I'm scared of that fool!"

"Mister, I just do."

"Come on, Polk. My woman's got breakfast on and she's madder'n hell at me as it is!"

"You coming, Loy?"

And heard the hoofs going softly down the dust as if dust alone of all the earth's substance were silently forgiving them for their atrocity upon it. Five remained now, sullen in hangdog disorder, while their mounts, smelling the sour man anger in the air, pawed the yard restively.

"Wait!"

And only then did Isaiah turn in fear at that new voice and see in the long morning shadow of the barn the shape of Toby moving slowly toward the five Klansmen by the gate.

"Wait!"

But he kept still, not stopping him, watching him move toward them with his big hat held across the ragged check of his gingham shirt; watched Toby come and felt fear for him like a frost on his heart, but not stopping him, thinking: Yes, he has a right. Whatever he has to say or do he has the right. He kept still longer than any of us. He is a man, too, and I have no right to stop him.

"Please," Toby was saying in a low, steady voice and his face, however supplicant, was neither cringing nor retaliative "dead, my son, compadres? Where? If you tell me at least where, compadres. Then I can take him away. Compadres, my boy must not lie in a ditch. You are men. Some earth should be his."

Drugged with this new astonishment they watched him with a curiosity so compelling that they could not resist it: saw him moving beneath the noses of their snorting mounts begging, cajoling, pleading. Watched him with a certain extravagance of clemency, as teasing children might watch a hurt insect which they might, at any moment, extinguish with a shoe-heel. And something else holding them back, something making them think: What the hell breed is he anyways? Is he a nigger or ain't he? Is he half-breed, mulatto, quadroon, octoroon? Maybe he ain't no nigger at all and we was all just drawed into something tonight that wasn't no affair of ours at all but something purely twixt Loy and that daddy of his! Maybe he ain't no nigger at all but some breed of a Jew or Arab or Injun! Maybe this is all just a family squawl and that damned, crazy Loy just drawed us into it to spite his daddy. How does a man know where a family thing like that begins and where it leaves off? How does a man know where these damned family things is everybody's affair or just their own?

Loy was gone with Polk and the others. The five left behind to witness Toby's anguished immolation were men of tepid conviction from the very outset; they had taken part in the night's squalid and unglorious expedition merely because they were men ashamed not to follow slogans and dares.

"Okay then!" he shouted. "Then I will do the thing I have held myself back from doing! Okay then! I will make you sorry! You and the rest of your riders and everyman in Kingdom County—all your women and your children, too! I will make you sorry for the thing you have done! Oh, how sad you will all be when you know what you have lost! What sorrow will fill your hearts when you see what is gone! One hour from this hour you will see—you will know! One hour from this hour! In the square at Goshen! Before the courthouse! Oh, you will be sorry then!"

And none moved a muscle to stop him as he turned and walked with stiff dignity into the barn and it was perhaps their curiosity at knowing what this queer creature would be about that saved his life. Because they could see he had not gone to fetch a rifle; all they could make out in the stable shadows was this strange, raceless man in the greasy sombrero, weeping and speaking softly into his big mustaches, while he hitched the mare into the buggy and then went about heaping things into it with gentle, crazy hands.

"What do you reckon he's up to?"

"Be dog if I know. He's loading things in the buggy."

"He's crazy. He drive that buggy into Goshen and start any trouble he'll sure as hell get it."

"Well, I don't think he cares."

"What's them things? What's he fetching into the buggy?"

"Be dog if I know. Maybe it's firewood to burn down the courthouse!"

"Let's get on t'hell back to Goshen. If he drives in and starts up any trouble, we'll need every man of us!"

Without a signal each man spurred his mount gently, and turning, rode out of the yard onto the road for town. The hoods flapped on their shoulders, preposterous somehow by morning light: like the pillow-case ghosts of Hallowe'en children. They trotted slowly toward Goshen.

In the square at Goshen, men and women had gathered to await Toby's coming.

"Yonder! Yonder he comes! The mare and the buggy!"

"Hahhhh!" sighed the crowd.

The buggy rocked slowly behind the mare into the very center of the square before the courthouse and stopped and Toby got down and took off his big, stained hat. He stood looking around the ring of all their faces for a moment, the breeze stirring his dark, long hair; he looked at all the faces as if to be sure that everyone was there.

"He ain't got no gun," some man whispered through a chew of tobacco.

"Well then, what's his game?"

"I say one of us ought to throw a slug into him anyways."

"What for?"

"For being an uppity nigger. That's what for."

"Nobody even knows that for sure. Whether he's nigger or part-nigger or what?"

"I say Loy Wilson got everybody stirred up over nothing!"

"Yes, and where's he now!"

"Gone! Left town! And us left here to face this crazy fool!"

"What's he going to do?"

"Dog if I know! He told some of the boys he was coming to town to make us sorry!"

"Well he's come to town and I ain't sorry!"

"At least it wasn't no lynching last night!"

"No," said a voice among them. "It was worse."

"Listen! He's saying something!"

Toby began speaking in a voice so low that the mob held its breath to catch the words. His dark face streamed with tears but his voice was so steady that he might have been addressing no one there but the wind: "I hoped I could spare you! I hoped I could keep it from you! I swear by God that I meant to keep the sorrow of it all inside myself so that none of you would know and be sorry, too! But this thing—this evil that was done last night! My boy!—my Luke!—torn up like a dead weed and thrown into some ditch without a flag or a stone with words on it or a flower to mark that he was ever here! No! Now you deserve to *share* my suffering! All of you!"

And before the agog faces of them: bonneted, quid-sagging, beet-red, livid, hangdog, wrathy and purely confounded, he began fetching Luke's paintings, one by one, from the buggy and standing them out where all could see them in the public square propping them into the grip of cobbles or between wagon ruts, against lamps, trees, and hitching posts and along the boardwalk against the courthouse steps and against the wheels of the rockaways and buckboards of the mob themselves, sobbing gently as he transformed the whole square into a gallery of those strange works, each glowing as if from some intrinsic light, more than they might have ever reflected beneath the hot sun of that mid-morning or before the bewildered and gawking jaws of Kingdom County folk. No one breathed. No one cursed or coughed or signaled yet an uproar of contemptuous laughter.

"There!" cried Toby, when the last was out. "Look! You see now? God help you! Look! It is only justice that you *know*! See what we people of Kingdom County might have had to be proud of someday if my Luke had lived! Look! Someday he would have made beautiful pictures—more beautiful than these! Look! This is my revenge on you! To make you know what I know! But now! Look and see! And be sad, sad like me! And now, God forgive you, be ashamed!"

And without hurrying he climbed back up into the buggy, whipped the mare's rump lightly and rode slowly out of the square toward Goshen road while the mob, pop-eyed and stunned with their astonishment at this bathos, breathed in slow angry air, preparing for its unison uproar of hoots and howls of savage laughter; yet no one raised a rifle, nor made a move to stop him; none pursued this man to punish him for an impudence, for a gesture which their wits, numbed to any but the reflexes of violence, struggled now to translate. The people glared at Luke's gaudy paintings, glowing in his wake like a garden of fires around the courthouse square; seeing these as if they, and not Toby, constituted the patriotic slur, the civic peril, the spittle of treason in their eyes. They grew angrier yet at not knowing why. Then someone resolutely moved.

"Haaahh!" breathed the crowd, as Polk Lowther stepped manfully forward and smashed a boney Madonna to splinters beneath his boot-heel, and the square stampeded into pandemonium as men and women surged in to get their turn at smashing the paintings with heels and hands. In a moment the square was a dust-boiling forest of polished boots and whirling skirts, wheels of lurching wagons and the delicate legs of rearing horses. In a quarter hour it was all over. By noon the town had stilled to a puzzled and suspicious stupor: Goshen, breathless in a hot glaze of summer light that shimmered still with the aftermath of roused dust, fell back to a sullen, torpid pulse. Negroes stayed out of town that night. White men spat and whittled and kept apart, on their own porches. Their women went upstairs with sewing baskets and shut the bedroom doors.

Something had been said that day: something that had no right to be said by someone who had no right to say it. No one was sure exactly what it was but they knew that it was dangerous, eloquent, and personal. It stayed in the air that night like the smoke of a burning that no one could locate.

While in that enormous night Loy pellmelled down a road far from that place, into the years to come, his fevered eyes sometimes discerning, unmistakably, the identity of that dark child who races ahead of him: shadow of himself; no, soul of himself propelled out of himself and beyond himself, surrogate forever, down the moon-white road: a figure darker than shadow, dangerous as love. Someday, then. Somewhere, he knew. In a place sometime he would catch up to him at last and see him plain in that same cold and bitter revelation of moon. And he would know the dark child for who he really was. And he would have a gun in his hand and he would know what to do with that gun until the dark child's face went away. So that he could, at last, rest safe. So that he could sleep.

LOY

"Verge, I guess this is kind of a silly question, but why did you bring me out here to Loy Wilson's country club?"

"Instead of to the County Jail? Why, you'd have been booked at the jail."

"But I won't be booked here, will I, Verge?"

"Sure not. We don't want a nice, clean, young American boy like you with a criminal record."

"Nor any other kind of record—is that right, Verge?"

"That's right. I doubt if anybody will ever find much of a record on you after tonight, George."

"Well, you've got the gun. Why don't you get it over with."

"We wait for Mister Wilson, boy."

"You mean Loy Wilson wants to shoot me himself."

"Mister Wilson just wants to supervise the job personally, that's all."

"And I'll be shot in cold blood."

"No, not in cold blood. You're going to escape. A little bit."

"I'm to be shot—escaping."

"That's the ticket. As of tomorrow, boy, you never existed."

"No one wants to die," George said childishly, softly, and to himself; it was a sudden, candid comment and he made it without a tremor in his voice.

"Well, boy, you're gonna die."

"And leave the world to darkness and to you—"

"What's that—a line from a church hymn? You want to pray, boy?"

"If I pray, Verge, your ears wouldn't hear it."

"I didn't think you would, you fucking atheist."

God? George thought gravely to himself. Is there still a Thee? He wasn't sure of that. But suddenly in his mind, in his heart, in all his consciousness there was a Carmel.

"Ever see a Colt Magnum, boy? Here. Ever see one? A boy your age oughter be interested in guns."

"What?"

"A Colt Magnum. Ever see one? Here. It'll put a bullet through the motor-block of a car."

"No."

"Mister Wilson has one, too. So does Lowdy. I hope we get to use them on you. We won't need so much quickline if we do."

"What kind of gun will you use on me when I come back, Verge?"

"Son, you ain't a-comin' back."

"What caliber gun do you need to kill a mistake, Verge?"

"You're commencing to give me a pain in the ass, mister."

"A bad mistake, Verge. Will quicklime destroy the tactical error of leaving a man's memory still alive in a woman's heart?"

He felt the first pain when Verge hit him across the face with the gun barrel, but the blows beyond the first one were only faint, dumb, swift pressures falling somewhere against his darked-out, descending face. In the indemnity of that oblivion the image of a girl shifted through, luminous with love, and the hands of his consciousness reached out to stay it, though it would not be stayed. And then he seemed only to be sleeping, though without dreams. His face hurt sorely when he woke, his tongue cut and bleeding on some sharpness in his numbed mouth. When he opened his eyes he saw shoes inches from his head: beautiful, polished, handmade oxfords, glittering with droplets of rain. He knew they did not belong to Stafford. He sat up. He stared from one to the other to the last: Loy, Verge Stafford, Lowdy Kelts. He thought to himself foolishly how he wouldn't want Amy there then because he couldn't kiss her properly with his broken mouth. There were revolvers like the one Stafford had in the hands of Lowdy Kelts and Loy. The men stood without speaking, their faces fixed in stiff expressions which appeared neither cruel nor angry. They were rather the faces of a businessman and his two accountants about to address their signatures to a document terminating a long and unsatisfactory lease. A fragment of gold from his mouth twinkled on the floor by Stafford's toe. His eyes moved across the little space to the open door and the freedom of night and rain beyond it. He wanted to say something to all three men to the effect that he somehow understood their own predicament to be, curiously, as hopeless as his own. But he didn't try to speak; the condition of his mouth would make it sound like something else. He got up painfully, walked to the open door, stood a moment with his eyes closed, halfway through its threshold, feeling the cool rain of autumn on his poor lips. Then he moved out without looking at the men again, without looking back at anything. In the illumination of floodlights from the roof of the country club's main building he surveyed the long, velvet rise and fall of the golf course which Loy and his friends had made there for the entertainment of themselves and their guests. The unwounded mouth of his mind spoke, without impediment, the name the night had made him love. Amy. Amy. The sound of her name in his mind made him aware suddenly in his nose of the scent of perfume from a sister named Carmel he had loved. Far down the plush dip of the golf green lay the white gravel road and Loy Wilson's truck. He walked a little faster, as if hastening toward an appointment for which he was already discourteously late. The wind and the rain mingled in a furious, crystal smoke all round him on the barbered, immaculate grass.

He thought he might have heard Loy Wilson's voice scream something in the years behind him, but its words were drowned in the downpour. Then it seemed as if the great, jovial palm of a friend struck him twice across the shoulders and he hurtled forward in sudden agony. Now something seemed to sweep him up in a healing and forgiving wind, into a darkness mid whose simple mercy all of man's most frail and simple promises seem to prevail beyond even the most anguished, desperate, and futile of his trials.

Dark, in the almost dawn. Nell awakens and hurries down-stairs with her naked footsteps pattering quick as the years. Decades vanish like a flight of birds in that night's moon. Every-thing had happened so long ago. Yet now Loy's daughter cries and hammers in terror at that same door. And in her own room that morning Nell looked at Amy's face, exhausted but softened now into some little respite, a transitory peace, sleeping on Nell's pillow, her dark, lustrous hair brushed out over the puckered sleeves of Nell's good nightgown: the manclothes she had come running in bundled into the box in the hall closet for the Christ-mas poor. Nell, looking, saw Amy's face for the first time in a decade, and saw, it seemed to her, some long-dead ghost of herself reborn again in love and courage.

"George? George?"

"No, dear. George isn't here. Amy, you're sick with fever and running. Rest, child. You're half delirious with fear."

"Aunt Nelly! It's not for me that I'm afraid. It's for George! Aunt Nelly, you don't know what they'll do to him—knowing what he knows!"

"I know, dear. But rest now, Amy. Get back your strength so we can all think together—so we can all do what must be done to help your George! Rest, child."

"There's not *time*! Aunt Nelly, there's not *time*! Oh, God, you don't know what they could do! Those two! And Daddy! Aunt Nelly, you don't know what kind of man my daddy is! He. . . !

Listen to me, Aunt Nelly, it's been so long since you knew Daddy! Aunt Nelly, you don't know what kind of man Loy Wilson is! I couldn't begin to tell it all!"

"Amy, I know what he is!"

"You don't! You couldn't! All you have is a pretty, happy memory of your childhood and Daddy a fine young man! You're all alike! Older people *never* know! And there's no way to tell them how people change!"

She struggled in Nell's bed like a weak and captive animal for the three days of that autumn week while the story of the Negro boy's murder spread like streaks of blood poisoning throughout the land: Loy Wilson and the two other men facing indictment for murder in Augusta County Court's September assizes in Elizabethtown. While the land's and the world's eyes watched, smirking, or crinkled with revulsion, or hot with vindictive alertness, dark face and light face watching, listening, and all knowing how it would end, how it had always ended, and must surely always end: a week—no more than that—of judicial travesty and court would adjourn without indictment unless, of course, the chuckling, winking, tongue-in-cheek of prosecution could prevail upon moon and stars to sit as witnesses to the boy's murder. No, there were no witnesses. No one had seen what, therefore, had not happened.

"Aunt Nelly!"

"Amy, I called. I called the County Court in Elizabethtown."

"Aunt Nelly, *they* wouldn't tell you! Did you. . . ?"

"I called the Criminal Court. There's no record of an arrest!"

"God! God!"

"Amy, I called the State's Attorney's office. They said they'd look into it. They talked to me—"

"I've got to go back! Go back!"

"—like I was some crank—some queer old maid. They talked like they didn't believe there was anyone named George. Because, I guess, they'd find it hard to believe that anyone down here would ever dare testify to such a just murder. Amy, dear child, we'll do all we can! Don't think I don't *know!*"

"You don't know! You don't begin to know! You're what you said, Aunt Nelly! A crank! An old maid! You've never loved anyone in all your loveless life! Not a man! You've never loved a man and had him touch you and want you and feel you and want him to get you pregnant! No! That's what's wrong! Never!"

"Amy, maybe I've forgotten all those things! Remind me, dear."

Amy raved on in a wild, loose-tongued fever of delirium for the three days of that week and none of them could help; Isaiah, listening to the girl's ravings in the shadow of his tree, in the stiffness of his years, stared grieving into the downfall of that autumn as if he were hearing the voice of Time returned, of old judgments settled in the courts of generations before his birth. When Amy slipped into a mumble of feverish sleep Nell would go listen to the night newscast from Baton Rouge and wonder what she could do, what any of them could do, what anyone could have ever done. Everything, even now, seemed so long ago. Even the moment of now seemed like a thing remembered, a thing happening over again, and that would happen again so long as there were any man alive. Sometimes in the dark Amy would waken to some luminous hallucination and cry the name of George, who had, in those weeks, become to Nelly someone so urgently real that it almost seemed as if it had been her own flesh that had loved him so.

On the fourth day the fever broke and when Nell came to the room that morning she saw that Amy had found an old dress in the clothes closet and was dressed in it, sitting wanfaced and weak in the rocking chair by the window, staring out into the soft yellow of the autumn day.

"Aunt Nell, is there any word?"

"No, dear."

"You've done all you can, Aunt Nell. It's all up to me now— for me to think—to know what to do now."

"I called the district office of the FBI in Atlanta."

"I suppose they're keeping nicely out of it, aren't they?"

"They called me back. They said there was no record of any arrest of a George Purdy in Calhoun. I said that didn't matter—that we knew he'd been arrested. That something might have happened to him."

"I know. I know, Aunt Nell."

"Amy, they said that something couldn't happen to someone who never was. They said they were keeping in touch with the situation. They said they'd keep in touch with us."

"Do they know about me? No, that wouldn't matter either, I suppose. I guess they're keeping clear of it as much as they can."

"Amy, what do you feel that you must do?"

"Die! Die! What's left? What matters now?"

"Amy, you don't think I've ever felt this way, I know. You—"

"Did I say terrible things to you while I was sick, Aunt Nelly?"

"It's all right, child. Whatever happened to me in my life that really mattered has been so long ago that I've half-forgotten. Loving. That was so long ago. Maybe you were right. But I do know about your father, Amy. I haven't seen Loy Wilson for twenty years but, believe me, dear, I know how he is."

"What are they *doing*? Back home. Is there a trial, Aunt Nelly?"

"Loy," she said, looking at her old, tired hands. "My brother and the other two—"

"Lowdy Kelts," whispered Amy, in a shiver of dreadful memory. "Verge Stafford."

"Yes. My brother and those two. There's a grand jury sitting. They're making a show of trying to indict the three of them for the lynching."

"But no one saw," whispered Amy, with widening eyes. "No one living saw."

"No one," said Nelly, "has come to court to say they saw."

"Because," whispered Amy, "no one *dares* say they saw! No one in this land has *ever* dared to say they saw!"

Amy's face grew hard suddenly.

"Yes," she cried. "But what does it have to do with me? What should I care what Daddy did! What should I care? Why let it ruin my life? Nothing could concern me less! But Daddy thinks—he thinks I'd come back and testify against him. But I wouldn't! All I want is to be with my George again!"

Isaiah had come into the room in the middle of her outburst and stood patiently listening by the doorway.

"We know, child," he said quietly when she was finished. "We understand that feeling."

And then the soft autumn night which enclosed them seemed to pause for an instant and the faintest of sounds broke the stillness and then another, unmistakable, and suddenly Amy's heart seemed to rise to her throat as she ran to the kitchen window and saw the headlights of the truck that had slowed to a standstill by the gate and watched the shadowed manshape of the hitchhiker slip down from the cab and hold a cigarette lighter flame to the mailbox stencilled "Wilson." Her breath was coming too quickly now even to cry out his name, to urge him on up those last few yards of space which separated them; she could not even move for that moment, nor race crying, barefooted, down the porch and across the lawn; she could hardly get it through her mind that it was really true that he had gotten free, escaped somehow and gotten to her somehow; that, at the very moment, her true love moved up the lawn toward the door upon whose threshold she now, trembling, stood.

After the first sucked-in breath of shock and her face draining to whiteness in the poor light of the hallway, her eyes searched his face as if it were a statement she were trying to read in a language which she had not yet learned.

"Hawk," she murmured.

"That's right, Amy."

Nelly stood by, her face a mask of sorrowful understanding.

"Hawk, you wouldn't be here unless something has happened to him," Amy whispered. "George—"

"What are you supposed to say at times like this," he said bitterly. "You've got to be brave?"

"George is dead," she said evenly.

He nodded and sat down at the kitchen table, staring at his knuckles.

"How—how do you know?" she stammered.

"I hitched rides all the way here," he said flatly. "There was a car radio in one of the cars. I heard the late news. A farmer near Elizabethtown found a new grave on his place. He dug."

"Oh," she said, simply, quietly, without tears.

And they sat around the table in the kitchen, making Nell remember another night, another time and season; herself and Hannah Jane Christmas, who in that other night drank coffee in the quiet consolation of silence and faced the deaths and decisions of another age.

"Why?" whispered Amy. "Why?"

"Why is he dead?" said Hawk. "Because he wouldn't keep his mouth shut. That's the only reason."

He stared hard at her.

"And what will you do, Amy?" he said.

She said nothing.

"I'll do what I have to do," she said, her eyes queerly bright.

"Well," he said. "I stuck around town a while. I listened and watched until I started to get too sick at the stomach to even hold down black coffee at the farce of a trial they're holding. You see there's no evidence—no witnesses."

"Yes," she said. "There's a witness."

"Oh, Amy," Nell said softly.

Isaiah sighed as if something heavy had suddenly been lifted from his chest.

"So you're going back," Hawk said.

She nodded swiftly, shaking tears free from her lashes.

"I guess I always figured you would," he said. "You've got to go, don't you?"

"Yes."

Isaiah moved suddenly to her, raised his giant hand and

cupped her face, lifting it gently in his great fingers so that he could look into her eyes.

"You've always known you had to go, Amy," he said.

"Yes," she said.

"Even before you knew your young friend was dead," he said.

"Yes."

"You think it matters, don't you?"

"Yes, Grandfather."

"Why?" he said. "Now tell me why, my child."

"I don't know why," she said, after a moment's frown. "I just know it matters."

"Good," said Isaiah. "That's the only answer that could make any sense to any of us, I reckon."

He turned tired, strong eyes to Nelly, eyes that made her remember other, stranger nights as sad and brave as this one was. Then he looked back to Amy.

"Listen to me, child," Isaiah said. "Tell me—are you frightened?"

She bit her lip and nodded fast.

"Yes," she whispered. "Frightened."

"Good," said Isaiah. "You can't be brave until you know you're frightened."

He lowered his fingers from her cheeks and moved away to stare out the window into the firefly dark.

"So you're going back," he said. "You're going to talk. You're going to make your try to break him once and forever. You're going to do the thing that we here so long ago should have done. Should have done and maybe could have done and somehow lacked the good courage or the wits to do. Or was it merely the chance? No. No, not chance. No, we lacked something elemental, didn't we, Nelly?"

He was still a spell and then went to the row of hat pegs on the wall above the kitchen pump and fetched down his old, pale Stetson. Slowly he fitted it over his white locks, brushed them back under the brim above his ears. Then he walked slowly to Amy and held out his right arm for her to take in a gesture that was quaint in its courtliness. He led her to Nelly and held out the other arm for her.

"Grandfather, what are you doing?"

"Child, you can't go back there alone," he said.

"You don't have to come with me, Grandfather," she cried. "Oh, I thank you, I do! But I can go alone. I won't need you and Aunt Nelly to hold me up."

"I rather think it's otherwise," said Isaiah, with a sorrowful smile. "That it's you holding us up."

"But, Grandfather—"

"Amy," whispered Nelly. "Can't you understand it, Amy? There's more than one conscience involved in this returning."

"Yes."

"Then come along, my dears," said Isaiah, lifting his still proud shoulders. "We mustn't tarry. It's getting late. It's been late for far too long already."

And so they moved out into the darkness and the stars.